HIRST

THIRST

THE SHADOW
OF DEATH

CHRISTOPHER PIKE

Hodder
Children's
Books

a division of Hachette Children's Books

A Catalogue record for this book is available from the British Library

ISBN-13: 978 1 444 90278 5

Typeset in New Baskerville by Avon DataSet Ltd,
Bidford-on-Avon, Warwickshire

Printed and bound in Great Britain by
CPI Bookmarque Ltd., Croydon, Surrey

The paper and board used in this paperback by Hodder Children's Books are
natural recyclable products made from wood grown in sustainable forests.
The manufacturing processes conform to the environmental
regulations of the country of origin.

Hodder Children's Books
a division of Hachette Children's Books
338 Euston Road, London NW1 3BH
An Hachette UK company
www.hachette.co.uk

When I was a junior in college, I dropped out of a strict pre-med program and started painting houses for a living, writing whenever I had free time. My decision grieved my mother; she had lost her 'son the doctor'. But she kept her disappointment to herself and supported my choice without complaint. The passing years and my growing collection of rejection slips did not discourage her. Her faith in me was absolute. It was stronger than my faith in myself. She knew I would succeed as a novelist, it was just a matter of time. For that reason, and a million others, I would like to dedicate this book to my mother.

1

I hug Seymour and whisper in his ear.

'It's me, Sita. I'm still here. I'm in Teri's body.'

Seymour Dorsten does not know how to respond. I can't blame the guy since I'm basically telling him that I have just reenacted the resurrection and risen on the third day, if it has in fact been three days since Matt shot me in the chest. I'm not too sure of the date. The last few days have been a blur. Sometimes I felt like Teri, other times I thought I was Sita. But most of the time I felt as if I was wandering lost in a twilight realm without any clear sense of self. One thing is for sure: Even though I did technically die, I never went to heaven. I never saw Krishna, which weighs heavily on my heart.

I'm not sure I'm happy to be alive again. When I

threw myself in front of the laser beam that was about to slice Seymour in half, and shouted out to Krishna, I believed deep in my soul that I would soon see my Lord. That didn't happen. Indeed, I don't know what happened. I have no memory whatsoever of what occurred immediately after I got shot.

Nevertheless, I'm grateful to John, Paula's son. It was only after the funeral ceremony, when John took my hands and gazed into my eyes, that my confusion lifted and my personality crystallized. With his help, I'm myself again, except for the rather important fact that I'm no longer in the body I was born with.

Where is Teri, I wonder? How did I displace her soul? When Matt shot me, she was deep in the unconscious phase of the conversion cycle from a human being to a vampire. In order to save her life, I had already replaced a large portion of her blood with my own. Matt had been furious at my decision to change her, but he had not fired his weapon at me out of malice.

No, he had shot me in the chest because the Array had overshadowed his will and forced him to kill me. I can only assume Cynthia Brutran had grown weary of me and activated her mind-warping tool in order to rid the world of my presence. I can't imagine she'll be happy to see me again, although I suspect she won't recognize me. But see me she will for I swear I'm going to kill her the first chance I get.

'It can't be you,' Seymour says.

'It is.'

'But that's impossible.'

'I know,' I agree.

'You're confused. Changing into a vampire – I've never been through it myself. But it must be a disorientating experience.'

'I'm telling you the truth.'

'It was Sita who changed you. It's her blood that now flows through your veins. I'm not surprised you've inherited some of her memories. That's what must be throwing you off. You just think you're Sita.'

'I am Sita.'

Seymour shakes his head firmly. 'No. Sita's dead. She died in my arms, in Matt's arms. That's screwed you up as well. She should have been here to teach you what it means to be a vampire. But she's gone and you don't have anyone to talk to. I mean, you can talk to me but I just write about vampires, I don't know shit about them. Not when it comes to the real thing.'

I reach out and hug him. 'You know me.'

'Teri . . .'

'Shut up. You know it's me. We're too close, you can *feel* that I'm here. Quit trying to convince yourself otherwise.'

Seymour doesn't hug me back. Yet his face is suddenly stricken with grief and he is close to tears. 'No. I can't go there. I can't let myself hope. It hurts too much. Get out of here. Go back to Matt. He's half vampire, maybe he can tell you what to do.'

I continue to hold on to him. 'Matt's the last person I can talk to. He knows there's something wrong with me but he's nowhere close to guessing the truth. Plus he was furious that I gave Teri my blood. Now if he finds out I've stolen her body, he'll want to kill me all over again.'

Seymour does not reply. I feel him trembling in my arms. His breathing is suddenly erratic, his heart pounds. But as I stroke his head and press my lips against his neck, I feel him slowly begin to calm down. It is only then his tears start to flow, their damp saltiness washing over me like an elixir of pain. I know intuitively he has not been able to cry during the last few days. When we're close like this, we're practically one mind. I know his grief has been too intense to allow it to come to the surface. For that reason I keep touching him, soothing him, until finally his tears stop. Only then do I release him and take a step back, the heel of my right foot accidentally bumping into my coffin. It's weird to look at it, from the outside, and imagine what's on the inside.

My dead body.

'Why did you decide to bury me?' I ask. 'Why didn't you have me cremated?'

He shrugs as he slowly collects himself. 'I guess there was a part of me that kept hoping you would rise from the dead. Like a normal vampire.'

'Cute. Was that the real reason?'

'I couldn't stand the thought of putting you in the fire.'

'Well, if it's any consolation, I'm glad you left me intact.'

'Do you think you can get back inside your body?'

'Seymour. I'm a goddamn vampire. I'm not a divine avatar. I can't work miracles.'

'Maybe John can help. You need to talk to him.'

'John's the one who just locked me tight in this body. Before he got ahold of me, I was drifting around the ozone.'

'What do you mean?'

'I don't know exactly. I remember being up in the mountains with you and Matt, outside that cave where Teri was resting. Then I felt the Array coming and saw Matt's face change, like he was possessed, and I knew Brutran had caught him in her web. I'm sure you saw the same thing.'

'I did. But what happened when you jumped in front of the laser and got shot in the chest?'

'I died. I felt myself dying.'

'What was it like?'

'It was quick. I felt my heart explode. I saw my blood pour out. But it was weird. My blood suddenly turned to gold dust, and floated up to the sky. At least that was how I saw it.'

'I saw the same thing. So did Matt. What happened next?'

'Nothing.'

'What do you mean, nothing?'

'That's exactly what I mean. There was a long gap where I didn't experience anything. Not that I can remember.'

'What is the first thing you do remember?'

'Waking up in bed beside Matt.'

5

Seymour frowns. 'Were you naked?'

'Why do you ask?'

'Just curious.'

I snort. 'Here we're trying to solve one of the greatest mysteries of all time and all you can worry about is whether I've been having sex with Matt the last few days.'

'Have you?'

'That's none of your business.'

'I know you're attracted to him.'

'Seymour, please, you've got to help me. I don't know what's going on. I'm in someone else's body. It's freaking me out. I don't even know if that means Teri's dead or not.'

Seymour considers. 'Do you have access to all her memories?'

His question shocks me. Because suddenly I feel as if a computer file has opened deep in my brain – separate from the Sita file – and I can recall the details of Teri's life. The sudden flood of her nineteen years on earth staggers me and I almost fall over. Seymour reaches out and steadies me.

'Are you OK?' he asks.

'I remember!' I cry out, recalling a dozen Christmas mornings and birthdays in the Raines' happy household. I see Teri's parents so clearly, they could be standing right in front of me.

'What's that like?'

'Confusing. I feel like two people. But it's sort of nice, too. I feel closer to her than ever.'

6

'That could be the answer. It's possible Teri's gone nowhere. Maybe you're overshadowing her personality. I don't mean this as an insult but you always were an egomaniac.'

'You're saying the two of us are in this same body?'

'Yes.'

I shake my head. 'No, that's not right. Even though I have her memories, I feel like they happened to someone else – to her, not to me. Trust me, I would love to feel her soul inside. But she's gone, Seymour. She's just gone.'

He sighs. 'Then chances are she is dead.'

I nod weakly. 'That's what I fear.' The words sound so simple and plain. But a mountain of grief stands behind them. Even though I was with Teri when she was dying, I still can't accept her death.

'You have to talk to John,' Seymour says.

'John doesn't talk to people. He just hangs out and plays computer games. You remember on Santorini, he wouldn't even see me.'

'True. But he came to your funeral today.'

'He came because his mother brought him.'

'Then talk to Paula. She's a seer. Tell her what's happened.'

'What good would that do?'

'What harm would it do?'

'Paula warned me to stay away from Teri. She said nothing good would come from the relationship and she was right. She's always right.'

'I hear ya. Hey, how come you keep putting your

7

hands over your eyes?'

'I didn't know I was.' I realize he's right and lower my hands, but I raise them a few seconds later. The glare is bothering me. It appears Teri's body is more sensitive to the sunlight than my own. Yet she – or it – is not nearly as susceptible as a newborn vampire generally is.

I wonder how much my mind is affecting the new body I'm in, and vice versa. Specifically, I wonder if I'm as strong as I used to be. Going by the way I walk and talk, and the acuity of my senses, I don't feel nearly as powerful as I normally do.

That worries me. I'll have to be at full strength to deal with Brutran and the IIC, never mind the Telar. However, there might be some advantage in their thinking I'm dead. I tell Seymour as much but he is doubtful.

'The only way we can deal with those two groups is to hide from them,' he says. 'That battle we had with the Telar three days ago proved that. You and Matt hit them with everything you had in your arsenal and they kept coming. Their organization is too big, too deeply entrenched in too many countries. The same with Brutran and the IIC. There's no way we can fight them. At least not directly.'

I point to the blisters he has on the back of his right hand.

'Are you forgetting about the X6X6 virus the Telar are planning to release? If we sit back and do nothing, seven billion people will die.'

'I didn't mean we should find a cave in the Rockies

and hibernate. We still have a vial of the T-11 vaccine and we have Charlie on our side. We need to put him in touch with other scientists who can help him reproduce the vaccine on a massive scale.'

'Is that vaccine even working?' I study his blisters more closely. They're dark and look plump with dead blood. 'Have you given yourself another shot?'

'Yesterday. It slowed down the spread of the blisters but it didn't get rid of them. Shanti has blisters as well, on her face, especially on the skin that she had grafted on. I was planning to give her another dose today.'

'Have you talked to Charlie about what's going on?'

'I haven't had a chance. It took all my time to plan your funeral.'

'I suppose I should be grateful.'

'Don't mention it. But I'm serious when I say we have to keep a low profile when it comes to the Telar and IIC. We can't fight ten thousand immortals and we can't fight Brutran's Array.'

'I wonder how Brutran was able to lock the Array on Matt.'

'Why should he be immune?'

'First off he's a Telar/vampire hybrid, and his father, Yaksha, was not just any vampire. Matt's stronger and faster than I am. Also, we assumed Brutran was able to attack because she collected blood from me at her Malibu office. But I can't see how she could have got hold of a sample of Matt's blood.'

'The relationship between your blood and the Array is just a theory of yours. It might be wrong. We're still not sure what the Array is or how it works. Brutran might be able to target whoever she wants.'

'Brutran went to a lot of trouble to get a sample of my blood. Then she went out of her way to avoid me until my blood had been disbursed to her people. That I'm sure of.'

'Matt could have run into her people in the past, without knowing it. Ask him when you're in bed tonight. He might remember something.'

'I can't ask him that. It's not a question Teri would ask.'

'So you're going to keep Matt in the dark? How long do you think that will last? You have to tell him the truth.'

'No.'

'Why not?'

'I'm afraid. He has a temper. I told you, he was furious at me for trying to change Teri into a vampire, even if it was to save her life. Right now, he's probably just learning to accept her as a vampire. Now, if I tell him that not only did the change not work, but I just happened to steal Teri's body in the process, he'll explode. I wouldn't be surprised if he tried to kill me.'

'He's not going to kill his old girlfriend's body.'

'He might if he's convinced she's not coming back.'

'But you didn't choose for this to happen.'

'He won't care! He's not going to react logically. He's emotionally on fire.'

'I understand all that. But he needs you and you need him. You two are the only ones who can save the world from these maniacs. It doesn't have to be now, but at some point you're going to have to risk telling him the truth.'

'Agreed. Later. A lot later. Let's give it a few days. Or weeks.' I stare down at my coffin. 'I need to be alone for a few minutes.'

He hesitates. 'All right.' He turns and walks toward his car. 'Don't do anything disgusting,' he calls over his shoulder.

When he's gone, I kneel beside the coffin and put my hands on the top. I'm sitting in the same position John was when he did whatever it was he did to my body. Or should I say my old body? Chances are this change is permanent.

The coffin has been nailed shut. Even though I lack my old strength, I'm still a vampire with Sita's blood flowing through my veins. That makes me stronger than a dozen men combined. I snap the top off without effort and set it aside. For the first time in my long life, I stare at myself from the outside. The effect is overwhelming. I shake, feel a wave of dizziness, and for a moment I fear I will faint.

I look so much like me, and yet I'm a stranger to myself. It frightens me to gaze at my face. I could be staring at a mirror that lies under a foot of water. I look like a ghost.

I have a hole in my chest, in my heart. The long white dress the morgue has dressed me in does not hide the fact. There is a dark red and gold stain where the material brushes the skin near my left breast. I know I

11

should not touch the wound but feel I must. My shaking hand reaches out and pops two buttons off the dress as my fingers probe the rim of the wound that ended five thousand years of life.

The hole feels narrow, too narrow. Of course I have no clear idea how wide it should be, yet it doesn't seem right. Plus my dress is stained because the wound is still damp, when it should be dry.

I smell not a hint of formaldehyde. I know Seymour would not have allowed me to be embalmed, on the off chance someone might have tried to steal my blood.

There's just something about the wound that's unnatural.

I get the impression it's slowly healing.

Yet the dead do not heal.

Not even dead vampires.

On impulse, I let go of the bloody hole and reach up with my other hand and open my eyes. Leaning forward on my knees, I stare down into them, and here I note a definite change. They are darker than before. The blue is closer to black, and they gaze back at me with a reflectivity that no mirror could match. However, I don't see myself in them.

I see Krishna. I see his face, his eyes, his divine dark-blue light. The weight on my heart partially lifts and I shed my first tears for dead Sita. I finally realize I'm alive only because he wills it, and that this respite won't last forever, or even a great many days. He has sent me back for a purpose and I have a limited amount of time to accomplish it.

Seymour volunteers to take me back to my hotel, where I share a room with Matt. Almost immediately after leaving the cemetery grounds, I begin to feel physically worse. I don't know if my sensitivity to the daylight has suddenly increased or if it's just because we're driving east, in the direction of the sun, but the bright glare hurts my eyes. Pulling down the car's visor and closing my eyes helps, but the irritation remains.

And I have a worse problem.

My guts are cramping. It is as if two maniacs have grabbed hold of opposite ends of my intestines and decided to play a game of tug-of-war. The spasms are so intense I feel they'll cause internal damage.

I haven't had such a sensation in a long time. Around five thousand years. Yet I recognize it immediately. I'm experiencing hunger pangs. A vampire's hunger pangs. I need blood, Christ, I have to have it soon or I'll go insane.

Seymour glances over at me. 'Are you all right?'

'Fine. Why?'

'You're squirming in your seat.'

'The sun's bothering my eyes.'

'Close them.'

'I tried that. It's still bothering me.'

'Is that all that's bothering you?'

'You are. Shut up and drive.'

'Sita. Tell me what's wrong.'

Another spasm strikes. I feel as if my stomach's trying to tear itself in two. 'I'm thirsty,' I whisper.

'It's not the Array?'

'It's this body. It's young, it has to be fed.'

'Oh shit.'

An uneasy silence settles between us, disturbed by the loud pounding of his heart, the pulsing of his blood through thousands of veins, millions of microscopic capillaries. It's like the sound is promising me it will provide instantaneous relief – if I just reach over and rip open his skin.

'What are we going to do?' he asks.

'Drop me at my hotel, let me worry about it.'

He's scared but not as scared as he should be.

'You're going to have to tell Matt. You're going to need his help. At least when it comes to getting blood.'

'I've been a vampire a long time. I can handle it,' I say.

My hotel is a Hilton. It's rated four stars and stands on the outskirts of town. Seymour is staying at a Sheraton two miles away. He tries to walk me to my room but I convince him I'll be OK. The sound of his blood is like the song of the Sirens in my head, calling us both to our doom. My thirst has entered the insane region where I'll do anything to satisfy it.

I practically run from Seymour's car.

Matt's not in our room. He's left a note. It says something about needing to scout the area for Telar. I hardly read it. I don't care about Matt or the Telar. Now it's my own pulse that pounds in my brain like a primal drum that knows only one message: *FEED ME!*

Perhaps if I was in my old body, and had all of my ancient power, I might have resisted the urge longer. Alas, I've inherited Sita's soul, I *am* Sita, but for some reason I lack her strength of will.

I pick up the phone and push the button for room service. I order something, anything, it doesn't matter what's on the menu. It's the person who will bring the meal that counts; they are what I'm having.

Nevertheless, waiting for the food to arrive, pacing like an addict in need of a fix, I promise myself I won't commit murder. I just need a drink, a pint or two, to satisfy my thirst. I'm not going to hurt anyone. I suspect my mind – and therefore my new brain – retains a measure of its old power. When I finish feeding, I can always hypnotize my victim with my eyes and make him forget there's a vampire in room 1227.

No one need know. Not even Matt.

A knock at the door. I answer in an instant. The odours of rare steak and a baked potato fill the air. Along with the sound of another pounding heart. The guy delivering my meal is six-six and weighs three hundred pounds. His muscles bulge. He belongs on a professional football team. He has sandy hair and trusting green eyes. He smiles when he sees how cute I am.

'Hi. Name's Ken. You hungry?'

'Yes. Please come in.' He pushes the sheet-covered cart past me, and even though his head is bent low, he still towers over me. The guy doesn't just pump iron; he looks like he eats it, in between shooting up with steroids.

Why on this of all days did Superman have to deliver my food? Ken's size means he has more blood to spare, sure, but it also means he is going to be harder to subdue. It is high noon, the weakest time of day for a newborn vampire. At the moment I'm stronger than him but not by much. I need to use my wits as much as my raw strength to get his blood.

But I've lost it, totally, I'm way beyond the point of control. The second he goes past me, I kick the door shut and grab the steak knife from the cart and stab the tip in the side of his neck.

Unfortunately, the knife is for cutting steak, not for killing people. The tip isn't as sharp as the side of the blade. I cut him, true, but his jugular remains intact. Ken whirls on me with fear in his eyes, and anger. To say I've lost the element of surprise would be the

16

understatement of the year. Pressing his hand to his neck, he quickly backs up. Yet his back is not to the door, and in his haste he moves deeper into my room.

'What the hell's wrong with you?' Ken shouts.

I still have the knife in my hand. I stare at it like I don't know how it got there. It is only now, in this moment of crisis, that I realize my mind is moving as slow as my body. The old Sita would have hit him with the perfect answer in an instant.

'I'm sorry,' I say, the smell of his blood overwhelming all my senses. 'I didn't mean to do that. I'm a mental patient. I just stopped taking my meds. My boyfriend's supposed to be here. He's taking care of me.' I pause and wipe at my eyes as if brushing aside a tear. 'Did I hurt you? I truly am sorry.'

He realizes he's not bleeding too badly. The blood is only trickling out, staining his white collar with red drops. Yet the guy is either awfully stupid or amazingly compassionate. These days, the way the world is, it's hard to tell the difference. Maybe he's just a sucker for a pretty face. Ken holds up both his palms and tries to calm me with his words.

'It's OK, you're going to be OK. But you have to put the knife down. Can you do that?'

Again, I look at the knife as if I have no idea how it came to be in my hand. 'Where should I put it?' I ask innocently.

He shoves the food cart back towards me. 'Put it there, next to the hot plate. You're going to be all right. I'll call the front desk and get you help.'

'No, please don't,' I say as I set down the knife. 'If they see what I've done, they'll call the police. I could go to jail. I can't do that, I can't stand to be in enclosed places. I'm sick, you see, I need my meds.' I pause. 'Can you get them for me?'

'Where are they?'

'In my suitcase, it's there in the corner.' The suitcase belongs to Matt but that doesn't matter. The guy is not quite as dumb as I thought. He gestures to the case.

'You get them,' he says. At the same time he reaches over and picks up the knife. 'Let me read the bottle before you swallow anything.'

I stroll lazily towards the suitcase, walking past him. 'Why?'

'I just want to make sure you're taking the right amount.'

'That's thoughtful of you. You're a nice guy, really.'

He shrugs. 'I know what it's like to suffer from depression. I take Prozac. Been on it for five years. You should never come off all of a sudden. I tried it once and I thought I was going to lose my mind.'

'That's exactly how I feel.' I kick up with my right foot as I speak, aiming for the knife. I still possess the knowledge of a dozen systems of martial arts, but my nervous system doesn't recall the precise moves. I feel as if I move in slow motion. My foot manages to connect with his hand and knock the knife away. Unfortunately, as I try to scissor my kick, strike with my other leg and put him down, I stumble in midair and hit the floor.

Ken has had enough of this crazy blonde bitch. He

runs for the door. But he is tall, with long legs, and has trouble accelerating. I stick out my foot and trip him. He falls face-first on the floor and in a moment I leap on to his back.

'Sorry,' I say as I grab the back of his head, a handful of his sandy hair, and smash his nose into the stone tile floor. My insane hunger adds fuel to the blow. The cartilage in his nasal cavity cracks and he goes limp in my arms. 'I really am sorry,' I repeat.

Blood. Ken's blood, it is all I see, all I can think about. He spouts from his nose and only dribbles from his neck. But I sink my teeth into the latter spot because, well, that's what vampires do. It's risky, though – at the back of my mind I know if I drink too deep I'll open his jugular.

Indeed, I'm only sucking on his neck a few seconds when I feel the pressure of the large vein beneath the tip of my tongue. The pounding of his heart no longer drives me insane. I am beyond that. It possesses me, as does the taste of the warm, lush fluid that fills my mouth. As I let my teeth sink deeper, I feel the jugular slowly split open . . .

Then I am in heaven, lost on a red river of blood.

I lose the ability to plan and reason. My lust is too primal, it leaves no room for thoughts. I'm no different from an animal. All I know is the desire to feed, to keep feeding until I'm full. The room vanishes from view. Even the pounding of Ken's heart seems to disappear. Far off, I hear someone moaning. Only later do I realize it was me, lost in the throes of pleasure.

Time goes by. I'm in no condition to count the minutes. It's possible I pass out. When I do become aware of the hotel room again, I hear a noise. A ringing sound. Groggy, lying facedown on top of Ken's back, I pick up the phone.

'Hello?' I mumble.

'Hi. This is Mike down in room service. We sent an order up to your room thirty minutes ago. We'd like to know if you received it.'

I sit up suddenly and feel for a pulse at Ken's neck.

There's nothing. No heartbeat, no Ken. He's dead.

'No,' I say. 'I ordered a steak but it never arrived.'

'Are you sure? I was here when our server left with your food.'

'I'm quite sure.'

'Is it possible you were in the shower or asleep and didn't hear him knock?'

'I've been sitting here wide awake this whole time. But you know what, I'm no longer thirsty, I mean, hungry. I want to cancel my order.'

'That's not a problem. It's just that our server is missing and you sound like I just woke you up from a nap. I was just wondering if—'

'You know, you're being awfully pushy. What kind of hotel is this anyway? I've told you I haven't seen Ken and I meant it. Now cancel my order and quit bugging me.'

I go to hang up but hear him ask, 'How did you know his name is Ken?'

Shit! How could I be so stupid? The old Sita simply

did not make such mistakes. I struggle for a way to cover my error.

'You just said his name, Mike. Or did you forget already?'

Another long pause. 'I suppose I must have. You have a nice day, Ms Fraiser.'

He hangs up the phone before I can respond. It is just as well. With every remark I make, I keep burying myself deeper.

I stare down at Ken's body and realize I'm going to have to bury him, and quick. I have to get him out of my room before Mike grows impatient enough to call the police. Hell, for all I know, he's already dialed 911.

The one plus in all this madness is that I have left few blood stains on the floor. There's a small puddle beneath his nose that I'm able to wipe up with a napkin. In the last fifty centuries, I've done this thousands of times – cleaned up after feeding on victims. Yet I'm shocked at the emotion that shakes me as I turn Ken on his back and stare down at his extraordinarily pale face.

I weep, salty tears, made of water, not blood. My vampire body is too young to shed red ones. Too young to enjoy the calm detachment I'm used to. Ken really was a nice guy. Even when I hurt him, he still wanted to help me. It kills me that I killed him.

Yet my instincts are old, they take over. The food cart, with its rubber wheels and cotton tablecloth, is an ideal tool to use to dispose of the body. There is a steel tray that blocks the centre portion of the cart but I'm able to use my Swiss knife and remove it. Squeezing Ken into a ball tight enough to fit beneath the white sheet is a task but the freshly dead are extremely limber. I bend him until the bones in his back crack but I finally fit him in place.

I don't have a car. I'm going to have to borrow one, or steal one, as the case may be. With the cart, I need the elevator, but the only one I can find in my wing, on the miniature map posted to the back of the door, makes it clear that it passes through the lobby on the way to the garage. Great. With the luck I've been having lately, I'll run into Ken's mother.

I move fast. When it comes to murder, to hesitate is to get caught. I can grieve over Ken later. Physically, I actually feel a lot better than I have at any point since my transformation. Despite the Prozac, Ken's blood was strong.

After peering out the door and making sure the exterior hallway is empty, I push the cart outside and casually wheel it towards the elevators. From the outside, I probably look cool. But inside I'm a nervous wreck. I pray for an empty elevator.

I'm on the top floor of the hotel, in the expensive suites. I push the button and wait for the elevator to arrive. It appears quickly, and it's empty. I push Ken inside and select the lowest button on the panel. Best to steal a car from the bottom floor of the garage, there will be less traffic.

My elevator stops on the fifth floor. A mother and father, and four rowdy kids, pile inside. The kids are between the ages of six and twelve, totally hyperactive.

The family is obviously on vacation but Mom and Dad look burned out. The woman turns to me.

'Do you know where the Pepsi Center is?' she asks.

'No,' I say flatly.

'It's the arena where the Denver Nuggets play. You must know where it is.'

'I'm not from around here,' I reply.

The woman persists. 'What do you mean? You work for room service, don't you?'

'Nope,' I say. The youngest boy tries to lift up the cart's tablecloth. The kid is short. He might see a dead hand or finger hanging down there. I come close to slapping his hand away but change my mind at the last second and reach down and grab the kid's hand. 'Please don't touch that,' I say.

The woman really is a pain in the ass. She pulls her kid close and scowls at me. 'Why are you returning the cart if you don't work here?'

I go to snap at her but turn to the husband instead. Our eyes meet and I smile sympathetically. 'Is she always this way?' I ask.

The man smiles back and nods faintly. The woman gives us both a look to kill but I have finally shut her up. I silently wish the husband well.

They get off in the lobby. The door stays open forever, probably because it's the main floor. I feel naked standing there with a dead body inches away. Finally, though, I'm on my way to the bottom floor.

I've stolen hundreds of cars in my time. I'm good at it but once again I usually rely on my strength more often than my knowledge of how ignition systems work. The last thing I want to do is set off an alarm that won't stop. For that reason, an older car or truck would be best. Too bad I'm staying at a rich hotel and there's a shortage of jalopies. After scanning the two lowest levels, I settle on a Camry that has been in a serious accident but had tons of body work. My eyes are sharp enough to detect the damage and repairs. I shatter the driver's window with the back of my elbow. The blow stings but I don't care. I'm just happy the horn hasn't started blaring.

I'm inside in a moment and have no trouble breaking the steering column and pulling out the ignition wires. The wires spark as I rub them together and the engine turns over. Only when I have all systems working do I pop the trunk. I wrap Ken in the cart sheet before I dump him in the back. I leave the cart and its supply of utensils behind, but I put the plate carrying the steak and potato in beside the body. I slam the trunk tight. I'm fortunate I'm able to lower the broken window. A cop might have spotted it.

Denver is one of the few major cities in America I know almost nothing about. Rather than drive around aimlessly, I stop at a mall where I buy a map of the area, a shovel, a box of heavy-duty garbage bags, and two rolls of duct tape.

What a miracle God created when he invented duct tape! It would take a vampire who has a constant and annoying need to get rid of bodies to fully appreciate how important it is. I know that once I find a place to bury Ken, I'll be able to seal his body in several layers of garbage bags and attach them so tight that a bloodhound could walk over the grave site and not smell a thing.

The map is useful. It leads me to a small national park not far outside the city. The softness of the soil and the site's proximity to the road factor in my decision of where to bury Ken. I don't fancy digging through rocky dirt, and I'm not strong enough to carry the body far. Still, Ken deserves a decent grave. I bury him as best I can and take a few minutes to pray over his grave.

'I'm sorry about this, Krishna. What can I say? I screwed up. Please take care of Ken. I just met him but he seemed like a nice guy.'

After wiping down the stolen car thoroughly, I park it two miles from the hotel and take a bus back to the Hilton. I have to walk the last few blocks to reach my room. I don't mind the exercise. The day is getting on; it is near evening. The air is fresh and brisk. The walk gives me time to figure out what I should tell Matt. Should I try to conceal what happened in the room? That would probably be best, I decide.

Yet the instant I open the door, and see his face, I know he's already figured out what's happened.

3

Matt's face. A thousand years old and he still has the look of a young god. Gazing at him now, at the faint but intense lines that create his varied expressions – along with his sensual lips, his strong jaw, and the depth of his dark eyes – I don't understand how I didn't recognize him the moment we met.

Yaksha's son – it's so obvious to me now. Yet maybe it was the sheer power of his gaze that hid his true identity from me. He's a sorcerer. As with his father, I seldom know what he's thinking or how he feels.

'You've been gone a long time,' he says.

'Yeah.'

'You're having trouble adapting.'

He's not asking. 'That's putting it mildly,' I say.

He gestures to where the blood stain was. 'The front

desk called. So did the police. It appears the hotel has lost an employee. Someone from room service.'

I sit on the couch not three feet from where I broke Ken's nose.

'What did you tell them?' I ask.

'Nothing. They insist on talking to you. You might want to give them a call.'

I sigh. 'I'd rather not.'

Matt crosses the room and sits beside me, taking my hand. 'You're shaking,' he says.

'I'm OK.'

'Do you want to talk about it?'

'There's nothing to say. My thirst overwhelmed me and I attacked the guy. I thought I could drink a little and stop the craving, but I couldn't stop myself.' I let my eyes flood with tears. I need to appear upset, as Teri would. 'He was dead before I knew it.'

Matt moves to hug me. 'I should have been here. I could have helped you.'

'Did your father help you when you were young?'

'I don't remember having such cravings. It must be my Telar half.' He pauses. 'It's too bad Sita's not here to give you advice on how to get through this transformation.'

I don't trust myself to answer. I close my eyes and shudder.

'How do you feel?' Matt asks softly.

'Like a murderer.'

'You're not a murderer.'

I open my eyes and stare at him. 'What am I then?'

He stands and starts to pace. 'It's something you'll

27

learn to control. You don't have to kill to get blood. As far as I could tell, Sita almost never killed her victims.'

'She was five thousand years old. I'm an infant compared to her.'

'But you have me to help you. I may not have gone through what you're going through right now, but I'm stronger than Sita was. I also have many of her abilities, ones I haven't told you about. If I stare deeply into someone's eyes, I can make them forget what's just happened. That means you can drink from someone and I can hypnotize them and make them forget the whole thing. Then we can send them on their way with no harm done.'

'Have you ever used that ability on me?'

He stops in mid-stride. 'No,' he lies.

He lies because he's embarrassed to tell the truth, and he believes that Teri, as a newborn vampire, cannot detect his lie. He doesn't suspect who he's talking to.

Yet his lack of suspicion doesn't make me cocky. I know from experience how perceptive he is. If I'm not careful, if I make even the slightest mistake, he'll be on to me.

'Why do you want me to talk to the police?' I ask.

He resumes his pacing. 'You're an Olympic gold medalist. You have an all-American look. If they meet you and find out who you are, they'll lose all their suspicions.'

'Why didn't you just tell them who I am?'

'It will have more impact coming from you.'

'Fine. Should I call them now?'

'Let's talk a little. What did you do with the body?'

28

I explain how I buried Ken in the woods, but I don't go into every detail. I don't want to sound like an expert. Yet I walk a thin line. I tell Matt just enough to make him relax. He nods as I finish.

'You did well,' he says.

'Thank you.'

'I still should have been here to help. And you should have told me how much your thirst was bothering you. These first few weeks, you have to tell me everything that's going on with you.'

'It came on all of a sudden, after the funeral. By the time I got back to the hotel, you were gone.'

'Did Seymour drive you back?'

'Yes.'

'Did he know you were struggling?'

'Sort of. I played it down.'

'You didn't play it down enough. He's called a few times. He's worried about you.'

'It was scary, Matt. I almost grabbed him.'

'Seriously?'

'I can't describe it. It was like I was going insane.'

'You went too long without drinking. Three days. I'm surprised your thirst didn't hit earlier. It must have been the power in Sita's blood. She was so old. Plus my father gave her his blood before he died. Sita wasn't a normal vampire. The fact that she made you might spare you a lot of grief. I'm sure you've inherited a lot of her strength.'

'I wish she was here.'

Matt hears the longing in my voice, and the weird

thing is, it is genuine. But the longing comes because I miss my old body, as much as I miss Teri. Still, the feeling in my voice does much to reassure him that I'm being sincere. When he speaks next, there is pain in his voice.

'I miss her too,' he says, sitting back on the couch, further away this time, looking weary, troubled. I reach over and touch his leg. He has such beautiful legs, I used to find it hard not to stare at him. Now, I don't have to hide it.

'Tell me about your day,' I say. 'What did you do?'

He shakes his head. 'Tried to find out how much fallout there is from that small war we had a few days ago. But as far as I can tell, the Telar have kept it out of the media. It sounds impossible but it's true. It just goes to show how influential they are.'

'Can we stop them?'

'It's going to be harder without Sita. She was so shrewd, so fearless – we're going to miss her more than we realize. But even if she was here . . . I don't know. We're going to have to make some difficult decisions.'

'Does that mean you're going to get in touch with your mother?'

The question disturbs him. It's a dangerous question, it's something Sita would ask, not Teri. But I put it out there because I need to know the answer.

'What do you know about my mother?' he asks.

I shrug. 'Only what Sita told me. She said you two have not spoken in years. That you have stayed apart to increase your chances of survival.'

'When did she tell you this?'

'A few days ago. In the house in Goldsmith.'

Matt considers. 'Maybe it's time I spoke to her. I haven't decided yet.'

Again, he is lying, and his lies are easier to pick up than before. He's not being as careful with me as he would be with Sita. For the first time I suspect his mother has set up a situation whereby she's able to contact him but he isn't able to contact her – not when he so chooses. Umara is a lot older than Matt. From the sound of things, she may be older than me. I'm confident there are things about her that even her son doesn't know.

'You know, Shanti and Seymour still have blisters from the Telar's virus,' I say.

He nods. 'Today, I had a long talk with Charlie about that. He's going to give them another shot of the vaccine but he admits it's not the answer. The vaccine was designed to protect the Telar, not ordinary people. I've put Charlie in contact with some scientists that might be able to help him modify the vaccine. He sounds optimistic but I don't know. Even if he comes up with a new formula that works, how are we going to distribute it in time?'

'We could appeal to the IIC for help,' I say. Another remark that Sita would make, instead of Teri. Yet I feel I cannot totally hold back. I need to know where Matt's head's at.

My remark startles Matt. He studies me closely.

'How much did Sita tell you about them?' he asks.

'Enough to know they're not to be trusted. But she did say, "The enemy of my enemy is my friend."'

'Not when it comes to the IIC. They're monsters.'

'It might take a monster to kill a monster.'

'They're not an option. Especially with Sita gone. We have nothing to offer them. If they find us they'll kill us.'

'Do you say that because of what happened up in the mountains?'

He looks away. 'I don't know what you mean.'

'If you don't want to talk about it, Matt, I understand. It's just that Seymour told me on the drive back from the cemetery that the IIC was able to use their Array to control your mind.'

'Seymour has a big mouth.'

'That's not fair. I need to know what's going on, especially now that I'm no longer human.'

'Don't say that!' he snaps. 'Don't ever say that!'

'Goddamn it, it's true. I'm a vampire. If you can't accept it, then how am I supposed to? I'm not your cute all-American Olympian anymore. I'm a bloodthirsty killer. Get used to it.' I stop and add the most dangerous words of all. 'Or else get rid of me.'

I have hurt him, I realize, and I suppose a part of me wanted to. To get revenge on him for the fierce argument he had with me because I wanted to save Teri by giving her my blood. Just three days ago, he had threatened to enter the cave where Teri was sleeping – while her body was undergoing the transformation that would turn her into a vampire – and put a bullet in her head and heart. He even threatened to kill me if I got in his way.

Then the Array came and his mind fled.

And he did kill me. He shot me in the heart.

Matt has walked over to the window. He stares out at the dirty haze that hangs over the city. Here we are, a mile high in the Rockies, and there is smog. Who would have thought. But I've been told the mountains act like a surrounding bowl that keeps the pollution from escaping.

'Seymour saw what happened. That doesn't mean he understood what happened,' he says, and this time there's a deadly note in his voice. It makes me wonder if he would ever hurt him. Certainly, if he wanted to, I wouldn't be able to stop him.

'Sita told me she trusted him more than she trusted herself.'

'Sita's dead.'

Now he hurts me, or Teri, or both of us. His stroke is masterful. My eyes burn and I have to struggle to stop the tears. Yet I suppose one good stab deserves another.

'I don't blame you if you want to let me go,' I say.

He lowers his head. 'How can you even suggest such a thing?'

'Because it's what you wanted. For me to be dead.'

I'm really raking him over the coals, but the weird thing is, I can't stop myself. It's only now I realize how angry I am about his behaviour on top of the mountains. How he acted *before* the Array appeared, when he was still in control of his mind.

'I'm grateful you're still alive,' he says softly, and for the first time since we met he sounds totally exposed. He's trembling, and just like that my anger switches and

33

I feel an overwhelming wave of love for him.

I don't remember crossing the room but suddenly I'm in his arms and he's kissing me and I'm kissing him and it's like drinking Ken's blood all over again. Except this time I feel myself drowning in a clear, warm river rather than a sticky, red one.

Matt sweeps me off my feet with his powerful arms and takes me into the bedroom. We don't take off our clothes, we tear them off. And our lust is good, it's better than good, it's natural and spontaneous. I'm not betraying Teri and he's not betraying her because in that moment I am her.

I don't say that casually to excuse what I do next. I honestly lose track of myself. It's like the entire storehouse of Teri's memories that are ingrained in my physical brain break like a tidal wave against my soul. As his tongue slips in my mouth and his hands grasp my breasts, I feel as if Teri rushes into the room and reclaims her body. Suddenly there are two of us. One rides an ecstatic wave of physical pleasure, while the other floats on a plane where bodies are unnecessary.

Because I experience both worlds, hers and mine, the personality split is disorientating and delicious. As my physical form begins to moan with pleasure, my spirit sings with joy. I'm a saint and I'm a sinner. We both make love to Matt, Teri and I, and because he knows his lover so well, nothing I said to him in the other room makes any difference. My lies are forgotten and his suspicions flee. He believes his girlfriend is not dead, and for a time it's true.

4

Late in the night I awake to find Matt sound asleep beside me in bed. All awareness of Teri has vanished. Inside at least, I'm alone again.

In the first century after Yaksha changed me into a vampire, I used to sleep as much as six hours. But that was during the day, never at night. At night I was at my strongest and I hunted.

It was only as the centuries passed that the need to sleep diminished, until I required as little as an hour of unconsciousness to recharge myself. I'm used to taking an hour nap at midday. Yet I know Matt prefers to rest for three or four hours at night. I can't imagine lying silently beside him for that long. I feel restless and slip out of bed and go in the other room.

I try watching TV, the news, but nothing holds my

attention. The suite's living room haunts me, the area where I killed Ken. Immediately after his murder, I was too busy dealing with his body to dwell on what I had done. Then, seeing Matt, making love to him for the first time, I forgot about Ken altogether.

However, now my eyes keep straying to the spot where I shattered his nose on the tile. I notice the phone has been left off the hook. Matt must have disconnected it at some point, I don't remember when. The police have probably tried to call. Chances are they'll come to the hotel, probably early in the morning. It might be wise to leave before they arrive, yet that might make me look more guilty.

I'm unsure what to do. I only know that a young man, with his whole life in front of him, has been wiped off the face of this earth just to satisfy my thirst. Viewed objectively, from a state where I feel not the slightest need for blood, to kill a person simply to satisfy an unnatural bodily urge seems ridiculous. The pettiness of my motive coupled with the brutality of my act makes my guilt feel all the deeper.

I recall having the same thoughts five thousand years ago. Immediately after my first kill, I shared them with Yaksha, and what did he do? He just shook his head and said I would get used to it. And I did.

Now it looks like I'll have to get used to it all over again.

'No,' I whisper aloud. I can drink without killing. I can take a pint from a person – preferably a large person – then hypnotize them, make them forget. Matt can help me, he promised he would.

Yet the thought of having to depend on another, when I have taken care of myself for so long, depresses me. I don't want to be Matt's pet, always having to follow him around. I have to find another way.

I feel the urge to go for a run. My body does, at least. The desire should not surprise me. Teri ran every day of her life. Changing into shorts and a sweat top, lacing up a pair of Nikes, I slip my card key and a credit card in my pocket and leave the hotel.

It's after midnight. The streets are relatively empty. I run without direction, without purpose, and yet it feels good, so I suppose that is reason enough. I run fast and don't feel tired. Surprisingly, a portion of my endurance comes from the rigors Teri subjected her body to as a mortal. The girl just won the gold medal in the metric mile at the Olympics. Teri's legs are longer than my old ones and I enjoy the longer stride. Sweat pours from my hair and into my eyes. My heart pounds. I feel as if I fly over the ground.

An hour goes by. Two.

I'm twenty miles from the hotel when I spot the cemetery.

And here I thought I was running aimlessly.

I have come back to my grave for a reason. Something is happening with my body, something that calls to me. I remember studying my chest wound that morning, how it appeared to be closing, to be healing, despite the fact the body was dead. But is it truly dead? Why should it draw me so intensely if there's no living spark left inside it?

I don't stop running until I stand beside my grave.

The plot has been disturbed.

Hell, forget disturbed. Whoever replaced the dirt was in a hurry and didn't give a damn how suspicious it looked. I don't have to dig the coffin up to be sure. I know that someone has stolen my body. The mud and dirt are strewn all over the place and I can actually hear my violated coffin groaning under the weight of the earth dumped on top of it. Whoever tore off the lid of the box used a crowbar or an axe, some such subtle instrument, obviously, and cracked the wood in a dozen places.

On the far side of the cemetery, half a mile away, I hear a car start. Summoning every bit of Teri's finishing kick, I race toward the sound. But I'm too late, all I do is catch a glimpse of a vanishing station wagon.

Yet I see the license plate, a California plate, HJK2622. The IIC and Ms Brutran have offices in California, a fortress I've been to. And faintly, I catch a glimpse of the driver. He looks like a she, like a woman.

'What the hell?' I mutter.

Why would someone want my dead body?

My vampiric blood would be of no use to them.

Who knew I was dead?

Did we have a spy in our group?

A wave of fatigue sweeps over me. I've had enough exercise for one night. Outside the cemetery, I flag down a taxi and ride back to the Hilton. I'm practically at its doorstep when I redirect the cab to the Sheraton, where Paula Ramirez and her son are staying. It's time I talked to John. I feel he owes me an explanation.

Paula answers the door, wearing red and white cotton pajamas. As usual, she doesn't look surprised to see me. It's hard to take a psychic by surprise. At the same time, she doesn't look happy to see me.

'Teri. It's late. What can I do for you?'

I push her aside and she gives way before me.

'I'm not Teri and you know it, so drop the act,' I snap, glancing around, looking for her son. I can hear him in the adjoining room. He sounds like he's playing a computer game. Does the kid do anything else?

Paula folds her arms across her chest. 'I sensed it. I wasn't sure.'

'Right.'

'Believe what you want.' She pauses. 'How did it happen?'

'That I switched bodies? Gee, I don't know, isn't that more up your alley?'

'Sita, stop. I had nothing to do with what happened to you.'

'Can your son say the same thing?'

Paula hesitates. 'I don't know.'

'I want to talk to him. And don't tell me he's busy or he doesn't want to talk to me. I saved his life. My daughter died saving him. Even if he is a divine incarnation, he can stop playing his goddamn game for ten minutes and answer my questions.'

My rudeness is left over from the last time I tried to

talk to John, on the Greek island Santorini. That was only a few weeks ago. He wouldn't even see me.

Paula considers. 'All right, let me talk to him, tell him you're here. But I warn you . . .'

'No threats, Paula, I'm not in the mood.'

She leaves and is gone longer than I expect. But when she reappears she nods and gestures for me to enter the last room on the right, the master suite. As I trudge down the hall to confront John, my anger and impatience vanish. Either I hold the kid in too much awe or else he deserves it. My heart pounds harder than when I was running. My mind goes blank. What does one say to a god?

John sits cross-legged in the centre of a king-sized bed with a laptop resting on his thighs. He's a nice-looking guy, sixteen, close to seventeen, with a mature demeanor that makes him appear older. His hair is longish, dark and wavy, and his eyes are big and dark. He has lowered the laptop screen and removed his pair of headphones and is no longer focused on the computer. His eyes rest on me, or perhaps on a place ten million miles behind me.

I'm in the room two seconds and I cannot escape the feeling that he sees right through me. I stand at attention, waiting for him to make the first move. He gestures to a chair on his right.

'Have a seat,' he says in a calm voice, or should I say a magical tone. Three simple words and a wave of peace washes over me. My frantic heart slows, my whole body is suddenly at ease. I have to grope with my hands to find the chair because my eyes refuse to look anywhere other than at him.

Yet he's just a kid. It makes no sense. Nothing does.

He stares at me a long time. I stare back.

'John,' I whisper.

He gives a faint nod. 'What do you need?'

'I need to know who you are.'

'You ask with words. That's natural. Your mind is filled with words. Most people think with the language they were first taught. You know many languages, but still, every concept you carry with you, every idea you have, is created from words.' He pauses. 'But words cannot describe what I am.'

The way he speaks, the beautiful simplicity of his words, he sounds like Krishna. 'Are you Krishna?' I ask.

'Krishna is a word.'

'Krishna is more than an ordinary word. It's a mantra that's supposed to embody the vibration of the supreme. Do you represent that vibration?'

'Of course. As do you and everyone else you know.'

'I can think of a few people who have nothing to do with Krishna.'

'You refer to the Telar and the IIC. You consider these people evil. To be disconnected from the supreme.' He shrugs. 'But they're no more separate from the whole than the Light Bearer.'

I gasp. 'Lucifer!'

'Yes.'

'How did you know I was thinking of him?'

'I can see it on your face.'

I hesitate. 'Something terrible happened to me ten days ago. I took a Telar captive, a woman named Numbria. While I was interrogating her, I fell asleep and dreamed about being trapped in hell. Only it was much more than a dream. I felt like I was really there, as if I was having a vision. At the end of it Lucifer came to me and I saw into his heart, or else he told me what he was. And I understood that he really was the Light Bearer, the greatest of all the angels. He knew it, that was the weird part, but he denied it because he hated God so much, even though he knew he was one with God.'

'Why was the dream so awful?'

I cannot stop the harshness from entering my voice. 'It was awful because when I awoke from it I committed an atrocious act. The woman I was questioning – I ate her alive, slowly, horribly, with her screaming for mercy.' I stop. 'I haven't been the same since.'

'You were under the sway of a powerful compulsion.'

'I know, the Array invaded my mind and forced me to do it. But it makes no difference. Ever since I did it, I feel tainted somehow, like I'm now linked to Lucifer and everything he represents.'

'You are. He's the Light Bearer. He's one with his God.'

'That's . . . that's sick.'

'It's true. It's a paradox. The truth often is.'

'Can you take this tainted feeling away?'

'You experienced it for a reason. It will help you later. Best you hold on to it for now.'

'How the hell can it help me?'

John doesn't answer, but smiles faintly.

I ask the question I should have started with.

'What did you do to me at the cemetery?'

'You were ready to die but you were afraid to die. A part of you wanted to go on living. It was the same with your friend. Only your will was stronger than hers.'

'So you put me in this body?' I ask.

'I strengthened your hold on it. You were already attached to it.'

'But why? If you had just left things alone, Teri would have grown accustomed to being a vampire. She would be here instead of me.'

'When you were alone together in the cave, she asked you to let her be. She did not want to die but she accepted it was her time. But you refused to let her go.'

'Are you saying I'm stuck in this body because of karma?'

'That's one reason.'

'What's another?'

'You've lived a long life, through an entire age. You've done many deeds, some great, some not so great. But there are still a few tasks left for you to accomplish. Your soul knew that, and for that reason, it was reluctant to leave this world.'

His words are hard to accept. I want to argue with him. But a part of me knows he speaks the truth. 'What's to become of Teri?' I ask.

'She's dead.'

'But I feel her around me at times.'

'That feeling will pass.'

'That's not fair. You have to bring her back.'

'You've read the Gita. You know the answer to that.'

I nod sadly. 'All who are born die. All who die will be reborn.'

'Yes.'

'The Gita also says that whoever thinks of Krishna at the moment of death goes to his abode. What happened to me when I died? How come I didn't see him?'

'You don't remember what you saw.'

'Then help me remember!' I plead. 'I need to see him again.'

'What will you do if you see him? Will you be able to leave him?'

I understand what he is trying to tell me. 'You're saying I have to complete these tasks before I can go to his abode.'

He nods. His computer beeps and he raises the screen and hastily pushes a button. He turns back to me and sits silently.

'Why do you play that goddamn game?' I remember that Seymour had played the game with John. It was called Cosmic Intuitive Illusion, CII; IIC spelled backwards. I remember what Seymour said when I asked what the goal of the game was.

'*Survival. But all games are about that. It starts on earth and you have to fight your way out of here to higher, more exotic worlds. The ultimate goal appears to be to reach the centre of the galaxy.*'

'To let the others know I'm here,' John replies.

'Who are the others?'

'You'd do better to ask what is behind the Array.'

'If I discover that, will I know who you're playing against?'

'You'll have a better idea.'

I feel frustrated. 'Is all this a play to you? Our struggle with the Telar and the IIC? Do you just watch and wait? At the last moment are you going to make everything all right?'

'This is a world of choice.'

'You're saying you cannot interfere with our freedom of choice?'

John nods. His computer beeps and he hits another button. I hear an electronic explosion and hope one of the bad guys has bitten the dust.

I know he is about to ask me to leave, so I persist with my questions. But I phrase the next one differently. I make it a statement and verbally force him into the position of Krishna.

'But you do interfere,' I say. 'You've saved me a number of times.'

John stops playing his game, pushes down the screen, reaches out, and brushes the hair from my eyes. Our eyes lock and I feel I never want him to let go. His eyes are no longer dark brown but a black blue, and so deep, so bright, I feel that if I fall into them I'll fall forever and never want to stop. His love is blinding; it obliterates everything else. I almost forget why I came to him, what I asked or how he answered. I just feel safe, eternally protected, and he confirms the feeling when he tells me the same thing Krishna did five thousand years ago.

'Sita. My grace is always with you.'

5

The next morning we hold a war council in Seymour's hotel room. I don't know what else to call it. The world is threatened by two rival groups, both powerful, both mad, and we're the only ones who are foolish enough to try to stop them. I suspect if the Telar or the IIC were to eavesdrop on our meeting, they would laugh their heads off. There are so few of us and our wills are totally divided.

However, everyone in our group comes to the meeting except John. I'm surprised to see Paula present and briefly worry if she plans to expose me. But she gives me a look early on that tells me to relax. She's there to help, not to break Matt's heart or get me killed.

The first topic of concern is the X6X6 virus. Haru, the leader of the Telar, has indicated he's going to release it worldwide, with the hope of wiping out the bulk of mankind. Charlie, a nerdy scientist who has worked with the Telar for two hundred years – but who has recently joined our gang – has with him vials of the virus and the vaccine, which he calls T-11.

Unfortunately, Seymour and Shanti have had shots of the vaccine and are still showing signs of the infection. Naturally, this makes us wonder if T-11 even works.

'Why are Seymour and Shanti still sick?' Matt asks Charlie.

The scientist doesn't look a day over twenty, but he's an amusing example of an immortal. He has a facial twitch that causes his right eye to blink whenever he speaks. He paces anxiously as he answers.

'A vaccine isn't usually a cure, although most people think of it that way. You see it all the time on the news. People say, 'When are they going to come up with an HIV vaccine so all the people with AIDS can be cured?' But a vaccine is designed to prevent a disease, not to cure it. And Seymour and Shanti were already infected with X6X6 when they got their first shot of T-11.'

'But the shot seemed to stop the virus dead in its track,' Matt says. 'All of us got better at first, and Teri and I continue to feel fine. It's only Seymour and Shanti who are showing signs of a relapse.'

'You have a few black blisters,' Charlie says to Seymour and Shanti. 'But you two feel OK, don't you?'

'I feel fine,' Shanti says. 'Except my face itches where I had plastic surgery.'

'My hands itch like crazy,' Seymour replies.

'Do you feel better since I gave you another shot this morning?' Charlie asks.

'I do,' Shanti says.

'I'm not sure,' Seymour says, doubtful.

Charlie continues to pace. 'Your case is unusual. I gave you guys the vaccine just a few minutes after you got infected with the virus. The two compounds overlapped in your bodies in ways we won't see in the general population.' Charlie pauses when he realizes what he's saying. 'That is, if we're lucky enough to duplicate the vaccine and get it out to the world in time.'

'A big if,' Seymour grumbles.

Matt holds up his hand. 'Let's not go there yet. I want to know if the vaccine works, period. If it doesn't, then there's no point in trying to get help to spread it globally.'

'T-11 is definitely effective on Telar,' Charlie says. 'It was designed with them in mind. After personally vaccinating five hundred Telar with T-11, I exposed them to the virus and nothing happened. They were immune.'

'So Telar and vampires like me are safe,' I say. 'What about the other seven billion people on the planet?'

Charlie stops pacing and shrugs. 'It must work to some extent on humans. Otherwise, Seymour and Shanti would be dead. It just has to be tweaked to accommodate a mortal immune system.'

'That's the bottom line,' Matt says to Charlie. 'Can

you alter it to protect everyone?'

Charlie hesitates. 'Yes.'

'But . . .' Seymour says, letting the word hang.

'But I'll need a state-of-the-art laboratory and time,' Charlie says. 'A few brilliant chemists and microbiologists helping out wouldn't hurt.'

'Can you make up a list of human scientists that can help you?' Matt asks.

Charlie considers. 'I have Telar friends that would be more helpful.'

Matt's face darkens. 'Who can you trust?'

'Those close to me. They're not fans of Haru or anyone connected with the Source,' Charlie says.

I recall that Numbria, the Telar woman I interrogated and murdered, referred to the Telar high command as the Source. I got the impression there were only a dozen or so people on their high council.

'But they still fear the Source,' Matt says.

'Of course,' Charlie says. 'We all fear them.'

'I want to stick with human scientists for now,' Matt says. 'It will be safer. Later, if you're not making progress, we can consider contacting your Telar friends.'

'How do we approach these scientists?' Seymour asks. 'We can't run around saying the world is ending. We need proof that the Telar exist and we need proof that they intend to release X6X6.'

'The contagious effects of the virus are easy to demonstrate,' Charlie says.

'In a lab, sure,' Seymour says. 'But how are we going

to get these brilliant men and women into your lab?' He turns to Matt. 'You've been kicking around forever. You must have contacts in the government.'

'I know important people in this country and across Europe. They'll take my calls if I contact them. But the moment I do, the Telar will know about it and they'll come after me and whoever I talk to.'

'Then we're screwed,' Seymour says.

Matt gives him a hard look. 'That's helpful. Give up at the start.'

'I'm just being pragmatic,' Seymour says. 'Charlie's told us that he and his Telar buddies have been working on the X6X6 virus for over twenty years. Do you seriously think he's going to be able to modify it in two weeks so that it works on mortals?'

Matt turns to our resident scientist. 'Charlie?'

Charlie is so hyped, he's close to pulling out his hair. 'I don't know. I could stumble on a cure in an afternoon. Or it could take six months.'

'When does Haru plan to release the virus?' Seymour asks.

'No one knows for sure,' Matt replies.

'We heard it was going to be soon,' Charlie adds.

'We're screwed,' Seymour repeats, not afraid to look Matt in the face when he says it. Yet it's Charlie's last remark that deflates the room. Our timetable for stopping the virus appears to be a fantasy.

It's time for me to speak what's on my mind.

Time for me to sound dangerously like Sita.

'We can't stop the Telar without the IIC's help,' I say.

51

'I disagree,' Matt says. 'We have vials of T-11 and X6X6. We have Charlie, who helped create the virus and the vaccine. The IIC has nothing.'

'Then we should give them what we do have,' I say.

Matt studies me closely, alert to my tone, my choice of words, my way of thinking. There are so many ways for him to penetrate my disguise. But I'm careful; I'm good at mimicking Teri.

'Explain,' he says.

'The IIC and the Telar are already enemies. When it comes to power and influence, they're about equal. More important, the IIC already know about the Telar. We don't have to prove to them how dangerous they are, or their virus. The IIC will take one look at X6X6 and understand the threat it represents.'

'They'll also immediately take it out of our hands,' Matt says.

'Maybe they should. They have resources we can't imagine. I say we warn them about the coming plague.'

'That's insane,' Matt snaps.

'It sounds reasonable to me,' Seymour says.

Matt stands and the force of his presence seems to fill the room.

'Are you forgetting the IIC is every bit as evil as the Telar?' he asks. 'They have the Array. They have even used it on us a few times.'

'So?' Seymour says. 'If they force us to jump off a building, what does it matter as long as they're able to neutralize the virus?'

'The enemy of my enemy is my friend,' I say quietly.

'That's bullshit and you know it, Teri,' Matt says. 'If Sita was here she'd agree with me. The IIC may have the means to alter the vaccine and manufacture enough of it to save the world. But they're the last group we should put in charge.'

'Why?' Seymour asks.

'Because we can't trust them,' Matt says.

'You don't like them because they forced you to shoot Sita,' Seymour says, in a slightly mocking tone. I wonder at his motives. Throughout the meeting, I have felt he's trying to push Matt's buttons. I know Seymour well enough to realize he must have a reason. But I fear for him. Like his father, Matt has a temper.

Matt stares at Seymour. 'Maybe you're right. Until you've had your free will ripped from your grasp, you can't imagine what it's like. Trust me, if it had happened to you, you'd want nothing to do with them either.'

Seymour meets his gaze. 'How did they get their hooks in you?'

'What do you mean?'

'Did they have a sample of your blood?'

'I don't know what you're talking about,' Matt says.

'I'm sure you don't,' Seymour says. 'Let's move on. The danger of this virus is too big for us to handle. If we have to make a deal with the IIC or the devil himself to make it go away, then so be it. No offence to Charlie and his pals, but we can't rely on them to alter the vaccine and spread it all over the world in time to stop this plague. It's not going to happen, not in the real world.'

'Seymour,' Matt says, "the vials of virus and the vials of the vaccine all represent power. We can't just hand that power over to the IIC when we have no idea what their ultimate goals are. We would just be strengthening their position while we weaken ours.'

'Will that matter if millions start dying?' Seymour asks.

It's my turn to stand and speak. 'Matt does have a point, and so does Seymour. I still think we're going to be forced to appeal to the IIC to help us stop the Telar but we may as well use what time we have to gain a better understanding of what the IIC's up to. I know Sita was anxious to explore their background.'

'How do we do that?' Shanti asks.

'By researching how the company came to be,' Paula replies. 'I wouldn't mind helping in that area.'

'Really?' I ask, astounded. It's hard to imagine Paula taking an active role. 'Can you talk John into helping?'

Paula catches my eye. 'Let's not bring him into this.'

'Our time would be better spent helping Charlie build and stock a laboratory so he can alter the vaccine,' Matt says. 'Let's not take our eye off the immediate threat. X6X6 is what will destroy humanity. It's all that matters. We have to discover how to stop it.'

'It's just as important to stop the people who invented it,' Seymour says. 'Your focus is on the virus, Matt. That's good, you should follow your heart. Stick with Charlie. The girls and I can go after the IIC.'

Matt shakes his head. 'I don't want Teri getting near those people.'

'That's Teri's decision to make,' Seymour says.

Again, doubt appears to flicker across Matt's face as he studies me. His gaze is so intense, I feel as if he literally peels away layers of skin, tissue and bone until he reaches my psyche. I feel him inside, probing, and I can only pray that our lovemaking the previous night has deflected any misgivings he has about me.

'Teri?' he says.

I lower my head. I don't have the strength to look him in the eye.

'I want to go with the others,' I say.

6

I call several of my old-time associates in the detective field to help research the origins of the IIC. To my surprise, they are not thrilled to hear from me. The problem is simple; I should have anticipated it. They're not sure it's me they're talking to. Teri and I look more alike than we sound. As a result, on the phone, I'm far from convincing. A couple of my trusted allies actually threaten to investigate me instead of the IIC. I'm off to a great start.

But with Paula's help, we start to make our own progress. The IIC is controlled by a board of directors made up of five people: Thomas Brutran; his wife, Cynthia Brutran; Noel Brent and his wife, Wendy Brent; Fredrick Wild. These five have been with the company since its inception, forty years ago.

It's interesting that, before founding the company, the board members attended a graduate programme at the University of California, Berkeley. Their curriculum was taught by a Professor John Sharp. On the surface it seemed to be connected to the psychology department. But a closer examination reveals that it was focused almost exclusively on parapsychology, on proving the existence of ESP, or extrasensory perception.

That was pretty much all we could learn about the programme, other than the fact that it had lasted three years before suddenly being cancelled when Berkeley decided Professor Sharp was performing studies of 'questionable moral value'.

The four of us, Seymour, Paula, Shanti and myself, are intrigued. We find an address for Professor Sharp online. He appears to be living in the Bay Area, in San Mateo. He's retired, and based on how long ago he taught, we assume the man must be in his eighties.

We decide to visit without calling ahead. If he's still friendly with Ms Brutran, she might invoke the Array before we can reach him, and God only knows what will happen to us. Yet it's not a big worry. Professor Sharp appears to be living in a modest apartment, and if he's connected to the IIC in any way then they are not paying him.

Before leaving Denver for the Bay Area, the police question me about the disappearance of Ken. They come the afternoon after our war council, when I'm alone in the hotel suite and feeling the first stirrings of my *thirst*. The police are lucky to show up in pairs, or else I might have had one of them for dinner.

They knock on the door as if they would prefer to kick it in.

I answer wearing the sweats Teri wore in the Olympics, and leave my gold medal on the living room table. I'm shameless, I know, but the glint of the shiny medal has a powerful effect on them. Their eyes are immediately drawn to it and they smile when I invite them inside. Already, I believe, I'm halfway home.

They sit on the couch across from me and talk about how they saw my world-record race on TV. They're detectives; they have on sports coats rather than uniforms.

'How did you feel going into the last lap?' the taller and older of the two cops asks. His name is Lieutenant William Treach. He's close to forty, with a thin build but a wiriness that projects strength. He's friendly but alert, very much in charge. I may have made a strong initial impression, however, I quickly notice that the man prefers clear answers.

'I was hurting and I was at the rear of the pack. Plus I was boxed in. It looked pretty hopeless. But in running, there's a burning pain and then there's a weak kind of pain. The burning kind can actually feel worse than the exhaustive kind, but it means you've still got something left. You can still go for it, and that's what I did. I had to shove two women out of my way to get out of my box. If the race had been in America, I would have been disqualified. But European runners treat races like soccer matches. When it comes to the metric mile, they see pushing and shoving as part of the race.'

'It must have been a thrill to hit the straightaway and know the gold medal was waiting for you if you could just get in front of that Russian,' Lieutenant Sean Astor says. Short and stout, ten years younger than his partner, he has a boyish innocence that tells me he'll be easy to fool. He adds, 'What was her name?'

'Olga Stensky. I'm never going to forget Olga. She elbowed me and cut me off in the last eighty yards. I was lucky it backfired on her. As she swung into the second lane to try to block me, I moved inside. She lost a stride trying to stop me, and I won by a stride. Most track experts say if Olga had just ignored me and run her race, she would have won.'

'How did it feel to stand on the winners' podium and hear our national anthem?' Treach asks.

'I felt like I'd died and gone to heaven. I still haven't come down from the high.'

'I imagine you've received a ton of endorsement offers since the Olympics,' Treach says. I notice how he studies the room.

I shake my head. 'Not as many as you would think. I just won one gold medal. Sure, it was in a big event, but it's like I had my fifteen minutes of fame and now it's over.'

Astor is sympathetic. 'A lot of Olympic athletes say that. One week they're getting invited to the White House and the next week they're back home and bagging groceries.'

Treach clears his throat, signaling that he wants to get down to business. 'What brings you to Denver, Ms Raine?' he asks.

'Teri, please. I'm here with my boyfriend. We're bumming around the country. Taking a break after all the stress of the Olympics.'

'That's Matt Fraiser, isn't it?' Treach asks.

'Yes.'

Matt signed in under a fake name to hide us from the Telar. A minor strategic move that has swollen in size and danger now that the police are looking at me. Treach takes out a tiny notebook and jots down a few words.

'It's our understanding that Matt wasn't here when you ordered room service?' Treach asks.

'That's correct. I was alone and starving. But the room service guy never showed up.'

'Do you mean Ken?' Treach asks.

'Yes.'

'Did you call to complain?'

'No. I was about to but then they called me.'

'Was that Michael Pollak? The head of room service?'

'I don't know his title. He said his name was Mike.'

'Why did he call you?'

'He was looking for his server.'

'What did you tell him?'

'That I hadn't seen any food or server.'

Treach consults his notes. 'Mike says that you identified Ken by name even while you were insisting that Ken had failed to deliver your order.'

60

'That's true. I called the guy Ken right after Mike called him Ken.'

'Mike says he never mentioned Ken by name. Not until you did.'

'He did so the second he got on the phone. But I don't think he's lying. I think he just forgot.'

'That happens,' Astor adds for my benefit.

'Why do you say that?' Treach presses.

I shrug. 'When I spoke to Mike, he seemed like a nice guy. I think he was just worried about his employee. Is he still missing?'

'That's why we're here. Ms Raine, Teri, are you absolutely certain Ken didn't come to your door? Is it possible you were in the restroom and he knocked and left because you failed to answer?'

'It's possible. I think I went to the bathroom at some point while I was waiting for my food. But I wasn't in there very long.'

Treach makes another note. 'What did you do after you spoke to room service?'

The way he asks his question, I realize Treach has something up his sleeve. It must be the family I ran into on the elevator. He's probably talked to them. I'll have to admit to leaving the hotel, which I hate to do. It looks odd.

'Well, I was still hungry so I went out to get a bite.'

'Where did you go?'

'I don't know, somewhere local. A deli a few blocks from here.'

'Do you remember the name of it?'

'No.'

'Was it two blocks from here? Or three or four?'

'I'm not sure. It could have been as many as five or six blocks away. I don't know the area. I just went walking.'

'How come you didn't eat at the hotel?'

'Well, as far as I could tell, their service wasn't very good.'

'How did you pay for your meal?'

'With cash.'

'Do you do that often?'

'What? Eat?'

'Pay for your dinner with cash. Most people use a card these days.'

'I had some cash on me and I just bought a sandwich so I used it.'

'I try to use cash when I can,' Astor says.

Treach gives him a hard look before he continues, and I realize I've underestimated the detective. He's experienced and my story does not ring true to his ears. The more we talk, the greater his suspicions grow. I wish he was alone and I could try using the hypnotic power of my eyes on him. Unsure of my abilities, I don't dare try it with both of them in the room. I realize that I have to end the interrogation soon.

'Teri, when you were leaving the hotel, you ran into a family that's staying here. They said they tried to talk to you but you were rude to them. They also said—'

'I wasn't rude.' I interrupt. 'They thought I worked for the hotel and kept asking me directions to the Pepsi

Center. Even after I explained that I didn't know the area, they kept bugging me, especially the wife.'

'The husband and the wife said you had a room service cart with you. Is that true?'

'Why would I be walking around with a room service cart? It was in the elevator when I stepped inside. I had nothing to do with it.'

'The couple's youngest boy thought he saw a man's body stuffed beneath the cart.'

I stare at Treach. 'You've got to be joking.'

The man shrugs. 'It's what the boy told us.'

I laugh softly. 'That's cute. I mean, it would be cute if Ken wasn't missing. But no, Detective Treach, I can assure you I didn't kill Ken after he delivered my steak to my room. And I certainly didn't stuff his body in a room service cart.'

'It's not like any of us really believe that,' Astor says.

I smile. 'Well, that's a relief.'

'Did you get out of the elevator with the family?' Treach asks.

'I waited until they left. Then I got off.'

'Why did you wait?'

'I think I already explained why. They kept asking me questions I couldn't answer. And the wife seemed to get mad I couldn't answer them.'

'Did you by any chance ride the elevator down to the garage?'

'No.'

'The Johnsons said you remained in the elevator,' Treach says.

'Who are the Johnsons?'

'The family you bumped into.'

'I'm sorry, they didn't introduce themselves. No, I didn't stay in the elevator. I got off at the lobby. But I waited a minute until the Johnsons left the area.'

'I would have done the same thing,' Astor says.

'Lieutenant,' Treach says, annoyed.

Astor is not quite the puppy dog he appears. 'With all due respect, I think Ms Raine has explained her actions extremely well. I believe her.'

'Thank you,' I say.

'I'm not saying I don't,' Treach continues. 'I just have a few more questions and I'll be done. Would that be OK, Teri?'

'Sure. I know you have a job to do.'

'The reason I ask about the garage is because a Camry was stolen from the lower level about the same time Ken went missing. Furthermore, the cart Ken took to your room was found abandoned beside the parking spot where the Camry was parked.'

I nod, act interested. 'That sounds like an important clue. How do you know the cart belonged to Ken?'

'We found samples of his hair attached to the cart tablecloth.'

'Wow. That's kind of scary. Maybe the boy was right. Maybe we were all standing together in that elevator and his body was crammed inside the cart.'

Astor shakes his head. 'It's doubtful. Ken's a big guy. To squeeze him into that kind of space, it would take an awfully strong person.'

'But the scenario is not out of the question,' Treach says.

'I know this is none of my business, but have you guys managed to locate the Camry?' I ask. I worry about them finding samples of hair on the driver's seat.

Treach shakes his head. 'It's disappeared.'

He's lying! Damn, they found the car already. His people are probably going over it with a fine-tooth comb as we speak. I assumed I would have had more time to get out of town.

'That's too bad,' I say casually.

Treach appears to have run out of questions. He gives me his card and heads for the door. But he suddenly stops and faces me and there's no mistaking the suspicion in his voice and expression.

'Will you be staying in Denver the next few days?' he asks.

'We plan to leave tomorrow,' I say.

'Where are you headed?'

'Nowhere in particular. We're just going to get in the car and drive.'

'So you do have a car?'

'Yes.'

'Is it a rental or does it belong to you?'

'It's a rental. Matt got it at the airport.'

Treach nods. 'Please, Teri, before leaving, let us know where you're heading next.'

I give him a cold smile. 'I'll try.'

When they're gone, I feel like I need a nap, or at least to lie down and rest. It's clear to me that I've made an enemy, and that Treach is going to dog my steps in the coming days. True, I don't possess my usual power, but deep inside I'm still ancient Sita. I still have a pretty sharp intuition and it's telling me my best bet is to kill him.

I need to drink. I'm not feeling psycho or anything but my thirst is starting to aggravate me. It's probably one of the reasons I was so short with the police.

I call an old private-eye friend of mine who is up in years and hard of hearing so he doesn't notice anything odd about my change of voice. I ask him to get me Lieutenant William Treach's personal information and the PI calls back within the hour with the cop's home address and other assorted details.

Matt told me before leaving that afternoon that he would help me hunt that evening but I'm in no mood to wait for his return. Also, I want to make it clear that I don't need his help. Otherwise, he'll try to stop me from going off with the others when they travel to the Bay Area. I leave him a brief note saying I've gone out and not to worry.

Matt's rented me a car and I drive to Lieutenant Treach's neighbourhood and park two houses down from his residence. The sun has recently set and the shadows are lengthening. Rolling down the window, I sit quietly with my eyes closed. Before entering Teri's body, my hearing was my most potent sense, the one tool I could always rely on when things got tough. Although Teri's ears are not nearly as keen as my originals, I'm relieved that I'm able to hear what's going on in the Treach household.

Treach is not home yet. I listen as Mrs Sandra Treach talks on the phone with her sister in New York. From the conversation I'm able to discern that Sandy, as her sister calls her, is the head of surgery at a nearby hospital. This interests me because surgeons often do transfusions during operations, and the head of the department would probably have relatively easy access to the clinic's blood bank.

From experience I know about blood banks and the quality of blood that can be found in such places. In the past, for the most part, I've stayed away from that source of nourishment. It's not merely the components of blood that feed a vampire, but the life essence itself in the blood.

What this essence is would be difficult to describe scientifically. In the West, they don't have words for it. A Chinese acupuncturist might call it *chi*. A yogi from India would refer to it as *prana*. Whatever it is, it exists, and blood that has been stored for several weeks usually has a low charge. However, it is better than nothing and if I can get hold of a few gallons it could save me a lot of grief while we travel to California. I hate the thought of constantly having to put my life on hold to satisfy my thirst.

I decide to strike now while William is out. But I wait until Sandy finishes talking with her sister. I don't want to be waved away at the door because she's on the phone. Leaving my car, approaching the house, I listen as Sandy fiddles with an assortment of pots and pans.

This venture is something of a test for me. Finally I'm going to see how much of my psychic abilities I have left.

Sandy answers quickly, after I ring the doorbell. Like her husband, she's about forty, tall and slender, but there the resemblance ends. The woman has bright red hair – it is close to orange – and wonderful green eyes. They sparkle; she is the kind of person that glows. And here I expected to find a stuffy old doctor.

'Hello. Can I help you?' she asks.

'Hi. My name's Teri Raine. I met your husband today. He came to the hotel where I'm staying. He's investigating a missing employee there.'

'Teri, yes, I know who you are. Bill called me after he spoke to you. He said you were delightful. You were in the Olympics, weren't you?'

'That seems to be my main claim to fame.'

'Well, of course, you won a gold medal and set a world record. How many women your age can say that?'

'Not many, I suppose. Look, I know it must seem kind of weird to stop by your house, but I was sort of short with your husband today and I wanted to talk to him about something I remembered from when that guy vanished. Would he be home by any chance?'

'He's not here right now but I can give him a call. Would you like to come in a sec? I'm just starting dinner.' She opens the door wider and gestures for me to enter.

'That would be great, thanks,' I say as I cross the

threshold. The home is three storeys tall, custom designed, with lots of open wood beams. I assume it's Sandy's salary that paid for the place. The woman bubbles with energy. I follow as she leads me into the living room and offers me a seat. Once again, I'm not surprised she trusted me enough to invite me into her home. Teri's fame and her wholesome looks work wonders with complete strangers.

Yet the inevitable question quickly comes up. Sandy wants to know how I happen to know where her husband lives. I'm sitting across from her when she asks and I catch her gaze and let my power flow through my eyes.

'Bill gave me your address,' I say softly. 'He told me to contact him if I remembered anything about the missing young man.'

Sandy stares back without blinking, and I know I have her to some extent. Yet it is all a question of degrees. I need to start with small orders and lies and work my way up.

'Bill is puzzled about the missing boy,' Sandy whispers.

'The case is puzzling. But I'm here to help Bill.'

Sandy smiles faintly. 'That's good you can help.'

'I want to help because I'm a good person.' Although I channel the energy through my eyes, I experience its source as a magnetism that radiates from my forehead. It projects out from me like an invisible hand. My grip on Sandy is not nearly as firm as it would have been in my old body, but I'm pleased that she's repeating what I feed her.

'You are a good person,' she says. 'Can I get you something to eat? To drink?'

'Soon. Tell me, when will Bill come home?'

Sandy blinks and frowns, not a good sign. 'He'll be home soon. But he'll wonder why you're here.'

'I'm here because Bill invited me here.'

'Oh.'

'When you say he'll be here soon, how soon do you mean?'

'I'm not sure. In a half hour.'

'Good, that's good. Now close your eyes, Sandy.' She immediately shuts her eyes as I continue. 'Listen to the sound of my voice. My voice is all you hear. Do you understand?'

'Yes.'

'You work at Springfield Hospital. You're a surgeon there. In fact, you're the head of the surgery department.'

'Yes.'

'Do you have access to the blood bank at your hospital?'

The woman frowns again and I fear I've made my question more complicated than it needs to be. Of course, as a surgeon, she would not get the blood herself.

I'm not used to taking so much time to hypnotize a victim. Usually I just say a word or two and people do what I want. I feel my hold on Sandy wavering. However, I know if I weaken her physically – and I can think of the perfect way to do that – she'll respond to my commands more readily.

'The blood is there,' she says. 'The nurses bring it when we need it.'

'Good. If I drive you to the hospital, will you be able to get me in the blood bank?'

'Yes.'

'In the evening, how many people work in that department?'

'Usually there is one person on duty. Sometimes two.'

'Good, we'll drive there soon. You want to drive to the hospital. You want to go with me.'

'I do.'

I get up and stand above her. 'Before we leave I want you to relax in your chair. Just relax and go to sleep for a few minutes. You won't awaken until I tell you to. All right? Now sleep, Sandy. Sleep deeply.'

The woman doesn't speak but her breathing grows heavy and I know she's out cold. Ideally, I would have waited until after I had her out of the house to drink her blood. The threat of her husband coming home cannot be taken lightly. Yet my thirst clouds my judgment. I figure if I can just drink a pint or two, and take the edge off my discomfort, I'll be better equipped to handle the situation at the hospital.

Sitting beside Sandy, I tilt her head back and expose her jugular. Her skin is thin and pale – I can see the pulse of the vein through her flesh. I'm hungry but I'm in control. I'm not going to make the same mistake I did with Ken. That's why I turn away from her neck and reach for her right wrist instead, twisting the back of it upward, towards my mouth.

I don't possess the fangs the popular vampires always seem to be flashing but Teri's teeth are sharp and as I bite down a delicious flood of red fluid fills my mouth. Like Ken, Sandy must take care of herself – her blood is intoxicating. I've opened the vein most depressed people slit when they try to commit suicide. The flow is ample but it's nowhere near the flood I unleashed when I bit into Ken's neck. I'm able to monitor to the ounce how much blood I suck from Sandy's body. I do catch myself moaning, though, unconsciously, and have to make a point of stopping.

I'm through drinking and spilling a few drops of my own blood on Sandy's wounds – which instantly seals them – when I hear a man coming up the front steps. I know who it is for I remember the sound of William Treach's gait from a few hours ago.

'Damn you, Sita!' I swear at my own foolishness. I should have listened to my head, not my thirst, and got Sandy out of the house before feeding. Now I will have to deal with Bill quickly, not necessarily an easy task. He's not just an armed cop, he's smart, and he won't be lulled by my enchanting eyes and sweet voice. If he catches me standing over his unconscious wife he'll draw his gun and shoot.

I can't let him see me. I have to knock him out quick, or else kill him. But I'm suddenly troubled. I don't want to kill him, not now, not after being in his home and meeting his wife. Since I specifically came to his house to eliminate him as a threat, the feeling is totally illogical. Yet that doesn't make it any less real. I can't just make it go away. At the very least, I need more time to think about the situation. As he reaches for his doorknob, I rush across the room and hide behind the front door.

'Sandy, I'm home!' he calls as he opens the door. His focus is towards the rear of the house, in the direction of the kitchen. I'm able to come up behind him and wrap my right arm around his neck before he can so much as blink. There is a curious irony to my tactic. The choke hold I apply to his neck is the one most often used by the police. But with my strength, it works extremely fast and I'm able to close off the blood supply to his brain and render him unconscious in a few seconds. He sinks quietly to the floor.

Duct tape! Don't leave home without it. I have brought my duct tape with me from yesterday. It's on the front seat of my car and I hurry outside and hastily retrieve it. I bind Bill to a leather chair in the living room. It's heavy, not easy to move around, and it's comfortable. I tie him up before he has a chance to regain consciousness, going so far as to tape his eyes shut.

But I worry about my binds. No matter how thorough I am, he's a cop and he might escape. The best thing to do would be to drug him but I have not brought any narcotics. Then it strikes me. I'm in a doctor's house! Chances are they have some kind of drugs on hand. Rushing upstairs, I check out their medicine cabinet and find a bottle of Ambien, a popular sleeping pill, plus a bottle of Percocet, a relatively strong painkiller.

I discover an enema bag beneath the sink, and crush four Ambiens with four Percocets, and pour the powder in the bag with twelve ounces of water. The advantage of the enema bag is that it comes with a rubber hose I can directly feed into Bill's stomach. This way I don't have to resort to using needles, which Sandy does not appear to have on hand anyway.

I run into a small problem when I cut the tape on Bill's mouth open. He must have woken up when I was upstairs preparing the drugs and now he's only pretending to be unconscious. He almost bites my finger off when I try to slip the tube into his mouth.

'Stop! Who are you?' he snaps.

I have already told his wife my name. I told her because I'm a public figure, and my name was the quickest way into their house. But I made that decision a half an hour ago, when I was planning to kill them both. Now I'm not sure what to do.

I grab a pillow and muffle my voice. 'I'm not here to harm you. But I need to knock you out. It will be easier if you cooperate.'

'Where is my wife?' he demands.

'She's resting on the living room couch. She's unharmed. If you listen closely, you can hear her snoring.'

He does stop to listen. Sandy snores loudly.

'Why are you doing this?' he asks.

'I can't explain right now. But you have to trust me, I mean you no harm.'

He struggles in his chair. 'Who are you? You sound familiar.'

'You don't know me. You don't want to know me.'

I drop the pillow and slip behind him. He hears me move but there's nothing he can do to stop me from slipping my arm around his neck again. He goes out quicker this time, and a minute later I'm sliding the petroleum jelly-coated rubber tube down his throat and holding the bag above his head so gravity will drain the solution of drugs into his stomach. I leave his duct tape slit open. I don't want him vomiting in the night and choking.

When I'm done with Bill, I return to Sandy. I don't shake her awake but use the power of my voice. I instruct her to open her eyes and lead her outside to my car. Night has fallen and the street is old and devoid of lights. The dark provides us with plenty of cover. I steer her by her arm and once she's seated in the front, with her seat belt on, I ask her for the hospital address. I know it already but I want to start engaging her, getting her ready for the performance she's going to put on at the hospital that will hopefully bring me to the blood bank.

'At the hospital you will tell people that I'm your niece,' I say as she sits fixed-eyed beside me.

'You are my niece, Teri Raine.'

'No. Say I'm your niece, Kim Treach. Say Kim, Sandy.'

'Kim Sandy.'

'No. I want you to call me Kim. From now on, that's my name.'

'Kim.'

'Yes. Kim Treach. And when we reach the hospital, if anyone asks what you're doing there, say you have to catch up on some paperwork.'

'I do have to catch up on my paperwork.'

'When we reach the hospital, I want to go to your office first.' Sandy is dressed for a casual night at home. I want her to get her doctor's coat on her, have her badge in place.

'We will go to my office,' she repeats.

We reach the hospital ten minutes later and our entry goes off without a hitch. Sandy's office is on the fourth floor and she has brought her keys. While she is changing into her hospital clothes, I hurry back down to the security area and find a sole guard overseeing a bank of monitors. Before he can even get a good look at me, I belt him in the temple and knock him out cold. Then I turn off all the hospital cameras and remove the digital cards they were transferring their data to. Now the hospital will not even have a record of Sandy and me entering the hospital.

I return to Sandy and find her dressed and ready to go.

Yet I run into a mental block I find difficult to overcome.

Sandy is a surgeon and like most surgeons she's used to calling down for blood before or during an operation. She's too important to actually run to the basement and collect it herself. The habit is so ingrained in her that when I suggest we're ready to pay the blood bank a visit, she reaches for the phone.

'I'll call them and tell them we need blood,' she says.

'There's no need. We'll get it ourselves.'

'I can call. They'll take my call.'

I take the phone from her and put it back down.

'This is a special case, Sandy. We need to get extra blood and we need to take it out of the hospital.'

She frowns. 'Why?'

One simple word, but it's enough to shake my world. The woman should not be questioning my orders. I struggle to come up with a scenario that might fit a pattern already locked into her brain. It doesn't help that my thirst has returned and I'm feeling pissed off. Obviously, I didn't drink nearly enough of Sandy's blood.

What's so cool about craving blood and having the urge drive you crazy half the night? I remind myself to tell Seymour that he's crazy to want to be a vampire, especially a newborn.

'There's been a major train accident outside of town,' I say. 'Many people have been injured. It's so serious that triage units are being set up near the track. A lot of people are so badly hurt they can't wait until they reach a hospital. They need immediate care. It's your job to get as much blood as possible and take it to the scene and start operating on people.' I pause and focus on her eyes. They have turned bloodshot, another fact I'm not wild about. Could I be damaging her? 'Do you understand?' I ask.

'How did this happen, Kim?'

'Teenagers were fooling with the track controls and derailed a train. We need the blood and we need it now. Let's get it.'

I manage to get her in a nearby elevator and push the button for the basement. It's half past eight. Most of the patient visitors have gone home but the hospital isn't as empty as I would like. It probably would have been wiser to wait until midnight to try to steal the blood. Tell that to my thirst. The blood I drained from Sandy is beginning to feel like a mere mouthful.

There is only one guy manning the blood centre. At first glance I feel relieved. He's young, maybe twenty. He looks neither very strong nor very intelligent. He just looks bored. Unfortunately, he flashes a smile when he sees Sandy, and it's obvious he knows and likes the woman.

'Dr Treach, I thought you went home hours ago,' he says. His name badge reads GARY STEVENS. 'What are you doing here?'

Sandy replies like a zombie robot. 'There's been a major train accident outside of town. Many people have been injured. It's so serious that triage units are being set up near the track. A lot of people are so badly hurt they can't wait until they reach a hospital. They need immediate care. It's your job to get as much blood as possible and take it to the scene and start operating on people.' She turns and gestures to me. 'This is my niece, Kim Treach.'

Oh shit, I think. Could there be a worse example of

crossed brain circuits? Now, it's clear my psychic abilities only go skin deep.

On the plus side, Gary must not be a sports fan. He couldn't have watched much of the Olympics. He doesn't appear to recognize me.

At the same time that doesn't make Dr Treach's request any less unusual. Gary stands and comes around his desk, and as he does so a cloud of doubt crosses his face. He scratches his head.

'I've been online most of the night and didn't see anything about it. And no one's called down from the nurses' station. Dr Treach, are you sure about this accident?'

'Teenagers were fooling with the track controls and derailed a train. We need the blood and we need it now.' She stops and seems to glance at me for support. 'Let's get it.'

I would laugh if the situation wasn't so dire. Gary does chuckle but it sounds forced. He glances at his phone like it might be a lifeline to a saner authority.

'How much blood do you need?' he asks.

'As much blood as possible and take it to the scene,' Sandy says.

He nods uncomfortably. 'I heard you the first time.'

I catch his eye. 'Show it to us and we'll take care of everything,' I say softly but firmly. Unfortunately, I don't feel much power in my voice or in my head. Also, Gary appears to be one of those people who are simply difficult to hypnotize. I run into them every now and then.

'That sounds like a pretty screwy plan if you ask me,' Gary replies and suddenly reaches for the phone. I have no choice. In a flash I take two steps forward and slug him in the jaw, in the sweet spot, as the boxers like to call it. I catch him as he falls and then let him down gently. Sandy stares at me with a bewildered expression.

'Why did you hit him?' she asks.

I grip Sandy by the shoulders and focus on her face as best I can.

'Forget I hit him. What's important is the blood. We have to get the blood so we can help the people who were hurt in the train wreck. That's all that matters.'

The suggestion appears to strike home. Sandy nods vigorously.

'We have to get the blood,' she says.

Being a vampire, I'm not unfamiliar with blood banks. I know the variety of forms doctors store it in. A common one is blood plasma, which I've sampled in the past with disastrous results. Plasma is blood with the red cells centrifuged out of it. When it comes to vampires, it would seem the red stuff is essential.

Yet straight blood platelets are of no use when it comes to satisfying my thirst. I need whole blood, preferably from a healthy donor.

Sandy leads us into a long narrow room packed with exceptionally large refrigerators. The room is warm; the coolers give off heat. It's not hard to identify the refrigerators that hold the blood that's been tested for diseases. Everything in the space is clearly labelled. Opening the cooler nearest the door and seeing row after row after row of plastic baggies filled with dark red fluid, I feel a rush of excitement that is almost sexual. I have to restrain myself from ripping open a bag and downing it in front of Sandy. The fewer disturbing images I put in her mind the better. Also, blood tastes much better warmed to body temperature.

I'm fortunate there's a large metal cart in the room. With its wheels and steel compartments and narrow crossbars that are ideal for hanging filled baggies, I know I'm looking at the very tool the hospital uses to make blood deliveries. I quickly load it to capacity – about ten gallons' worth of whole blood – before covering it with a couple of white sheets I find in a closet. The sheets help give the cart the vague appearance of a gurney.

We leave the hospital without incident. Just stroll right out the front door and no one asks us a single question, although almost everyone says hello to Dr Sandra Treach. Yet I worry about leaving Gary Stevens lying unconscious on the floor. He is the worst of loose ends. He will assume I helped steal the blood. He will wonder at the amazing punch I gave him. He will almost certainly end up talking to the police.

But the thought of snapping his neck, before leaving the hospital, repulses me. For years now, centuries actually, I've striven only to kill those I consider evil. I've not always succeeded with the vow but I have drawn a line at murdering the completely helpless. And quietly sleeping off my right uppercut, Gary could not be more helpless.

And since I no longer desire to kill the Treaches, my idea is to plant the most powerful 'FORGET ME' hypnotic suggestions I can summon in both Sandy and Bill's minds. Yet my plan has two weaknesses. I have drugged Bill heavily. I'll have to hang out at least until morning to take care of him. Plus my powers are questionable. Actually, they are pathetic and Bill is very strong-willed. He won't be easy to control.

Of course I could call for Matt. He would help his dear love Teri Raine in an instant. I've no doubt he could make the Treaches forget their first and last names. But running to him for help will reinforce his belief that I'm too weak and inexperienced to be left alone. With the important trip to California coming up, that's the last thing I need.

Inside Sandy and Bill's home, I plop the good doctor in front of the TV and turn the channel to the Shopping Network and order her to enjoy herself. Then, after checking on Bill to make sure he's breathing easily, I heat up a quart of blood and sit on the back porch and slowly sip it. The blood may not be fresh from a human vein but it goes down awfully smooth.

I instruct Sandy to get ready for bed and when she's finally ready to slip beneath the sheets, I have her sit on the edge of the mattress. Her pupils swell in size as I focus my eyes on her. She appears much more relaxed now that she's back in her bedroom.

I kneel beside her and speak in a quiet but forceful tone.

'You're to forget me, Sandy. You're to forget everything that happened after I came to your door. You never met any Kim or Teri or Olympic runner. You never returned to the hospital, nor did you speak to Gary Stevens tonight.' I pause. 'Do you understand?'

She stares. 'Yes.'

I repeat the instructions several times before I tuck her into bed. Now I have to wait for Bill to awaken so I can repeat the process. Unfortunately, sitting around has never been my strong suit. I soon grow impatient. Then it strikes me that if I pump his stomach, I can probably get the majority of the medicine out of his gut before it can enter his bloodstream.

I free him from his chair, undress him, and carry him upstairs to the bathtub. There I use the enema bag to force a stream of warm water mixed with Epsom salts down his throat. Even though he's unconscious, I'm able to trigger his instinct to vomit, and he throws up a large amount of white guck. When I turn the cold shower on his face, he quickly wakes up.

But the good news is he's stoned out of his mind from the drugs he did absorb, and they've put him in a very suggestive state. I lock eyes with him and command him to forget about me, not only being in his house, but as a possible suspect in the mysterious disappearance of Ken. I realize his partner will eventually remind him about me at some point but I load him with suggestions about how innocent Teri Raine truly is.

I don't know if it's the drugs or my own wishful

thinking but Lieutenant William Treach seems to swallow everything I say. He repeats my orders back to me word for word.

I dry the detective off, tuck him into his pajamas, and slide him into bed beside his wife. Then I go downstairs and collect my ten gallons of blood and leave the Treaches to their dreams. The evening has had its ups and downs but I feel confident that I'm ending on a positive note.

Time will tell.

Paula and Seymour introduce themselves to Professor John Sharp as freelance reporters. Shanti and I are close friends along for the ride. Sharp seems to absorb our lies with a kindly, grandfather-like smile that slightly droops from a long-ago stroke.

He invites us into his house, which is crammed with books and old photographs, and offers us a pitcher of iced tea and a plate of chocolate chip cookies. We gather in his kitchen. I take that as a good sign. Decisions are more often made in the kitchen than any other room in the house.

There's a feeling of unreality to Sharp's greeting but I keep my mouth shut and help myself to his refreshments. I figure his motives for letting us into his house so easily will become clear in time. I'm tired of sitting in the car; it's good to stretch and nibble. We have driven straight through from Denver to San Mateo. Along the way we decided Seymour would take the lead when it came to questioning Sharp. However, we have hardly sipped his iced tea when the professor surprises us with a strange remark.

'I've been waiting for you people,' he says.

We exchange puzzled looks, although the eyes of the others come to rest on me. I'm not surprised they want my advice as to how to proceed, even Shanti. Since we were all cooped up in a car for so many hours with Shanti – an extremely intuitive young woman – it got to the point where the truth just spontaneously burst out and I had to admit that I was Sita and not Teri. The news should have blown Shanti's mind but she seemed to take it in stride. Indeed, she seems relieved that I'm still alive.

'What makes you say that?' Seymour asks.

Sharp is in his eighties and looks it. I'd wager to say his life has been difficult but interesting. On the surface, he appears to have largely mended from the stroke that I assume forced his retirement but he still walks with a limp and the left side of his face lacks a clear expression. He's a character, though – I can tell he has secrets he's going to make us work for.

But I'm not worried. I know how to handle his type.

He studies Seymour. 'You're not a reporter,' he says.

'No?'

'You've never interviewed anyone in your life.'

'How do you know?'

'I just have to look at you. Experienced reporters have cold eyes. They don't care what they expose, who they hurt. They rationalize it all away by saying they're just searching for the truth. You have too much heart to be in that business.'

Seymour stays cool. 'You're right, I'm a novelist. But that doesn't mean my interest in IIC isn't genuine.'

'Explain,' Sharp says.

'There's a mystery behind that company. Its founding, its rapid growth. I think there's a book there, a book that should start with you.'

'Why me?'

'I Googled IIC to get a list of their board of directors. It can't be a coincidence that all of them were once graduate students of yours.'

Sharp appears satisfied. 'Very good.'

'Your turn,' Seymour says. 'Why did you say you were waiting for us?'

Sharp shakes his head. 'I haven't been waiting for you per se. Just for someone to come along and ask about the mystery surrounding IIC.'

'We're the first?' Seymour says.

'Yes. Odd, don't you think? I kept expecting someone from the government to at least get suspicious about my old students. But no one has.'

'It's possible others have begun to wonder about the company,' Seymour says. 'But something stopped them from pursuing the matter.'

'Such as?' Sharp says.

'Money. Nosy people could have been bought off.'

'Or else killed,' I say.

Sharp turns and looks me over. He could be a dirty old man but I feel his gaze goes deep. A glance from Paula has already told me the man is sensitive, perhaps a psychic in his own right.

'You know something about that,' he says finally.

'I've met Cynthia Brutran. It doesn't take a mind reader to know she's a killer,' I say.

Sharp hears the bitterness in my voice. 'Has she hurt anyone close to you?' he asks.

I think of Jeff Stephens, the boyfriend of Lisa Fetch, a member of our small group who is teaching maths back in Truman, Missouri, and waiting for the IIC to make her disappear. Jeff Stephens was the first victim of Brutran that I knew. I also think of my own dead body, out there somewhere, maybe in the hands of Brutran and her monsters. To be frank, I think about it every few minutes.

'Yes,' I say.

Sharp digests the news slowly. 'I'm sorry,' he says.

'Do you apologize because you're to blame?' Seymour asks.

Sharp doesn't appreciate the question. 'You've got a lot of nerve, young man.'

Seymour realizes he's overreached and looks to me for help. I hold up my hand by way of apology. Sharp's anger is real and I don't want to lose him before we can begin.

'It was Brutran who stole your life's work,' I say.

The insight startles Sharp out of his anger. This is

how to get the truth out of him. Shake him up, make him realize he doesn't have all the answers. Like many intellectuals, particularly the elderly kind, he suffers from arrogance. That's why he invited us so quickly into his home. He wants us to hear his story.

'What makes you say that?' he asks.

'I've felt the sting of her Array,' I reply.

Sharp sucks in a breath. For him, just hearing the word is like a slap in the face. My guess is correct. Brutran and pals must have used whatever they learned from their teacher to smash him down.

'I'm sorry,' he repeats.

My tone is sympathetic. 'The woman has made us both suffer. Isn't that enough for you to share your story with us? That's why we're here, to listen to what you know. And based on what you said a minute ago, I think you have been waiting for us.'

Each of my remarks is carefully designed to save us an hour and cut right through his armour. It doesn't matter that Sharp probably knows that. I believe I've sized him up correctly. Especially when he sits back in his chair and smiles at me. He's been waiting to tell his story before he dies.

'Now you could have been a reporter,' he says to me.

I act hurt. 'I hope I don't come across as cold.'

'That's not what I meant. I was simply acknowledging that you're shrewd enough to succeed in the business.' He pauses and scans the rest of us. 'What do you want to know?'

'Everything,' Seymour says. 'Take us back to

Berkeley. How did you manage to create a graduate programme focused on paranormal abilities?'

Sharp sighs and reaches for a spoon, which he uses to drop a hefty dose of sugar in his iced tea. He stirs it slowly and I can tell his mind is travelling back to another era.

'That was forty years ago,' he begins. 'The UC system was much more liberal then. Particularly when it came to Berkeley. The school wasn't stuck in the free love of the hippie days but at the same time it had never really lost that flavour. And I was the perfect candidate to explore the weird and wonderful. I don't know how thoroughly you have researched my past. I have a PhD in psychology and I was in fact the head of the psychology department at Berkeley. But I also have an equally prestigious degree in anatomy and physiology. It was an early goal of mine to be a psychiatrist. But the allure of pure research kept me in an academic world.'

'What sparked your interest in ESP?' Seymour asks.

'The need to know. The most basic desire of all. I had read about the research Dr J. B. Rhine of Duke University had conducted on psychic phenomena, back in the thirties and forties. When I came across his work, I couldn't understand why other scientists hadn't followed up on his findings. Of course there was a stigma attached to such research. Many of my colleagues failed to see it as real science – whatever that's supposed to mean. But to me there was no question Dr Rhine, with the help of his wife, had established that ESP definitely existed.' Sharp pauses.

'Are any of you familiar with his work?'

'I am,' I say. 'He developed the standard deck of ESP cards psychic researchers use to this day. They consist of five symbols: a circle, a cross, wavy lines, a square, and a star. He wanted to keep the symbols simple. He felt that would make them easier to transmit from one person's mind to another. I know he used a large body of statistical analysis to back up his claims that ESP existed. He would go through thousands of people to detect the tiniest statistical variance.'

Sharp nods his head in appreciation of my summary. 'You bring up the main strength and the main weakness of his research. With the five different shapes, a test subject should be able to guess what card another person is staring at twenty percent of the time – by chance. But Dr Rhine showed that certain individuals exceeded that average. They'd guess the correct card thirty percent of the time.'

'That's not very impressive,' Seymour says. 'They were still wrong over two thirds of the time.'

'Yes!' Sharp says, excited enough to pound the kitchen table. 'Congratulations, Seymour. You just summed up the problem with the entire parapsychology field. The results of Dr Rhine's research were real. No one with an open mind could study it and not acknowledge that ESP does exist in certain people. Statistics don't lie. However, they don't get people excited, either. I just made an extraordinary statement. I said a select group of people could telepathically read the cards correctly thirty percent of the time. And you responded exactly as most people do. You said, "So what. Big deal."'

'I'm sorry, it doesn't sound like a big deal,' Seymour says.

'That's where you're wrong. If the deviation was as little as one percent of what it should be – as predicted by chance – then it would be important. Because no matter how weak the ability to read another person's mind is, it still proves that ESP exists. And that seemingly small truth, if contemplated seriously, and viewed from every branch of science, should force us to rewrite every science book we have on this planet.'

'I'm not sure I agree,' Seymour says carefully.

Sharp waves a hand. 'Don't worry about hurting my feelings. Surely you can see I've had this argument a thousand times over the years. But I'm telling you the truth, and it explains why I devoted a large portion of my life to this field. Take for example physics. If ESP exists in human beings, then every law of physics that we have identified so far is suspect.'

'I don't follow,' Seymour says.

'Our laws of physics cannot account for telepathy. Despite the advances in the field, the wild implications of string theory and black holes, we've still only identified four forces in the universe. Electromagnetic forces, gravity, and strong and weak nuclear forces. Ask any physicist and he'll tell you that there are no other powers at work in this world. Yet ESP, even if it exists to only a slight degree, says that's not true. There has to be another form of power in this universe that we cannot explain. I'd even go so far as to say that the existence of ESP supports the argument that we have a soul. Do you follow me?'

Seymour hesitates. 'I see where you're coming from.'

'That's good enough for now. I know I've belaboured this point but it's important that you understand that I approached parapsychology from a purely scientific point of view. And I didn't have to conduct much research to come to the same conclusion Dr Rhine did. Let me state it in one clear concise sentence: ESP exists in certain people – perhaps in all people, to a degree – but it's either a very weak force or a very dormant one.'

'I'd imagine such a conclusion would have depressed you,' Seymour says.

Sharp shakes his head. 'On the contrary, I was delighted with what I'd discovered. Because it occurred to me that if I could assemble a large enough group of psychics, then I could use them the same way astronomers use groups of radio telescopes to boost the faintest signals given off by the most distant galaxies.'

'Oh God,' I whisper.

Sharp nods in satisfaction. 'You see where I'm going. Astronomers call such groups of radio telescopes "arrays". No one telescope picks up much information. But when their data is fed through a computer and scanned for patterns, they prove to be remarkably accurate.'

'You created a psychic array,' I say, my blood turning cold, never mind that I drank two pints of warm blood this morning.

Sharp beams. 'Yes.'

'Wait,' Seymour says. 'I don't get it. I don't care how large a group you assembled, it should only be as strong as its strongest link. I mean, you must have gotten a bunch of answers that were all over the place. That must have happened when you applied your array to reading the ESP deck, didn't it?'

'You're jumping the gun, Seymour. We're not all as bright as Teri obviously is. Let's take it step by step. When dealing with a large group, all you need is a one percent deviation by chance to construct a workable array. Let me give you an example. I took a female student who knew nothing about my work and had her focus on the ESP cards one at a time. Usually there are twenty-five cards in a deck, five of each basic shape. I gave her twenty decks to work with. Enough to get a statistically sound average but not enough to exhaust her. At the same time I borrowed four hundred students from the school's general population. Their job was to try to read the woman's mind. To see what shape the woman was looking at. I stationed her in an isolated area and put my large group in an auditorium. They could see her via remote camera but she couldn't see them. They knew when she picked up a fresh card. They knew how long she held it for. They were not allowed to talk to each other. I discouraged them from even looking at each other. I wanted them to focus on the woman and try to guess what shape she was seeing.'

'Guess?' Seymour says. 'They were still guessing.'

'Of course. And they were wrong most of the time. But I quickly noticed that there would be a certain shape the group would lean towards with any one card. For example, when the woman was staring at a square, often a hundred people in my array would guess a square.'

'The other three hundred would be wrong?' Seymour asks.

'Yes.'

'That doesn't seem to prove anything.'

'You're not thinking this through!' Sharp snaps. 'According to the laws of chance, only eighty people should have guessed a square. A hundred people guessing it correctly was very significant. Ninety people guessing it correctly was significant. Eighty-five guessing correctly was also significant.'

'Come on,' Seymour grumbles. 'How can you say eighty-five people getting it right meant anything? They could have done that by chance.'

'In any one trial, chance was always a factor. But I performed hundreds of trials with each test subject. And my array of four hundred students would lean towards the correct answer one quarter of the time.'

Seymour struggles to be diplomatic but he is stuck on this point. 'By chance they would have got the right answer one fifth of the time. I'm sorry, I'm still not impressed.'

'I'm not offended. That was the identical response I received from my colleagues when I showed them my results. But with the help of my grad students – five of whom were close to me – I began to experiment with my array. I soon discovered that kids were accurate more often than adults. I also learned that concentration didn't improve accuracy. Kids did better when they relaxed and answered with whatever popped into their minds. Finally, and this was a big key, I discovered that the ESP signal was still weak in the most psychic person I could find. The bottom line was, I had to use a giant array to get accurate results. It was only when I began to use three thousand kids that I was able to create a workable array.'

'How accurate was that group?' Seymour asks.

'They would lean towards the correct answer almost every time.'

'The word "lean" is ambiguous. How many of the three thousand kids would get the correct answer?' Seymour persists.

I feel I must interrupt and defend what Sharp is saying.

'It doesn't matter, Seymour. All that matters is he was able to create a group that had a *tendency* towards accuracy. That not only proved that ESP existed, it created a situation where it could be tapped for other purposes.'

Sharp nods. 'Thank you, Teri.'

Seymour is wary. 'What do you mean for other purposes?'

I turn to Sharp. 'I assume you began to use your array to see things other than the shapes on the cards.'

'Yes,' Sharp says. 'At the urging of my graduate students, I tried to see if my array could predict swings in the stock market.'

'Of all the things the kids could predict.' Paula jumps in suddenly. 'Why did you have them focus on the stock market?'

'It wasn't my idea. It was Cynthia's. But her reasons must be obvious. She wanted to see if the kids could help make money.'

'Up until this point your research had an innocent quality to it,' Paula says. 'You were a scientist seeking the truth. But when you allowed your group of kids to be exploited to make money, didn't it worry you that such an intent would distort your experiments?'

'We never told the kids what they were predicting. We wanted them to remain innocent, as you say. We just fed them stock symbols and asked if they felt "positive" or "negative" about them. Understand, none of these kids recognized the symbols. I didn't recognize them. They were from obscure stocks. Cynthia was the only one who knew what companies they belonged to.'

'Professor,' Paula says, 'I don't wish to hurt your feelings but you're avoiding my question. The intent of your experiments was controlled at the top. It was you and Cynthia and the other grad students who were in charge. All of you knew you were using the kids for personal gain.'

Sharp is offended. 'Never in my life have I put money at the top of my list of what's important in life. Look at the path I chose. I could have made a substantial salary as a practicing psychiatrist. With wealth, I could have purchased a large home and attracted a beautiful wife. But I stayed in an academic environment, and remained single, so I could devote my life to teaching others what I knew, and continue with my research. How dare you accuse me of exploiting my subjects for selfish purposes.'

'I apologize,' Paula says. 'The fact you didn't exploit the kids is admirable. Still, you knew your graduate students weren't as altruistic. I get the impression you did little to rein this Cynthia in.'

Sharp snorts. 'You don't know the woman. No one told her what to do.'

Paula persists. 'You still haven't answered my question. Weren't you concerned that the intent to make money on the stock market would distort your results?'

Sharp is a long time answering. The left side of his face, the injured part, seems to tremble. 'At that time, I didn't realize that intention was important in this work.'

'But later?' Paula asks.

Sharp holds up a hand. 'I'll get to that later. For now, the main point is we'd made a major scientific discovery. In my mind the most important discovery of our time. My array was not only able to prove the existence of telepathy, it was able to show that people could actually predict the future.'

'Were you able to publish your research?' I ask.

Sharp's shoulders sag and the life goes out of his voice. 'No. The fools. I had in hand absolute proof of a force of nature that had been under our noses since we first lived in caves, and no one wanted to hear about it.

I should say, no one in the scientific community. Sure, there were fringe groups that were willing to publish my work, but you have to understand that given my position with the university, I couldn't be seen as avoiding the scrutiny of my peers. Yet they wouldn't even look at what I had discovered! They joked about me behind my back. I was no longer Professor Sharp but Professor Dull.'

'Was Cynthia upset your work wasn't accepted?' I ask.

He hesitates. 'I suppose.'

'I don't think so. I think once she and the others saw what you had stumbled upon, they were anxious to keep it quiet. Come on, Professor, isn't that the truth?'

He's still lost in the past, in his anger over the rejection of his years of research. 'I don't know what you're talking about,' he mumbles.

I give the others a look telling them that I want to take control of the questioning. I especially don't want Shanti to speak up and admit she's recently been a member of Cynthia's Array. For all I know it might make the old man clam up with fear.

Seymour nods, indicating he doesn't have a good feel for the subject matter. Yet Paula frowns. She's worried about something I'm missing. That's fine, she can question him when I'm done.

'Professor Sharp, please look at me,' I say and he raises his head. 'You've done a wonderful job of explaining the theory behind your work and how the original arrays first came to be. But you've told us almost nothing about your grad students who went on to found the IIC. They're the reason we're here. They're dangerous. You know that as well as we do. Isn't that true?'

He blinks as if shaken but his eyes come back into focus.

'They're more dangerous than you can imagine,' he says.

I smile. 'I think you're going to discover that I have a pretty vivid imagination. Help us take a close look at the players involved here. I get the impression Cynthia was the boss when it came to this group?'

'I was in charge. I taught them everything they knew.'

'That might have been true in an academic sense. But already you've admitted it was Cynthia who came up with the idea to use the large group of kids to predict changes in the stock market.'

Sharp nods reluctantly. 'Cindy was the smartest of the lot, the most driven. She was the first to grasp the implications of my work. She helped me a lot when it came to tinkering with the arrays, improving how the kids did. In the beginning, we were very close.'

'Did you have a falling out later?' I ask.

He shrugs and lowers his head. 'It wasn't that way. I got a stroke, I got sick. I was in bed for over a year. The university forced me to retire, although I think they used my illness as an excuse. They never appreciated my work.'

'Was Cindy married to Thomas Brutran at the time?' I ask.

'To Tom? No, they got together later. When I met Cindy, she was with Fredrick Wild. You must have seen his name listed online. He was on the original IIC board.' Sharp smiles wistfully as he recalls the good old days. 'We used to call him Freddy or Fried Freddy. He was a huge devotee of LSD, mushrooms and other mind-expanding drugs. He used to worry me, I was scared he would damage his brain. He was the exact opposite of Cindy. They were an odd couple, to be sure. But she loved him. I never saw a girl so much in love. And boy she was jealous! If Freddy so much as looked at another girl she went on the warpath.'

'Did Freddy feel the same about Cindy?' I ask.

Sharp hesitates. 'He loved her, sure, intensely. They were very close. Unfortunately, they weren't compatible. Freddy was a laid-back hippie and Cindy was driven to get ahead. They wanted to be together but it didn't work out. And so Cindy ended up with Tom, Thomas.'

'Does Cindy love Tom?' I ask, although I already know the answer.

'He loves her but I doubt she ever got over Freddy.'

'Then why did she marry Tom?'

Sharp shook his head. 'Tom was rich and handsome. They had more in common than Cindy and Freddy. Tom was clean-cut, well disciplined. He wore a sports coat to campus while most kids his age had on shorts and sandals. I knew that one day he'd be president of a company. And you see, that's what's happened.'

'IIC is not a normal company.'

'You'll get no argument from me on that point.'

'Were Noel Brent and Wendy Brent married when they were your students?' I ask.

'They got married shortly after I came up with the array. They had to. Wendy got pregnant and Noel pretty much did what she told him to.'

'It sounds like the women were the real power when it came to your graduate students.'

'That's true about Cindy and Wendy. But you couldn't say that about Freddy. No one told that guy what to do. He was a free thinker. I've told you that Cindy helped me refine the early arrays, but Freddy was a big help as well. He was the one who figured out how to get them to talk.'

My heart skips. 'Talk?'

Sharp suddenly looks as if he's been caught with his hand in the cookie jar. 'I didn't mean that literally.'

'How did you mean it?' I ask.

Sharp is distinctly uncomfortable. 'Freddy came up with a list of experiments that allowed us to extract information from the kids.'

'What kind of information?'

'Your usual New Age drivel. I didn't think it was important at the time.'

'But later?' I ask.

Sharp brushes the question away. 'Don't get hung up on that part of our research. There was nothing there we could prove.'

'Professor, I'm afraid you contradict yourself. On one hand you say Freddy was a big help. He had insights into the early arrays and got them to talk. Then you act like the information he came up with wasn't important.'

'I don't think it was important.'

'At least tell us how he got the arrays to talk.'

Sharp shrugs. 'None of his techniques were scientific. It was more along the lines of spiritualism. The type of people drawn to those cults are always trying to get messages from beyond the grave. They gather people around a table and try to get the table's legs to tap once for yes and twice for no. Or else they sit with Ouija boards and channel all kinds of bizarre information. Freddy was drawn to that sort of thing. It impressed me that he was able to adapt our arrays so the power of a large group could contribute to what was being channelled. But, once again, the quality of the information was usually poor.'

'Give us an example of the type of information you received.'

'It was no different from the junk you can find in a hundred channelled books at the store. A spirit would arrive with some high-sounding name and profess to have the secrets of the universe. He or she would dictate pages of information on reincarnation or higher dimensions, none of which could be tested. I'm telling you, it was a waste of time.'

'Professor Sharp, do you believe in God?' I ask.

My question catches him off guard. 'Why do you ask?'

'With all your experiments, it sounds like you were

trying to tap into a kind of collective unconsciousness –
if you want to use Carl Jung's label – or a universal
consciousness. Would you say that's fair?'

'We were trying to tap into a power that had no
name. Some people might have called it God. I'm not
sure I would have been one of them.'

'Why not?' I ask.

He shakes his head. 'How can I answer that
question? As a scientist, I could only work with what I
could prove.'

I lean forward and take his shrivelled hand in mine.
'Are you afraid to answer because you think Cindy used
the arrays for evil purposes? To give you a stroke?'

'No.'

'When we first arrived, you gave that impression.'

He shakes free of my hand. He acts trapped, restless.
'You don't understand,' he says.

'Then help us understand.'

'The arrays were designed to solicit information. To
prove we had hidden senses beyond the five obvious
ones. I didn't create them to hurt people. The idea is
preposterous.'

'That's not true,' I say.

'It is true!' he shouts back.

'But you've admitted how dangerous the IIC is. You
said it was more dangerous than we could imagine.'

Sharp struggles to answer and I fear I might have
pressed him too hard. He's old and frail. His voice
cracks as he answers and I worry he's going to have
another stroke.

'That company is dangerous but not because of the big Array Cindy eventually created. That's not what stung you and that's not what put me in bed for a year and destroyed my health.'

'If it wasn't the Array, then what was it?' I ask.

Sharp hesitates. 'The Cradle.'

'What's that?' I demand.

The man lowers his head and trembles as he speaks. 'I can't talk about it, it's too dangerous. Find Freddy, talk to him. I'll put you two in touch. He knows more about it than I do.'

I feel frustrated. I have finally managed to steer him to the secret of secrets and now he refuses to tell us what it is. I try pushing him harder but finally have to accept his fear is genuine. It's not like he is refusing to talk about what happened next, it's like he *can't.*

However, when we're about to leave, I ask, 'At least tell us why it's called the Cradle?'

He stares at me closely, as if seeing me for the first time, and his face darkens. 'You know,' he says. 'It touched you. It's just begun to grow.'

It's my turn to clam up. I don't ask what *it* is. I already know it's that horrible thing that attacked me in that crummy motel in London.

8

It's not difficult for us to find Fredrick Wild. True to his word, Professor Sharp gives us his address and phone number. It appears the two are still on speaking terms. Freddy lives with his girlfriend, Mary, in Santa Cruz, an hour's drive from San Mateo. We climb in our car and head for the coast. Seymour drives while I sit in the back with Shanti. She keeps giving me uneasy looks.

'Relax,' I say. 'We're not trying to play a practical joke on you. It really is me.'

'If I had any doubts, you got rid of them at the professor's house,' Shanti replies.

'Was I too hard on him?' I ask.

Shanti is at pains not to offend me. 'You did what you had to do.'

'I think you were too easy on him,' Seymour says.

'What makes you say that?' Paula asks.

Seymour rolls down the window, which means he's about to light a cigarette. 'I worry we didn't learn anything that will help us defeat Brutran and the IIC.'

'We learned how the Array came to be,' Paula says. 'I found his talk fascinating.'

'But it's like he switched boats on us,' Seymour says. 'He talks about the Array for an hour but when push comes to shove he says it's the Cradle that's the problem. If you ask me, he's still trying to protect the idea of the Array. It's his baby, he invented it. I think he's still proud of it.'

'He did prove the existence of ESP,' Paula says. 'He made a major contribution to science. I think he has a right to be proud.'

Seymour lights his cigarette and blows smoke out the window. He glances over at Paula in the passenger seat. 'Then why did you jump on him for using his knowledge to predict stock prices? If it had been me, I would have done the same thing.'

Paula gazes out the window at the lovely scenery. The road between San Mateo and Santa Cruz leads us through a rich forest. Yet the beauty of the countryside doesn't seem to comfort her.

'You've all heard the quote in the Bible, "Knock and the door shall be opened". As you know, I've had experience when it comes to praying to the universe for guidance. And I can tell you that you have to be extremely careful what doors you decide to knock on.'

'Is that why you brought up the issue of intention?' I ask.

'Yes. Like I told him, at first his research was noble. He was trying to demonstrate the hidden potential we all have. But later, when Brutran wanted to use the Array to make money, the intention became self-serving.'

'And that's bad?' Seymour asks.

Paula hesitates. 'It can be.'

Seymour isn't convinced. 'I write novels to make money. Each time I sit to write, I indirectly depend on the universe to inspire me. No offence, Paula, but I've never been possessed.'

'You create out of your own imagination,' Paula says. 'Out of your own soul, if you like. Or, when you worked with Sita to write her story, you spontaneously sought out a writing partner, even if you didn't know it at the time. But it's my belief that the Array is designed to tap unnatural powers.'

'What do you mean by unnatural?' Seymour asks.

'There are many doors in this universe,' Paula says.

'You're saying you have to be careful what higher power you turn to for help?' Shanti asks.

'Exactly,' Paula replies.

'Krishna says the same thing in the Gita,' Shanti says.

'But Krishna is flexible when it comes to who a person worships,' I say. 'He said that whatever god a man or woman worships with love, it is the same as worshipping him. I think that line is one of the keys to the Gita. The worship is for the sake of the devotee, not for the sake of the god.'

'I can't argue with you,' Shanti says. 'I mean, you met Krishna, I've just read about him.'

She continues to look troubled, and I think I know why.

'You're wondering why I gave you the evil eye every time you went to talk to Professor Sharp,' I say.

Shanti hesitates. 'I assume you knew what you were doing.'

'You worked with Brutran's Array as little as a month ago. I was afraid he might see you as one of her spies.'

'Is that the only reason?' she asks.

'Yes,' I lie. The truth is, my gut told me to keep her quiet, and I'm not sure why. Shanti continues to look disappointed and I try changing the subject. 'Speaking of Krishna, did you happen to bring a copy of Yaksha's book? I wanted to study it some more.'

Shanti nods. 'I have the original in the trunk.'

'The original copy I gave you?'

Shanti hesitates. 'I thought I had Yaksha's copy.'

I smile and squeeze her hand. 'I never gave you that one. The Telar have it. But let's not worry about it now. I'll look at it after we get to Santa Cruz.'

Seymour isn't ready to let go of the meeting with Professor Sharp. He glances at me in the mirror. 'Sita, you told us you met Brutran twice, and that she was about forty. But everything Sharp told us happened forty years ago. How can that be?'

'The Telar are immortal,' I reply. 'How can that be?'

'Are you saying the IIC have tapped into the same

secrets as the Telar?' Seymour asks.

'That's my working theory,' I say. 'That's why I pressed Professor Sharp about what kind of information the group channelled.'

'Which is when he started to clam up,' Seymour mutters.

'That wasn't a coincidence,' I say. 'The two groups have a lot in common. They're both obsessed with power and control.'

'But Matt made it clear that long ago the Telar lost the secret of their immortality,' Paula says.

'Then how can they still be immortal?' Shanti says.

'They're immortal and their children are immortal,' Seymour says. 'They're born that way. But they can no longer make other immortals. They continue to benefit from their original secret, they just don't know what it is.'

'It's strange how they could have lost it,' Shanti says.

'Is it?' I ask. 'Over time, people forget almost everything.'

'Let's return to Cynthia Brutran's age,' Seymour says. 'She doesn't look sixty-five like we'd expect, but she has aged. She's no longer twenty, and I don't know a woman who would willingly add twenty years to her face.'

'What does that tell you?' I ask.

'That the IIC have figured how to slow ageing but not how to stop it.'

'Which tells you they've probably only begun to scratch the surface of the Array's power,' I say.

'Or the Cradle's,' Seymour adds. 'I still wonder why they named it that. It was obvious he didn't want to tell us.'

'Maybe they use babies somehow,' Shanti says.

I shake my head. 'I don't think that's it. The way Sharp spoke about the Cradle, it was like it was connected to the Array, but also separate from it.'

'I got the same impression,' Paula says.

'I think we should take a closer look at what Krishna told Yaksha about the Telar,' Seymour says. 'Krishna didn't bring up the fable of the Hydra by chance. It's got to be related to the Telar's and the IIC's arrays.'

'Assuming the Telar used to have one,' Paula says.

'I think that's a safe assumption to make,' Seymour says. 'I can't be the only one who was reminded of the Hydra story when Sharp was talking. He kept saying that the more people he had to work with – the more heads, in other words – the more accurate his results were. I don't think that's a coincidence.'

Shanti laughs. 'Hey, I used to be one of the kids they called up for answers. What are you going to do, chop off my head?'

'It was Krishna's idea, not mine,' Seymour says cheerfully. Everyone in the car knows how protective he is of Shanti.

'You're forgetting that in the Hydra fable,' I say, 'Hercules couldn't destroy the monster no matter how many heads he chopped off. It just kept growing new ones.'

Shanti gives Seymour a playful shove and then puts

her hands around her neck. 'I guess I'm safe for the time being,' she says.

Freddy's girlfriend, Mary, isn't surprised when we knock on her door. Apparently Professor Sharp called ahead of time and warned her and Freddy we were coming. Nor does Mary appear to mind our visit. She invites us in and immediately offers us dinner. It is near midnight, an odd time to eat, but that does not seem to bother anyone. With the exception of me, our gang is starving. I just downed two pints of blood, after heating it in a steel thermos with a Sears blowtorch. Like I planned, the ready supply is saving me a lot of grief. I keep the blood out of sight in the trunk, in a cooler packed with ice.

Mary has made a large pan of vegetarian lasagna, which suits Shanti, who's from India and never eats meat. Mary explains that Freddy is out for a run, but she doesn't bother waiting for him to return. She starts serving us as soon as we're settled in the living room. Once again I find the greeting unusual. Mary is exceptionally friendly. But it seems her nature; I don't feel like she's trying to put us at ease for any devious reason.

'This is fantastic,' Seymour gushes as he digs into the food. 'You should open a restaurant.'

'He means it,' I tell Mary. 'Seymour's from New York and knows all the finest restaurants. He's hard to please.'

'I've already tried that,' Mary says. 'A restaurant

requires constant care. It's worse than a man. I loved the cooking and treating people to a fun night out, but I had no life.' Mary notices how little food I have on my plate. 'Teri, is that all you're eating?'

'I don't like to stuff myself before I sleep.'

She appears to study me for a moment, and I do likewise. Even though I have yet to meet the man of the house, I know Freddy is a lucky guy. Mary is not only a gracious host, and kindhearted, she is an exotic beauty.

Her hair is a bright blonde, cut short, and her brown eyes are clear and sharp. She has amazing skin. She's naturally white but she's somehow managed to bake herself brown in the sun without picking up any wrinkles. Close to thirty, she's on the short side but has a lush figure. She moves the way I used to, in my old body, with a smooth confidence that makes all eyes go to her. She appears to be a natural leader, and yet her dress could not be more casual: jeans and a T-shirt. She wears no bra or underwear, and I know that Seymour notices, and approves.

'Can I get you a drink?' she asks me.

'I'm fine, thank you,' I say.

Mary loads her plate and sits on the floor beside me. There's only a small couch and a single chair in the living room, and the others have taken over them. I note the absence of a TV, but am intrigued by the number of paintings on the walls. Mostly abstract art that borders on the psychedelic. Mary explains that they belong to Freddy, and given what Professor Sharp told us about the man, I'm not surprised.

'Freddy must have a vivid imagination,' I say.

'He's always been intuitive,' Mary says. 'I'm sure Professor Sharp told you that.'

'He didn't mention it,' Seymour says. 'Was your boyfriend an actual participant in Sharp's studies?'

Mary nods after biting into a slice of garlic bread. 'That's how the two got together. The professor was randomly testing students at Berkeley when he stumbled on to Freddy. Sharp said he had the highest degree of ESP he'd ever recorded.'

Seymour smiles. 'Don't tell me. He scored better than thirty percent with Dr Rhine's standardized ESP deck of cards.'

Mary chuckles. 'I can see the professor is still trying to keep Freddy a secret. No, Freddy scored a lot higher than that.'

'How high?' Shanti asks.

'He would guess correctly over eighty percent of the time.'

Seymour frowns. 'But we just listened to an hour lecture on how weak and impractical the ESP signal is when it comes to the individual.'

'I suppose that's true. Except when it comes to Freddy.'

'I'm surprised Sharp didn't tell us about his abilities,' Seymour says.

'Are you?' I ask. 'The whole basis of his research was his discovery of the array. If he went around talking about Freddy, people would have just wanted to go to him and get a personal reading.'

'Are the four of you students of parapsychology?' Mary asks.

'In a manner of speaking,' I say. 'Right now we're researching the firm that a few of Professor Sharp's graduate students founded after they left Berkeley. Infinite Investment Corporation, IIC. Have you heard of them?'

Mary's expression darkens. 'Freddy knows all about the firm. He might even still be connected to them legally. But he'll have nothing to do with IIC, and my advice to you is to stay away from them. They're not nice people.'

'Because they're rich and successful?' Seymour asks.

'Because they're ruthless. Freddy used to date their leader, a woman named Cindy Brutran. I met her once. It was like meeting the serpent that killed Cleopatra.'

I find Mary's choice of simile interesting.

'So Freddy never talks to any of them?' I ask.

Mary shrugs. 'He talks to Cindy on the phone now and then. But that's for personal reasons. He has nothing to do with the company.' She turns to Seymour. 'Professor Sharp said you want to write a book about them.'

'Yes.'

'Don't. They won't let you publish it.'

'I've published a number of books. I doubt they could stop me.'

'I'm giving you a friendly warning. I hope you heed it. I'm not a gloom-and-doom sort of person. But I feel obligated to tell you that you'll regret it if you don't listen.'

'You must have a reason for your concern,' Seymour says.

'Talk to Freddy when he gets back. He'll tell you the whole story.'

The man of the hour arrives minutes later, hot and sweaty from his run. Before showering, he greets each of us individually. Freddy appears as polite as his girlfriend, and in his own way he's just as striking. He has lost the hippie look Sharp mentioned, but he's kept his long maroon hair, which drapes over the hood of his sweatshirt. And it doesn't take a vampire's eyes to see that he looks no older than thirty, the same age as Mary. He reminds me a bit of Matt, with his handsome features and large dark eyes. But he is on the thin side, jerky in his movements. It's like he's seen things in his life he wishes he could forget. The man is friendly, yet he looks like he needs a friend.

He has Mary, though, wonderful Mary. She should be enough.

Freddy showers and returns dressed in black pajamas. After fetching a plate of lasagna and garlic bread, and a cold beer, he sits beside Mary and me on the floor. Mary isn't into sports, but Freddy is a track fan and he's excited to talk to me about the Olympics. He says he's got a video of my gold medal race on his iPod.

'I even recorded your trial races in London,' he says.

I smile. 'It's nice to meet a true fan.'

'Hell, I followed your career all the way from the US trials in Oregon. But to be honest, despite your great times, I was sure the Africans were going to eat you up. They practically own all the middle- and long-distance races.'

'They train all day,' I say. 'They don't do anything else.'

'Do you think that's their secret? I can't say I agree.'

'You think it's the altitude advantage.'

'Altitude can only help you so much. And don't forget that plenty of American and European runners are living at altitude year-round and they're still getting their butts kicked by the Kenyans and the Ethiopians, especially in the marathon. No, I think the answer is genetic. They're better runners because their ancestors were great runners. They had to be to survive. There are more wild animals in Africa than any continent on earth.'

'That's an interesting way of looking at it,' I say.

'You can't deny the evidence. You were the only white person to win an endurance race in track.'

'I got lucky,' I say.

Freddy's interest in track makes for an excellent ice breaker. Too bad it's all he wants to talk about. It grows late, and Seymour and Shanti start to yawn. I try steering the conversation toward IIC with no success. Near two o'clock in the morning, Mary bluntly informs her boyfriend that we have stopped by to discuss the IIC. Freddy doesn't flinch. He offers to talk about his college days tomorrow.

'We would appreciate anything you can tell us,' I say.

Freddy nods as he stands, although I notice his jerkiness increases the instant Mary mentions the IIC.

'That will be great,' he says. 'To tell you the truth, I'm flattered to have a famous person in my house.'

'I'm far from famous,' I say.

'Get off it. I'd rather meet you than Madonna or the Dalai Lama. Hey, I have an idea. Why don't you guys stay here tonight? We have an extra room at the end of the hall, and we're almost finished remodelling our guesthouse. It's out back beside a well that supplies us with incredible drinking water. You've got to taste it.'

'Which means you've got to stay,' Mary says.

'We'd hate to put you guys out,' I say.

'You're not,' Mary says. 'Besides, you might have no choice but to stay here. It's the weekend, and Santa Cruz is a resort town, at least to those who are from out of town. Unless you have reservations, you're not going to find a room this late.' Mary pauses. 'I'd be honoured if you'd be our guests.'

I turn to the others, who nod their heads. I especially seek Paula's approval. Like myself, she mustn't sense any danger. Still, there's an odd feeling in the air, a sense of the unknown that I can't place, and that has me on guard. It's not a sense of malice, it's more like a mystery.

'Thank you. We'll stay,' I say.

9

An hour later Seymour and I sit on our respective beds in the guesthouse. Both Paula and Shanti were exhausted from all the travel and wanted to go straight to sleep. For that reason they took the room in the house. Besides, Seymour and I, we belong together. He sits nearby, smoking a cigarette and scratching the blisters on the back of his hands.

'How bad are they?' I ask.

'Bad enough. I could use another shot.'

'I have a small vial of T-11 and syringes in the car. I can get them for you.'

'It can wait until morning.'

'There's no reason you should be uncomfortable.'

'If Charlie and Matt don't get their lab up and running, a lot more of us are going to be feeling

119

uncomfortable real soon.'

'You don't put much stock in them.'

'Hell, Matt's like Superman. And I'm sure Charlie's a genius in his field. But we're asking too much of the guys in too short a time. The Telar have been around forever. They didn't design a virus and vaccine that can be reconfigured in a few days. They designed it to destroy humanity. When you're that pissed off at seven billion people, you're going to come up with a pretty complex formula.'

'I hear ya.'

'Then how come you didn't fight Matt to abandon his plan?'

'I would have fought him. Teri couldn't.'

Seymour takes a drag on his cigarette. 'Yeah, I guess you're right. I'm sorry.'

'I can't complain. I'm still here, ain't I? Besides, with Matt and Charlie off doing their thing, I can do what I have to.'

'Can you? You don't have your invincible body any more. How are you going to face Brutran as a newbie vampire? Even when you were Sita, she practically wiped the floor with you.'

'Your faith in me is overwhelming.'

'Sorry. I just never had the end of the world staring me in the face before.'

'It did in a few of your books. That must have helped you get used to it a little.'

'Let me tell you a secret that only writers know. All the stuff we write about, we're glad it happens to other people. Because if it happened to us, we couldn't handle it.'

'And that's why you write about it.'

'Yep.' Seymour coughs and grinds out his cigarette in a plastic cup. He scratches his hands before feeling the hardness of his mattress. 'What do you think of our hosts?' he asks.

'They look great together. But something doesn't add up.'

'His age sure as hell doesn't. Going by what you said, he looks even younger than Brutran.'

'That's one point.'

'Are you worried that he's a true psychic?'

'A little. He gave me a few funny looks. I wonder if he could read my mind.'

'Could you read his?' Seymour asks.

'No. I doubt the old Sita could, either. But that's not what's bothering me.'

'What is it then?'

'It's the two of them together. It's the way they took us into their home. To a certain extent, I felt the same around Professor Sharp, but I could understand his desire to talk. He's old, he lives alone. He wants people to know about his discoveries before he dies.'

'He's afraid of the IIC. I don't think he wants too much publicity.'

'Sure. But you know what I'm saying. Sharp doesn't want to go to his death bed without being acknowledged. I can understand his desire for company. Freddy and Mary are not the same kind of animal.'

'Why link them? They're together now, sure, but she doesn't have his history.'

'I just have this feeling . . . I don't know.'

'Tell me.'

I sigh. 'I've had it before.'

'When?'

'A long time ago.'

'Everything with you was a long time ago. When?'

'When Krishna was on earth,' I reply, and I don't realize the words are true until I speak them aloud.

'You might be feeling that way because you spoke to John.'

'It didn't come over me until . . . tonight.'

'You're not making much sense.' Seymour keeps scratching. 'You can get that medicine if you're dying to take a late-night stroll.'

I jump up. 'You poor dear. I'll be back in a minute.'

'Try not to get mugged.'

I reach for the door. 'You don't have to worry about me.'

'I'm more worried about the mugger.'

I point a finger at him. 'You. I should let you suffer.'

'I'd stop suffering if you made me a vampire.'

'You don't want Teri's blood. You don't want to go through this awful thirst every night.' I open the door. 'I'll be back.'

The medicine is in the trunk. I have no trouble locating the vial of vaccine but I have to search for the package of syringes. The bright moon helps, the white beams peering over my shoulder. In the end, I find the needles under a book. A big fat book with a thick leather cover. I can hardly believe it. My hands tremble as I lift it clear.

It seems impossible but it's Yaksha's book. The original.

I hurry back to the guesthouse and show Seymour what I've found. He's interested but he's even more interested in the vaccine. I give him a high dose. I have suspected for some time that Charlie was being stingy with his injections. I shoot the blue liquid directly into the vein on Seymour's left arm and he feels immediate relief. The black blisters on his hands begin to recede.

'Better?' I say.

'Yeah. I think Shanti and I both need the higher dose.'

'I wonder if I should wake her and give her a shot.'

'Not if she's already asleep. I don't think she's suffering as much as I am.'

'I noticed that. I think the girl's tougher than you.'

He ignores the dig and gestures to the book. 'What did you find in the book that was so exciting?'

I stare at him. 'You've seen this book before?'

'When I picked Shanti up at JFK. Isn't this Yaksha's book?'

'Yes,' I say feeling a slight overlapping of Teri's memories with my own. The phenomena is happening less and less but it has not gone away. 'I haven't found anything new in it. I was just about to start looking. But I got this interesting idea today. It was when we were in the car. No, it might have been tonight. It doesn't matter. I got the idea that there's more to this book than meets the eye.'

'What do you mean?' he asks.

'There are parts where Yaksha goes into great detail. Like when he travelled to the New World and found Jamune and the Aztecs, and fought the bulk of the remaining vampires to the death. He narrates those battles blow by blow. But when he comes to other important matters, he skips over them quickly. Like the section where Krishna tells him the story of the Hydra and how to kill the Telar. It's like important parts are missing. And he never writes about meeting his wife, Umara.'

'You must have skipped that section. It is there. I remember when Shanti's uncle was translating portions of the book, when you were being held captive by the Telar. He told us about Umara back then.'

'I'm not saying Yaksha doesn't mention her in the book. He doesn't describe the day they met. He just starts talking about her like she's always been a part of his life.'

'Maybe he met her earlier than you think.'

'He shouldn't have met her until he reached Egypt. But even if they did meet before then, he should have written about it. After all, she was the love of his life.'

Seymour hears the change in my voice. I can't hide anything from him. 'You were the love of his life,' he says.

'It's not like we were in competition. I hardly saw him.'

Seymour strokes my head. 'Sita. He loved you and you loved him. You can't measure that love by how many days you spent together.'

I'm moved by his concern for my feelings. The truth is, I haven't accepted the fact that Yaksha had a wife. Five thousand years of daydreams don't wash away overnight.

'Thank you,' I whisper.

He kisses my cheek. 'Besides, I'm the one who should be jealous. You're my dream girl and I've never got to have sex with you.'

'You know, I'm not myself these days. And if Matt ever found out, the only question would be which one of us he would kill first.'

Seymour drapes his arms around me. 'Matt's not here and you're not his girlfriend.'

'I'm not really Sita, either. You'd be making love to a ghost.'

'As long as you're a friendly spirit, I don't mind.'

I can't help but laugh. 'Look at you, Seymour. You don't care if I'm Sita or Teri. You'd sleep with either of us. True?'

He shakes his head. 'You're the love of my life. That's never going to change.'

'I know.' I give him a quick kiss on the lips. 'Thank you.'

He points to Yaksha's tome. 'Tell me more about your idea about the book.'

'I've been trying to put myself inside Yaksha's mind. He knew that the Telar were interested in the story of his life. He knew they were anxious to study it. Eventually, he must have realized, they would get their hands on it. How could he protect its deepest secrets from them?'

'He could have placed a hidden code within the pages.'

'Clever. Unfortunately, Yaksha knew how smart the Telar were. No matter how brilliant his code, he must have figured they would eventually break it. But that wouldn't have stopped Yaksha. When it came to the parts of his life he was anxious to keep secret, he must have written it in such a way that only a vampire could retrieve it.'

'Logical. But how did he do it?'

I hold up a portable sprayer that either Mary or Freddy uses to water their plants. I spotted it on the porch while walking back to the house from the car.

'Watch this,' I say to Seymour, and squeeze the handle on the sprayer. A mist fills the air between us.

'It's just plain water, isn't it?' he asks.

'Yes. Now let's try an experiment.' Unscrewing the sprayer cap, I set it down and open a vein in my wrist with my nails. As my blood drips out, I hold my wrist above the lid of the sprayer. I don't put too much blood in it; I don't think it will be necessary. A minute later I replace the cap and shake it a few times. Then turn the sprayer towards the book. 'I hope this works,' I mutter.

'If it does it's ingenious,' Seymour replies, quickly grasping the principle. Once more, I squeeze the handle, and a fine mist, tinged slightly red, fills the air and settles over the open pages.

Instantly a series of words appears between the sentences.

Seymour claps. 'Bravo, Yaksha! He designed it so that his secret notes could only be retrieved by a vampire. And since you were the last vampire, besides him, he wrote those sections for your eyes only.' He pauses, impressed. 'How the hell did you figure that out?'

'It always bugged me that Yaksha wrote his autobiography in the heart of enemy territory. Now I realize he did it to throw them off. He conned them into thinking they have all his secrets.'

'Cool. What do the secret messages say?'

I lift the book and hold it to my chest. 'Sleep, Seymour, and let me study it tonight. If I find something important, I promise, you'll be the first to know.'

'I'm too excited to sleep. We should study it together. I might see something you miss.'

'In ancient Sanskrit? I hardly think so.'

Seymour gives me a knowing look. 'You're just hoping to find sections where he talks about how much he's missing you.'

I point at his mattress. 'To bed. Now. I have a feeling we're going to have a busy day tomorrow. You're going to need your strength.'

Shaking his head, Seymour trudges over to the bed. He strips down to his shorts and slips under the blankets. 'I have trouble sleeping with a light on,' he says.

'No problem. The moon's out. I was thinking of reading outside.' I cross the room and lean over and kiss his cheek. 'You have my permission to have sex with me in your dreams.'

'Since when do I need your permission?'

Mary and Freddy's home is located on the edge of town, more in the woods than the city proper. The residence looks like an old hippie abode but the property is lovely, filled with tall pines and thick grass. I find the well Freddy spoke of. It stands in the centre of a meadow and is exposed to bright moonlight. I sit on the ground with my back to the stone and lightly spray more pages. Once my vampire blood has had its alchemic way with the mysterious ink Yaksha used to create the hidden passages, it appears that the words are permanently revealed. It's an important point. I cannot let the book fall into the hands of the Telar.

Again.

I could have sworn I gave Shanti a copy.

I assume Teri's memory is playing tricks on me.

I find the section where Yaksha first meets Umara, his future wife and Matt's mother. I'm shocked to learn the encounter takes place in India, in the days after the battle at Kurukshetra, where Krishna revealed the holy scripture known as the Bhagavad Gita to Arjuna.

It's soon after the battle. Yaksha is wandering alone in the woods, his heart both heavy and joyous. He describes how he's happy because he got to spend time with Krishna and is now more convinced than ever that he is the supreme being. Yet the tasks Krishna has assigned him are intimidating. Yaksha not only has the responsibility to destroy all the vampires, Krishna has given him a new job. To travel to Egypt and try to contain an immortal race of beings called the Telar.

Yaksha is thinking of the Telar when he first sees Umara.

I read the passage with great interest.

I stared at the woman transfixed, feeling I had stumbled into a dream. She was the most beautiful creature I had ever seen. At the same time she looked familiar, and I didn't understand how that could be. Surely I would have remembered meeting her.

She was alone, dressed in the garb of a gopi, a female devotee of Krishna, wearing a saffron-colored sari. Yet her skin colouring set her apart from the rest. It was lighter; to me it shone like polished bronze. Her hair was long and dark, her eyes as brown as the earth after it has been washed by a storm.

She sat on the stump of a long-dead tree, a small book in hand, and moved her lips as she read its words aloud. She continued to do this even when I had moved close enough to be heard. It appeared the book meant more to her than my company. But she nodded in my direction as if to say she would talk to me soon.

It felt like an eternity before she closed the book and looked at me. 'Hello,' she said. 'You are Yaksha, the demon warrior. I've heard of you.'

'Then you have heard wrong. I am no demon. In this last battle I fought alongside Arjuna and Bhima, and helped them defeat Dhuryodhana.'

'I meant no offence. I embrace the dark the same as I do the light. I care nothing about your mysterious birth.'

She smiled. 'You wonder how I know so much about you.'

I felt exposed. It was her eyes. I could not gaze into them without wanting to confess all the deeds of my life, both good and bad. 'I feel we've met before,' I said.

She nodded. 'Long ago and far away. In Vrindavana, near the banks of the Yamuna, when you and your kind sought to invade Krishna's land. I was there the day you challenged Krishna and descended into the cobra pit.'

There were many gopis present that day, at least a few hundred. I must have missed her in the woods.

'That was many years ago,' I said. 'Were you a child?'

'I was as you see me now.'

'How is it that you haven't aged?'

'You haven't aged, either.'

I shrugged. 'I'm different from other men.'

'But you're not a monster?'

'If you want me to leave, I will be on my way,' I snapped.

'That's not necessary.' She made room for me on the stump. 'Come, sit beside me, rest. You fought hard the last few days. You must be weary.'

I almost left. She enjoyed teasing, a quality I especially despised in women. I suspected if I stayed she would continue to taunt me. Yet she was so beautiful; it would have been difficult to walk away. I sat and gestured to her book.

'What are you reading?' I asked.

'A copy of *The Lord's Song*, the Gita. I daresay it's the first copy.'

I thought that I alone, besides Arjuna, had heard what Krishna said before the battle. 'How did you get it?' I asked.

'I wrote it down with my own pen.'

'So you were there that day.'

'The whole world was there that day.'

'You could not have heard what was said.'

'No?'

'You should destroy that book. What Krishna taught was secret. It was sacred. It wasn't for the common man.'

'If Krishna isn't here for the common man, then why has he come to this godforsaken planet?'

'What's a planet?'

'A world. Krishna chose to come to this world. But there are many others like it, in the sky, circling the stars you see at night.'

'That's a strange idea. He told you this?'

'He didn't have to tell me. I knew it long before I came to India.'

'You're from another land. Now I understand. I have never seen a woman who looks like you. Tell me about your home.'

'It's called Egypt, and it belongs to this world. Our culture's more advanced than yours. We have vast farmlands and are able to feed tens of thousands. We have brilliant artists, engineers, mathematicians and healers. We have built many wonderful cities alongside a great river called the Nile.'

'What is it you do in Egypt?'

'I'm a teacher and a priestess. I teach the young how to read and write. I also teach them about Isis, the Universal Mother.' She stopped and smiled. 'But now that I've met Krishna, I'll have to teach them about him as well.'

'How can you worship two gods? There can be only one.'

'Krishna says the one are the same as the many. Study the Gita. Krishna doesn't care for our human laws. The world he comes from was old before our sun burned in the sky. We're lucky to grasp a fraction of what he tells us.'

'That I can well believe.'

She was a bold woman. She had the nerve to pat me on the back. 'You look troubled, Yaksha. What is it? Have I said something that upset you? It's a bad habit of mine, to make fun of strangers. Of course, if you knew me better, I'd probably still make fun of you.'

'Who are you?'

'My name is Umara.'

'How is it you know my name?'

'The snakes hissed it aloud when you entered the pit.'

'Your mocking grows tedious.'

'I apologize. You were most impressive that day. No man had ever challenged Krishna before.'

'I was young, I was a fool.'

'Perhaps. Kidnapping Radha was a strange way to say hello.'

'I regret that. I wish I could find her and ask her forgiveness.'

'You can't, she's dead.' Umara eyed me curiously. 'You still haven't told me what's bothering you.'

'You. I'm not sure if you're to be trusted.'

'You obviously haven't met many strong women.'

'A strong woman doesn't disturb me. But I find you out here in the middle of nowhere, after so many years, and you haven't aged. You say you are from Egypt, and Krishna has already told me about a group of immortals who live there, called the Telar. He says they're dangerous.'

'Some are. Not all.'

'Are you Telar or not?'

'I am.'

I stood and reached for the hilt of my sword. 'Damn you, I knew it. I should take your head.'

'Don't you find it more attractive attached to my body?'

'It doesn't matter what I think. I have taken a vow. Your kind must be destroyed.'

She stared at me. 'The same is true of vampires. Krishna told you to kill them all. Remember, I was there that day. I heard what he said.'

'How? He whispered in my ear.'

'Is it true or not?'

'I've killed thousands of vampires since that day.'

'No doubt. But I saw one the other day. She was present at the great battle. I watched her as she watched you. You saw each other, although you tried to pretend that you didn't.' Umara paused. 'Her name is Sita, if I'm not mistaken.'

I shook with anger. 'She is no concern of yours!'

'She's a vampire, and you've taken a vow to destroy them all. Tell me, Yaksha, with Sita so near at hand, why didn't you spare a minute and sneak up on her and cut off her head?'

'It is . . . She's someone I once knew.'

'Now she's someone you must kill.'

'Not yet.'

'Why not?'

'The time's not right.'

'You can't do it, can you?'

'Silence!' I yanked my sword free and put the tip to her

neck. 'You will not speak of her again.'

Umara was unafraid of my sword. She casually brushed the blade aside and stood. I couldn't understand how warm her eyes were when her words were so harsh.

'I can do it for you,' she said.

'What?'

'Kill her. Help you fulfill your vow.'

'Now you speak nonsense.'

'Are you afraid I'll do it?'

'You wouldn't stand a chance against her. She's stronger than she appears.'

'The same is true of me. I'm old, Yaksha, very old. You're the first vampire, the most powerful, but I'm one of the first Telar. I'm from the beginning. The stars in the sky have changed since I was born. To me you're but a child.'

There was strength in her words. I sensed it came from the fact she spoke the truth. My grip on my sword wavered.

'If I'm such a child, why do you speak to me?' I asked.

'I'm here to help you fulfill your vow. I'm the only one who can. Krishna spoke to me about this yesterday. He knows I'm the last of the original Telar, the only one who still knows the secret of their origin.'

'Tell me their secrets.'

'Not now. But I should warn you that a handful of the Telar know how old I am and have ordered my death. They fear me.' She paused. 'But think how much more they will fear me if I return to Egypt with you.'

'Has Krishna ordered you to help me?'

Once again she shocked me. She threw her head back

and laughed. 'He's never ordered me to do anything. I volunteered to help you because I want to.'

'Why?'

'It's the right thing to do. Besides, I like you.'

'You can't care for someone you don't know.'

'Really?' She touched my hand that held the sword. 'Are you saying you have no feelings for me?'

'We've only just met.'

'You only care for Sita?'

'We spent a lifetime together.'

'Fair enough. What are you going to do when the day comes that you have to kill her?'

The question filled me with pain. It was only the soothing quality of her touch that made it bearable. I realized then she was as old as she boasted. She could see right through me.

'That won't be for a long time,' I said.

'If you want to give her that time, then let her go.'

'And leave with you?'

'Yes. And stay with me.'

I close his book and close my eyes.

I have read enough.

I'm not jealous.

I'm happy Yaksha got to be with such a wonderful soul.

10 ~~

In the morning, I check my cell and find three pressing messages. One is from Teri's parents, who are now my parents. The next is from Lisa Fetch, a fringe member of our group, back in Missouri. Finally, Matt has called. God knows where he is. He wants me to call immediately.

I should call Matt first, he's the boss now that I'm not.

But Matt intimidates me. Humans, Telar, vampires – we all put off what we don't want to do.

I call Lisa Fetch to start. I figure hers will be the shortest call. Lisa's a mathematician; she's sort of hyper, smart, quick to get to the point. She's presently teaching maths at Truman College, a school Teri is supposed to return to in the next two weeks. I wonder how I'm going to get out of that commitment.

Lisa and Teri are not close, although Sita was a friend of hers, a point I have to keep in mind while talking to her. In a way, I'm surprised Lisa did not ask for Shanti, until I realize Lisa's call is about Shanti.

'Did Sita talk to you about how the two of us puzzled over why Brutran wanted to eliminate Shanti when the girl appeared to contribute to the accuracy of the Array?' Lisa asks.

'Yes. Sita and I talked about Shanti's relationship with the IIC in Goldsmith. She said you had come up with mathematical data that proved Shanti both helped and hurt the Array.' I pause. 'To be frank, it confused me a little.'

'Don't feel bad, Teri, it confused us. Why did Brutran want Shanti dead when she was one of their most accurate psychics? That was the mystery Sita wanted me to solve. There was stuff I had discovered that I wanted to talk about at the funeral, but it didn't seem like the time or the place. Everyone looked too bummed out. Plus I had to get back to my classes here.'

'I understand.'

'If I explain my findings to you now, can you pass them on to the others?'

'Sure.'

'Ever since you guys ran off to Europe, I've been studying the data the IIC fed me when I worked for them. I discovered that when Shanti joined the Array, as an individual, she gave a high percentage of correct answers. At the same time, her connection to the Array caused it to falter.'

'Why?' I ask.

'I don't know why. I just know that it did. As soon as the IIC hired Shanti, the Array dropped four-point-three percent when it came to picking successful stocks. That might not seem like a lot, but it's staggering when you think how many thousands of kids make up the Array.'

'Did the IIC know it was Shanti's fault?'

'They must have thought so. They hired a hit man to kill her, didn't they?'

'Sita told me about that guy. Marko.'

'What else did she tell you?' Lisa asks.

'She had a theory that Shanti's goodness somehow short-circuited the Array. It was just an idea of hers, but it sounds like you've proved it.'

'Maybe. There was another kid who joined the Array the exact same day as Shanti. This kid also scored real high individual numbers.'

'What was the kid's name?' I ask.

'He or she is designated by IIC's computers as M3014. We'd have to hack into their system to get personal data on the kid. But you know what happened to my ex when he hacked into their computers.'

'I'm sorry, I don't,' I lie.

'He got killed.'

'Oh.'

'Look, Teri, the main reason I called was to let the gang know the Array can be weakened. At the same time, I'm not a hundred per cent sure Shanti's the magic bullet we've been looking for.'

'Because of M3014.'

I wonder who this kid might be. I want to find him.

'Right,' Lisa says. 'I'm sorry I can't give you guys a conclusive answer. But I'll keep studying the data, see what I can come up with.'

'I'll tell the others you're working on it.'

Lisa hesitates. 'How is everyone doing without Sita?'

'It's rough. She was our leader. I'm not saying Matt's not doing a good job, but it's not the same.'

'I understand. Stay in touch. I still want to bring that bitch Brutran down.'

'Don't we all,' I say.

Mr and Mrs Raine are up next. I procrastinate ten minutes before making the call. I feel like I'm screwing with my own mind when I talk to them. This won't be the first time since I took over her body, but I can't say I've got used to it. I have all of Teri's memories inside. I can recall every birthday party they ever threw me.

Dad's what people call 'salt of the earth'. He works as an engineer at a local aluminum factory. Mom's soft-spoken. She takes care of the house and spends a lot of time helping at church. They couldn't be more harmless, or more divorced from the world I live in. That's why they sound upset on their message. It seems Detective William Treach has called and is looking for me. Just what I need.

'The detective told us you left town without telling

him where you were going,' my father says after I explain the misunderstanding about room-service Ken. My mother is on the line as well but generally lets Dad do the talking when it's important.

Damn! My hypnotic suggestion didn't work.

'I don't have to report to him,' I say. 'I gave him a full statement about what happened at the hotel. And I warned him I wasn't going to be staying in Denver. I don't know why he keeps bothering me.'

'He said he's going to keep calling us until you call him.'

'Did he say why?'

'He's always polite, always brief. But he's firm. He doesn't sound like the kind of man you want to get on the wrong side of. Call him, I'm sure it's just a formality.'

'I don't know. I wonder if I should speak to a lawyer first.'

'What do you need with a lawyer?'

'I didn't say I needed one. I'm saying I'm tired of this detective. This guy named Ken disappears and the cops don't have a suspect so they go after me because I just won a gold medal. That way they automatically get their face on TV.'

'Detective Treach doesn't sound like that kind of person.'

'Well, you might be right.' I dislike putting Detective Treach down, because I happen to like the man.

'Do you want me to call Fritz Chandler for you?' Dad asks.

140

Fritz is an old friend of the family, a lawyer from church. He can set up a living trust and help with a DUI, but he's way out of his league when it comes to a murder case, which is what this is, even if my parents can't see it.

'Let me think about it,' I say.

'You're a big girl, you take care of it.' My dad often defaults to that line when he doesn't know what else to say. 'The agencies keep calling as well. ICM, CAA, and William Morris Endeavor all want to represent you. They think you've got to strike while you're hot. But they say you're not returning their calls, either.'

'The Olympics were only two weeks ago. People haven't forgotten me. They're pushing for me to call because they're in competition with each other. That's good, I'm flattered. But I'm not sure if I want to go that way. Selling shoes and cereal on TV. What kind of doctor does that?'

'The endorsement money could pay for medical school.'

'I know. I haven't dismissed the idea. I just want to take it slow is all.'

My mother finally speaks. 'Is this the best time to be travelling all over the country with Matt? You know Mayor Spender still wants to throw you a town party. He wants to give you the key to the city. That's an honour, Teri. I think you should come home.'

'I will. But I promised Matt this time together before the games, when I was training night and day and hardly talking to him. I owe him, Mom. And I need this time to unwind. Really, I'm having a great time. Just be patient with me. I'll be home soon.'

That's good enough to pacify them. After hanging up, though, I realize I have to stop Detective Treach from calling. I wonder what state of mind the detective and his wife are in. I worry I might have started a 'loop' in one of their brains, where they fixate on an idea and keep repeating it to whoever happens to be nearby. At the hospital, Sandy had shown definite signs of looping.

I decide to give the cop a call and feel him out.

'Detective Treach. This is Teri Raine. I heard you were looking for me. What's up?'

'Teri, thanks for calling. I appreciate it. How's all the newfound celebrity treating you?'

'Fine,' I say, already worried about the man. He only has to say a few words for me to know he sounds tentative, like something's bothering him that he can't explain.

'Good, I'm glad. The reason I called, well, it's sort of complicated. You know about the young man who disappeared at the hotel?'

'Sure. Has he turned up yet?'

'No. And it's beginning to look like he's not going to, if you get my drift. But he's not the reason I called. I no longer think you had anything to do with his disappearance. I'm sure of that.'

Shit, I think. The detective is repeating word for word the suggestion I placed in his mind. Not a good sign.

'Why did you call?' I ask.

'There's another man, his name is Gary Stevens. He works with my wife at her hospital. He's in charge of their blood supply. The other night, at work, he says he saw someone who matches your description.'

'When?'

'The day we met.'

'Detective Treach, I don't know your wife or this Gary Stevens.'

Detective Treach sounds embarrassed and confused. 'I believe you. I told him that my wife's never met you and she's certainly never been to the hospital with you.'

'This hospital must have some sort of security.'

'We have a problem in that area as well. That night, the man in charge of the security cameras was knocked unconscious and his digital records were removed. When we add to that Gary Stevens's accusation that you assaulted him, just before you stole a large quantity of blood, then we have a problem.'

I chuckle lightly. 'This is getting more complicated all the time. Does Gary Stevens say your wife stole blood as well?'

'He says she helped you steal it, which is of course ridiculous. My wife would never do such a thing. The entire case is a mystery, but I'm still required to investigate it, especially since my wife stands accused.'

'This is obviously a case of mistaken identity. I'm not a vampire. I have no need to go around stealing blood.'

'My partner's working on the case as well. He's sitting across from me right now. He'd like to talk to you. It's his understanding that many endurance athletes do what's called 'blood doping'. They store up their blood months before a big race and then inject it into their veins to boost their red blood-cell count. It's supposed to heighten their endurance. I'm sure you've heard about the procedure.'

'Sure. I know athletes who've done it. But they withdraw their *own* blood before a major event like the Olympics. They don't just stroll into your local hospital and steal a few gallons of strangers' blood and inject it. If the blood types didn't match, it would probably kill them.'

'That's exactly what I told them. That the hospital's blood couldn't possibly help you. But that's the only motivation they can come up with for why you might have wanted the blood.'

'Lieutenant Treach, to be blunt, it doesn't sound like Gary Stevens or the hospital has a shred of proof that your wife or I was involved in this theft. For that reason, I'm not going to worry about it. I suggest you do the same.'

Lieutenant Treach is slow in answering and I feel bad for him. He can't point the finger at me without pointing it at his wife. And besides the fact that he doesn't want to get her in trouble, nothing about the case makes any sense.

'I told you, I'm inclined to take your word that you're innocent. But Gary Stevens is pressing charges against you, and my captain wants you to return here for questioning. I tell you this as a friendly warning. If Gary Stevens should go to the papers and associate you with blood doping, even if you're totally innocent, it could damage your name. That's why I prefer we nip this in the bud.'

'I can't return to Denver at this time. I'm busy and I'm innocent. Tell Gary Stevens that if he does speak to the media about this incident, I'll sue him for slander. Impress upon him how serious I am. Also, please stop calling my parents. If you need to speak to me, call me.'

'I tried your number. I only went to your parents when you didn't return my calls.'

'From now on, I promise to call you back. But right now I have to go. Tell your partner I'll speak to him later. OK?'

'He just needs a minute of your time.'

'Not now. I'll check in with you in two days. Bye.'

I hang up and groan. For centuries I fed my thirst without raising eyebrows. Even when modern times arrived, I adapted and kept my need for blood hidden. Largely because I required so little and because the power of my gaze was so formidable. Now I slip up a couple of times and I've set a whole mountain of suspicion in motion. The only positive in this whole mess is that these are mistakes Teri would make.

I finally call Matt and confess to him the mess I'm in. The guy has his sources. They are much more extensive than my own. He already has a fairly clear idea about my legal problems. He reminds me that it's all my fault, that I should have turned to him for help. But he doesn't spend a lot of time scolding me. He probably considers Detective Treach and Gary Stevens minor irritants. Matt has power. If and when he returns to Denver, he'll visit both men and look them in the eye and they won't even remember who I am.

'I'll take care of them when I get a free moment,' he says. 'For now, Charlie might have fixed the T-11 vaccine to work on your average person. He's anxious to try it out on Shanti and Seymour.'

'That's incredible. How did he do it so rapidly?'

'The guy's a genius. We underestimated him because of the way he carries himself. Also, he admits that the Telar did experiment with normal people while they were developing the X6X6 virus, mostly in small villages in Africa where it was easy to hide the atrocious results. Before Charlie joined our team, he was already thinking how the vaccine could be adjusted. But he didn't want to admit it until he had something concrete to show us.'

'Shanti and Seymour will be relieved to hear this news. I'll get them back to you tomorrow. The next day at the latest.'

'What's wrong with today?'

'We're investigating an important IIC lead. A guy who was part of the company at the start, but who has carefully separated himself from Brutran and the others.'

'I'm surprised she let any of her key people go.'

'When she could just kill them, yeah, I know what you mean. It's odd. But let us finish investigating this guy. We think he has the answer to many interesting secrets.'

'Is he willing to share them with you?'

'That's just it, he's a great guy. He has heart. You can't imagine he would have anything to do with Brutran.'

'Be careful, Teri. It might be a trap.'

'I will.' I pause. 'Hey, have you heard from your mother yet?'

He hesitates. 'No.'

'But you've tried to contact her?'

'Yes. I told you we haven't spoken in ages. I would have been surprised if she'd got back to me right away.'

He's lying, I can tell. I can hear the disappointment in his voice. He fears his mother is avoiding him, or worse, that she's dead. I know nothing about their relationship. Perhaps I can spray more of Yaksha's pages with my blood and see if I can find any hidden messages that talk about Umara and Matt.

'Where are you?' Matt asks.

'Santa Cruz. You?'

'The East Coast. I'd rather not be more specific right now. Tell me what you learned from Professor Sharp.'

'Let me tell you tonight, after we finish questioning his student. To me, they're two sides of the same coin. We'll have a much better idea of the IIC when we're done.'

'Whatever you discover, I still think it's a mistake to go to the IIC for help.'

'I understand. You have a rare insight into how evil they are. Like Sita, you're one of the few people who has lived through an Array attack.'

He is silent a long time. 'Why do you bring that up now?'

'I know it upset you. It would upset anyone to have their mind ripped away from them.'

'Yeah,' he says softly.

'But there is one thing I don't understand about what happened that morning up on the mountain. I've been talking to Seymour and he said that Sita believed the IIC needed a sample of her blood to turn the Array against her. How did they get a sample of your blood?'

'No one connected to the IIC has my blood.'

'They must have it. Seymour said—'

'I don't care what he said. From the time I was young, my mother and father taught me to guard my blood carefully. In the last few years, since the IIC came into existence, I've never let anyone close enough to me that they could have taken even a microscopic amount of my blood.'

'Then the Array shouldn't have worked on you.'

'Sita had a theory the IIC needed her blood in order for it to work. She was obviously mistaken. I know you idolized her, Teri, but she wasn't always right.'

'I know.' He's wrong. They must have his blood.

'However their Array works, the IIC are monsters. We can't go to them with our hat in our hand. Chances are they'll cut our hand off.'

'I don't totally disagree. Professor Sharp made it clear Brutran's a witch. It's just an option. Let's not close any doors until we know what's behind them all.'

Once again he takes a long time to respond.

'You're beginning to sound like Sita.'

I fight not to freeze up. 'I'll take that as a compliment.'

'Seriously, Charlie has got to see Shanti and Seymour immediately. He's confident he can get rid of their symptoms. You know how much is riding on this vaccine.'

'If we don't fly out tomorrow, maybe you can fly here.'

'I already have Charlie set up in a temporary lab. I don't want to take him away from his work, not even for an hour. The fate of the world might rest with that guy.'

'That's a scary thought.'

'I trust him. I know he helped the Telar create the virus, but he's working himself to death to make this right.'

'Tell him we're all rooting for him.'

'I will.' He pauses. 'I miss you.'

'I miss you.'

'Do you?'

'Of course, silly. How can you ask that?'

'You're a vampire now. You've gone through a major change. Your feelings towards everything must have changed.'

'They have. Except when it comes to you. My love for you will never change.'

He draws in a deep breath. 'That's nice to hear. Will you call soon?'

'Of course. Take care, Matt. Watch out for the Telar.'

'Watch out for the IIC. You're poking your heads in their backyard, questioning these people. Make no mistake, Brutran's going to hear about it. My advice to you is, finish questioning this guy as fast as you can and charter a plane and fly into New York tonight.'

I tell him I'll consider his suggestion. When I put down the phone I discover my heart's pounding. The strain of talking to him and keeping up the façade is immense. I can't maintain it forever. A single mistake and it could all be over. He's faster and more powerful than lightning. In his rage, he could snap my neck before I saw him coming.

11 ~~

It takes until after lunch to get Freddy settled in one place so we can talk to him. I suppose we can't complain. We have dropped in on Mary and Freddy without warning. They have fed us and given us a place to sleep for the night. When they go shopping for fresh produce at an organic market, on the other side of town, all we can do is wait.

I convey Matt's news to the others, and suddenly Seymour and Shanti are more interested in Charlie and his research than the IIC. I guess I'd feel the same way if a plague of black blisters kept reappearing on my body and itching like crazy. I give Shanti a double dose of the vaccine we have and her symptoms improve but don't vanish.

Finally, Freddy is all ours. The group, Mary included,

squeezes into the cramped living room to hear the parts of the IIC's birth that Professor Sharp was too frightened to tell us about. It's probably a good thing Mary's present. Freddy, looking nervous, downs three beers before he even starts.

I just want to get him talking. There's no way I'm going to start with the Cradle. I can be patient, if the need is there. By the time I'm done with Freddy, I'll know everything he knows.

'Mary says you're super psychic,' I say. 'That you tested better than anyone Professor Sharp had ever met before. Is that true?'

Sitting on the floor next to Mary and me, Freddy stares at his bottle of beer, takes a sip, and then nods. 'That's how I met the man. He was always canvassing the campus for people to volunteer for his experiments. One day I decided to give it a try. I remember it vividly because he scheduled me for an odd hour – from twelve at night to one in the morning. Cindy was there. She sat across from me in a small room. She'd pick up a card, stare at it for thirty seconds, then set it down and wait fifteen seconds before picking up another card. I can't say she was totally professional. She winked at me a few times during the test. She was so damn pretty, it was hard to focus on the cards. But I guess I did great. When the hour was up Professor Sharp burst in the room and shook my hand. I thought it was a weird thing for a professor to do. He said he wanted to congratulate me, that I'd gotten sixty-five correct hits out of seventy-five cards.'

'That's better than eighty percent,' I say. 'Were you able to keep up that average?'

'That's the first thing Sharp wanted to find out. He had me come back the next day and tested me all over again, this time using two hundred and fifty cards. I didn't mind, the research was funded by the university and they paid us five dollars for every hour we sat in one of his chairs. I made twenty bucks that second day. Back then, that was a lot of money. I don't know who the tester was, except it wasn't Cindy. But I remember I scored around seventy-five percent and the professor said I could be the next Uri Geller.'

'Who's that?' Shanti asks.

'A famous psychic from the seventies,' Freddy says. 'He was supposed to be able to bend spoons with his mind. A lot of people said he was a fake, a smooth stage magician. But there were many scientists who believed he was genuine. I don't know, our paths never crossed. I had my hands full with Professor Sharp. I was close to finishing my undergraduate degree in chemistry. I was thinking about becoming a doctor. But Sharp told me it would be a waste of my talents. He wanted me to get a master's in parapsychology, in a programme he was starting up. I told him no but when he came back to me with a full scholarship – that included room and board – it was hard to refuse.'

Mary sighs. 'Never mind that you were dating Cindy at the time.'

'I admit she influenced my decision. I fell for her big-time. We were together night and day. Cindy was full of life back then. But my interest in the professor's work was genuine. I could see that he'd hit on an amazing tool with his array. The more people we brought aboard, and the better we got at screening them, the more impressive were our results. We didn't just prove the existence of telepathy, we were able to do the same when it came to precognition.'

'When you talk about proving precognition,' I say, 'you're talking about playing the stock market, aren't you?'

'When Cindy brought up using the stock market, it seemed a clever way of testing whether the array could predict events. Understand, we didn't start down that road until after we'd been together a couple of years. Noel and Wendy were already married by then and had a kid, Angela. We were all surviving on our scholarships – except for Tom, Thomas Brutran, who had his own money – but we were living on the edge. We were often broke. When Cindy showed us how we could take a small sum and multiply it several times over, it seemed like manna from heaven.'

'Did Sharp approve of using his research to make money?' I ask.

'We didn't tell him. At least not at first.'

'Why not?' Paula asks.

'Cindy asked us to keep it secret so we could prove that it worked before showing him the results. I felt kind of funny going behind his back, but I have to say Cindy wasn't the easiest person in the world to argue with. She was so strong-willed, she had to have her way.'

'I believe you,' I mutter.

'When we finally did tell him, he yelled at us that none of the other academics would take us seriously now. The truth is, I think he was just looking for someone to blame for why he couldn't get his results published. He said that Cindy's money-making system had made his peers think he was operating a Ponzi scheme. Those were tense times. We'd been together for over two years and there was talk among the other teachers that Sharp was squandering the university's money. He was still having to pay everyone who volunteered. When the array reached a thousand heads, you can see how funds started to be a problem. Ironically, it was Cindy who kept the experiments alive with the money she made on the market. That was true even after Berkeley shut us down.' He pauses. 'I don't suppose Sharp told you that.'

'He didn't mention it,' I say.

'How did the Cradle come into existence?' Seymour asks, growing impatient. I sympathize with his mood. Freddy has begun to repeat several points Sharp has already told us. It's time to cut to the chase. He tenses at the question and stares at his beer bottle. He doesn't respond, not at first. Mary strokes his back and whispers in his ear.

'Tell them, honey. It'll be good to get it off your chest.'

Freddy sighs. 'It's hard. It was my fault.'

'It was Cindy's fault,' Mary says.

Freddy looks up. 'Two unrelated events led to the

creation of the Cradle. The first was definitely my fault. I'd heard a rumor that Tom – the man you know as Thomas Brutran, the president of IIC – had been seen kissing Cindy at some restaurant. I don't know why I didn't confront her about it. I guess I was afraid she'd tell me it was true. Suffice to say I was pretty upset to get the news. To make matters worse, I heard about it two hours before we were supposed to have a full gathering of the array. Back then we didn't usually get everyone together in the same room to conduct our experiments. We'd discovered that a person could be on the phone and give us practically the identical support, as long as we were all on one line together.

'That day was different. Sharp wanted to get everyone together to see if we could boost our results. I forget his reason. I just know it was a pity I was chosen to lead the group. My brain was on fire. All I could think of was Cindy in Tom's arms. And here I was the guy in charge of helping everyone focus.' Freddy stopped and shook his head. 'I know that's why it happened.'

'What happened?' I ask.

'During the session, Tom started having trouble breathing. His skin took on a bluish tinge. He gasped for us to help him. He felt as if he had a mountain on his chest, crushing him down. The professor was sure he was having a heart attack. We called for an ambulance. It goes without saying we broke up the array. After that, we were all afraid to do any psychic work. Especially me.'

'Why you?' I ask.

'Isn't it obvious? I was the one who hurt Tom. I was the one who almost stopped his heart. I didn't mean to, I couldn't control myself. I already told you the state of mind I was in. Then, when I took my place in front of the crowd, and they closed their eyes, I felt this huge magnetic web encircle me. I can still recall how it felt to this day. It was like a huge spider entered the auditorium and spun a hideous web that somehow linked us together. It was real, it was as tangible as a physical object. There was only one thing that kept me from running screaming from that auditorium. The one thing that overshadowed the horror I felt.'

'It was a sense of power,' I say.

Freddy stares at me, stunned. 'How did you know?'

'It's a long story.'

He nods. 'It was like my anger towards Tom got magnified a thousandfold and transformed into something else. Into an evil I'd never dreamed could exist.'

I suddenly have trouble breathing. I cannot stop thinking of Numbria in that crummy London motel room, and what I did to her. I know the evil he is talking about.

'What happened to Tom?' Seymour asks.

'He had a heart attack. He ended up spending over a month in the hospital. A twenty-five-year-old guy who didn't smoke or drink and who played tennis before breakfast. He couldn't have been in better shape. Yet somehow my mind, in connection with the array, almost killed him.'

'That's quite a leap from answering yes and no questions,' Seymour says.

'You're telling me. It was a power we just stumbled on to.'

'Did you tell Sharp about your state of mind during the experiment?' Seymour asks.

'I confessed to the others what I'd done. My guilt haunted me. But ironically the professor didn't blame me. He felt it was a fluke. Still, to be on the safe side, he made it a rule that no one was to join an array if they were feeling emotional.'

'Did you confront Cindy?' Seymour asks.

Freddy hesitates. 'No.'

'Why not?' Seymour persists.

'That's none of your business!' Freddy snaps.

The room suddenly feels tense enough to prompt another visit from the psychic spider. I let Freddy calm down before I gently encourage him to explain about the other half of the Cradle. I have a feeling I've waited a long time to hear what he has to say.

Freddy finally tell us the big secret.

'Six months after Tom had his heart attack, the professor had a stroke and was forced to retire. For a time the members of our group went their separate ways. Except for us couples, Cindy and me, and Wendy and Noel. There were no more experiments with the array. There was no longer an authority figure to get the thousands of people together. I was glad. After my contact with that evil power, I lost all enthusiasm for the work.

'I told you that Wendy and Noel had a child, Angela. She was five years old when Cindy got pregnant with our child. Unfortunately, this was in the days before routine sonograms, although it's debatable that knowing about the baby's situation ahead of time would have made any difference.

'When Henry was born, he had a condition where his liver, his gallbladder and portions of his small and large intestines were outside his body. The surgeons operated immediately. They skillfully shifted Henry's tiny organs into their proper place and sewed him back up. For a few days it looked like he would make it. But the trauma of the surgery or else the pressure of the organs themselves was too much for the boy. He died and it broke Cindy's and my heart.

'We didn't have a funeral with a coffin. We didn't believe in them. Cindy and I had Henry cremated. The old gang rented a boat and took it out on the San Francisco Bay. We prayed, sang songs and sprinkled his ashes on the dark water. My heart felt so heavy that day. I kept thinking how unfair it all seemed.

'It was while I was driving home that night with Cindy that an idea struck me. I wasn't a major follower of astrology, but I dabbled in it from time to time, largely because I'd noticed that many of the events the array predicted, the stars were also able to predict.

'I couldn't stop thinking of Henry and it made me wonder if there was a sign in his astrological chart that would indicate that he was meant to die. Like so many people who had suffered a loss, I suppose

I was looking for meaning in his death.

'The Internet was on the horizon but it didn't yet exist. However, personal computers had begun to appear. The first were primitive Apples, which we all thought were miracles in a box. My point is that computers and their endless streams of data had begun to spread around the globe, and it struck me that this incredible wealth of information might somehow be harnessed to prove whether astrology had any validity to it or not.'

'You just lost me,' Seymour says.

Freddy explains in a patient tone.

'Consider the case of Henry. He died six days after he was born. If astrology had any truth to it at all, then surely there must be something in his chart that would indicate his days would be short. To see if this was the case, I drew up his chart the same day we spread his ashes on the bay, and I stayed up all night studying it. To my surprise I found not one but four clear markers that he was doomed the instant he took his first breath. To this day, I remember what they were. He had Mars in the eighth house, the house of loss. Mars is the planet of death. Then he had both of them in Scorpio, which gives great power to the negative influence. Worst of all, he had been born during a solar eclipse. It's true it was a partial eclipse but it had been noticeable. Outside, I recalled, the light had dimmed just as Cindy pushed our son out of her body and Henry drew his first breath.

'All of this seemed an incredible coincidence. It

made me wonder if it was possible to create a more accurate astrological system than anyone had come up with in the past. Trillions of bits of data on millions of people would be the key. I proposed using computers to scan the charts of living people, to identify astrological patterns that matched what was already going on in their lives.'

'I'm still lost,' Seymour says.

Freddy grows animated. 'Let me give you an example. Say you took a thousand successful CEOs. Men and women who had worked their way to the top of the largest companies on earth. What if you threw all of their astrological charts together into a computer and programmed it to look for characteristics in the heavens that they all shared. What if the computer began to spot patterns. They could be anything. Venus in the second house, the house of wealth. The sun in the ascendant. With Jupiter and Uranus trine with Venus.'

'Did you just list the astrological signs of successful people?' I ask.

Freddy nods. 'Yes! I began to spot patterns everywhere I looked. Some matched the ancient texts on astrology. That surprised me. It meant that either someone in the distant past had come up with the same concept as me and implemented it without the help of computers, or else there had been a handful of psychic people back then who'd cognized the patterns out of thin air. But no matter how insightful those ancient seers were, they couldn't compete with modern computers and trillions of bits of data.'

'Fascinating,' Seymour says, finally grasping the concept. 'Why do I get the impression you created this system by working backwards?'

'Because that's exactly what I did! To understand the compassionate nature of someone like Mother Teresa, I took her astrological chart and the charts of thousands of other people who had devoted their lives to service. Then I fed their birth data into a computer and searched for qualities in the sky that they all shared. Do you see?'

'Gotcha.' Seymour nods.

'My goal was to discover the perfect place and time for an infant to be born on earth so they would embody the exact qualities their parents were hoping they would have. I sought for patterns that would create the greatest scientist, statesman, dancer, writer, artist, actor, doctor. With my system, I imagined a day would come when every parent could choose what kind of child they wanted.'

'That was a lofty goal,' I say. 'It's amazing, working alone, that you were able to identify all these patterns.'

'I worked on the system for years, night and day, without rest.'

I pat his arm. 'It was the pain of your son's death that drove you.'

Freddy stares at me with tremendous feeling in his eyes. 'I'm glad you understand. The system was to be Henry's memorial.'

'What went wrong?' Seymour asks.

Freddy drops his head. 'Cindy,' he whispers.

'You have to tell them,' Mary says gently when a minute goes by without him speaking.

He shrugs helplessly. 'After we lost Henry, Cindy and I grew apart. We'd go days, even weeks, without speaking. She didn't tell me that her grief had inspired her to head in a totally different direction. She went back to the professor's experiments. She gathered together an array that was far more powerful than any of Sharp's creations. She used every dollar she'd saved from her earlier ventures with the stock market to first identify the kids that were most psychic, then to pay them to work for her at predicting the moods of the market. I should have known what she was up to because suddenly we had money. But I didn't want to know. My research consumed my every waking moment and frankly I needed her funds to continue with my research. To this day I don't know if she supported me because she had faith in what I was doing. Or if she simply saw the potential of my idea and planned from the start to steal it.' Freddy pauses. 'Of course, that's exactly what she did.'

'*How* could she steal your system?' Seymour asks.

'Every single computer disk, every hard drive, every scrap of paper that dealt with the Cradle . . . she took it all. Now I know what you're going to ask. Didn't I have backups of my work? I did. Unfortunately, she knew where they all were. It's not as if I tried to hide them from her. After all, she was the one who was supporting me.'

163

'First she stole Professor Sharp's work,' I say. 'Then she stole yours. You don't need to check her stars. Her pattern is obvious.'

Seymour nods. 'She's a user.'

Freddy shakes his head. 'She's more than that. She's a monster.'

'What did she do with your astrological system?' I ask.

Freddy appears stunned, as if the answer were obvious.

'She used it to create more monsters,' he says.

'Huh?' Seymour says.

'It all goes back to that day I sat before the professor's array with my mind in turmoil. Cindy spotted an important secret that day that none of us noticed. She realized if you took a person who had exceptional psychic gifts – in this case, me – and connected them to the array, he or she could focus its power so that it caused physical harm. In other words, she saw a way to allow the array to transcend the confines of the mental realms. Make no mistake, I gave Tom a heart attack. My mind struck him down like the hammer of Thor. It's a miracle he didn't die, although, as things eventually turned out, it's a shame he didn't.'

'Tom helped Cindy steal the Cradle from you?' I ask.

'He took everything I had. I don't know exactly when Cindy left me for Tom. I'd ask if she still loved me, and she'd say sure, but she had always been a great liar. All I know is that when they stole my work, I was left with nothing and the world was in terrible danger.'

'What did they do with your Cradle?' I ask.

'I'm sure you can guess. They began to seek out the qualities that defined a psychic child. Not only that, they sought out the qualities that made a person empathetic.'

'They wanted to draft people with empathy?' Seymour asks.

Freddy smiles bitterly. 'The opposite. They wanted to know which qualities gave rise to love and compassion so they could avoid them at all cost. By this time they probably had so much money and power their reach stretched across the world. I know they set about testing children in the most remote corners of Africa, India, Mongolia, South America. In these places they identified *future* astrological charts that would produce children more psychic and cold than anything the world had ever seen. Then they made it a point that a child was born in the right place at the right time.'

'How?' Seymour asks.

'Cesarean section,' I say.

'Right,' Freddy says. 'It was these children, as they took birth – according to the stars, and according to Cindy's will – who eventually became the most lethal members of her Cradle.'

'How many are there?' Seymour asks.

'My best guess is the IIC has twenty thousand kids in their central Array. While another three hundred children make up their Cradle.'

'Interesting,' I say.

'That they have so many kids?' Freddy asks.

'That you know how many they have,' I say.

He acts innocent. 'It's an educated guess.'

'Freddy, get off it. Mary told us the truth. You know way too much about what Cindy's been doing since you guys broke up not to still be in touch with her. If I had any doubts on that score, I just have to recall the face of the five-year-old girl I met in Cindy's house. She looked a hell of a lot like you.'

Stunned, Freddy goes to deny my accusation, but then Mary touches his arm. 'I told you not to lie to her,' she says.

'I didn't lie,' Freddy says.

'How can you still see her after all she's done to you?' Seymour asks.

Freddy shakes his head. 'She's the mother of my child.'

'Does Tom know the kid's not his?' Seymour asks.

'He's not stupid,' Freddy says, annoyed.

'Are you?' I ask gently.

'I know what you're thinking. That I'm obsessed with her. OK, maybe I do still care for her. But I know how dangerous she is. I see her for what she is.'

'Do you see your daughter for what she is?' I ask.

'Huh?'

'Isn't she a member of the Cradle?' I ask. 'One of these preplanned super-psychic children?'

Freddy appears stunned by the idea. 'Jolie? No, she can't be one of them. Cindy wouldn't use her that way. Not our own kid.' He turns to Mary. 'Would she?'

Mary is sympathetic. 'It's not your fault if Jolie is. Nor is it Jolie's fault.'

'I'm surprised you let the relationship continue,' Paula says to Mary. If she's thinking of getting a rise out of Mary, she doesn't know the woman. Mary doesn't bat an eye.

'I encourage the relationship,' she says. 'It helps Freddy keep an eye on them.'

'So you know all their secrets?' I ask Mary.

She looks me straight in the eye. 'I've seen what that Cradle can do.' She pauses. 'Tell them, Freddy.'

He shudders. 'It happened in this house, not long after Cindy learned I was seeing Mary. We had just finished making love. Mary was dozing and I came into the kitchen to get a glass of water. Then it struck, I didn't know what the hell it was. It swept over me with a force that's difficult to describe. Suddenly, my will was no longer my own. I was a puppet. I picked up a knife. I needed it because all I could think about was how good it would feel to stab Mary. To see her bleed. To hear her scream. I returned to the bedroom and held the blade over her like a guillotine. Right then, there wasn't a soul on earth that could have talked me out of killing her. Fortunately, I stumbled as I neared the bed and bumped the mattress. Mary woke up, saw what was happening, and shouted my name. It didn't help. I tried to stab her, but she rolled off the bed and jumped up.'

'I kept calling his name but something in his eyes told me he was gone,' Mary interrupts. 'Yet it was more than that. There was something in that room that wasn't human. It was a devil. It wanted me to suffer because it craved my pain. I sensed its hunger.'

'How did you stop him?' Seymour asks her.

'I ran out the back. He chased after me with the knife but he was so crazed, he kept bumping into things. I didn't know what to do. I acted on instinct. When he ran into the well, I snuck up behind him and pushed him over the side. I knew he'd survive the fall into the water. The shock of it must have cured him of his madness. A minute later he was calling for me to throw him down the rope.'

'That's an amazing story,' I say, feeling a huge piece of it was missing.

'It's true,' Freddy says. 'The IIC doesn't just have enough money to take over the world. They have a tool that can control the most powerful men and women on earth. They have to be exposed. That's the only way they can be stopped.'

'Do you honestly feel that will do any good?' Seymour asks.

'You have to try. Someone has to,' Freddy says weakly.

'But we should warn you that they own several major newspapers and TV stations,' Mary says. 'The instant you speak against them, your lives will be in danger.'

'Is that why you've kept silent all this time?' I ask.

Freddy looks away. 'I wanted to keep Mary safe.'

It strikes me then that I'm missing something very important in our conversation. It's right in front of me but I can't see it. The not knowing drives me nuts.

I stand. 'This is all very interesting, but I need time to digest it. Would it be possible if we spent another night here?'

Mary smoothly climbs to her feet, leaving Freddy on the floor with his assortment of beer bottles. Mary gives me a shrewd look. Yet she appears genuinely happy with my request.

'We were hoping you would stay,' she says.

12 ~~~

Another night with Seymour in the guesthouse. He sits smoking, unhappy that we're not on a plane to New York to try out Charlie's new vaccine.

'What are we doing here?' he asks.

'We're here because they want us to stay.'

'You invited us to stay this time.'

'You have to look deeper than what was said. Mary is anxious to keep us here. So is Freddy. Why? What's their motive?'

'Freddy has a long history with Brutran and the IIC. He knows they're dangerous. So does Mary. I think they were telling us the truth when they said they want to help us expose them.'

'They barely asked about our credentials.'

Seymour hesitates. 'That was odd, I admit. But they

know I'm a famous writer, and Professor Sharp obviously gave us a thumbs-up.'

'Why?'

'I don't know why. If you doubt them so much, then let's leave. We can drive to the airport now, charter a plane.' He scratches the back of his hands. 'The vaccine we have is not doing the trick.'

'I'll give you another shot.'

'Paula already gave me one. She gave Shanti a booster, too. Matt's right when he says Charlie's got to try out his new vaccine on someone who's infected. It's the only way he'll know if it's working. And we can argue all you want about Matt's list of priorities versus yours, but Matt is not stupid. The Telar pose the immediate threat.'

'Even if Charlie's developed a working vaccine, our position has not changed. We're still small and weak. We need an ally, a powerful one. It's got to be the IIC.'

Seymour shakes his head. 'The more I hear about that bitch, the less I want to knock on her door.'

'I'll do the knocking.'

'Yeah, right, the rest of us will just wait in the car. Sita, this isn't like you. Usually, you see a problem and you deal with it. The last few days, you seem like a different person.'

'I am different. Do you know how much I hate being handicapped like this?'

'You still have the strength of a dozen men.'

'When I died, I had the strength of a hundred.'

'That's not what I meant.'

'You want me to take over, I know, lead the troops forward. But we're missing something here, I feel it.' I pause. 'There's no way Mary freed Freddy of the Cradle by shoving him in that well.'

'That did sound awfully convenient. So they lied to us on that point? That's what people do, they tell white lies. I still think they're good people, and Freddy did give us a profound insight into the Cradle. Frankly, that part where he explained how he developed a working astrological system blew my mind.'

'It was impressive. But he never explained how he got the arrays to talk. He barely spoke about Tom, Wendy and Noel. They were always in the background, like props.'

'I noticed that. It made me wonder.'

'Do you think Freddy's still under Brutran's control?'

Seymour sucks on his cigarette. 'I think he's still in love with her, and he's not as ready as he thinks to bring her down. He suffered big-time when he lost Henry. I can see how he would be attached to Jolie. Even if her mother is the Wicked Witch of the West.'

'That little girl gave me the creeps.'

'I remember. Still, this is all talk. I want to leave. So does Shanti. Why don't you let us fly back to New York and try out the new vaccine? If you think you still have something to learn here, then stay here with Paula.'

'I'm not ready to break up the group yet.'

'What's that supposed to mean?'

'Let's give it one more day here. I feel . . . I feel like something's going to happen.'

'Good or bad.'

'Both.' I pick up Yaksha's book and hug it to my chest. 'I'm going to search for more secret sections. I can do it outside, the moon's bright. Do you think you can sleep?'

He starts scratching before I finish my question. 'When I get tired enough, I'll pass out. You remember to sleep, too. Teri's body needs to rest.'

I step towards the door. 'I won't be gone long.'

'Good night, Sita. Love you.'

'I love you more,' I say.

Outside is a dream. The branches on the surrounding trees sway in a warm breeze. A myriad of moonbeams dance like at a celestial party where angels mingle with intoxicated fairies. There's a sweet odour in the air I've not been treated to in ages. Jasmine; it reminds me of Vrindavana, Krishna's forest. There, the jasmine flowers grew wild on the banks of the Yamuna River. It's been centuries, and yet I remember those woods as if it was yesterday. The cows grazing in the meadows. The gopis laughing in their saris, talking endlessly about their Lord.

I wished right then I had been one of them, a gopi, free to leave this world for Vaikuntha, Krishna's supreme abode, at the end of a normal life. Yet I recall how Krishna left Vrindavana and the gopis when he was still a young man, and never returned. Later, it was said he did it to force them to suffer the pangs of separation, so they would think of him and nothing else. Even at the moment of death.

'I called your name when I died,' I whisper to the mysterious night. 'Why didn't you take me?'

No one answers and I'm not surprised. I don't really care what John said about my duty being left unfinished. I still feel I've been cheated.

The night is filled with unanswered questions that call to me. All my doubts, my fears, my hopes – I feel as if they have gathered nearby but still hide in the shadows so I can't easily confront them. The fragrant air feels pregnant with the possibility of discovery, but I'm not sure I want it to speak to me, for I fear that whatever it reveals will kill what little hope I have left.

Like the previous night, I take the spray bottle that contains a mixture of well water and my blood and sit with my back beside the stone well. Yet I have hardly opened the book when I close it again. The smell of jasmine is stronger here than elsewhere, and I realize it's because it's coming from the well.

Standing, I peer down into the hole, the sharp angle of the moonlight allowing me to see no deeper than thirty feet. Even with my vampire sight, I cannot pierce the darkness beyond that point. Plus I hear a trickle of water, and it would seem a foolish idea to climb down into a well that's already flooded, even with help of the nearby rope and bucket.

Yet I wonder at the source of the smell.

Why it should come out of the earth. Why tonight.

As I mentioned, my hearing has been my most trustworthy sense over the years. I suspect if I simply drop the bucket, let the rope spin out at full speed, the sound of it hitting the water might tell me something about the structure of the well. There are a hundred yards of wooded land between the well and the house. I doubt the others will hear the splash, and if they do it won't be the end of the world.

I untie the knot that holds the bucket in place and let it drop. The well's wooden shaft spins wildly, for a long time. The well is deep, more than fifty yards, half a football field. Finally I hear the splash as the bucket strikes the water.

How does the noise echo in the deep?

To my surprise, the sound doesn't bounce around the stone hole and pour out the top. Rather, the noise dissipates at the floor of the well as it spreads out underground. It makes no sense. Of course, neither does the smell. It's decided . . .

I have to climb down and see what the hell is going on.

I return Yaksha's book to the car before I proceed.

Teri's body is a hundred and twenty pounds of solid muscle. Before I changed her into a vampire, the girl had less than 5 per cent body fat and spent a fair amount of time in each workout stretching. She was addicted to yoga and used to brag that her stride was as long as it was because of her flexibility.

Bottom line – Teri left me with a perfect physique for rock climbing. Grabbing the rope, I hoist myself over the edge, plant my feet on one side of the well and my back on the other. I'm able to adopt this stance thanks to the well's narrowness. It's less than four feet across.

I'm in no hurry, I descend slowly. As I pass out of sight of the moon, my vampire eyes adapt further and I can still see the perfect spots to jam my rubber soles against the uneven rocks. The pressure on my upper back is uncomfortable but bearable. My arms remain strong, although I find myself breathing hard. The humidity in the air increases as the sound of the trickling water grows louder.

Approximately ten feet from the water's surface, the walls of the well suddenly vanish and I'm left hanging in mid-air, clinging to the rope. There's a reddish glow off to my right, but it's so faint it doesn't allow me to see my surroundings. Nevertheless, I think I've already solved part of the mystery of the well. Its source of water is not your normal underground stream. I'm in a cave, with an open brook running beneath my feet.

I can't tell how deep the stream is, but I hope it has a shore. Like most newborn vampires, I can't stand the cold, and I sure as hell don't want to get wet. I grip the rope tightly and kick out with my legs, trying to build up enough momentum so I can swing back and forth. Since I have nothing to kick off of, I struggle like an astronaut caught in weightlessness. Nevertheless, after a few minutes of hard kicking, I'm swinging freely, and I finally build up enough courage to let go.

I land on smooth *dry* stone. The underground stream does indeed have a shore, although it's narrow, two feet wide at best, good enough to support me. I take a few minutes to stretch my arms and legs, and free myself of the cramp in my upper back.

The glow fascinates me. I hike along the bank of the stream, drawn by its haunting color. The glow would be invisible to most humans, but there's a reason for its faintness. The cave winds left and right, making it impossible for the light to travel in a straight line.

As I turn a particularly sharp corner, it suddenly grows in intensity and I recognize its source. The light is created by a torch, or a series of torches. Its colour and a faint crackling sound give it away.

Minutes later I enter a well-lit cavern.

It's possible the cave's a natural structure, but this space is definitely the work of human hands. The dome-shaped roof is too smooth; it expands steadily in width and height, creating a large egg-shaped grotto. The six-foot-wide stream flows through the centre, while a dozen burning torches reach out from the curved walls.

To my left, on the other side of the stream, is a stone altar. Its design is primal and powerful. Three steps rise to an oval-shaped platform, over which stands an inverted triangle, a six-foot-tall etching encrusted with a thousand glowing rubies, with a single large pearl in the centre, a symbol of Mother Kali. Near the bottom tip of the triangle someone has kindled a bonfire, and close to it, lying on her back on a white cloth turned blood red by the light, is the body of a young blonde woman.

It's me lying there. I knew it would be me.

I don't recall crossing the stream but I must have leapt over it. Suddenly the body is within arm's reach and I'm staring down at her face. She looks at peace; it's a lie. She looks almost alive; maybe that's not a complete lie. On the sheet that covers her, near the heart, is a red stain. It looks fresh.

I drop to my knees as the strength drains from Teri's body.

'Krishna,' I whisper. 'Why?'

I close my eyes and weep. I'm not sure for who. It doesn't matter, my sorrow is real, why should I be ashamed to share it with myself?

Time passes. It passes slowly when your body's dead.

I hear a sound at my back.

Someone breathing. Someone alive.

I don't turn. There's no need. I know who stands there. I probably knew the truth from the start. I had seen the wisdom in her eyes. And it was that wisdom that had told her to position herself as the lover of the one man who still had the love of her enemy.

'Hello, Umara,' I say to Mary.

She moves until she is standing over my left shoulder.

'I took it here to protect it,' she says.

I open my eyes and stare at my body. 'Do the dead need protection?'

'Yaksha died once and came back. You can do the same.'

I turn and look at Mary, at Umara, the oldest living creature on earth. She still wears her blue jeans and a plain red blouse. Her feet are bare. But the way she stands, so carefully balanced on those feet, she gives off a sense of incredibly coiled energy. I wonder if I, even at my peak, could have taken her.

'I didn't see that story in his autobiography,' I say.

'You'll find it. I notice you've begun to use your blood.'

'Did you put that idea in my mind?'

Umara gestures. 'Perhaps this place did. It's very old.'

'How old?'

'I've been coming here for three thousand years. The Native Americans built it for me. A wonderful people, you would have liked them. They called themselves the Rulan, although that name has become lost in history.'

'Did they worship you?'

'They tried but I forbade it. They were a simple people, attuned to nature.' She gestures to the triangle. 'I taught them about Isis, the Great Mother. They had their own gods but they were wise enough to understand they were all the same.'

'India. America. Egypt. It sounds like you got around.'

'I can say the same for you. I've watched you, Sita, since you were young.'

'I know. You offered to kill me.'

'Couldn't you tell I was teasing him? Yaksha would never have allowed that. And there was no need. When Yaksha took his vow, you became the forbidden fruit, whereas Krishna wanted me to help Yaksha.'

'Lucky you. God blessed your union.'

Umara sighs. 'It wasn't that way. Our lives were filled with struggle. From the day I met Yaksha, I was never again to know peace.'

'But it was worth it.'

Umara is reflective. She nods.

I stand and face her. 'When did you last see him?'

'It's been over a hundred years.'

'Matt saw him fifteen years ago.'

'He was fortunate.'

'Why would he see his son and avoid you?'

'He didn't allow Matt to have much contact with him, not towards the end. But I think he found it harder to say no to his son.'

'Yaksha was afraid the Telar would find all of you.'

'Of course. It was the primary reason for our separation.'

'What was the other reason?'

'You.'

'I don't understand.'

'Yaksha knew his time was approaching. He didn't want to leave the earth without fulfilling his vow. Yet he couldn't imagine killing you. It tore him apart.' Umara pauses. 'In the end, you tore us apart.'

'You say that like I should be pleased.'

'You're obviously jealous that I was his wife.'

The need to challenge her feels silly. Still, I find it hard to resist. 'I could have been with him if I wanted,' I say.

Umara treats my petty emotionalism with more respect than it deserves. 'He often spoke of you. He kept better track of you than you realize. He was never at ease unless he knew you were safe. At the same time, he used to boast that you were invincible.'

I nod towards my body. 'It seems he was wrong.'

She reaches out and touches my arm. 'You're a living miracle. Even in death, you found a way to survive. You stand before me in another body, true, but I believe your original form can be saved. Have you studied your chest wound? It's almost healed.'

'How did you know I was in Teri's body?'

'Matt tried to contact me as soon as you were killed. He left a long message for me describing what had happened.'

'Did you respond?'

'No. But I flew to Denver to watch over you.'

'And you knew I was in Teri's body?'

'The second I saw you.'

'Are you a healer as well as an immortal?'

'You misunderstand. I brought you here to keep you safe from Haru and Brutran, and to help preserve your form. Up until this evening, I've kept your body anchored in this water. I kept you near freezing, as I did to Yaksha when he was fatally injured. The cold halts the decay. At the same time the water gave your body the time it needed to regenerate.'

'What's so special about this water? Besides its temperature?'

'The Rulan had a legend that said the source of this river was located deep in mountains that overlook this part of the coast. In a chamber filled with massive crystals that shine with their own light. There may be some truth to the story. Long before I came here, this cave extended deep into the earth. I was able to confirm that fact with my own excavations. But it soon became clear to me that a massive quake had closed off the bulk of the cave and I'd never be able to reach the stream's source. Still, we're lucky the water continues to flow. It has healing properties.'

'It can restore me to life?'

'No, but it has given your body a chance to recover. Now, with your blood, nothing is impossible. I know your history. Yaksha, Kalika and John have all contributed their blood to yours. Think about it, Sita, that's a remarkable trinity.'

'How did you resurrect Yaksha?'

'It's better I show you than tell you.'

'How was he killed?'

'That's a story for later, when you're back in your own body.'

I shake my head. 'You can't do it. You're not Krishna.'

Umara grabs me by the shoulders. 'But I knew him. I spent years with him. I can't draw a breath without feeling his grace, and the instant I met you, I felt it as well. He's still with us, you know in your heart he is, and I believe it was he who brought you here.' She pauses. 'You can't defeat the Telar or the IIC unless you reclaim your full power.'

For some reason I find myself staring at Teri's hands. 'If it works, what will become of this body?' I ask.

Umara lets go of me. 'It will die.'

'No. You don't know that. Maybe she could come back.'

'She's dead, Sita. She died the day she was supposed to die.'

I stare at her face. 'Matt doesn't know I'm in here.'

That startles her. 'You never told him?'

'He was furious when I tried to change Teri into a vampire. I only did it to save her life, and still he didn't care. He threatened to kill her in the middle of her transformation. That's when the Cradle struck and he shot me instead.'

Umara frowns. 'The Cradle couldn't have controlled Matt.'

'Why not?'

'Brutran would need a sample of his blood to get a hold on him.'

'I figured the same thing. Somehow, she must have got that sample.'

'From where?'

'I don't know. It worries me. And it terrifies me how Matt's going to react when he discovers I've swiped his girlfriend's body.'

Umara turns and wanders around the cavern. 'I only saw him with Teri from a distance. He seemed to care for her. But I never got to spend time with them. Tell me, was it a deep love?'

'She was the love of his life.'

Umara nods to herself. 'He knew she was your descendant. It makes sense. I'm glad he got to experience a love like that at least once. It's a pity she died so young.'

'I loved her a great deal. I wish I could have died instead of her. But what's happened has happened. I need to get back in my real body before he discovers the truth. Even then I don't know if I'll be able to handle him.'

'He's not going to hurt you.'

'How do you know?'

'Because I'm his mother.'

'Then you know how strong he is. How fast.'

Umara shakes her head. 'I'm not going to fight him. I'll talk to him, he'll listen to me. Trust me. But we're going to have to tell him what we're doing beforehand. The one thing Matt can't stand is to be lied to.'

'You don't get it. When it comes to this point, I don't trust you. There's no way I'm going to call Matt and say hey, guess what, I'm not really Teri. I've just been pretending for the last week. He's not going to accept that.'

Umara stops pacing and stares down at my body. 'He's still trying to reach me. He's left messages warning me about the Telar and a supervirus they've developed. Of course I've known about it for years.'

'Do you still have friends among the Telar?'

'Contacts. People who report to me. Telar who don't trust Haru or the Source. You'd be surprised how many there are.'

'Have they told you when the Telar plan to release the virus?'

'Soon.'

'Why haven't you tried to stop Haru?'

'I've been waiting for you.'

'Don't bullshit me, Umara.'

'I'm not. My intuition is unlike Freddy's. I seldom

see things that are going to happen. But occasionally I'll have something akin to a waking dream. I usually don't see many details but I can sense the truth of these visions, if that's what they are. And whenever I've considered attacking the Telar directly, I always remember a vision I had the night after the Battle of Kurukshetra ended. That was the day I saw you from across the battlefield.'

'What did you see?'

'I saw you chopping off the heads of a Hydra.'

'Krishna told Yaksha about the Hydra. That's why you dreamed it.'

'I hadn't met Yaksha yet, and Krishna never said anything to me about a Hydra, although I would have understood if he had.'

'Because you're one of the first Telar. You were there at the start.'

Umara hesitates. 'Yes.'

'You lied to your son when you denied that you were one of the original Telar.'

'That lie was necessary to protect him. None of the Telar alive today know how old I am.'

'Not even Haru? I heard he was your brother.'

She sighs. 'Please. I don't wish to speak of him. Now now.'

'Did the original Telar develop an array?'

'Yes.'

'Did they have a cradle?'

'Now is not the time to explain what happened then. You heard what Freddy said. Between him and

Sharp, you've gained a basic understanding of how large groups can be used to tap into a vast field of psychic energy.'

'Sure. The two of them gave us an insight into how the IIC is making trillions of dollars while twisting people's brains into mush. But I still don't have a clue how to destroy Brutran or the Telar. Our time is short. You've got to come clean with me. I need to know what you know.'

'I can't tell you. Not until you're back in your body.'

'Why not?'

Umara kneels beside my body and puts a hand on its head. It's strange – I feel her fingers on Teri's forehead. We share similar blood. Perhaps that explains the link between our two forms.

Umara speaks in a dark whisper. 'Because what I know could be used to destroy this planet. Literally, it's possible to unleash a power so great it could detonate the earth's core and transform this world into a second asteroid belt. And you're not strong enough to protect such secrets, not in your current form.'

I kneel beside her and squeeze my ancient hand. It's probably due to the nearby fire, but it still shocks me to find my flesh is warm. There's no pulse, though, and my dead eyes remain closed.

'Put me back in my body,' I say.

Umara nods. 'Tomorrow night. When the moon is full.'

'Does that matter?'

'Freddy's system would say that's when the energy of

the Goddess is at its strongest.'

'Tomorrow night is fine with me. But you can't bring Matt here.'

'I have to. If you're right and she was the love of his life, then he has to be given a chance to say goodbye to her. He'll never forgive either of us if we deny him that.'

'She's dead! He's not going to get a chance to talk to her.'

Umara strokes my body's arm and I continue to feel the sensation on my own arm. 'I'll speak to him before he sees you. We have much to catch up on, and when we're done, I'll make sure he understands that you didn't choose to enter Teri's body. And I'll explain why you kept the truth hidden from him.'

'Who else will witness this exorcism?'

Umara smiles sadly. 'Is that what you think of it? I don't know. Who do you want there?'

'Paula and Seymour.'

'They're mortals. They won't understand.'

'They're my friends. They understand plenty.'

'Anyone else?'

I hesitate. 'John, if he'll come. Have you heard about the boy?'

'Of course. The Telar and the IIC are searching the four corners of the earth trying to find him.' She pauses. 'Are the prophecies about him true?'

'I don't know. I doubt he's Krishna, but there's something about him that's wonderful. I'll ask Paula to bring him. He helped anchor me in this body. Maybe he can help anchor me in my old one.'

Umara nods as she stares down at my body. 'What we're attempting to do is dangerous. I suppose you've guessed that. For this body to live again, the body you're in must die.'

'How will it die?'

'Simple. We'll kill it.'

13 ～

Twenty-four hours later I sit in the guesthouse with Seymour and await a visit from Matt. I figure one of two things will happen. Matt will either come in and give Seymour a shot of Charlie's new vaccine. Or else he will kick the door down and snap my neck.

The possibilities make the wait interesting.

Seymour smokes, when he's not scratching.

'I can't believe that chick's ten thousand years old.'

'More like twelve thousand,' I say.

'Christ. She's such a fox. Do you think she really loves Freddy or is she just hanging out with him because of the Brutran connection?'

'She befriended Freddy to keep an eye on Brutran. But I think over time she's come to love him.'

'Does he know who she is?'

'Umara would never trust her secrets with a mortal.'

'But you've told me and Paula.'

'I know neither of you will talk. Besides, it's too late in the game to worry about who's who. Soon, very soon, humanity is either going to live or die.'

'Even if you get your body back, you're not going to be able to stop the Telar.'

'You're wrong. I have a plan.'

'One you might share with a lowly mortal?'

'Not yet.'

'Fine. Be that way. I have an idea what your plan is anyway.'

'I'm sure you do,' I say.

'Shanti's excited Matt's bringing the new vaccine. At the same time she knows something big is happening and she's being kept out of it.'

'Shanti is young. You better believe Umara sees her that way. What she doesn't know won't hurt her.'

'I agree. She's sweet but she's led a protected life. She shouldn't be burdened with too many secrets.'

'God, it feels weird for you to agree with me.'

'Don't get used to it. Hey, I heard you on the phone with Charlie. Asking for large bottles of the new T-11 vaccine and the X6X6 virus. I assume that has something to do with your plan.'

'Don't spy on my private conversations. You never know who might kidnap you and try to torture the information out of you. Besides, the new vaccine is called C-1.'

'After Charlie?'

'He invented it. He should be allowed to name it.'

Seymour studies the black blisters on his hands and arms. They are not only larger, they're spreading. 'Did Umara go alone to pick up Matt?'

'Yes. Remember to keep calling her Mary around Freddy.'

'I hope she arranged for Freddy to be out of the way tonight.'

'She sent him off to see his daughter.'

'Brutran's child? Isn't that sort of risky at a time like this?'

'The visit was planned far in advance. Neither of us thought it should be changed. We don't want to raise any unnecessary suspicions.'

'If you ask me, Brutran knows exactly where we are and is just biding her time.'

'It's possible. But if Cindy tries to attack with the Cradle, she's going to run into a big surprise. Umara can block it.'

'Like Shanti?'

'Better.'

'How does she do it?'

'That's a secret she's keeping to herself. I'm sure it's something that can't be taught.'

'How was she able to mask her heartbeat from you?'

'Like Matt, she has complete control over all her bodily functions.'

'I guess a woman like that wouldn't be interested in a guy like me.'

'She does have Freddy and he's not a bad guy. Then

191

there's the age difference, that might be a problem. Besides, she knows you're in love with me.'

Seymour is too damn perceptive. He hears something in my voice. 'Is it hard for you to be around her?' he asks gently.

'She's the most amazing woman I've ever met.'

'More the reason to hate her.' He pauses. 'It's not like Krishna gave Yaksha a choice to be with you.'

I sigh; it does hurt, and it shouldn't, it's so childish. 'Yaksha made his own choice. He met her and fell for her. The years were not a barrier between them. Their love was real.'

'But he never stopped loving you. He was with you in the end. That means a lot.'

'He was with me then because he knew I would not stop him, that I would let him die. I doubt Umara would have ever let him go.' I stare down at Teri's hands and try to imagine that they will be dead before the night is through. 'Can we talk about something else, please?'

'I'm sorry, Sita. I just meant . . .'

'I know, I know.' I rub my palms together, enjoying the warmth of Teri's flesh. 'There's a call I should make before Umara and Matt return.'

'Are you worried if John is coming?'

'Paula called from the road. They're on their way.'

'Great. John is finally taking an interest in you, after all.'

'I'm grateful. I have this feeling that everything will go smoothly if he's around. But the call I brought up . . .'

'It's to Teri's parents,' Seymour interrupts.

'It's hopeless, I know, what am I going to say? I'm saying goodbye to them while I'm still alive. Yet I feel I owe it to them. I don't talk much about Teri's memories. I try not to dwell on them. But they're a part of me now. Even if this switch works tonight, I'll take them with me. Mr and Mrs Raine will always be Dad and Mom to me.'

Seymour stands. 'I assume you want to be alone.'

I reach out my hand. 'I want you right here beside me. I want you to hold me, and if I get stuck, whisper in my ear and tell me what to say. Can you do that for me?'

He takes my hand and sits beside me. 'Just let them know how much you love them. That's the most important memory you can leave them with. And tell them that winning the gold medal in the Olympics was the thrill of a lifetime. That will comfort them in the days to come. Teri didn't have a long life but it was a rich life. You need to know that, too.'

For some reason I hug him. 'Thank you.'

Two hours later, I'm alone in the guesthouse. Seymour is in the main residence with Paula and John, who have only just arrived. I could hear what they're saying if I concentrate but I don't feel the desire. My hearing is focused on another car that's turning into the long driveway. Umara and her extraordinary son are here.

I assume Matt will go in the house first, say hello to the others, maybe give Seymour a shot of the new vaccine. But the instant he steps out of the car, he walks towards the cottage. I swallow. The long wait is over.

Moments later he stands in the doorway. He's dressed in a white shirt and grey pants, with a charcoal sports coat. His expression is impossible to read. It appears empty of all emotion, which does not reassure me. I try to form a welcoming smile but my lips are frozen. I have to cough to speak.

'This is not easy for either of us,' I say.

'No.' He enters and sits on the corner of Seymour's bed. I curl my knees to my chest. At least he has sat down.

'Your mother insisted on speaking to you. That was not my wish. I wanted to tell you myself.' I pause. 'When I leapt in front of your laser, this was the last thing I expected to happen.'

'It just happened? You had no role in it?'

Now that he's alert to the situation, it will be useless to lie to him. His truth sense is equal to my own. 'No conscious role, although John says my soul wanted to remain here.'

'You talked to him about what happened?'

'I felt confused. I had to talk to someone.'

'Did John say Teri wished to leave?'

'He indicated it was her time.'

'That's what I told you. Her body should have died that night.'

'I know. But . . . it was hard, too hard, to let her go.'

He nods. 'And if you had, then we would have lost you both.'

'Probably.'

'I wish I could speak to John and ask him these questions.'

'He's in the house. You could try talking to him. But he's difficult to approach. The other night was the first time we really spoke.'

'But you trust him.'

'Yes.'

'He says that you remained here for a reason. That you have an important task to accomplish.'

These are points I passed on to Umara to improve my case.

'Essentially,' I say.

'And if I kill you, I go against the word of God.'

'The child is not God. Kill me if you wish. I won't fight you.'

'You can't fight me. Not until you're back in your original body.'

'Is that why you're here? To wait until the switch is complete so we can have a fair fight?'

'The idea did cross my mind.'

'Better kill me now and save everybody a lot of trouble.'

'You know I can't harm Teri.'

'You don't have to worry about that. Teri's gone.'

My words sting him and he grimaces. 'Is that definite?'

'According to your mother and John.'

It takes time for him to absorb his girlfriend's death sentence. But finally he asks the question I have most dreaded. 'Why didn't you just tell me the truth?'

'At first, I went through a period of disorientation. You were with me, you knew I wasn't myself. It was only at the funeral, when John gazed into my eyes, that things came into focus. It was then I knew who I was.'

'You could have told me when you returned to the hotel.'

'I wanted to. I took no pleasure in deceiving you. But I remembered your anger on the mountain. I was afraid how you would react.'

'We made love that night.'

'I know. I'm . . . I'm sorry.'

'That's not it. Teri and I made love. She was there, I felt her.'

'I know. When you took me in your arms, I felt her, too.'

Matt sits up. 'Then there's hope.'

'You can't think that way. It kills me to keep saying this but she died on that mountain.'

'But you have all her memories. A part of her must still live inside you. If we could reawaken it . . .'

'Matt. Please. I understand little of what's supposed to happen tonight. Your mother refused to give me any details. But I do know she brought you here so you could let Teri go. Your mother understands how painful this is for you. She wouldn't put you through this anguish unless it was necessary.' I pause. 'Teri's dead.'

He closes his eyes and grips his hands together so hard they shake. His internal struggle is palpable; it heats the room. A part of him wants to scream in anguish. Another part wants to fight for her life. And what's left wants to strike out at me for putting him through such agony.

'This is your fault,' he whispers.

'It's both our faults.'

His eyes pop open and he glares at me. 'How dare you!'

I meet his furious gaze. 'We both dared, Matt. We both contacted Teri and interfered with her life without asking her permission. Without telling her what we were. You're half vampire, half Telar, and you brought the whole threat of the Telar into her life when you chose to pursue her. At least I didn't know about the Telar or the IIC when I first made contact with her. But that's no excuse. I knew from experience that death follows me. I had no more right than you to involve myself in her life.'

He leaps to his feet and is suddenly inches away. I feel the fire of his breath, the choking ash of his loss. He's so close to killing me I know it will be over before I'll feel it begin. He raises a hand above my head.

'I've read your history,' he swears. 'Everyone you've ever loved, everyone you've ever touched, has always died. That's your legacy, not mine. There was never a chance I would have harmed her.'

My fear has left me, my death feels inevitable. For that reason I'm able to look up at him and speak in a calm voice. 'That's not true. You can fool yourself but you can't fool Teri. You're right, part of her does still live inside me. Her memories are all there, and I have only to glance at the day you met her and the days that followed to know that you were constantly battling with yourself whether it was right for you to let her fall in love with you. Well, you convinced yourself the answer was yes, when it was no. No, Matt, I'm no more to blame than you for what happened to her. So if you decide to rip my head off please be a sport about it and end your own life when you're done with me.'

The life goes out of him right then and he plops down on my bed. He sways as if he's been stabbed and I instinctively reach out to steady him but I end up hugging him. He seems to melt in my arms, or perhaps it's our tears that create the sensation, as they mingle and flow together and drop into the lap of a young woman we both loved more than we could say. It seems he accepts my words, or else Teri's memories, since he stops threatening me and falls into a cold and lonely silence.

14

My body lies in front of me on the altar. I sit on my knees to the left of it, near my head. John is beside me, above my long blonde hair, and Umara is to the right side of my body, a puja kit near her crossed legs. At the feet of my body is Matt. At the last moment John stopped Paula and Seymour from attending. No one asked him why.

Umara has built up the fire, and the last of the chill of the icy stream has left my body. The thousands of rubies embedded in the inverted triangle sparkle; the central pearl glistens. The Kali symbol reminds me of my daughter, Kalika, and how fearlessly she offered her life to save John. I wish to imitate her courage now but a thread of fear has woven its way back into my heart. I wasn't afraid when I leapt in front of the laser that originally killed me but I had no time to think then.

Now I wish I could stop thinking and turn off my mind. I have no idea what is to happen next but I'm overwhelmed with a strange sense of the abyss. Kali is supposed to represent extinction, the loss of all individuality. At another time and place I might have viewed such a state as related to enlightenment but now it just feels like another form of death.

I know who I am and I want to go on being me.

I don't like the odds Umara plays with. She has only done this once before. She doesn't know whether it's going to work any more than I do. Nevertheless, I watch closely as she removes a small blue bottle from the folds of her red robe. As she uncorks it, I smell blood and give her a puzzled look. She nods.

'It's Krishna's,' she says.

'Did he give it to you for this purpose?' I ask.

'I was with him when he left this world.'

'But you were in Egypt with Yaksha.'

Umara shakes her head. 'I was with him.'

'But—'

'Silence. He's here. We must begin.'

For several minutes Umara closes her eyes and sits in silence. Unsure what to do, I follow her example. The feeling of the abyss grows, but out of nowhere a wave of love expands inside it and suddenly I don't feel so alone.

I hear Umara's eyes open and peep over to see what she's doing.

Her puja kit is used to perform Vedic ceremonies.

It's similar to a variety of ceremonial kits from all over the world. There's a brass candleholder, which holds a narrow white candle, and two small brass dishes: one for rice, the other for water. There are three other pieces: a tiny vase that supports a burning incense stick; a small dish equipped with a handle that's filled with camphor; and a two-inch plate smeared with sandalwood paste. To Umara's right, in a neat pile, are fresh fruits, flowers and a brand-new white handkerchief.

I saw these same items a thousand times when I lived in India. But I don't understand why she's defaulting to the trappings of that tradition when she's originally from Egypt. I wonder if it has to do with the blood she carries. It's strange but I don't doubt her extraordinary claim, although it's no different from a Christian priest or minister saying they had a bottle of Christ's blood. Of course there aren't many priests or ministers who can boast they've been alive for thousands of years.

Umara begins to sing in a language I don't wholly recognize. I say wholly because there are a few words that are familiar – a combination of ancient Egyptian and Sanskrit mantras and hymns. The tune is melodious and her voice is nothing short of enchanting. I know now where Matt inherited his voice. I find myself drifting along with it like a leaf in the wind. I feel as if I'm being hypnotized and don't really care. Umara waves her candle and lights her camphor as she sings, and I wish the song would never stop.

Yet at some point she falls silent. It puzzles me

because I'm not sure when it happens. I become aware that the loving feeling in the chamber has grown in intensity and I cannot free myself of her remark, 'He's here. We must begin.' Someone sure feels like they've stopped by for a visit.

I glance at John and Matt. They both sit with their eyes closed, so deep, so settled, they could be asleep. Umara is the only one who is busy, slowly dripping the blood from her vial on to the forehead of my dead body. What's remarkable about it is that it doesn't spill into my hair or eyes. It's simply absorbed by my skin. Drop after drop strikes the space between my eyes and vanishes. It's as if my dead brain hungers for it.

Or maybe it's my body hungering for life.

I blink and my old body suddenly jerks.

Umara looks over at me. 'It's time,' she says.

'For what?' I whisper.

'To die, so that you may live again.' She turns to her son and gently shakes his knee. Matt opens his eyes, his gaze a million miles away. 'She will need your help.'

'Mother?' he mumbles.

'It's time to set Teri free,' Umara says. 'To do that, you must let her experience the death she was meant to have. Her leg must shatter, the bone must pierce the skin, the artery inside must rupture, and her blood must flow. You can help Sita, and Teri, by doing this to her.'

'No,' Matt says.

'I can do it myself,' I say, although the thought unnerves me.

Umara shakes her head as she continues to address her son. 'You're her love. You are what binds her to this world. You should be the one to set her free.'

Matt gasps. 'Then she's here! She can be revived!'

'No. She's passed on. Only a portion of her is still trapped. With your love, you can free her, but only if you're willing to let her go.'

Matt is distressed. 'I can't hurt her. Let Sita do it. She's the one who caused her injury in the first place.'

'You can't blame Sita for what happened. You can't blame yourself. Teri's death was destined. Sita's rebirth is also destined. But there's only a narrow window in which this can all happen. Sita, lie down on your back with your left thigh near the head of your body. Matt, move between them and lift up her left leg. You know your strength. A single swift crack and it will be done.'

'Why do I need to put my leg near her head?' I ask.

'No questions!' Umara says, holding up the vial of Krishna's blood. 'We have only a limited supply, and limited time. Get in position, both of you.'

I lie back on the stone altar so that my left thigh bumps against the head of my body. By chance I have on a white dress, and I instinctively pull it above my knees so Teri's skin is in contact with my old skin. I sense the contact is important.

Matt's another matter. He's moved into position so that he's kneeling between me and my body. He's managed to lift my leg several inches off the ground. But his grip is weak and he trembles. I understand. He holds the soft flesh of his true love in his hands and he's being asked to desecrate it. I'm not looking forward to the pain of the break but I know his task is more difficult.

'Do it!' Umara snaps.

Matt shakes his head. 'Mother?'

'Do it for Teri, my son. Do it for love.'

'I can't hurt her. Not her leg. She was a runner. Her legs were everything to her.'

'Now!'

Matt practically sobs. 'It's not fair. She was so young.'

'Enough!' I cry as I sit up and put a hand over Matt's. I glance at Umara. 'You're asking too much. I loved her, too. I can do it, and together we'll let her go.'

Umara stares into my eyes, then into the vial that is supposed to hold Krishna's blood. 'Very well. But it must be a fatal blow.'

'I understand.' I turn back to Matt and squeeze his hands. 'It's OK. Teri will find her way to Krishna's abode.'

Matt stares at me with red-shot eyes. 'I'm sorry,' he whispers.

I smile and reach out to rub his face. 'I always knew you were a softy. You . . . Aaahh!'

He's not so soft. He just broke my leg.

The scream bursts from my chest and tears out my mouth. Yet it is not loud enough to drown out the crack of my bone. Or the sickening sound as the jagged edges of my femur rip through Teri's flesh. No, it's my flesh, my goddamn skin, I'm the one who's in agony. What kind of idiotic ceremony is this? My body's dead, this one's alive, nothing's going to change that. I don't know how in the world I let Umara talk me into . . .

'Lie down!' Umara orders. 'You must be on your back.'

'Leave me alone, you stupid bitch!' I yell.

'Matt, help her to lie down. Hold her down if you have to. Turn the head of her body towards the blood. Her body will seek her blood.'

Now Matt is keen to do whatever Mommy wants. He shoves me on to my back and twists the head of my dead body so my mouth's pressed against the red gore. From the way the blood is spurting, I know the artery has been severed. My old face drowns in my new blood.

But neither my new body or blood will last long.

I feel faint, the torch-lit chamber spins. What I feared to face on the mountaintop is finally happening. With the rip in the femoral artery, Teri's body is rapidly bleeding to death. I try to sit back up, vainly reaching for the break with my left hand, but even though Matt does nothing to stop me, I'm too weak to find it. My vision goes out of focus, the fire and the faces and the blood blur into a single red wave. Nausea sweeps through my guts. Every cell in my body screams in protest. The tiniest parts of my anatomy know that without blood, my major organs will close down and fail.

My heartbeat hammers, then the beats start to skip, to flutter, to miss. I gasp for air. There's plenty of oxygen in the chamber but not enough red blood cells in my lungs to extract it. Only then, as I begin to choke, do I finally accept the fact that I'm going to die. It doesn't matter that my death is the point of the ritual, the realization brings its own special bitterness. Because it was all for nothing. Umara is crazy. She should have left well enough alone. Now both our bodies will be dead.

My eyes close. The darkness is deep. I hear the fire burn but I feel cold. My pulse begins to slow. The feeble sounds fade. I want to speak, to weep, to say something, but I'm too weak. I struggle to breathe but I know it's a fight I'm going to lose. Despair, that's what I feel most of all. Death is despair for it is both dark and empty.

Far off, I hear a strange sucking sound.

And feel a weird tickling sensation.

The sound and the sensation seem to originate in the identical spot. Where my life pours through the hole in my leg. With my last fibre of strength, I open my eyes and look down, and see the impossible. My dead body is drinking from my dying body. It seems like a dream but it is true.

Sita is taking back the blood she gave to Teri.

'Well I'll be damned.' I don't know if I say it or merely think it. I have lived five thousand years and was confident I would never see anything new. But this outdoes it all, and I figure if I do end up dying, then at least I got to witness a miracle before I left.

My eyes fall shut. My chill turns to ice.

My pulse fades to a whisper.

The dark is deep and there is suddenly no pain.

I feel as if I'm floating, before I feel my 'I' float away.

Nothing. There is nothing for a long time.

From the other side of the galaxy I hear someone call my name.

'Sita . . . Sita . . . Sita.'

Whoever summons me, they make my name sound like a holy mantra, a sacred word. I assume it's Krishna and when I open my eyes I see his wonderful blue eyes. Only the face that holds them is different. He looks like a boy I once knew, like John, and when I blink his eyes change to a dark brown.

'Hello, Sita,' he says, and smiles.

'Hi,' I hear myself reply.

Yet there is another conversation going on, another miracle that I'm about to witness. Taking the white handkerchief, John wipes the blood from my face and helps me up. I see Matt holding Teri in his arms and she is dying. But it is Teri, it's not me, because I'm back in my old body.

'You're here,' Matt whispers as he cradles her in his arms, stroking her head. 'I knew you'd come back to me.'

'Thank you,' Teri says.

Matt seems to blush in the red light. 'Why do you thank me?'

'For now. For this moment.'

Matt nods. 'This moment is forever. You can live forever. You have Sita's blood . . .' He suddenly stops as her eyes close and her head rolls to the side. He shakes her. 'Teri?'

She struggles to open her eyes. A part of me is still

attached to her and knows what that struggle cost her. 'Oh, Matt. I have to go now but it's all right. This body dies but our love is forever.'

Matt is suddenly desperate. 'No! Your body will heal. It has to heal. It has vampire blood in it. It's immortal.'

Teri forces a smile. 'But I'm not a vampire, you never wanted me to be one. Now please, Matt, let me go. Let's be grateful we got this chance to say goodbye.'

Matt shakes his head. 'No! You can heal. You just need time.'

'Time.' Somehow she reaches up and touches his lips. 'Yes, I see it. We will meet again in a world without time.'

'Wait!' He grabs her fingers and kisses them but it's one kiss she doesn't feel. Her eyes have closed and the life has left her. No longer does her leg bleed. Her heart has stopped. Once again, I have returned to life, but it's to a suddenly lonely world. My child is gone.

15

Thirty hours later, I sit down the hill from the IIC's primary office in Malibu. Beside me in the driver's seat is Umara. It's early morning, nine o'clock, and our car is located on the lone road that leads up to the office building, if it can be called that and not a fortress. For the last six hours I've been alone in the car with Umara. During that time I've learned a great deal about the ancient Telar that she helped create and the modern Cradle Brutran and her associates now wield.

The parallels are striking but not exact.

'How do you feel?' Umara asks.

'Strong. Ready.'

Umara studies me, smiles faintly, nods. 'You understand now why I had to wait for you.'

'But you know so much more about their psychic rituals than I do.'

'Knowledge is not the key to this victory, experience is. Only someone who has died and been reborn can face what you are about to face.'

'Then I wish Yaksha was here.'

My remark is too flippant. I see I've hurt her and try to apologize but she stops me. 'He didn't want to leave either of these monsters behind for us to destroy but he wasn't given a choice in the matter. Krishna dictated much of his life and I never saw Yaksha disobey.'

'Yet Yaksha spent centuries fighting the Telar.'

Umara shrugs. 'He fought to contain them. He knew he would never stop them.'

'How am I supposed to?'

'You've already said it. It takes a thorn to remove a thorn. Until the IIC matured and developed the Cradle, there was nothing on earth that could wipe out the Telar.'

'Then I guess I better get my butt up that hill.'

Umara eyes the steep climb from the Pacific Coast Highway. 'I'd give you a ride but they have external cameras. I can't risk them obtaining a photo of my face. Besides, it's better I stay here. Once you enter the building, I won't let any cars enter or exit this road.' Umara reaches over and hugs me. 'Call if they start to gain the upper hand. Matt and I will come quick.'

It feels good to hold her. 'I'll only do so as a last resort.'

She kisses my cheek and lets go. 'Time to kick ass, Sita.'

I laugh as I climb out of the car.

I suspect it will be a long time before I laugh again.

I hike the road to the centre of the IIC's power at a casual pace. The sky is a brilliant blue and the morning sun feels good on my reborn flesh. Of course, if I wished, I could reach the structure in seconds. But it's my goal to use as little force as possible to achieve my goal. Cunning will serve me better with Brutran and her people than force. Still, in the end, I know blood will be spilled.

I've been in the IIC's main building before. It's four storeys of bulletproof glass, and was designed by an architect who was so in love with the primal shapes – cubes, spheres, pyramids and such – that he couldn't help but combine them all into his design. Surprisingly, the structure is pleasant to look at, nestled as it is in a wide patch of green almost two miles back in the brown hills.

I don't bother to knock but walk in like I own the place. The same young woman sits at the reception desk: the secretary who insisted I use the company's bandages to stop my fingers from bleeding. The woman flashes a bright smile, and I doubt she was in on the plot to collect my blood.

'You were here a few months ago. I'm sorry I've forgotten your name.'

'Alisa Perne. You are?'

'Janice Walker. How can I help you this morning?'

'I'm here to see Cynthia Brutran.'

'Do you have an appointment?'

'Just tell her I'm here.'

'I will. But I must warn you that you might have to wait. Ms Brutran's in the middle of an important meeting.'

I smile but my eyes add an extra punch to my next remark. 'Then be sure to add that I don't want to be kept waiting.'

Turning, I walk towards the seats. As I do so, I reach in my pocket and remove a glass vial filled with a clear liquid and pop the cork. I allow the fluid to spill across the tile floor. The amount is so small and I leak it so quickly I doubt the receptionist notices. I hear her on the phone. It's good to have my hypnotic powers back. She fights to make sure Brutran gets my message.

I'm sitting for perhaps five minutes when Brutran's handsome male secretary exits a nearby elevator. He glances at me uneasily, he knows I'm dangerous. He has a high-tech metal detector in his hand.

'Ms Perne. Ms Brutran would be happy to see you now.'

I stand and walk towards him. 'Thank you. Fourth floor?'

'Yes. I'll take you up. But first let me apologize for a new security measure we have instigated. I have to scan you for any metal you may be carrying.'

I casually raise my arms, for I am not armed. Not with a gun.

'Scan away,' I say.

Minutes later I'm led into Brutran's corner office on the top floor. The woman doesn't stand to greet me but remains seated behind what she probably considers legitimate shelter, her beautiful walnut desk, which she keeps crowded with computer screens. She wears a charcoal blouse, an elegant gray pantsuit, and a bright string of pearls. Like before, she'd appear to be thirty at a glance, perhaps six years older with a closer look. Yet I know she's at least sixty years old and has a daughter that's five.

With my left hand in my pocket, I remove the top from another vial and allow the liquid to seep into my pants. Since that particular leg is turned away from Brutran, I'm not worried she sees it. Besides, I have on black, and it's difficult to see a water stain on my favorite color.

Not that the liquid is water.

Brutran forces a smile. 'Alisa. What an unexpected surprise.'

'A pleasant one, I hope.'

'Of course. Except for your bad habit of not calling ahead of time. Like a normal person.'

'I apologize. I was in the neighbourhood. I thought I'd stop by so we could catch up.'

'I heard through the grapevine you've been travelling since we last spoke. London, Arosa, Colorado – you've had quite the summer. Did you have fun at the Olympics?'

'That was the most enjoyable part of the trip.'

'I can imagine. I watched the night your friend ran the 1500 metres. It was an exciting race. The experts were all surprised when Teri won the gold medal.'

I'm careful to keep my voice steady. 'Teri's a gifted athlete.'

'I'm sure she is. And she had you there to cheer for her. She's a lucky girl.'

'How was your summer?' I ask.

'Busy. I was hoping to get away but there's too much happening here that requires my attention.'

'I can imagine. You've got Wall Street on one side and the Telar on the other side.'

'The Telar are an old annoyance of no consequence.'

'I agree with the old part. But you have to admit they're your most lethal enemy.'

Brutran's face quickly hardens. 'Are you sure this is the time and place to rehash such matters?' she asks.

During my last visit, Brutran had indicated that our conversation was being monitored. At the same time, she had hinted that I was in danger just by being in the building. Before, I took her warning seriously and quickly excused myself.

Today, Brutran is trying to give me the same warning. But unknown to her or her associates, it's already too late for me to leave. Nevertheless, I don't completely ignore the heavy weapons that are pointed at me from the other side of the walls. Even with the building's extensive soundproofing, I can hear the clips being loaded, the laser sightings being aligned, the fingers sweating over the triggers. Plus the hushed whispers, all asking the same question:

Why is she here?

'I'm afraid we have to talk,' I say. 'You already know I was in Switzerland. You must know I had a run-in with the Telar. But what you don't know is what happened when we met.'

Brutran sighs. 'We have a general idea. We know they took you prisoner and that you managed to break free. With outside assistance.'

So they know about Matt. I assumed they did but now I am sure. They must be watching him closely to have a sample of his blood and be able to aim their Cradle at his brain.

'But you don't know what the Telar and I discussed,' I say.

Brutran glances at a computer screen that's turned away from me. Someone is sending her a message. 'All right, Alisa. Tell me your secrets, I'm listening.'

I smile faintly. 'Surely you don't expect me to reveal everything I know. At least not until we've come to an understanding.'

'I don't follow.'

'The last time we spoke you offered me a job. You wanted me to work for you.' I pause. 'Well, I'm here to accept your offer. On certain conditions.'

Brutran holds up a hand to stop me. 'That offer was time sensitive. I made it in good faith and you spurned me. I can no longer see us working together. I'll go so far as to say that there are many people in this firm who see you as a liability.'

'Is that a warning?'

'Take it as you wish.' Again, Brutran glances at the

screen. 'But we'd still like to hear about your conversations with the Telar.'

'You want intel.'

Brutran scratches her right hand. 'Yes.'

'But you don't want to pay for it. That hardly seems fair.'

Brutran is brisk. 'What if I told you that your compensation will be your life. We'll let you walk out of here in one piece.'

I shake my head. 'Cindy, Cindy, I'm disappointed in you and your people. Do you honestly think you can use brute force against me and live to talk about it?'

'Yes,' she says flatly but with confidence.

My smile grows. 'Then maybe I should rephrase my question. Do you think I was stupid enough to come here unarmed?'

Brutran considers. The armed people behind her do as well. They send her messages on her screen but I get the impression they're not sure what to do next. Brutran scratches both her hands before answering.

'You were scanned downstairs. We know you're unarmed.'

'You scanned for metal. You forgot to search my luggage.'

'You're not carrying any luggage.'

'It's small, pocket-size.'

Brutran acts bored. 'If you have some type of plastic explosive on you, what good will it do? At best you'd kill us both and nothing will be accomplished.'

'I'm not carrying plastic explosives.'

'Then how are you armed?'

'With the most deadly weapon this world has ever seen.'

'Drama hardly suits you, Alisa. Answer my question.'

'X6X6. Have you heard about it?'

Brutran hesitates, glances at her screen. 'Is that the name of the virus the Telar are working on?'

'Yes. I brought some with me.'

For a moment she loses her cool. 'Into this building?'

'Yes.'

'You have a lot of nerve.'

'Thank you. I wanted you to be totally clear about the danger this virus represents. To your organization, to the world. You may not know this, but the Telar plan to release it soon.'

'How soon?' Brutran scratches her hands vigorously. They're itchy, they're bothering her, but she's too focused on me to notice.

I give my best guess.

'Within two weeks, maybe sooner. If you and I can't come to an understanding, then you'll need to get your top chemists, biologists and microbiologists together under one roof and start working on a vaccine.'

'How do you know we don't already have a vaccine?'

'Because of the look of horror on your face when I told you I'd brought the virus into this building.'

Brutran stands. 'Enough. You've worn out your welcome. Either turn over your samples of the virus to me right now or a dozen men with high-powered weapons are going to burst through that door. You are fast but not that fast. At least one of them will put a bullet in your brain. Then we will take the virus from you at our leisure.'

Keeping my hand in my pocket, turning my back to her, I stand and casually walk to the window. I stare out at the beautiful coast and wonder if Umara is still waiting down the hill.

'You can try that,' I say. 'But I must warn you I've brought only one vial of the vaccine and right now I have my hand wrapped around it, along with a vial of sulfuric acid, which will neutralize it upon contact.'

'You're bluffing.'

'I'm afraid not. You must have noticed your hands are itching. You can't stop scratching. That's the first sign of the infection. In the next few minutes black blisters will form on your skin. Dizziness and weakness will follow. The X6X6 virus is highly contagious, and since I released it the moment I got here, it has spread to every floor in this building – the upper floors and the ten underground levels. You can try sealing your ventilation ducts but it's already too late. I strongly suggest that you stop anyone from exiting or entering this building. You're not ready for what will happen if this virus should escape into the city.'

Brutran stares down at her hands. '*Damn*,' she whispers.

A dozen men in special-ops gear burst into the room. At their head, wearing a blue suit and red tie, is Thomas Brutran. I recognize him from a photo Freddy showed me. He walks towards his wife, although his eyes never leave me. A handsome man with brown hair and dark eyes, he reminds me of the perfect political candidate, by which I mean his good looks only run skin-deep. He doesn't have to speak for me to know there's something awfully bland about the guy.

Standing beside Cindy, he glares at me.

'You had no right to bring that disease into our building,' he says.

'I'm sorry. I thought you would have been impressed.'

'Impressed? Are you insane?'

'I assumed that an organization that prides itself on using psychic tools to rape the minds of men and women would be impressed at the sheer boldness of my attack.' I stop and grin. 'You have to admit it does show a certain flair.'

Thomas, good old Tom, struggles to find the right words.

'You heard my wife. Turn over your samples of the virus or die.'

'We don't need the virus now!' Cindy snaps. 'We need the vaccine!'

'Here it is.' I take the vial containing the blue-colored vaccine and hold it up in the same hand as the vial containing the sulfuric acid. 'I'll be happy to give each and every person who's infected with the virus a shot . . . if we can come to an agreement.'

'We'll not be blackmailed,' Tom swears.

I smile. 'Without the vaccine, your skin is going to turn black pretty soon.'

Tom turns to his men. 'Prepare to open fire. We'll give her three seconds to surrender. One . . .'

I address his soldiers. 'Men! Listen to me! If you shoot me, the vaccine will be destroyed. And twenty minutes from now you'll be in the throes of an agonizing death.'

'Two,' Tom continues.

'Stop it, Tom!' Cindy cries. 'She's standing beside the window on purpose. If we open fire, she'll leap outside, and we'll lose the vaccine.'

'Very perceptive, Cindy,' I say.

'She'll be riddled with bullets,' Tom says.

'No. She's fast. She'll escape,' Cindy says.

'There's no way she can break that glass,' Tom protests.

'Want to watch me try?' I ask.

Cindy turns to the men. 'All of you, leave!'

'We can't let her dictate terms to us,' Tom yells.

Cindy ignores her husband and shouts again at the men. 'Now!'

'Leave your rifles!' I say. 'You can see the blisters forming on your hands. I've memorized each of your faces. Leave them or I won't give you a shot of the vaccine.'

The men look at each other, bewildered, afraid. Itchy blisters are worth a thousand threats. They set down their guns and leave the room. Cindy steps towards me.

'Do we really have only twenty minutes?' she asks.

'Yes,' I lie. I'm not sure how long the virus takes to

kill but I know it takes at least a few hours.

'Then you must start injecting us with the vaccine now.'

'There's time. I can move fast when I'm in a hurry, even when I'm playing nurse. I know you have a medical clinic here, five floors beneath the surface. I assume it's well stocked with syringes. If you're still worried about the time, you can send Tom to organize your people into a line outside the clinic door. I'll be down shortly.'

'Will the vaccine give us total immunity to the virus?' Cindy asks.

'Not this version. It's a weak form of the true vaccine. It will stop the spread of the infection and relieve the majority of your symptoms for a twenty-four-hour period.'

'Then what?' Tom asks.

'Then you'll need another shot. From me.'

Shaking his head, Tom pleads with his wife. 'Don't you see, we'll be at her mercy.'

Cindy struggles to be patient. 'All I see right now are black blisters forming on my hands. Go, organize our people, try to keep them calm. Alisa and I will talk.'

Tom leaves, closing the door behind him, and for once I don't hear people listening through the walls. Cindy and I are alone. I stroll over and pick up an automatic weapon – an AK-47, an old Romanian favorite of mine. I point it at Cindy.

'How does it feel?' I ask.

'I don't know what you mean.'

'I'm referring to me and two friends of mine outside a cave high in the Rockies. It was only eight days ago, you can't have forgotten. Your Cradle paid us a visit. You know what happened. Shots were fired and someone very dear to me died.'

Cindy doesn't flinch. 'I was given a report on the incident.'

I'm so close to shooting, it's scary. Despite the fact I need Brutran to complete my plan, to literally save humanity, my desire for revenge is overwhelming. I see the bullet striking her face, I see her head exploding, and the satisfaction I'd feel . . .

'A report? You ordered the incident!'

'That's not exactly true.'

I go to snap at her again but stop. She's speaking the truth. 'Who did order the attack?' I ask.

'It's complicated.'

'I have time.'

'We don't, thanks to you. Rather than drag up everything that I've done that you didn't like, why don't you state your terms and see if we can reach an agreement. Otherwise, I'll take my husband's advice and refuse your vaccine. And if you think I'm bluffing, Alisa, then you don't know me.'

The woman has guts, I have to grant her that. I lower the gun. 'I want to work with your Array and your Cradle,' I say.

'In what capacity?'

'I want to take control.'

'Why?'

'So I can use it to wipe out the senior members of the Telar.'

'That's not possible.'

'You better make it possible. Or else I'm through talking.'

'I'm speaking logistically. You obviously have some knowledge of the Cradle but you're a long way from understanding its inner workings. The number of people who can channel the Array's power against another human being is very small. We call them the Lens. The Lens controls the Cradle. It's made up of only two dozen people, and all of them have unique abilities.'

'You mean they're children who have been born and bred to be psychic mutants. They're unique not only because they can tap into a large field of mental energy but because they're devoid of empathy, love, compassion – and any other human quality that would prevent them from sodomizing the minds of innocent people.'

Cindy hesitates. 'Yes.'

I snort. 'You're not going to defend what you've created?'

'No. It's not just because we're short on time. The situation is more complex than you know. Besides the fact that you're not mentally equipped to control the Cradle via the Lens, you'd never be able to attack the inner core of the Telar, what Haru and his people refer to as the Source. We have tried in the past and failed. The only Telar we can harm are those who physically attack us, those we can see with our eyes. Otherwise, the Lens can't focus on Telar who are on the other side of the world. Especially if they are linked.'

'Linked?'

'The members of the Source are able to fuse their minds together and form what they call the Link. It makes them impossible to kill.'

'What if you had samples of their blood?'

'Dream on. Even you couldn't obtain that.'

'I already have them,' I say, telling her the truth. Umara gave them to me.

'How?'

'That doesn't matter. Just accept I have blood samples of the twenty oldest living Telar on this planet. Now I may not understand the intricacies of your Cradle but I know it aims its mental attacks using the principle of sympathetic resonance. To home in on an individual, you need something intimately connected to them. And nothing is more intimate than their own blood. Even when removed from the body and spread across the globe, it still contains the vibration of the original person. That's why you needed my blood to attack me. That's why you took two days to launch your attack on me. You had to send a diluted solution of my blood to every member of your Array, and as we know, they're spread all over the world.'

'You are partially correct. I had to get your blood to every member of the Cradle.'

'You don't keep your kids all in one place?'

'No.'

'Why not?' Unlike the huge Array, I assumed she would keep a constant eye on the Lens.

Cindy fumes. 'We don't have time for this. I can't meet your first demand. You can't control the Lens.'

'Why not?'

'You're too . . . human.'

'I'm a vampire. I've killed more people than you can imagine.'

'Your past is irrelevant. You're no longer a killer. But let's not fight over this point. If you have these blood samples, then that's reason enough for us to form a partnership. If we work together, we should be able to wipe out all the Telar.'

'All?' I say.

'Once we destroy Haru and the Source, the rest of the Telar should become vulnerable to our attacks.'

'But I don't want to kill all of them.'

'Why not?'

'The majority aren't evil.'

'You're wrong.'

'Really? You're the last person whose judgment I'd trust on this point. I bet the IIC isn't as evil as it appears, although we both know it's rotten at the top.'

'It's natural to compare us to them. It's also a mistake. They're old. Even the young Telar are generally so old that most of them have forgotten how to feel. And you want to protect them?'

'It's my decision to make. It's another reason I won't hand over the blood samples to you. You can use them but they'll remain in my control.'

'Impossible. I told you, I have to disperse a diluted form of the blood to all the members of the Cradle.'

'Gather all the kids in the Cradle in one place. We can do it in this facility. I know you have a large underground room. That way I can keep track of the blood.'

Cindy pales and I wonder if it's due to the infection spreading in her system, or something else. 'We've never done that before,' she says softly.

'You're not afraid of them, are you?'

She hesitates. 'I can meet that condition. For now let's agree to work together to solve whatever other issues come up. You can hear when I speak the truth. You know I'm being sincere.'

'I know,' I say.

'Now my people need the vaccine.'

'I'll start injecting them in a minute.'

'You must also guarantee we'll get the permanent vaccine when the Telar are dead.'

'As long as you agree not to steal my blood samples,' I say.

'Agreed.'

'You must also give me back my blood.'

'I'll have to gather it.'

'And I want my friend's sample back as well.'

'Which friend is that?'

'The one who shot Teri Raine on the mountain.'

Brutran acts puzzled. I assume it's an act. Yet, again, she appears to be telling the truth. 'So it's Teri who died. I didn't know. She's a celebrity. Why wasn't it on the news?'

'It will be. Don't change the subject. I want the blood of the person who you mentally attacked on top of that mountain. Swear to me you'll get it back.'

Cindy is still hesitant. 'I'll see what I can do.'

'Don't start acting like you're not in charge of this operation. You're the queen bee. You have a finger on everything the IIC does. For that matter, I know it was you who planted a spy in our group.'

'I don't know what you're talking about.'

'I warn you, Brutran, don't anger me. You know who it is.'

'I don't, I swear it.'

God, she sounds like she's telling the truth again.

I try to act more confident than I feel. 'Then you won't mind if I use your Cradle to kill this mole,' I say.

Cindy shrugs. 'It's your call.'

16 ～

I'm still getting used to my old body. Now I have to get used to a new phase of life that's so unpredictable and fraught with danger I can't drop my guard for an instant. I've intentionally marooned myself in the heart of the IIC's stronghold so I can destroy them, right after I destroy the Telar.

But doubts assail me.

Even Yaksha was unable to stop the Telar.

I wish I shared the faith Umara has in me. It's hard not to call upon her and Matt for help. I miss Seymour, his love and wisdom, and I miss Teri. I never had a chance to properly mourn her passing.

I feel so alone caged inside the IIC's headquarters.

Yet it's crucial I stay, and that I remain alone. If I brought in Umara and Matt, then all our cards would be on the table and we'd be exposed to the IIC. And if something went wrong with my plan, we'd have no backup. Even if the IIC should happen to kill me, if Umara and Matt are still out there, alive, then at least there's a chance the IIC and Telar can be stopped.

I stay inside the Malibu centre to keep an eye on everything the IIC does. Likewise, I force them to remain inside the building, all six hundred of the firm's employees that I've infected. I convince them that they're contagious, and they believe me. Why shouldn't they? At this point, they know little about the virus. They have barely spoken to Charlie – I have given them limited access – who's confident a person can't spread the virus as long as the black blisters haven't begun to pop and ooze their deadly fluid.

I stay in the building for another reason. The IIC know me and know a portion of my history. For two decades they have fought the Telar. Now that they have me on their side, it's strange but they see me as a leader of sorts. Not Cynthia and Thomas Brutran, but the rank-and-file members of the company. On the whole, they're normal people, and I go out of my way to treat them with kindness and respect.

I am, after all, their doctor, even if I'm the one who infected them. The simple act of giving them a shot every day that washes away their symptoms gives me a mysterious authority.

But that doesn't mean that other members of the IIC are not working behind my back at other facilities to try to develop a better vaccine. I'm alert enough to know there are scientists in our centre who are sending out data on their computers to other IIC sites. That I cannot control, and I'm not even sure if I want to.

Because I have two holds on the IIC, not one. They need me to stay healthy, and they need me because of the blood samples I carry. The blood Umara has so carefully gathered over the eons. My decision to infect the IIC was to get them moving quickly. But it's the Telar blood that gives me my true control over them.

Cynthia Brutran is still a mystery to me. She knows the danger X6X6 represents. She may crave power but she's wise enough to know there has to be someone left alive on the planet to have power over. She should be doing everything she can to help me destroy the Telar.

Yet, when it comes to the Cradle, she keeps stalling me.

It's like she's afraid for me to meet the children. I've been at the Malibu centre for three days and still only a trickle of the kids who make up the Cradle have arrived. I've met them, twenty teens and preteens, and they seem normal enough, although on the quiet side. But I suspect I haven't met any of the kids who control the actual Lens.

My patience with Brutran quickly runs out.

On the fourth night, I tell her we're going for a walk.

We sneak out through a hidden exit Freddy has already alerted me to. It's late, close to dawn, and the half moon has risen. It lights our way as we stroll along a path that leads through the hills behind the compound.

'Why are you afraid to talk inside?' she asks.

'Why are you? You act like every room has ears.'

'That's close to the truth. Security monitors every important area. They'll know we've left the building.'

'Don't worry. You must know Harold in security? He and I have become good friends. He's not going to talk about our great escape.'

'I've noticed the two of you talking. For a vampire who's brought nothing but disease, you've managed to develop quite a following.'

'The rank and file don't know I'm a vampire.' When I give the injections, I work fast but not at hyper speed. Nevertheless, the soldiers who broke into Brutran's office have spread the rumour that I'm no ordinary woman. I don't mind. I have gone out of the way to build their trust but a little fear can be a good thing.

'They don't think you're human, either,' Cindy says.

'But they like me more than they like you. Does that bother you?'

'No.'

'I think it does. It must get lonely working in a building where your nickname is the Wicked Witch.'

'No one calls me that.'

'Not to your face. You should have my ears. Do you want to hear some of your other nicknames?'

Brutran acts bored. 'You didn't bring me out here to taunt me.'

'True. I'm annoyed the Cradle's not here. And don't give me your usual excuses about their parents and the distances they have to travel and all that bullshit. You're keeping them away for a reason, even though you know the Telar can strike at any time.'

'I never agreed to bring the Cradle here.'

'Liar. You never agreed to let me join them. You did agree to bring them to this building.'

'I didn't say those exact words.'

'You gave the impression that bringing them here was not a problem. Now I'm through waiting. Why do you keep stalling?'

'Give me the blood samples and we'll kill the Telar for you. We'll start immediately. You can oversee the operation. You can have access to all our surveillance equipment. You can't imagine how sophisticated it is. We have a dozen satellites that can read a newspaper from orbit. You'll be able to watch each target that we select die. You can even tell us how you want them to die.'

'No.'

Brutran stops me in mid-stride. 'There's only one reason you would say no to my offer.'

I don't respond. I wait. She knows.

'You don't just intend to destroy the Telar. You intend to do the same to us.' She pauses. 'Deny it.'

'Why should I deny it? You're dangerous.'

Brutran sighs. 'At last we're able to speak the truth to one another. Why, from your perspective, is the IIC dangerous?'

'Too much power concentrated among too few. You're like the Nazis.'

'Hitler was insane. Do you think I am?'

'You have too much control. I was present when the founding fathers created this nation. There was a reason they split the government into three parts. The checks and balances were all designed to keep power-driven people from seizing absolute control.'

Brutran is thoughtful. 'How little you understand what's really going on here.'

Her remark sounds degrading but again I hear truth in it.

'We're alone. It's just us girls. Enlighten me,' I say.

Brutran continues walking. I follow.

'To understand you'd have to go back to the beginning days of the IIC. I know now that you've spoken to Professor Sharp and Freddy, and I assume they gave you a reasonably accurate idea of how the Array and the Cradle came into existence. At the same time, you have to understand their point of view is limited. They were always on the outside looking in.'

'Because you're the real founder of the company.'

Brutran hesitates. 'I thought so at the time. Freddy told you about the loss of our son. What he couldn't tell you is how the pain refused to fade with the passage of time. I think I went a little crazy during those days. I knew Henry for only a week, but I talked to him in my head for years. And I had but one wish. That he would talk back to me.'

I feel a disquieting chill. 'I don't understand.'

Again, she stops me. 'Before I go any further I need you to answer a question. It's the most important thing I've ever asked of anyone. Please be honest with me.'

'Ask.'

'We know your small group battled the Telar in Colorado, outside the town of Goldsmith, and that you escaped the area in a helicopter by flying into the Rockies. We're not sure what happened up there but our best information says that you were killed.' She pauses. 'Is that true?'

I'm silent a long time. Knowledge is power and I'm reluctant to tell this woman anything that could give her leverage over me or my friends.

Yet I see the desperation in her eyes. The loss.

'Yes,' I say.

'You died?'

'Yes.'

'How did you come back to life?'

'I don't know.'

'Alisa, please, this is important to me. What happened to you when you died?'

I tell her a *version* of what happened.

'I lost two days of memory. Then, when I began to experience the world around me again, I found myself floating near my body. Eventually that sensation passed and I was back inside it.'

'And Teri Raine was dead. How did she die?'

'It was in this morning's news. She fell and broke her leg. The shattered bone ruptured her femoral artery.'

'That must have been a hell of a fall. How did it happen?'

'Does it matter?'

'Yes. You're leaving out a huge part of your story. You

act like you were killed days before Teri.'

'I was.'

'How were you killed?'

A note of bitterness enters my voice. 'We've gone over this. Your Cradle possessed a friend of mine and forced him to shoot me in the heart.'

'Who?'

'It's none of your business. Besides, you must know.'

'I know nothing about this incident.'

'Gimme a break.'

'It's true, and you know it's true as I say it. How did you recover from the wound that killed you?'

I shrug. 'There are qualities to my vampiric blood even I don't understand. The wound healed and I recovered.'

'I find that hard to believe.'

'Your own spy saw that I was dead. You can see I'm alive. What's there to believe?'

Brutran is suddenly emotional. The change in her is so unexpected I'm shocked. 'What's there to believe? Alisa, you of all people must know the questions that haunt us above all else. Is there life after death? Does the soul exist? Is my son still alive somewhere?'

A mother's grief over the loss of her child. Even the Wicked Witch is not immune to it. For the first time since I met the woman, I feel sympathy for her.

'Krishna brought me back,' I say.

'What?'

'It was Krishna. That's all I can tell you.'

Brutran grabs my shoulders. 'Did you see him when you died?'

'I told you, I don't remember what happened. I wish I could. You have no idea how I've struggled to fill in the blank of those days. But I can't, they're just empty.'

'Then how can you say Krishna saved you?'

'You just have to trust me.'

'Trust you?' she shouts. 'Now you sound like a Christian asking me to believe in the resurrection of Christ. I can't believe something because someone tells me to believe it. Faith is for the foolhardy. Can't you see that's why I returned to experimenting with the array after I lost Henry?'

The pieces of her story are finally beginning to fit together.

'I thought you used it to make money,' I say.

Brutran waves her hand impatiently and resumes walking. 'I needed money to create a powerful array. So yes, in a sense, I focused on money to start with. But my ultimate goal was to find out what had happened to my son.'

'Was this during the time Freddy was creating his scientific form of astrology?'

Brutran snorts. 'He came up with the idea. He didn't create it all by himself.'

'Explain.'

'Freddy had his obsession, I had mine. We were both trying to drown our grief. Drugs and alcohol could only help so much. Once I had a new array up and running, and enough money to sustain it, I changed the focus of the work.'

'You wanted to get it to talk,' I say.

She glances over. 'It seemed a natural next step. After all, you would have asked the same questions I did.'

'Give me examples.'

'Who are we talking to when we ask the array for information? Who or what is giving us insights into the market?'

'You had grown weary of yes and no answers.'

'Yes. I wanted more, a lot more.'

'So how did you get it to talk?' I ask.

'You might find this amusing. At first I split my two thousand kids into a thousand pairs and gave them each an Ouija board. Then I posed the simplest question of all: "Who are you?" I allowed the answers to come just one letter at a time. It took discipline to stick with this programme.'

'Why?'

'Because many of the messages coming through the Ouija boards were fascinating. The spirits we channelled would say they were guides or angels, and they would give us page after page of esoteric knowledge. Most of it was garbage but some of it was heartbreaking in its beauty and with its insights. Still, I forced myself to only keep track of the responses the group as a whole generated.'

'You were sticking with Professor Sharp's idea that ESP is basically a weak signal that can only be picked up by a large array of minds?'

'Exactly. I couldn't trust individual or paired responses. They had never been able to predict the market accurately. Why should I trust them to talk to me about spiritual matters?'

'What answer did you get to your original question: 'Who are you?''

'The answer was disconcerting. It said, "I am no one."'

'Nothing else?'

'Not at first. Not for a long time. I tried switching our method of receiving the answers. I used applied kinesiology, or muscle testing. That's where you have a subject stick out their arm, ask a question, and then test the arm for strength. Generally, if the arm is strong, the answer is yes, and if the arm goes weak, the answer is no. In many ways that worked better than the boards. I'd have each person start at the beginning of the alphabet and have another person keep checking them until their arm muscle went strong. Then I would write down that letter and repeat the process with everyone in the group.'

'You did all that just to get one letter of one word?'

'Yes. I know what you're going to ask next. How many out of the two thousand would come up with the same letter? At first our results were dismal. We were lucky if any letter would stand out. But as we continued to work together; it was like a group mind formed and most of the kids started to get the same answer.'

'Another amazing example of ESP.'

'Yes. I thought Professor Sharp would have been proud of me.'

'Were you in contact with him at the time?'

'He was recovering from a stroke. But we spoke occasionally.'

'Your work had nothing to do with his stroke?' I ask.

'Don't be silly, Alisa. The Cradle didn't even exist at the time.'

I ask my next question as gently as possible.

'Were you able to contact your son?'

The question still hits her hard. She takes a moment to recover. 'It seemed, from time to time, that we would contact a kind spirit that said he was my son.'

'Why do you say it was kind?'

'It felt that way when he was in the room.'

'What did he have to say?'

'That he was my son and that he was happy where he was.'

'Did he give you any practical advice?'

'I don't understand.'

'Did he urge you to let go of your grief and get on with your life?'

Cindy lowers her head. 'I don't recall every message that came through.'

We walk for a while in silence, and it seems to me that no matter how hard Cindy tried, she never did get to talk to the son she had lost, not really. However, after a few minutes, she begins to describe a breakthrough of sorts.

'The being that came at the start, the one who said

he was no one, returned and took control of the sessions. He blocked any other beings from talking. I didn't mind because he began to give out information that I could validate.'

'Give me an example,' I say.

'Besides predicting fluctuation of the stock market, he began to foretell other worldly events. Bad weather in certain countries. Plane crashes. Huge fires. Earthquakes. His accuracy level was higher than ninety percent.'

'Your test subjects must have been blown away.'

'You misunderstand. When this being showed up, I stopped sharing what was being channelled with my test subjects.'

'How did you keep the truth from them?'

'I separated them. The experiments worked almost as well on the phone.'

'But kids are curious by nature. Some of the older ones must have tried to contact each other.'

'Of course. I put a stop to it.'

'Did this brilliant being have a name?'

'It's ironic you should phrase your question that way. It called itself Ta-Ra-Na. *Ra*, as you know, is the name for the sun god from ancient Egypt. It also means "light" or "brilliant". All together the symbols mean the "Light Bearer".'

I stumble on the path. Brutran has to reach out to steady me.

'What's wrong?' she asks.

'Nothing.'

'You've heard the name before. Tell me.'

'It just reminds me of the Bible.'

'About Lucifer being the Light Bearer?'

'Yes.'

Brutran stares at me in the dark. 'You know more than you're telling me. I wish it didn't have to be that way between us.'

'You're not exactly the sort I would confide in.'

'Right now, I'm telling you things I've told no one else. Not even my own husband.'

'But I'm your enemy. You said it yourself. I want to destroy you. Why are you confiding in me?'

She lets go of my arm and continues down the path. 'Let me finish my story. Tarana became the focal point of my research. The Array began to channel him exclusively. His knowledge was breathtaking. He taught me simple herbal formulas and physical and mental exercises to halt the ageing process. He explained how best to choose candidates for the Array. He even gave me lessons in management. The IIC was organized under his directions.'

'You speak of him like he was your mentor.'

'In a sense, he was.'

'He wasn't real! He was just your subconscious speaking. Or else the combined subconscious of every kid in your Array. He wasn't the Light Bearer.'

'You say that like you're trying to convince yourself. If you don't believe me, then maybe you should have another talk with Freddy. Oh, I don't suppose he told you how often he came to me for Tarana's insights on

241

how to make his astrological system work. It was Tarana who dictated the bulk of the planetary influences that Freddy came to depend upon.'

'Freddy said he pinpointed the influences by using the lives of thousands of people as examples. He told us how he wrote computer programs designed to find patterns in their lives.'

'Sure, Freddy did all those things. *After* he asked me, and Tarana, what to look for.'

'Freddy said you stole his system.'

'Nonsense. I stopped supporting him and he ended up on the street. I'm not saying he isn't creative. He has one of the most imaginative minds I've ever encountered. But when it comes to reality, he's a failure.'

'So says the woman who talks to spirits. If Freddy was such a failure, why did you have another child with him?'

'Jolie was an accident.'

'You forget, I've met Jolie. She was no accident. She was one of those kids that was designed to be born at a certain time and place so she could be used to focus the mind-warping power of your goddamn Cradle.'

My last remark is an educated guess but I can tell from Brutran's reaction that I've scored a bull's-eye. She looks devastated. I don't care. I take advantage of the vulnerable moment and try to discover what I need to know.

'Freddy was more than creative,' I say. 'He was your example of what a true psychic could do when channelling the full power of the Array. What he did to Tom's heart was your inspiration for the Cradle. I bet the same day Tom was fighting for his life in the hospital, you were thinking what an awesome weapon the Array could be turned into. If the others would just leave you alone to play with it.'

'The others you speak of all joined me when I founded IIC.'

'Which reminds me. Where are Noel and Wendy?'

'They left the company two years ago.'

'And they're still alive?'

'Yes.' She pauses. 'Don't look so surprised.'

'But I am surprised,' I say.

'That's silly. You know . . . Freddy has resisted me from day one and I've never harmed him.'

'He doesn't count! You love Freddy! You cheat on your husband to be with him.'

'What I do in my personal life is no concern of yours.'

'This entire conversation is about how your personal life has led you to create a monster that even you are losing control of. Admit it, isn't that what your story is leading up to? I've only realized it now myself. You're not lying when you say you don't know who the mole in my group is. Or who ordered the Cradle to attack my friend on the mountain. You don't know because others have taken over your organization!'

Brutran stops walking and stands deflated. The pin I hoped to use to pop her ego has struck deeper. My words are like a needle through her heart. She doesn't even try to fight me.

'You're right, I have lost control,' she says.

'To the kids in the Cradle? Or just to those who control the Lens?'

'Both and neither.'

'You're not saying it's Tarana?' I ask.

'I'm not sure. It's whatever stands over the kids when they gather to invoke the Cradle. It's that power, or those beings, that have taken over.'

'Those beings? What beings?'

Brutran shakes her head. 'It all goes back to the questions we asked Professor Sharp the first day he spoke to us about creating an array. What is the nature of the consciousness we'll tap into? Is it individual or universal? Is it good or is it evil? Back then we used to discuss these issues late into the night. We were like a bunch of pseudophilosophers, safe in the certainty that nothing really bad could happen to us.'

'Hold on a second. I'm not buying this one-eighty you're trying to pull. Suddenly you're acting like the victim, when you're the one who set all this in motion. Hell, the night I came to your house you forced me to put a loaded gun in my mouth. If not for Krishna, and maybe some dumb luck, I would have pulled that trigger. And I know damn well you wouldn't have shed a tear while you wiped up my bloody brains.'

'The Cradle ordered your execution, not me.'

'I don't believe you. You created the Cradle.'

'Professor Sharp, Freddy, and yes, I, Cynthia Brutran, helped bring it to life. But I see now that Tarana and creatures like him were behind it from the start.'

'Now you sound like one of those religious nuts who blames the devil for every mishap in the world. How convenient, Satan made me do it. Don't accept any personal responsibility for how many people the IIC has killed.'

'Stop!' Brutran shouts as she tries to slap me. But I'm much too fast for her, and catch her hand before it can approach my face. The fury in her eyes doesn't surprise me, but the stark fear does. Damn it, the bitch is still telling the truth, or at least her version of it.

'I know what I've done!' she says. 'I don't deny that I've always craved money and power. But that doesn't make me any different from the majority of politicians and CEOs in this country. And if you're thinking about giving me a lecture on how those people don't kill others, save it. They make decisions every day that result in more deaths than I have ever caused.'

'Fine. You're evil. But it's OK because all powerful people are.'

'Nothing in my life is OK. From the start, I chose a path that was selfish. I admit that. But I never expected to end up where I'm at now. My life has become a waking nightmare.'

'Don't be so melodramatic.'

She lets out a bitter laugh. 'You think I'm being melodramatic? When you burst in my office the other day and released the virus, there was a part of me that thought, "Thank God, it will soon be over". I almost didn't make a deal with you for that reason.'

'But you did deal. You can't be as depressed as you say.'

'Whatever you think of me, I still feel a responsibility for the people who work for me. They trust me with their lives. I made a deal with you to protect them from the virus. And I agreed to join forces with you because you're probably the only one who can destroy the Telar.' She stops. 'And the Cradle.'

'You would kill your own daughter?'

In response, Brutran slowly lifts the front of her blouse. She wears a bra underneath but it does nothing to hide the extensive scarring. Her entire abdomen is worse off than Shanti's face used to be.

'What happened?' I ask.

'When my daughter was three she asked if she could stay up all night and watch TV. Like any decent mother, I told her no, she had to go to bed. A short time later I felt a thick psychic fist descend. I lost all control. When the command came to light a candle and burn the skin off my abdomen, I obeyed. Jolie showed me no mercy. It didn't matter how much I screamed and begged for her to stop.' Brutran pauses. 'Do you still think I'm being melodramatic?'

'She did all this without the Cradle?'

'Yes. Or at least, I think so.'

'How long did it take for you to recover?'

'I'm still recovering. I'm in constant pain. I'm addicted to OxyContin. I've built up an incredible tolerance. I have to take three hundred milligrams a day just to cope.'

'I'm sorry, I didn't know.'

'You can see why I need your help.'

'You could have asked for my help at the beginning. Instead, you set yourself up as a foe, and it wasn't the fault of the Cradle. It was you, Cindy. You have suffered, I see that now, but you have caused me and my friends to suffer. I don't forgive that and I sure as hell am never going to forget it.'

'That's fine. As long as you stop them.'

'The Telar or the Cradle?' I ask.

'Both.'

'What makes you think I can?'

Brutran sounds sad. 'You came back from the grave. How many others can say that? If you can't stop them, then who will?'

17 ~~~

Two days later I sit in the centre of the Lens, on the floor of a virtual dungeon, deep in the bowels of IIC's main structure. I have never been to this floor before, so far underground, and yet there's another level beneath us. Because my floor is a large circular one-way mirror, I'm able to see the two hundred kids of the Cradle gathering below. Brutran was right when she described how few members make up the Lens. Including myself, there are only twenty-five of us present. Like gods peering down at their loyal subjects, we sit directly above the others.

The material we relax on is not simple glass. It appears to be an extremely hard plastic, a composite the rest of the world hasn't heard about. I've studied it with my fingers and know it's virtually unbreakable. I'm not sure why the Lens likes to secretly view the rest of the Cradle, but I assume they have their reasons.

It is obvious to me that these kids know each other, that they have all been together before, which once again makes Cynthia Brutran a liar. Unless they are able to gather without her knowledge.

Yesterday, as the bulk of the kids arrived at the building, they were immediately infected with the virus. They quickly showed symptoms, but I prevented them from making any calls in case they tried to alert their partners about the virus. A few complained about the blisters, but as a whole the group settled down as soon as they got a shot of the weakened vaccine. Brutran did nothing to stop me from giving them the virus. She didn't even try to protect her own daughter.

How to describe these children who might one day rule the world? Three quarters are young, five and under; the others are between fifteen and eighteen. The former were planned; they are the true products of Freddy's astrological system. On the surface, they look normal, but they're too quiet for kids their age. They don't run and play.

Jolie falls into this group. She sits in the corner holding a stuffed toy she calls Mr Topper. A clown with eyes and lips so red they look like they were stained with blood.

The older kids were discovered using the same astrological system. But they were already born before Brutran and her colleagues founded IIC. They are the products of an extensive worldwide search, and as a result, their nationalities all differ. But a high percentage of them are from Africa. Brutran has already explained how it was easier to search poor nations for raw material.

The leader of the Lens is an eighteen-year-old boy named Lark. He's from Florida, and at first glance he appears to be the most balanced one in the group. Fortunately, Brutran has already warned me about him. On his tenth birthday, before he joined the Cradle, he murdered both his parents, using the same knife his mother had used to cut his birthday cake. When asked by a judge why he did it, he replied, 'They told me to make a wish. And I wished that they were dead.'

Lark would still be in prison if not for the IIC, which quickly spotted his remarkable abilities. Naturally, the IIC had only to flex its muscles to free the boy. Lark's not simply psychic, he has all the qualities of a powerful leader. On top of that, he's a handsome devil. He has curly black hair, cobalt blue eyes, and cherub-like features that would melt the hearts of teenage girls nationwide.

It's Lark who welcomes me to the Lens.

'Alisa Perne,' he says cheerfully, offering his hand and looking me up and down as if he'd like to rape me. 'I've heard so much about you. This is a real honour.'

'The pleasure is mine,' I say, shaking his firm grip. His clothes are expensive: tailored Brioni gray slacks, a fine white shirt, a black cashmere sports coat, and a gold Jaeger-LeCoultre watch. Quite the digs for a punk who should be in the slammer.

'May I call you Sita?'

'Who told you that name?' I ask.

'Let's just say we've worked together in the past.'

In a flash I understand. Lark has been inside my head. Twice.

'If you know my name then you must know about my temper.'

He claps his hands with pleasure. 'Of course! You wouldn't be half the fun you are without it.'

I move close to him, until I'm breathing in his face. 'Don't make the mistake of thinking you're in charge here,' I say.

I don't scare him. His grin broadens. 'This is technically your first day so you don't understand how things work here. I forgive you. But at the same time, I must remind you that we put a gun in your mouth and forced you to play with the trigger. And the next time we met, we talked you into eating a poor little Telar named Numbria. Tasty, wasn't she?'

I move to grab him by the throat, to lift him off the ground, maybe crush his windpipe. Something holds me back. Perhaps it's the gleam in his eye. I've never seen such a dark light. Or else it's the shifting of the others. Almost without my knowing, they have formed a circle around us. I'm at the centre, I'm in their crosshairs.

Now is not the time to attack. I need the Cradle to destroy the Telar. Besides, my attack, when I do launch it, must come from within. Umara has taught me that much.

But God, how I hate to back down in front of this punk!

I smile at Lark. 'You're right, she was a treat. Hopefully we can play with other Telar in the days to come.'

Lark speaks in a soft, confiding voice. 'I know you're not human, Sita, and I know you've been around for a while. Still, let me give you a piece of advice. If you want to be my friend, I'll be your friend. But don't challenge me in front of the others again. Try it and next time we put a gun in your mouth, we'll make sure you pull the trigger.'

I back off a step and give a faint bow. 'Understood, boss.'

His grin returns. It's like something he sticks on his face. 'Boss. I like that. You've got spunk.' He raises his voice, speaking to the others. 'Hey, everyone, this is Alisa. She'll be working with us for a few days. She's going to help us dispose of those goddamn Telar.'

The children of the Lens stare at me.

They are not interested in typical introductions.

However, Cindy's daughter, Jolie, comes forward to greet me. She asks me to shake Mr Topper's hand. Close up, I see the doll's lips and eyes are not made of blood but lipstick. Indeed, it's the same lipstick her mother wore the day we met. It makes me wonder what goes on inside that child's mind.

Down below, through the clear floor, I see the larger portion of the Cradle moving to what seem to be assigned seats. They carefully form a spiral, while we sit in a circle. Most sit cross-legged. The light in our room is turned off but a dim glow reaches us from the bottom floor.

A crystal vase stands at the centre of our room on a copper stool. A tall red candle rises from its middle. The lit wick throws flickering shadows over the children's pale faces.

Jolie is on my right, Lark is to my left. He has an electronic device in his hand that allows him to be heard by the others below. Lark is 100 per cent serious now. He speaks the following words like an invocation.

'ALL WHO GATHER TODAY
ARE SERVANTS OF THE ONE
WE CALL UPON THE POWERS THAT BE
AS WIELDERS OF THE ANCIENT FLAME
WE PRAY TO THE DARKNESS OF OLD
WE ARE THY SERVANTS
WE ARE THY HANDS AND FEET
AND THY EYES AND EARS
LET THY FIRE
LET THY DARKNESS
ENTER US NOW AND FOREVER
SO THAT WE MAY DO THY WILL
AS SERVANTS OF THE ONE
WE INVOKE THE POWER THAT DESTROYS
FOR WE ARE ONE WITH THY POWER
NOW AND FOREVER
WE ARE ETERNALLY ONE.'

Like in Umara's cavern, a presence enters the room. But unlike the puja she performed to call upon the divine, this invocation has summoned a choking vibration that I have unfortunately experienced before: in Brutran's living room when the Cradle pushed me to commit suicide; in a cheap motel in London when I murdered Numbria; and high in the Rocky Mountains, when the Cradle invaded Matt's mind and forced him to kill me.

A cold tendril of fear touches my heart and with it I feel a mounting pressure at the back of my skull. I'm not sure how to resist but my intuition tells me it will only get stronger if I fight it. All I can do is let go and trust in the grace Krishna has promised will always be with me.

Everyone below us and around me sits with their eyes closed. Except for Lark, who stares at me with eyes suddenly so bloodshot the whites look as if they have been painted red. Even before he asks, I know what's going to be demanded of me to be a member of the Lens.

'Alisa Perne,' he says softly, 'it's the custom when joining our lineage to make an offering to the powers that be. The purpose of the offering is twofold. It strengthens the powers we call upon while at the same time it confirms your commitment to those powers. Do you understand?'

'No. What is this offering?'

'A blood sacrifice.'

'Can I offer a chicken?'

'It must be a human sacrifice. Whom do you wish to offer?'

Umara had hinted I might be forced to give up a member of my group to be accepted into the Cradle's inner circle. I consider a possible candidate. It's a grim business.

Lisa Fetch. I'm 99 percent sure she's the mole. True, the evidence against her is circumstantial, but there's a lot of it.

By chance, out of the blue, Lisa and her cop boyfriend, Jeff, came to my home the morning of the night the Telar first attacked me. Before Lisa showed up, I knew nothing about the IIC. But even when Lisa introduced me to them, told me how evil they were, she supplied me with not a single fact that helped protect me from them.

Lisa worked for the IIC but was able to leave their employ without suffering any repercussions. Her boyfriend, Jeff, was supposed to have died at the hands of IIC agents but I never did see his body.

Lisa supplied me with reams of computer data the IIC supposedly gave to her to help them find out why their Array was no longer working like it used to. However, the data was incomprehensible to me and the conclusions Lisa eventually drew from it sounded more like opinions than facts.

Lisa refused to come with the rest of us to London to watch Teri run in the Olympics. It didn't frighten her to be left alone in Truman, Missouri, despite the atrocities she knew the IIC had already committed. It was like she was sure no one would touch her.

Against my instructions, Lisa insisted on travelling

with Seymour when he went to pick up Shanti after Shanti left Switzerland with a copy of Yaksha's book. Lo and behold, not long after that, the copy changed back into the original.

Several times our gang had picnics in my backyard in Truman. While swimming in my pool, Teri snuck up behind her boyfriend and tickled Matt, causing him to accidentally slip on the deck and cut his scalp. I remember that it was Lisa, and Lisa alone, who helped bandage his wound. I suspect she saved his stained gauze, for the Cradle couldn't lock on to Matt without a sample of his blood.

It was odd Matt had been so careless with his blood that day.

Finally, Lisa was at my funeral, and Brutran told me flat out that she had a spy in Denver who confirmed that I was dead. Who told her if it wasn't Lisa?

She has to be the mole. There's no one else.

'Lisa Fetch,' I reply. 'But I don't have a sample of her blood. I have only a strand of her hair that I found on my clothing. Will that suffice?'

I had searched for the hair after Umara had given me her warning. I'm not happy about dealing with Lisa in this manner but it's not like I have a lot of options.

'Is she a normal human being?' Lark asks.

'Yes.'

'The hair contains the DNA of the one who is to be sacrificed,' Lark says. 'Since she is not Telar, it should be satisfactory. Hand it to Jolie, please.'

I give it to the little girl, who does a very

strange thing.

She puts the hair in her mouth.

She doesn't swallow it. Just holds it inside.

'Now let us close our eyes and hold hands,' Lark says.

I don't mind the closing our eyes part. But touching Jolie and Lark at the same time creeps me out. They both have cold skin. Jolie's hand is so small it almost disappears inside my palm, whereas Lark has unusually long fingers.

Lark continues to repeat a portion of his original invocation. In no special order but with a religious intensity. He sounds like he's talking to someone physically present, and he clearly believes every word he says.

'Enter us now and forever so that we may do thy will.' Lark waits a minute before adding, 'We invoke the power that destroys. For we are one with thy power.'

These lines must be key. He says each two dozen times and with each repetition his voice grows quieter. Soon I feel as if I'm hearing him only in my mind.

The pressure at the back of my skull mounts. Paradoxically, it has the effect of pulling me slightly out of my body as the pain increases. I suspect my suffering would be unbearable if I wasn't being forcibly removed from it.

Lark suddenly changes his tune. This line I hear with my ears.

'We invoke the power to destroy against Lisa Fetch.'

Lark waits a minute then repeats the line. Softer.

Again and again. I begin to feel dizzy.

My eyes are closed and still the room spins.

The skull pressure, the internal pulling, Lark's chanting – it all combines to make me feel as if I'm being sucked up into a tornado. There appears to be astral dust in the room, some kind of suffocating filth that my spirit chokes on.

But just as fast as it came, the tornado passes. I feel a yank at the back of my head. I don't open my eyes. I don't have to open them to see. To know where I am.

I'm in Lisa Fetch's condo in Truman. She is grading a handful of math exams. Lisa is a genius when it comes to her favorite subject. She teaches all kinds of courses. Algebra and geometry for undergraduates. Advanced calculus for engineering and science majors. She loves numbers as much as she does people. She's really not a bad person. I was surprised that she betrayed us.

The odd thing is, I reach her mind before the tidal wave does and find her thinking of Shanti and Matt. She often used to accompany Shanti to the hospital when the girl was having plastic surgery on her face. And of course Lisa always had a thing for Matt. Her thoughts of them both are loving. That worries me.

Then it strikes. We do. The Lens, the Cradle.

The sky is blue outside, the sun bright, but it is as if a black hole suddenly enters her world. Darkness descends and her vision dims as her individual will is swept away. The numbers on her test papers twist into grotesque symbols and the red ink in her teacher's pen begins to leak on to her desk like blood from a torn vein. Despair as heavy as a falling moon crushes her and she sees no escape except to kill herself.

Instantly, I regret my decision to sacrifice her.

Her mind . . . I can't find any guilt there.

I plead for her to stop and think what she's doing but a hundred other voices disagree and she raises her pen in her right hand and stabs the veins in her left wrist. Real blood flows over her papers and spills on to her desk.

Let the fun begin. So cheer the children.

The rest, for Lisa, a master of maths, is horror raised by a factor of ten. Her wrist is punctured in a dozen spots but that is too common a way to kill oneself, and besides, she might still be found by friends and saved. The Cradle can't have that. It has two goals: to maximize her suffering and to ensure her death. Pain feeds the powers that feed the Cradle, and death, why, death is its own reward.

The Cradle scans Lisa's mind for what terrifies her the most. It seems she has a fear of heights, but her condo is on the bottom floor of a two-storey building. Lisa, wearing only a robe she put on after showering, is forced to go outside. This order she resists – vanity can be strong even in the face of death. But her mortal will is like a bamboo stick trying to fend off a bolt of lightning. Resistance is ridiculous.

I hear them, all the kids' minds, as if they're one unit.

Yet I'm not one with them, not completely.

I still know who I am, and I know I want them to stop.

Lisa strides across the busy campus until she comes

to the chapel. A dozen students stop to stare, but only a few notice she's bleeding. I see a young woman off to her side lift her cell and call for help. But no one's bold enough to stop Lisa directly. They watch, they wait, they don't know what's going to happen next.

Yet the apathy of the students is not totally to blame. Lisa is in the grip of a force so awful, it repels all those around her. The students feel the evil and fear it. I can sense their thoughts. A few of the more sensitive ones are even able to glimpse the black cloud that surrounds her.

Lisa opens the door of the chapel and goes inside. A desperate part of me prays the cross on the altar will repel the children that control her steps. But that hope is quickly crushed. The cross is a sacred symbol to those who have faith, and right now Lisa doesn't even have a hope.

There's a stairway behind the altar that leads to a floor above the main hall. Lisa follows its winding steps slowly upward. Her loss of blood has begun to sap her strength. It's possible she'll lose consciousness before the Cradle can finish with her.

But again my hope is flattened when Lisa finds still another flight of steps that climb to the bell tower. Her leaking blood drips on the steps and causes her to slip and fall. But it's as if invisible arms reach down and drag her to her feet to face her doom.

A door opens and the glare of the sun momentarily blinds Lisa. She's back outside but high up now, at the very pinnacle of the chapel. The sight of the campus's central courtyard, far below, makes her dizzy and brings to the surface her old fear of heights. But none of this is of any help. She knows who she is. She knows something horrible is happening to her. But she can't stop it.

Lisa climbs over the edge of the cubicle that shelters the church bell. She stands on the rim of a spire so steep its incline is almost straight up, or down. Now there's nothing between her and the ground except a hundred feet of thin air.

Lisa takes a step forward. There's room for only one step. Yet in that last instant her will finally bursts to the surface and for a few seconds I think she's going to escape.

Unfortunately, the children are too strong. Lisa's outstretched leg wobbles. Try as she might, she can't bring it back in, she can't replant her feet, nor can she regain her balance. The wobble reaches her hips and sets off a tremor that flows down her other leg. She sways back and forth before finally pitching forward. She falls.

The Cradle releases its hold and watches. They take delight in Lisa's screams. They love the sickening moment of impact. The instant of agony. The slow fall into darkness. If they are even capable of love. It feels more like gluttony to me.

Suddenly, I'm back in the circular room with Lark, Jolie and the other members of the Lens. I see it through a thick fog and realize my eyes are still shut. The pressure at the back of my head is awful. A small part of my mind remains with Lisa as her blood leaks from her crushed skull. But the bulk of my awareness watches as the crystal vase at the centre of the room begins to fill with blood. I'm not sure if the blood is physical or if it's just an illusion. But it looks real.

Then I see them, the creatures Cindy warned me about, the beings I told her were all in her subconscious. There are two dozen of them, one for each child. They stand behind each of the seated kids, their hands resting on their shoulders. Umara has told me about them as well. She called them Familiars and equated them to a witch's black cat, the true source of the witch's power.

Umara said that a great deal of mystery surrounded the Familiars. They were the batteries that gave the kids their power, and in another sense they were the entities that possessed them. When I asked Umara who was really in charge, she said, 'In the end, the Familiar always claims the soul of its mortal partner.'

At first glance they look like oversized kachina dolls, something a Hopi Indian might make for a ceremony. But whereas kachinas represent friendly spirits or natural forces – like rain, wind, fire – there's something distinctly unnatural about these beings. In place of a crown of feathers, they have rows of impaled blades. They wear hides, although they are far from the carefully prepared skins of buffalo or deer. They look more like the raw scalps of human beings and other intelligent creatures from alien worlds. I get the clear impression these beings are not bound to our earth.

With a shock I've seldom known in my five thousand

years, I become aware of two hands resting on my shoulders. Apparently, with my sacrifice of Lisa, I've become an official member of the Cradle, and a Familiar has been assigned to me.

As I try twisting around to see what it looks like, its hand comes off my right shoulder and touches my head at my temple. The feel of it on my hair, and on my bare skin, is revolting and I want to vomit. It's as if a slimy mucus coating on its fingers has rubbed off on to me. However, it has an insubstantial quality; I'm not even sure if it's there.

But the hand stops me from turning around.

The creature isn't going to let me see it. Not yet.

My eyes are still shut. However, my vision is forced back towards the centre of the circle. My mind is no longer with Lisa. But just as her blood seemed to fill the vase, now I sense the Familiars emptying it. Even though they remain standing behind their respective wards, the level of the blood in the crystal vase slowly drops until it's totally drained. I hear a licking sound. Like they don't want to waste a single drop.

The pressure on the back of my skull eases up.

I feel my body sag forward. Someone squeezes my hand; it's Jolie. Someone else pats me on the back; that's Lark. I hear the noises of the real room and when I do open my eyes, the lights are back on and the kids are standing and stretching. I look up and Lark offers me his hand.

'How do you feel?' he asks as he pulls me to my feet.

'Weird.' I let go of his hand and touch the back of

my skull. 'Like someone just operated on my brain.'

'The first time can be rough but it gets easier.'

'I threw up the first time,' Jolie says, holding on to Mr Topper.

'When we sit together like this, our minds link,' Lark says. 'We become one.'

Their remarks confirm they meet regularly.

'Does that mean you were able to read my mind?' I'm curious because I wasn't able to pick up their specific thoughts, although I could sense their overall mood. For example, their feeling of satisfaction when Lisa struck the ground. Lark shakes his head.

'I felt your emotions more than your thoughts,' he says. 'I know you were shocked when you realized your friend was innocent.'

I frown. 'I wouldn't say she was innocent.'

'Then you didn't see into her mind. She never betrayed you.' Lark grins. 'You didn't have to offer such an innocent victim. Yet you have pleased the powers, and been accepted into the Cradle. A great being has been assigned to you.'

I feel sick at heart with what I have done to Lisa. I struggle to hide my pain.

'Are you talking about that thing that was standing behind me?' I ask.

'That Familiar is your master now. If I were you, I'd speak of him with more respect. He's very special.'

'How do you know? Did you see him?'

Lark's eyes shine. But he doesn't answer my question.

18 ~~~

Brutran wants to speak to me after my first-hand experience with the Cradle but I feel the need to be alone. There's a room on the fourth floor that was ordinarily used as an overnight suite for IIC executives that were working late and didn't have time to go home. I have appropriated it as my own private quarters. After speaking to Lark, I hurry upstairs and lock the door.

Already I feel I'm in deeper than I planned. Mentally linking with the Cradle reminds me of the time the Telar tortured me with a device called the Pulse. The purpose of the Telar's invention was simple – to induce agony. But in practice it caused so much pain it made me lose even my sense of 'I'. Sharing a psychic connection with the kids has a similar effect on me.

With both, I feel I'm no longer myself.

Yet I fear the long-term effects of the Cradle will be worse than the Pulse. Alone in my room, I don't feel alone. It's as if I have two shadows instead of one, and this second shadow doesn't conform to my movements. It follows me, it gives the impression it will never leave me, but it does what it wants. I worry that in time I will do what it wants.

I feel watched.

Eyes staring at the back of my skull.

Invisible hands on my shoulders.

Most of all I feel fear.

Yes, I, the fearless vampire – the thing terrifies me.

I throw myself down on the suite bed and try to sleep. Since I have entered the IIC stronghold, I have slept at most three hours, and my nerves are ragged from fatigue.

I feel a desperate need to hear a friendly voice. Matt has given me what he swears is a secure cell phone. I pick it up and give Umara a call. She answers right away.

'How are you?' she asks.

'I feel like I'm losing my mind,' I say.

'That's to be expected. Tell me everything that's happened.'

I give Umara a quick but thorough overview. It doesn't take long with her because she grasps situations quickly. Plus she was in a similar position thousands of years ago. When I finish, she asks if I want help.

'Not yet,' I reply. 'No matter how much Brutran opens up to me, I don't trust her. There's no predicting how she'll react when the Telar's top people have been killed.'

'When she's done using you, she'll try to get rid of you.'

'Probably. But she's more desperate than you would imagine. This will sound strange but it's like she clings to me.'

'It's probably an act. She's a master manipulator,' Umara says.

'It could be genuine. And she still might be planning to kill me.'

'The devil's at his most dangerous when he's telling the truth.'

'Speaking of devils, how do I get rid of this feeling that the Familiar is still attached to me?'

'You can't. It is attached to you. And it will grow stronger the more you feed it.'

'With pain and suffering?'

'I think for a creature as advanced as your Familiar, that's probably dessert. I'm sure it's listening to every word we're saying, while drawing up long-term plans.'

'For what? Me? The world?'

'Both. Sita, I'm sorry but I did warn you.'

'When you spoke in the car on the drive down, I don't know, it all felt like an old fable. I didn't really think I'd be battling demons.'

'The battle has yet to start. Right now you're allies.'

I groan. 'Tell me some good news.'

'Shanti and Seymour are a hundred per cent cured. That means we can start manufacturing Charlie's vaccine. The question is, who should we turn to for help?'

'I've been thinking about that. As soon as we attack the Source, the Telar will release the virus. We're almost out of time. I say send Charlie here and let him turn over his research to the IIC's best scientists. With a sample of the vaccine already available, I bet they can start mass-producing it within two days.'

'The Telar can kill half the population in that time.'

'That's why we should get it ready now,' I say.

'One point worries me. Without the need for daily injections, you'll lose the strongest hold you have over Brutran and her people.'

'I still have your blood samples. That's enough. They still need me.'

'I hope you're right.'

'Hey, you're supposed to be cheering me up.'

I feel Umara smile. 'Would you like to talk to Matt? He told me to tell him if you called.'

I hesitate. 'What's his state of mind?'

'The trip back to Missouri was rough. Teri's funeral, seeing her parents, having to invent a story to explain her "accident".'

'I wish I could have been there.'

'You look too much like her. You would have raised questions.'

'Put Matt on. I'll talk to him.'

Umara pauses. 'Sita?'

'Yes?'

'You had to sacrifice Lisa. It was your only way in.'

'I know. But it doesn't make me feel any better.'

Umara sets down the phone and while I wait I roll on my back and stare at the ceiling. It's almost as if I see a shadow hovering over me.

'Hello, Sita. Mom says you're going through hell.'

'I'm sure I deserve it.' I give him a quick rundown on what's been happening, almost a repeat of my update to Umara. The only difference is Matt doesn't ask any questions. He doesn't even object when I talk about sending Charlie to join me. That's a surprise. It's like he no longer cares, about anything.

'You have always been against going to the IIC for help,' I say.

'You're already there, it's done. Besides, you're right, you start to hurt the Telar and they'll strike back. We need tons of vaccine on hand. Let the IIC make it and distribute it.' He pauses. 'Isn't that what you want?'

'I guess I just miss our old arguments,' I say.

'They were all about nothing.'

'You miss her. I miss her, too.'

'I know. At least I got to . . . say goodbye.'

'That was fortunate.'

I hear Matt sigh. 'I just wish my mom had more of Krishna's blood. Or John could have kept Teri in her body. She was right there, you know, in my arms. She just slipped away.'

'I don't think we'll understand why it happened the way it did. But you know, even though her life was short, it was rich. She won the big race. She won your love.'

'Yeah. The love of a man who couldn't protect her.'

'Your love was wonderful. And who knows, perhaps we'll all meet again one day. All these battles I'm fighting with these demons, it makes me believe there's got to be a few angels out there, somewhere, looking over us. Krishna couldn't have stacked the deck totally against us.'

Matt draws in a deep breath and slowly lets it go. He sounds like he's relaxing. 'Your words help.'

'Your voice helps, Matt. Just the fact you're out there.'

'You get in a tight spot, give me a call. I'll be there in a heartbeat.'

'That means a lot to me.' I pause. 'I love you.'

He's silent a long time. 'You're always in my heart, Sita.'

We talk a while longer but it's just a bunch of words. He does tell me, however, that Lieutenant William Treach came to Teri's funeral. He says the man appeared confused. Worse, it appears his wife is in a mental hospital. Matt gives me the name of the clinic. He got it from the detective knowing I would want it.

When Matt and I hang up I call the police detective. I feel responsible for upsetting the Treaches' lives. I catch him at work, alone in his office. The man asks who I am and in an instant I know he's not well. Damn, I should never have used my psychic powers when I was in Teri's body. I definitely started a loop in his mind.

'I'm Teri Raine's cousin,' I say. 'She told me about meeting you in Denver. And I heard you were at her funeral in Missouri.'

'That's true. Our first meeting was serious. It involved a murder case. But we formed a bond of sorts the next time we spoke.' He stops and the confusion in his voice is evident. 'I felt close to Teri, it's hard to explain. I was saddened to hear about her death.'

'It was a tragedy.'

'I was never clear how she died.'

'I believe the accident is still being investigated. But it's not the reason I called. I'm concerned about you and your wife.'

'My wife? How do you know my wife?'

'I heard she was ill.'

'Who told you this?'

I allow a measure of my telepathic power to flow out. 'It doesn't matter. Lieutenant William Treach, Bill, please close your eyes and relax. Listen to the sound of my voice. You don't have to block out other sounds, you simply have no interest in them. You're not even concerned with your office. You hear my voice and that's all that matters. Do you understand?'

He sounds dreamy. 'Yes.'

'From the time you returned home to your wife after meeting Teri Raine, a series of suggestions were placed in your mind. They were placed there with the best of intentions. No one meant you any harm. But it's time those suggestions were erased. You'll feel better with them gone. Now go back in time to that evening. You walk in the house and you sense someone behind you. From that instant on, until six o'clock the next morning, I want you to purge all your memories.

271

Anything that happened during that time can no longer bother you. It no longer exists. From now on, you'll feel and act like your old self. Is that clear?'

'Yes.'

'Continue to sit with your eyes closed and take a five-minute nap. When you awaken, you will have forgotten that I called. But you'll feel rested and refreshed, ready to tackle any task that comes your way. At the same time, deep in your heart, you know your wife, Sandra, is going to be OK. She's going to make a full recovery. Is this totally clear?'

He hesitates. 'I don't feel . . . Yes.'

My mental powers are at full strength. I don't know why he hesitates.

'What don't you feel, Detective?' I ask.

He's a long time answering. His breathing sounds strained.

'Something's here,' he whispers. 'Something . . . dreadful.'

I go to ask him to clarify but stop. He's sensing the Familiar! Worse, the creature's trying to disturb the healing I'm doing on him.

'Hang up the phone, Detective, and take your nap.'

I cut the line before anything else can be done to the man.

I feel as if I've been psychically abused. I dare not call Sandra and try to repair her mind. In her disturbed mental state, God only knows how vulnerable she would be to a Familiar. I'll have to avoid acting as a healer until I'm rid of the creature.

The Familiar interference shakes me up. There's one thing I can't stand – it's the feeling of losing control. Now, with this parasite attached to my skull, or my shoulders, or wherever, I feel exposed to all kinds of dark and invisible influences. But I'm not sure if that's really the case or if it's just fear that's making the situation seem worse than it is.

Lying back on my bed, I try to recall any helpful clues Umara might have given me when she told me the story about the origin of the Telar.

'How did a primitive culture like the ancient Egyptians come up with something as sophisticated as Professor Sharp's array?' I asked as Umara and I left the enchanting town of Carmel behind and began to enter the even more magical redwood forests of Big Sur. The coastal route from Santa Cruz to Malibu took longer than the inland route but I wanted to enjoy the beauty of the rugged coast before condemning myself to a miserable imprisonment in Brutran's stronghold.

'Who are you calling primitive?' Umara said from the passenger seat. We had argued over who was to drive. Both of us were control freaks. In the end, we agreed to split the task.

'Sharp needed computers to be certain his array was working. The same with the IIC and their psychic army. How did the Telar manage to skip these steps?'

'You assume we stumbled across it the same way. That wasn't the case. You have to understand we were a deeply religious people. We worshipped many deities

273

but understood they were all manifestations of the one. We were especially grateful to what nature gave us and for that reason our names for God and Mother Nature were identical. My own name, Umara, means "the Mother".'

'I hope your parents didn't see you as a divine incarnation when you were born,' I teased her.

'Far from it. I wasn't a priestess when our array first began to appear. I was a pot maker. My hands were stuck in clay all day. Except when I was firing and painting my creations. Those were simple days filled with a great deal of satisfaction. My childhood was joyful.'

'Something must have triggered the creation of your array,' I said, with a note of impatience. Umara has only one fault. She's never in a hurry. I suppose it's a reasonable quality for a twelve-thousand-year-old woman to possess. But I find myself often wishing she would get to the point quicker.

'It started rather innocently. On our equivalent of Sunday, our day of worship, we used to gather near the banks of the Nile at nighttime and pray. We had maybe a dozen songs we all knew, and we used to sing them with great love and devotion. Thanking nature for rain, the river, our crops, our good health. Like I said, we were a devoted people. But as a race, we began to enjoy the silence that would follow our prayers, and for that reason we made it a rule that we'd sit quietly for a few minutes after every hymn.'

'How did you begin to 'enjoy the silence'?'

'I mean exactly what I say. We were a sensitive race and we found it pleasant to sit still after each prayer. A large number of us sensed a presence in the silence. I think it's the way we lived that made us so receptive. We had no enemies. When other tribes from the interior of the continent visited, we welcomed them with open arms. We never tried to take lands that didn't belong to us. We were content with our own village beside the river.'

'So what triggered the array?' I asked.

'While sitting in silence after our prayers, a few of us began to make sounds.'

'Involuntary sounds?' I asked.

'Well, they weren't planned.'

'You began to speak in tongues. Like the Pentecostal people.'

'That's a fair example. But I must add that we were by no means a dogmatic race. We embraced all religions as long as they were based on love and gratefulness. We saw gratitude as the key to invoking the grace we felt from our prayers.'

'Did you personally speak in tongues?'

'It started that way for me. I didn't do it because others were doing it. I was a shy teenage girl. I wasn't trying to show off. But imagine ten thousand people all singing in harmony, and then falling silent, and in that silence a few sparks began to ignite.'

'Sparks?'

'It was like an energy burst through some of us and we had to let it out by speaking. Only we didn't know what we were saying. We only knew that it sounded like a language. It seemed to have structure and syntax.'

'But you were just speaking gibberish.'

'No. It got to the point that one in ten of us started to talk like this. That was over a thousand. And when that number was achieved, the words we were spouting became clearer, and we began to sense their meaning.'

'Wait a second. Are you saying that nature itself began to teach you a language?'

'That's one way of putting it.'

'That's ridiculous.'

'Try telling that to the millions of people worldwide who go to Pentecostal churches. When they pray with fervour and start to speak in tongues, it's nothing they can control. It just happens.'

'I understand that. I've seen it. But they never make any sense. You're saying you were spontaneously given an intelligent language.'

'It happened. In time, we wrote down the words and realized that an intelligence greater than our own was trying to teach us things.'

'What kind of things?'

'Like how to sterilize our milk and water by boiling it. How to build aqueducts to channel the water from the Nile so we could grow ten times as many crops. It even taught us how to build a thresher to separate our wheat kernels from the stalks.'

'Right. I suppose you ordered the parts from the steel mill it taught you how to build.'

'You don't need steel to build a basic thresher.

All you need is rope, lumber, a saw, primitive spokes and wheels, and some ingenuity. I add that last word deliberately because the knowledge we were channelling didn't tell us everything. It was more a source of inspiration. It was for that reason we began to call the being who spoke through us the Source.'

'Hmm,' I said.

'You don't look impressed with my story.'

'It lacks the scientific basis Sharp's explanation does. His discovery was uncovered step by step. It produces results that can be mathematically measured. Your array sounds more like a revival meeting.'

'The creation of our spontaneous language is throwing you off.'

'Most languages are the result of a random searching for sounds to describe something. No, my problem with your tale is that you were taught so much so quickly.'

'Once again, it happened. Thanks to the Source, in a few short years our culture evolved tremendously. We discovered higher maths, algebra and geometry, and used them to help develop engineering principles that allowed us to build huge structures.'

'Don't tell me you constructed the Great Pyramid?'

Umara hesitated. 'That came later.'

'I would hope so.'

'But not as late as you think.'

'You forget, I was in Egypt five thousand years ago, not long after Krishna died. That's where I met Suzama. I know the Egyptians had pyramids even then.'

'Good.'

'But you're asking me to believe they had them seven thousand years before that.'

'We did.'

I considered. 'You were there. I can tell you're not lying. But it's hard to accept this channelled information – and that's what it was – was of such practical value.'

'Nothing I'm telling you is really different from what Sharp told you. Your prejudice against our discovery is the form it took. So we didn't use decks of cards and record hits and misses on calculators. The principle of using a group mind to tap into a faint ESP signal was identical. It didn't matter that our information came to us after praying. It still took thousands of us listening together to understand what we were being told.'

'Could your people hear this voice?' I asked.

'In time, yes. After many years the most sensitive of us discovered how to link our minds together so we could hear the language as clearly as you hear me speaking right now. Come on, Sita, you have to believe that we could become telepaths. You're a telepath yourself. Just look at how your mind melds with Seymour. He practically wrote your life story before he met you.'

'Seymour and I do have a special connection. And I can hear other people's thoughts, from time to time. But I've never had the universe speak to me.'

Umara sat back in her seat and nodded to herself. 'Ah. Now I see the problem.'

'Really? Why don't you wipe that smug expression off your face and tell me what it is.'

'Your problem stems from the fact that Krishna has never spoken to you in five thousand years.'

'How do you know he hasn't?'

'It's obvious. Otherwise you wouldn't protest how we came into contact with the Source.'

Her words stung. They hurt because they were true.

'Tell me more about how you linked your minds,' I said.

'Just as Brutran has the Array and the Cradle, we had a thousand of us who could sense the Source, a hundred who could channel information from it, and a dozen of us who could link our minds so they functioned as one. We called our inner circle the Link.'

'I assume you were the head of it.'

'My father was. But I was a member. I saw how it evolved over time.'

'How much time?' I asked.

'Now we come to the Telar's deepest secret. How did we become immortal? It didn't happen overnight. As a people, we were in contact with the Source for two decades before it gave us insights into how to extend our lives. These insights Brutran and her inner circle are already using. We were taught herbal formulas, yoga exercises and breathing techniques that greatly slowed down the ageing process. That's why the scriptures talk about people who lived to be several hundred years old.'

'Umara. I'm the last person on earth who needs a history lesson.'

She ignored me. 'But the secret of the Telar's immortality came from the Link.'

I waited but she didn't continue.

'So what was the secret?' I asked.

'A great white light came and blessed us.'

I groaned. 'Now I know you're a born-again Pentecostal.'

'You'll have trouble with this part of my tale. But I suspect after you leave Brutran's castle – if you manage to survive – you'll have no trouble believing every single word of it.'

'Go on.'

'The Link grew in power with the passing years. As a group we aged very slowly. We were together perhaps a hundred years when we had a great breakthrough. We were sitting in silence in our largest pyramid. We had been fasting on nothing but water for weeks and our physical bodies felt as if they were made of air. Yet our Link kept growing stronger and stronger and with it we were able to peer into realms you can't imagine. Prophets speak of angels and archangels and elementals and gods. But we actually saw such beings. We were able to communicate with them, learn from them, and at each step we were led higher and higher. Eventually we reached a point where we believed we might one day see God.' Umara paused. 'It was then it happened.'

'A great white light came and blessed you.'

'Don't ridicule me, Sita. You're alive in your original body. One reason is because Krishna gave me his blood. The other reason is because of the light I experienced that day. The glory and power of it has never left me. It's possible it's the same light the Bible refers to when it speaks of the Holy Spirit. I don't know, it can't be described. I only know that after it came, and left, all of us in the Link, and the majority of the others who were able to contact the Source, were immortal.'

I took time to digest her words. I knew she was not lying. I would have detected the falsehood in an instant. But her tale was so fantastic, it created more questions than it answered.

'What went wrong?' I asked finally.

'Why do you assume something went wrong?'

'It always does. Never mind the fact that you're the only one left of this Link.'

Umara's expression was sad. 'I think the light gave us so much joy it was hard to return to the physical world. Imagine, we felt as if we had been touched by God. But the next day, when we broke our fast, we still had to chew our food before swallowing it. We still had to urinate and move our bowels to get rid of our wastes. We still had to wash our skin to keep it from smelling. But it was difficult to go back to being simply human.'

'Were those in the Link the leaders of your people?'

'Yes.'

'I'm sure that created problems right there.'

'True. We were supposed to be leading our people but all we could think about was returning to the light.

Because our breakthrough had come as a result of much fasting and meditating, that was all we did for the next few years. But it had the effect of separating us from our people and in the end they began to resent us just as we resented them.'

'Didn't your better angels advise you to be more loving?'

'We continued to experience higher dimensions. Realms of light and bliss. But none led us back to the great white light. As our frustration grew, I think we began to attract beings that promised us they knew a secret way to the light.'

'Who were these beings?'

'Familiars. They came as the best of friends, and they looked very bright themselves. It was easy to believe what they said. But, looking back, I realize they never would have come if we had been more attentive to our people. We had become selfish, self-absorbed, interested only in our own level of achievement. We didn't pray and meditate for the sake of our people. We hardly spoke to them, especially after we met the Familiars. To us, they were the most wonderful beings. We began to see them as almost as valuable as the great light. You see, they gave us powers.'

'What kind of powers?' I asked.

'All kinds. We discovered we could move objects with our minds. It didn't matter how large or heavy they were, not if we were linked together. We learned how to bring walls of fire. This power proved especially useful when we were attacked.'

'Attacked? I thought you had no enemies.'

'We were attacked by our own people.'

'But you just helped make them immortal!'

'Those connected to the Source were made immortal. The rest of our people realized this and wanted to be given the same gift. We might have given it to them if we had control over it, but we didn't. They turned against us and since they now outnumbered us fifty to one, we had no choice but to call upon the Familiars to protect us.'

'Did they save you?'

'All of us in the Link survived. But many in the Source died, despite their gift of immortality and the fact the Familiars were able to create waves of fire that flowed through the streets. It was a horrible time. Even though I hid deep in our greatest pyramid, I could still hear the screams of my people as they burned to death. It seemed to me, even then, that the Familiars liked to kill our foes slowly. Of course, I didn't understand at the time that they actually fed off the agony they caused.'

'How long did this battle last?' I asked.

'Three days. When it was over, my father made himself king of all the land and set down stern laws everyone had to follow. We had never had a king before. We had never had a caste system. Now those who were in contact with the Source were the upper caste, while those in the Link were supposed to be treated like gods.'

'You must have enjoyed that.'

'I hated it, I knew it was wrong. I went to my father and begged him to let us return to our simple life, when everyone was treated as an equal. But he said that was impossible, the people would always be jealous of our immortality and would try to take it from us by force. Then I begged him to at least stop invoking the Familiars. I couldn't stand the feel of them in our chambers, never mind what they had done to our people during the war. But again my father said we couldn't go back. He believed we needed the Familiars for protection, and to continue our search for the great light.'

'It was a search for the divine that led to your damnation.'

'It's ironic, isn't it? Our goal was great. Our path was dark.'

'What happened next?' I asked.

'Horror upon horror. Now that the Familiars were our protectors, they began to make demands. They insisted on human sacrifices. At this my father finally said no. He would never do that. In his heart, he wasn't a bad man, although he had clearly lost his way. But he wasn't given a chance to redeem himself. A member of the Link named Hatram poisoned him and declared himself king. It wasn't long after that we were slowly burning to death a dozen people in honour of every full moon. The victims were chosen at random. They could be mothers, children, it didn't matter. The Familiars had to be fed. After all, they were going to show us the great white light.'

'Surely even Hatram didn't believe that,' I said.

Umara looked out the window. When she spoke next, there was pain in her voice. 'I was never to know what Hatram believed. Even when he raped me and ordered me slain.'

'The rest of the Link allowed this?' I asked, shocked.

'This was a thousand years after my father had been killed. Half the Link banded together to kill Hatram. There was no other way to stop him. But he became aware of our plan and plotted a horrible vengeance. The Familiars supported him and soon there were not many of us left. It was right after this I was raped.'

'How did you escape the death sentence?'

'Friends came to my aid and hid me. After Hatram completed his vengeance he discovered he could no longer link with anyone. He had sunk too low, he could no longer invoke even the Familiars. Eventually, I was able to catch him alone and I killed him with a knife.'

'But you had his child.'

Umara whirled. 'How did you know?'

'I hear it in your voice. That child was Haru. He was never your brother or half brother. He's your son, like Matt.'

Umara lowered her head. 'Haru is nothing like Matt.'

I nodded to the road in front of us. We had exited the redwood forest and were staring down at the cliff's rocky shore and the crashing waves.

'If everything goes according to plan,' I said, 'I'm

going to kill Haru in the next week or two. Are you sure you're all right with that?'

Umara stared straight ahead and nodded. 'It's like when I slit his father's throat. It's necessary.'

There's a knock at my door.

'Come in!' I call out.

Brutran opens the door. She has a FedEx box in her hands.

'This just came for you,' she says.

I nod to my desk. 'Put it there.'

Brutran sets the package down. 'I hope it's not more of the virus.'

'Your problems with the virus are almost over. I have sent word for the permanent vaccine to be sent here, along with the man who invented it. He's Telar but I want your people to show him every courtesy.'

'Of course. What do you want in exchange?'

'For your people to manufacture as much of the vaccine as possible, as quickly as possible. We'll begin to strike the Telar this evening. Chances are they'll strike back.'

'Our intelligence indicates the Telar are producing vast quantities of the virus in Rio and Tokyo. But they have yet to distribute it to other cities, at least not on a large scale. They may have operatives working on a small scale that are unknown to us.'

'We must assume Haru already has the virus out there. Does the IIC have connections to the Red Cross?'

'The president of the organization works for us. We

are their largest donor. If an outbreak occurs, we can move fast.'

'Excellent. Anything else?' I ask.

'I wanted to know how your initiation into the Cradle went.'

'Is this room secure?'

'You asked me that yesterday.'

'Yesterday was yesterday.'

'You can talk freely. No one is listening except me.'

'It was amazing. Like a descent into hell. The whole experience left me with a splitting headache. Your Cradle is a piece of work. You should be proud of yourself.'

Brutran looks too tired to defend herself. But she tries anyway.

'I told you, I have almost nothing to do with it nowadays.'

'I heard you the first time. What are the kids doing right now?'

'What they usually do in their spare time. They're feeding lines of code into a computer file they keep secret from the rest of us.'

I sit up with a start. 'Do these lines of code have any relationship to the computer game one of your subsidiaries puts out? A game called CII or Cosmic Intuitive Illusion?'

Brutran hesitates. 'How do you know about that game?'

'Let's just say I have a friend who's obsessed with it.'

'Paula Ramirez's child?'

'Answer my question.'

'Yes. Our best hackers have determined that the Cradle is building up a massive online program that's capable of moving in and out of almost any computer system. Each day, this program makes brief contact with the online game CII and adds lines of code to it, making it even more difficult to beat.'

'Have any of your hackers defeated the game?'

'No. They're not even sure what the game represents. But we have noticed that hackers who spend a long time playing it begin to suffer from paranoia and delusions. Rumours about it have spread among my staff and I'm having trouble finding men or women who are willing to study it. The game is considered poison.'

'How can a computer game cause mental illness?'

'I have no idea,' Brutran says.

'How come you didn't tell me about this earlier?'

'I knew you were joining the Cradle. I figured you had enough on your plate.'

'Don't tell me you were trying to protect me.'

'I was,' she replies, and she's telling the truth.

'Have you asked Lark or your daughter what's the purpose of the program?'

'I tried broaching the subject and was warned to back off.'

'Can't your hackers figure out a way to delete the program?'

'They've tried. It's heavily protected and very sophisticated. I have heard several of my best people describe it as extraterrestrial.'

'That's silly.'

'I'm surprised someone who just got a close look at the Cradle would have trouble believing in that possibility.'

'Contrary to what you may have been told, I didn't see any aliens in that room.'

'Yet you refuse to describe what you did see.'

I wave my hand. 'I don't want to talk about it, not now. Tell the children I want to reassemble in six hours.'

'I'll politely suggest that's a good time for you.' Brutran retreats to the door.

'Cindy?' I call.

She stops. 'Yes, Alisa?'

'I do understand how you lost control of all this.'

'Thank you.'

'But you should never have opened the door in the first place.'

She leaves and I quickly unwrap my package. Yaksha's book. I called Shanti yesterday to send it down. I did not worry they would lose it, nor was I afraid Brutran would open the package behind my back.

While staying with Umara and Freddy in Santa Cruz, I sprayed a lot of its pages with my blood and uncovered several hidden messages from Yaksha. But the most important ones, I assume, the ones that deal with the Telar, I was unable to find.

Then it occurred to me that the book starts and finishes with blank pages. Picking up a bottle the staff uses to refresh plants, I bite the tip of my finger and allow a few drops of my blood to fall in the water, before I replace the cap.

I spray a faint mist over the first blank page. Nothing.

I spray it over the back of the last blank page.

A quote of Krishna describing the Hydra appears.

'The Hydra was the offspring of Echidna and Typhon. His mother, Echidna, had the head of a beautiful maiden and the body of a serpent. Typhon, his father, had a hundred horrible heads that could touch the stars and change their courses in the heavens.

'The Hydra lived in the swamps near the ancient city of Lerna, in Argolis. Like his mother, he had the body of a serpent, and like his father, he had many heads, nine, one of which could never be harmed by any weapon. If any of his other heads were severed, another would grow in its place. The stench from the Hydra's breath was strong enough to kill any man or beast.

'The Hydra terrorized large sections of the earth for many years until man appealed to the gods for help. It was Hercules, the son of Zeus, the king of the gods, who volunteered to slay it. Hercules journeyed to Lerna in a chariot, and took with him his nephew and charioteer, Iolaus.

'When they finally reached the Hydra's hiding place, Hercules told Iolaus to stay with the horses while he drew the monster from its hole with repeated shots of his flaming arrows. This stirred the monster's wrath and Hercules boldly attacked. But he quickly realized that as soon as one of the Hydra's heads was severed, another immediately grew in its place.

'Unsure what to do, Hercules called for Iolaus's help, and Iolaus brought forth a flaming torch. This time, as Hercules cut off the Hydra's heads, Iolaus quickly cauterized the open wounds with his fire. This stopped them from growing back.

'As Hercules fought the monster, he was almost killed by its deadly breath, but eventually he severed all but one of the Hydra's heads. The last one could not be destroyed by any man-made tool, so, picking up his club, Hercules crushed it and tore it off with his bare hands. With Iolaus's help, he wisely buried it deep in the ground and placed a huge boulder over it lest it be disturbed by the future races of man.'

'Fascinating,' I whisper as I finish reading. Since discovering that Krishna told Yaksha a parable about the Hydra, I had searched Yaksha's biography, as well as the Internet, for any clues that might help me wipe out the Telar's Source and the IIC's Array. The many-headed theme obviously connected the Greek myth to my enemies.

Yet there were so many versions of the Hydra myth online, and Krishna's brief comments on the story that originally appeared in Yaksha's book didn't say much. I find this longer version much more satisfying.

For one thing, here Hercules and Iolaus are dead ringers for Arjuna and Krishna. There are numerous parallels. Iolaus was Hercules' nephew. Arjuna was Krishna's cousin.

At the start of the battle with the monster, Hercules

came dashing in with his fiery arrows. Arjuna, of course, was known as the greatest archer of his time.

Iolaus was Hercules' charioteer. Krishna was Arjuna's charioteer. And even though Hercules appeared to be the big hero, it was actually Iolaus who figured out how to destroy the Hydra. It was the same with Krishna and Arjuna's relationship. Arjuna was supposed to be the supreme warrior of his time, but Krishna had to kick his butt to get him to fight at the Battle of Kurukshetra.

It was clear to me that Krishna was trying to tell Yaksha that he was Iolaus, and that Yaksha was destined to fulfill the role of Hercules. Just as Hercules is able to imprison the Hydra but cannot truly kill it, Krishna clearly knew that Yaksha would contain the Telar but not actually destroy them.

But what about this head that can't be killed.

Who does that belong to?

19 ~

All my planning has led to this moment. Finally, I am going to use the IIC's thorn to remove the Telar's thorn. I'm about to walk the ultimate thin line, and if I'm unable to separate my weapon from my target, the world will die.

At last I have the perfect tool to go destroy the Telar. I have provided each kid in the Cradle with a vial containing a diluted mixture of Ruth and Hurley Marherr's blood – two high members of the Source. The blood will act as a form of energetic radar and allow us to lock on to the Marherrs.

I'm back in the room where the Lens meets. The kids are forming their circle, with Lark on my left, Jolie on my right. Below us, through the one-way glass, I watch as the rest of the Cradle creates their spiral. I don't know if the shape is significant and don't care.

Along with samples of their blood, Umara has given me a photograph and a brief biography of our first victims. Marherr is not their real name but a pseudonym they've been using for the last fifty years. The couple live in Geneva, Switzerland. Hurley is a member of the United Nations. Ruth works for WHO, the World Health Organization. Both work to feed starving children in Africa. In all probability it's a front.

The Cradle has killed Telar before but never at a distance. Certainly, the kids have never successfully attacked members of the Source. The blood should give them a big advantage. The same with my mind. Some of them may be as psychic as I am but none has my willpower, and unlike the attack on Lisa, this time I'm 100 per cent behind them.

The candle that protrudes from the central vase is lit, the lights are dimmed. We join hands and close our eyes. Our vials of blood rub together in our palms. Lark begins to chant the strange hymn. Today all the kids join him, on both floors.

'ALL WHO GATHER TODAY
ARE SERVANTS OF THE ONE . . .'

The pressure at the back of my skull returns. The spot feels delicate from the last session. I suspect this kind of psychic work is not good for the brain. None of the kids in the Cradle are going to live very long if they keep it up.

Once again the pain of the pressure is blunted by the separation the joining brings about. A part of me feels as if I'm being torn from my body. Yet a portion of my spirit remains bound in this accursed room. I listen as the group falls silent and Lark repeats the three lines that seem to be the key to the demonic invocation.

'ENTER US NOW AND FOREVER
SO THAT WE MAY DO THY WILL.
WE INVOKE THE POWER THAT DESTROYS.
FOR WE ARE ONE WITH THY POWER.'

The tornado strikes again. I feel myself simultaneously pulled up and struck down. The internal spinning makes me outwardly dizzy and I fear I will vomit. Lark's voice softens until I suspect his voice is just in my mind.

The weird grip I felt on my shoulders returns. Someone or something stands behind me. I'm not imagining it. *He* watches, he listens. He knows me while I know nothing about him.

Suddenly the tornado stops. My eyes are locked shut.

Yet I *can* see. I know where I am. Geneva.

The Marherrs' home is a mansion. I see signs they were entertaining earlier in the evening but now it's late, it's dark. The Marherrs are alone. Hurley is reclining in a hot tub next to an Olympic-size swimming pool. He must take his laps seriously to have such a large pool. His dark hair is cut short, almost to his scalp, his muscles are perfectly sculpted, probably from exercise. He floats on his back in the steaming liquid, his thoughts sleepy.

Ruth is in the garage, throwing out a bag of garbage, when she sees a beetle scamper into the corner. In a flash she moves to crush it; the woman obviously hates bugs. This is all the Cradle needs.

Leaving her husband alone, we go after her first. The Cradle crashes through whatever mental barriers she has cultivated in the last few thousand years and brushes them aside. Suddenly the beetle swells in *her* vision to the size of a human being. It backs her into the opposite corner, speaking in Lark's voice.

'Pour the chlorine in the hot tub filter or I will eat you,' the beetle says to the terrified woman. I feel her trying to convince herself it's not there but it looks so real.

'Please,' she begs.

'The chlorine!' The beetle hisses. 'Pour it into the filter!'

The Marherrs keep a large tank in their garage. It stores warm water generated by solar panels on their roof. A plastic pipe runs from it, and attached to the pipe, on the garage end, is the filter we're trying to force Ruth to pour the chlorine into.

Ruth continues to try to resist but with the beetle bearing down on her, she cowers. The Cradle has intuitively tapped into her fear of bugs. Feeling frantic, she snaps the lid off the filter and reaches for a gallon of chlorine. Given the size of their pool, I'm not surprised to see so much of the harsh liquid on hand.

Twisting off the top of the bottle, she dumps the chlorine into the gurgling water that will flow back to the hot tub where her husband is bathing.

'More!' the beetle shouts when she has finished draining the first bottle. I am not directing this portion of the Cradle's attack but I can see that it's clever. Lark – I assume he's in charge – has identified that Ruth is the weaker of the two, while Hurley is in the more vulnerable position. By combining her fear of bugs with her husband's carefree floating in the hot tub, Lark has created a fearsome two-pronged attack.

Ruth is unable to resist the Cradle. She pours bottle after bottle into the filter until she's used up a supply of over forty bottles. If the water was feeding the entire pool, it wouldn't have been so dangerous. But the valves are set so that all the chlorine flows straight to the hot tub.

'Now run! Run to your husband!' the beetle cackles.

Ruth flees. Maybe she thinks she can outrun the monster.

In her backyard, she finds her husband writhing in the water. Not only has the concentrated chlorine begun to burn off his skin, but the fumes from the steam are frying his lungs. He thrashes in vain to escape the hot tub, and it is only then that I realize the green-tinged water has blinded him.

'Ruth! Help me! Ruth!' he cries.

'Hurley,' she moans, seeing him in such a pitiful condition. To her credit she tries to pull him free, but Hurley is like a drowning man grasping at a rope. He grabs her arm and doesn't let go. Worse, for Ruth, the beetle returns and appears to kick her in the butt.

The blow isn't real. It's all in her head. It doesn't matter. She thinks it's real and that's enough. Falling into the hot tub beside her husband, crying, she inhales a lungful of the highly chlorinated water and begins to choke. Now there are two of them thrashing in the hot tub and it's no wonder when one of them bumps the rubber button that controls the cover.

A motor whirls to life and a mechanical device begins to drag a thick plastic sheet over the water. Ordinarily, the cover shouldn't be able to knock down a ten-year-old, but their skin is falling off in agonizing red strips and they're both vomiting blood. They're helpless.

Like a lid on a coffin, the hot tub cover seals them in the water.

The Cradle releases its grip so it can savour this moment of greatest fear and pain. Or perhaps it's the Familiars that take over at this point, I'm not sure. But once more I sense their gluttony.

My eyes are still shut, nevertheless I see them standing behind each of the kids. Like before, I'm unable to turn and see the Familiar that grips me. Yet I feel something akin to talons digging into my shoulders and I realize that each time we feed the creature, it gets stronger. At the very least, its hold on me gets strengthened.

The crystal vase at the centre of the room fills with blood. A series of loud slurping sounds follows and the blood begins to drain away. When it is all gone, the candle spontaneously flickers out and the pressure on the back of my head eases up.

I discover I can open my eyes. Like before, I sag forward and only keep from falling due to Jolie squeezing my hand and bringing me back to the physical dimension. I'm surprised to see blood trickling from her right nostril. I have a handkerchief and reach up to wipe it away.

'What is this?' I ask.

'Sometimes it hurts,' the little girl replies.

I turn to Lark, who is not jumping for joy like last time. He, too, appears drained. 'We got them,' I say as a form of congratulation.

He nods. 'They made for interesting prey.'

I stand and address the group.

'The Telar will soon hear of this attack. They'll band together and fight to protect themselves. The faster we can destroy them, the better our chances. For that reason, I want you all to rest now. We're going to strike again in three hours.'

Lark grabs at my leg as I go to leave.

'You're not in charge here,' he snaps.

'But I am. Did someone forget to tell you?'

Lark goes to stand but thinks better of it. He's exhausted.

'We should wait at least a day before our next attack,' he says.

'You heard what I said. The longer we wait, the more they will band together and the harder they will be to kill. But you don't have to lead the next attack. I'm getting a feel for how the Cradle works. I'll take over.'

Lark forces a smile. 'I can't wait to see what you come up with.'

Charlie's waiting outside my room as I get off the elevator on the top floor. He has brought four large suitcases. He is being guarded by some of the men that burst into Brutran's office the day I released the virus into the compound. I dismiss them and invite Charlie into my room. I lock the door behind us.

'Are you tired from your travels or can you work?' I ask.

Charlie saw me before I left Santa Cruz but he still struggles with the fact that I have come back from the grave. He has trouble looking me in the eye, and his facial twitch seems to act up in my presence. I hope he doesn't scare away the IIC's doctors.

'I'm fine,' he says. 'What do you want me to do first?'

'Hand over all your data on the vaccine to Dr Hayes. He's one of the world's foremost experts on viruses.'

'I've heard of him. I didn't know he worked for the IIC.'

'He didn't. They bought him yesterday for ten million euros. Teach him and his people any tricks you know to speed up the manufacture of the vaccine. Then I want you to inoculate all the people in this compound except for the children. Don't give anyone under the age of eighteen a shot.'

'May I ask why?'

'I'll explain later. Don't broadcast the fact that you're not taking care of the kids. They'll catch on eventually but it will take time.'

'But you are going to vaccinate them, aren't you?'

'Of course. Matt will take care of it when he arrives.'

'I didn't know he was coming.'

'I'm going to call him in a minute. Charlie, it's important while you're here that you avoid the kids. They're not what they appear to be.'

Charlie rubs his hands nervously. 'You're scaring me.'

'That's not my intention. I want to thank you for all the hard work you put in on this new vaccine. I know you haven't gotten much sleep lately.'

'Well, it's not every day you get to save the world.'

'You should get the Nobel Prize. Unfortunately, if everything goes according to plan, no one will know about your work.'

'Few geniuses are appreciated in their lifetime.'

'No one knows that better than me.' I pause. 'Charlie, you've never described to me the end result of the X6X6 virus in human beings. I know it's fatal but exactly how does it kill?'

'The virus causes a multitude of preliminary symptoms. The blisters are followed by dizziness and general weakness. But the virus was designed to destroy the central nervous system. It migrates to the spinal cord and the brain stem, where it causes severe haemorrhaging,'

I think of the Hydra myth. 'It sounds as if it causes people's heads to explode.'

'Internally, yes. It's not a pleasant way to go.'

'How long does the virus take to kill?'

'Between six and twelve hours.'

'Then get to work. Make sure it's stopped.'

When Charlie is gone, I call Matt, who happens to be with Seymour. They're both playing CII – Cosmic Intuitive Intuition. Or rather they say they're studying it, and that they've discovered some strange quirks. For one thing, Seymour says it's making him feel odd.

'Why didn't it make you feel odd before?' I ask.

'I never played it for any length of time,' he says. 'But now, I don't know, I feel depressed.'

'How do you feel, Matt?' I ask.

'Fine so far. But we've discovered that when it comes to this game, what you see and hear isn't what you get. Listen closely to this battle scene. Watch the screen on your cell. Tell me what you see *and* hear.'

He downloads a segment of the game to my phone. At first glance it looks like a hundred other video battle scenes. The hero is armed with an assortment of weapons. He's trying to fight his way to a spaceship that waits at the edge of a desolate city. A variety of alien creatures fight to stop him. He shoots and kills dozens of them but some don't die so easily.

As I've mentioned, my hearing is my most acute sense and I notice something weird with the soundtrack. I hear voices, in the background, but the words are either greatly accelerated or extremely slowed down. Even with my ears, I can't tell what's being said. I tell Matt and Seymour about what I hear.

'I had the same difficulty,' Matt replies. 'That's why I recorded it on to my computer. There I could speed it up or slow it down. Let me play what's being said in the middle of the battle, at high speed.'

> 'ALL WHO GATHER TODAY
> ARE SERVANTS OF THE ONE
> WE CALL UPON THE POWERS THAT BE
> AS WIELDERS OF THE ANCIENT FLAME
> WE PRAY TO THE DARKNESS OF OLD
> WE ARE THY SERVANTS . . .'

Lark's invocation is recited in an endless loop, but someone else is talking. Matt switches from high speed to slow speed and the words get even more disturbing. They sound like a dirge written for a demon.

> 'POWER FLOWS FROM PAIN
> CONTROL IS ACHIEVED THROUGH FEAR
> INFLICT PAIN AND BECOME FREE
> INVOKE FEAR AND BECOME THE MASTER
> CONTROL BOTH AND MERGE INTO THE ONE.'

'It's called masking,' Seymour says. 'The principle is actually old. It's a subliminal feed. The people who invented masking say the conscious mind doesn't recognize it but the subconscious does. It was used in theatres in the fifties to try to get people to buy more popcorn.'

'At first we were surprised they'd use such a primitive

technique to try to influence people,' Matt says. 'But this game is designed to play with headphones. You can't play it without them because many of the clues are given in your right ear, while actual instructions are fed into the left ear. The game forces you to listen in stereo. That made me suspicious.'

'Why do they want you to listen in stereo?' I ask.

'So you can pick up the binaural beats,' Seymour says. 'The human ear can hear between twenty and twenty thousand hertz. But say you play three hundred hertz in the right ear and three hundred ten hertz in the left. If the sounds are carefully synchronized, they cancel each other out and all that's left is the difference between the two – ten hertz.'

'But you just said the human ear can't hear that low,' I say.

'True,' Matt says. 'But the brain recognizes the sound and at some level absorbs what's being said. Furthermore, it's well known that binaural beats cause the waves in the two hemispheres of the brain to synchronize.'

'All this is going on while excerpts from the Satanic Bible are being read to the teen population?' I ask.

'It's no joke,' Seymour says. 'By placing the binaural beats in the background, anyone playing the game eventually ends up hypnotized and open to suggestion. It's no wonder the game put me in a weird state.'

'That's only half of it,' Matt says. 'There are images being fed to the players that are also masked. The themes are disturbing. The main image, that's played again and again, shows one person torturing another.'

'How is a human eye able to see this?' I ask.

'It sees it without the brain consciously remembering it,' Seymour says. 'The images are flashed for less than a hundredth of a second. There may be as many as a thousand grotesque images in any one minute.'

'The game is a sophisticated form of brainwashing,' Matt says. 'On top of everything else, the binaural beats stimulate the pleasure centres of the neocortex. Seymour may have felt odd afterwards, but while he was playing it he loved it.'

'You seemed to enjoy yourself, too,' Seymour says defensively.

'Brutran tells me the Cradle updates this game every day,' I say.

'Maybe they're trying to brainwash every teen in the world,' Seymour says. 'But the fact they keep changing it might mean they're experimenting with the technology.'

'I wonder why John keeps playing it,' Matt muses.

'He told me he does it to let them know he's around,' I say.

'Does that mean John's taunting them?' Seymour asks.

'Let's hope it's not brainwashing him,' Matt says.

'John can take care of himself,' I say. 'I'm more worried about another program Brutran told me about. The Cradle's somehow integrating it into the Internet. Her best hackers can't break into it. But the kids devote a lot of time to it. Until I came along and promised to help kill the Telar, it was their main focus.'

'You said it's an Internet program,' Matt says. 'Has it been activated yet?'

'Yes and no,' I say. 'Brutran's people have noticed that it can slip in and out of other companies' systems. But as far as she knows, it hasn't done any damage.'

'The program might be spying on other companies,' Matt says.

'I thought of that,' I say. 'Or on individuals.'

'Find out where it's located online,' Matt says. 'I'll look at it.'

'Will do,' I say.

'Now that we have the vaccine,' Seymour says. 'I wonder if we're going about this backwards. Maybe we should have the Telar take out the IIC first.'

'No,' I say. 'Haru will just invent another way to wipe out humanity. The Source has to go.'

Matt is concerned. 'You don't sound so good. Do you need help?'

'That's one of the reasons I called. How long would it take for you and your mother to get here?'

'We can charter a plane or helicopter and be there in two hours.'

I hesitate. 'Come in four hours, no earlier.'

'Why the delay?'

'I have my reasons.' I want to complete the next attack on the Telar before I bring Umara into the Cradle. She's my ace in the hole. I suspect I can only use her once. I add, 'May I speak to your mother?'

'I'll get her,' Matt says.

'Wait,' Seymour protests. 'What about me and Shanti?'

'Things are going to heat up here pretty fast. You'll be safer where you are.'

'To hell with that! You know Shanti gives you natural protection from the Cradle. You need her and she wants to come. And you need me because, well, I'm the smartest one in the group.'

I have to smile. 'Let me speak to Umara. I'll think about it.'

Umara comes on the line a minute later. I ask if she is alone. She says she is getting there. Finally she's ready to talk.

'What's wrong?' she asks.

'This is harder than I imagined it would be. I'm not in control, I think the Familiars are. I worry that they're playing me.'

'They use whoever comes in contact with them, that's their nature. It's time I helped protect you from them.'

'You've kept out of sight for ages. I hate exposing you like this.'

'I know you. You're proud. You wouldn't have called for help unless it was absolutely necessary.'

'It's hard for me to admit I need help.' I pause. 'One more thing. I've asked Matt to come. For reasons of security, I'm going to need his speed and strength.'

'And?'

'I'm going to ask him to perform a task only he can.'

'Then we'll come together.'

'What about Shanti?'

Umara sounds uncertain. 'She's young to take to such a dangerous place. But you know her better than I do. You took her with you to Arosa when you faced the Telar.'

'She has a natural ability to block the Cradle.'

'How?'

'I'm not sure. I just know she rescued me in London when I was in bad shape.'

Umara considers. 'I'd bring her then. But that means Seymour will insist on coming.'

'He already has.'

'What about Paula and John?'

'No. I don't want John near these people.'

'From what I've seen, he has more power than all of us put together.'

'His mother won't let him come. She doesn't trust me. She says people have a habit of dying around me. And she's right.'

Umara hesitates. 'We'll see you soon, Sita.'

'In four hours,' I repeat. 'No sooner.'

20 ~~~

I sit in the circular room with the Lens.

The more I get used to it, the more I hate it.

We have already called on the dark gods to help. In our hands we hold the blood of four highly placed Telar that Umara has said often work together in the United States. On a hunch, I have placed all of their blood samples together in the same vials. I feel they will be together. Word will have reached them from Switzerland. I'm sure the Telar are on red alert.

We are not long in our trance when I see the four in my head. My intuition is proving to be accurate. The four Telar, two men and two women, are together in the same suite. My internal vision of the room is so clear it is like I'm standing in the corner. I scan for clues of where they might be and see the name of a hotel on the phone. The Century Plaza in Century City.

The Telar are only twenty miles away from where I am!

The four sit on the floor of the suite, holding hands like we do. They have sensed our approach and have immediately gathered to form a Link. The mental fusion surrounds them like a fiery bubble and I see the faint images of the Familiars that support them.

These creatures don't resemble the ones that stand behind the kids. They are taller, more humanoid than the Cradle's, and they have broad wings and fearsome faces, from which radiates a haunting red glow. If I didn't know better, I'd say they looked like fallen angels. Whatever, their power is ancient and strong and I know we're in for a difficult fight.

Mentally, I warn Lark not to attack without my OK.

He ignores me and launches an angry mental bolt towards the bubble. I have to admit it's powerful. It contains not only the energy of the Cradle and the Lens, it has the strength of every member of the Array behind it. Brutran has brought in all her troops to help with the attack, although the scattered kids in the Array are not aware of what we are fighting.

The bolt strikes like a laser and it seems for several seconds the protective shield of the Telar will fail and we can ravage their minds. During this time I get a useful glimpse of their security.

But then the bubble hardens and our laser fizzles. Not only that, as if in response to our attack, a globe of what could be burning silver forms above the Telar's shield and launches itself in our direction. How it knows where to find us, I'm not sure. However, the Telar were able to obtain my blood while they held me captive in Arosa, and it's very possible I'm the homing beacon they are using to lock on to.

The globe strikes us like a psychic torpedo. Half the kids below let out a scream and the ones beside me all groan in pain. We're not dealing with the top level of the Source and already we're in trouble. Again, I send Lark an order to back off, to let me have complete control. It hurts to send him the message. The back of my skull throbs. It feels like someone hit me with a baseball bat that had a stick of dynamite attached.

I give the kids time to settle back down. I notice that the Telar are not in a hurry to hit us with another torpedo. I suspect the attack took a lot out of them, too. According to Umara, they're not accustomed to using the Link to harm others. Indeed, it was only with the appearance of the IIC and the Array that they began to revive the Link. For eons, the Telar believed they were invulnerable.

Staying deep in a trance state, I'm still able to open an audio line to the kids below us. I speak in a soft voice, it's all I can manage.

'This is Alisa, I'm taking command of the Cradle. There's no need to fear. These four Telar are strong but moments ago I got a clear picture of who's protecting them. Their guards are other Telar who have no form of psychic protection. They have guns and are stationed outside the door of those we're attacking. One of these guards is the granddaughter of one of the top four. That means we can lock on to her mind using the blood we're already holding. Give me a minute and I'll pinpoint this individual. Then we'll attack.'

It takes me only a few moments to regain my concentrated state and shift my focus from the corner of the suite into the hotel hallway. A dozen guards lounge on a row of chairs. It's obvious the Telar have rented the entire floor to ensure their protection.

I was being completely honest with the Cradle. I feel the blood we hold resonating with one of the female guards. She happens to be a slightly built woman who looks no more than twenty. She's probably like Charlie, one of the younger Telar. She looks more worried than her partners. But her fear isn't a bad thing, not from our perspective. Her fear can open the door wide for the Cradle to step inside.

Once again, I whisper to the entire Cradle.

'This is the plan. We want the woman at the end of the line to walk to the door where the principals are gathered. She's to knock and if no one answers, or if another guard tries to stop her, she's to start shooting. It doesn't matter if she gets through the door and kills the four. She'll disrupt their Link.'

For the first time, I feel the full power of the Cradle pour through me. I realize they trust me more than they do Lark. They know he disobeyed me, and they know his rash attack led to the slap we took. Now they're anxious to put an end to these Telar.

The woman, her name is Darla, feels a sudden

urge to walk down the hall and knock on the door of her superiors. She's been told they're not to be disturbed for any reason but at the moment she doesn't care. The other guards pay her little heed. Half of them are dozing.

Darla knocks on the door. Hard.

Her commanding officer jumps to his feet.

'Darla! Get away from there!'

Darla lowers the tip of her M16 and opens fire. Her CO wears a protective vest but Darla shoots him in the face so it doesn't do him much good. She rakes the line of guards, back and forth, and exhausts the clip in her weapon. Half the guards are dead, the others are wounded. While they try to gather themselves, I order Darla to toss a couple of grenades their way. She is young but she's fast. The grenades are flash-bangers. They send out a deadly shock wave, not shrapnel. Darla hits the floor as they explode.

The rest of the guards die, at least all the ones in sight. But I hear running feet, more are on their way. I order Darla to stand and the entire Cradle pushes her back to her feet. Pulling out a fresh clip, she reloads her M16 and fires point-blank at the door's deadbolt. The wood splinters and the door bursts open.

The fearsome four have broken their Link. They stand with their handguns drawn and shoot Darla the instant the door opens. It's strange to be in Darla's mind one instant and have it go blank an instant later. At the same time, I don't care. The laser mind of the Cradle is on the move and I'm guiding it.

I steer the kids into the mind of one of the ancient women and force her to turn her gun on the others. They shoot her in the head before she can pull the trigger. Inside of me, another TV screen suddenly goes blank. Very well, I focus the Cradle on a bald man with a huge head. His name is Kram and he's extremely old. His order is the same – to shoot his partners.

Yet he resists, for an instant, and manages to shout out a word.

'Tarana!'

The name has a strange effect on our group.

Our psychic laser suddenly flickers on and off.

Tarana? Isn't that the name of the creature Brutran spoke about? The one that taught her a bunch of secret knowledge? I didn't know it worked for the Telar as well.

Actually, for several confused seconds, I have no idea what's gone wrong. My vision of the hotel suite phases in and out, and I feel a horrible ripping sensation at the base of my skull. Before I know it, I'm on my feet with my eyes wide open, the rest of the kids staring at me.

We broke the Telar's Link . . .

Yet somehow they managed to break us.

It was that damn word, 'Tarana.' It has its own power.

I notice many of the kids have nosebleeds.

'Listen!' I shout. 'The Telar aren't far from here. I'm going after them with some of Cynthia Brutran's men. While I'm gone, you'll help keep track of their movements. Don't try to psychically attack them unless I order it. Just stay alert and follow them. They won't escape.'

I disconnect the line and kneel beside Lark. His nosebleed is bad, perhaps because he tried to lead the attack on the Telar's Link. Blood soaks his expensive shirt and he's lost his cocky grin. He's as pale as a ghost, this eighteen-year-old punk who is accustomed to commanding evil spirits.

'Lark,' I say. 'We need to stay in touch with each other. Can you talk and still stay connected to the Cradle?'

He nods weakly. 'I can help you track them.'

'Good. No more heroics. Don't try to take them down.'

The guy's been humbled. 'I hear you, Sita.'

I pat him on the back and turn towards the door. Jolie stops me by grabbing my pant leg. 'Don't go,' she pleads.

I crouch beside her. 'It's better I kill them with my hands than waste our mental powers trying to take them down.'

'Are there many more?'

'After this, we have only one more group to kill.'

Jolie nods to herself. 'I want them to die.'

Upstairs, I alert Cynthia and Thomas Brutran to the situation. I portray the Telar's close proximity as a major break, which I believe it is. They say they can scramble three helicopters in ten minutes.

'Make it five,' I say. 'And I want Charlie to give each of the men who are coming with me a shot of the vaccine.'

'I'll take care of that,' Tom says, and rushes off. His wife studies me critically.

'I watched your last session on remote,' she says. 'It looks like half the Cradle is about to stroke out.'

'That's not my fault. Lark disobeyed me.'

'Lark's not the one who worries me. It's the next round, when we go after Haru and his people. He won't make the mistake these ones did. If he sets up a powerful Link, I don't know how you're going to punch through it.'

'Leave that to me. I have a secret weapon.'

'I don't like secrets. Tell me.'

'Gimme a break, you live for secrets. Now get out of my way, I have work to do.'

Brutran tries to stop me. 'Wait. I'm going with you.'

'That's insane. These are Telar. Just one of them attacked my house in Missouri and I was lucky to escape alive.'

'I'll take precautions but I'm going. I'm still the head of this firm.'

I shake my head. 'It's your life.'

Ten minutes later we're airborne over Santa Monica with Century City only five miles in front of us. The latter is loaded with crowded but elegant skyscrapers. Its real estate is some of the most expensive on the planet. The Century Plaza Hotel stands a block away from the Fox building.

However, an intelligence update, from Lark and Brutran, tells us that our three prime Telar have already left the hotel and are heading towards one of the town's original twin towers that were built back in the seventies. They are only forty-four storeys tall, pale shadows of the World Trade Center towers that were lost on 9/11, and yet the other skyscrapers have quietly built up around them, almost as if they were the founding parents.

What's unique about the two towers is their flat roofs. Helicopters can land and take off from them. The Telar must have sensed me behind the Cradle. Otherwise, they wouldn't be so anxious to get out of town.

It's dark, after midnight, and the city lights are bright.

I sit up front with the pilot, with headphones on and six heavily armed men at my back. I'm in touch with Cindy and Lark via a cell plugged into my right ear. The boy sounds weak, his voice is faint. He's following the Telar with his mind's eye. Cindy's in the helicopter off to my right.

'I wouldn't get any closer than a mile,' I warn her. 'If the Telar have a sharpshooter like the guy who visited me in Missouri, then we'll be lucky to make it to the towers.'

'These copters are bulletproof,' Cindy says.

'The Telar have lasers.'

'We know. We have samples of them. They can't take down these copters.'

'They have disruptors,' I add.

'What are those?'

'I don't know. But they hit us with them in Colorado and I can assure you they are nasty weapons.'

The helicopter on my left suddenly lights up. A dozen lasers have focused on it. The pilot swears as if blinded but luckily he doesn't bump into us. The black paint on the exterior of the copter begins to peel. The vehicle looks as if it's caught in its own private ray of sunshine. It glows in the night sky like Santa's sleigh. If I were aboard, I'd be reaching for a parachute.

'Bravo One, this is Bravo Three. Our hull temperature is over four hundred degrees. Our fuel tank is rapidly heating. We might be forced to retreat. Over.'

'Bravo Three, this is Brutran. Under no circumstances are you to retreat. Over.'

'Cindy,' I say. 'Let them go. Gasoline can only get so hot before it explodes. It doesn't matter how fancy your shields are. Bravo Three can always return later.'

Brutran appears to consider my request, although I know she hates for me to question her orders in front of her people.

'Bravo Three,' she says. 'You have my—'

The helicopter on our left explodes.

The shock wave is deafening, the fireball blinding. Our main rotor, tail rotor, and tail fin are pounded with debris. Swearing, our pilot fights to keep us aloft. But as he pulls up on the controls I caution him to keep low.

'Stay down until we're ready to land on top of the building. Weave around the trees if you must. But keep those lasers off us.'

'Gotcha,' the pilot says, and I can tell he wishes I was in charge instead of Brutran.

'Bravo Two, this is Bravo One, what's your status?' Brutran asks.

I speak up. 'We're keeping our heads down, Bravo One. Suggest you do likewise if you don't want to join the Telar's next target-practice session.'

Brutran doesn't answer but her helicopter suddenly veers low and away. They are no longer heading for the building. Brutran's life can't be that much of a nightmare. She sure as hell doesn't want to die.

Lark informs us that the three Telar we are pursuing have entered one of the towers. He sounds confused and is unable to specify whether it's the north or south tower. Brutran calls to people she has assembling on the ground for an update. This is one advantage in having the IIC as an ally, even if it is temporary. They have lots of people you can call for help.

From studying the buildings when we were high up, I noticed there were more men and machines on the roof of the north tower. Yet there was a single helicopter on top of the south tower, and the buildings do connect underground. I wonder if it's a trick . . .

Brutran interrupts my thoughts.

'Bravo Two, the Telar have entered the north tower. Over.'

'Bravo One, copy that. Telar are in north tower,' I say.

From everything I've seen of the Telar, I know their technology is far superior to anything mankind has, and that includes the IIC. There's an excellent chance the Telar are listening to us now, and are going to try to take off from the south tower. I share my thoughts with our pilot. He frowns.

'They're running scared. Do you think they've had enough time to come up with such a clever plan?'

'I've learned never to underestimate them,' I say.

'But if your guess is wrong . . .'

'If it's wrong, I'll know soon enough and you can come back for me. Which brings me to another point. I don't want you to land on the south tower. You'll come under heavy fire from the other tower. Just fly over and I'll jump out.'

He looks at me like I'm crazy. 'We'll be moving too fast. I'll at least have to stop and hover.'

I don't have time to get in an argument. I touch his arm and let the power enter my voice. 'I appreciate your concern but I'll be fine. Just give me a rifle, plenty of ammo, a dozen grenades, and I'll be on my way.'

The pilot instructs his men to fill my order and pretty soon I'm jamming my pockets with everything I can carry. The pilot is skillful, he swoops low around the Fox building before suddenly crossing the street and climbing.

We're almost to the south tower when the lasers hit. They dance over our hull and pierce our armoured glass. The internal temperature jumps twenty degrees. The lasers make my eyes ache and virtually blind the pilot. I briefly grab his controls.

'I'm steering us, don't worry!' I shout. 'I'll turn our back on them just before I leap out. When you hear my door slam shut, you have to take back the helm.'

'It's getting hot in here,' he says, sweating, afraid.

'Their lasers have a limited range. Duck below the south tower as I leave and use it as a shield. Trust me, you'll be all right.'

The leap out of the helicopter reminds me of the last time I jumped from a helicopter to escape the Telar. Then I had Shanti in my hands, and Seymour was with Teri. It was that night, high in the Rockies, on top of a half-frozen lake, that Teri hit an ice patch in the water and shattered her leg. In that instant her death became inevitable, although I refused to accept that fact for a long time.

Now I leap alone, into a red corona of laser fire, and land rolling on top of the south tower. I watch with relief as my copter makes a quick dip, after passing the building, and escapes the Telar's bombardment.

I'm not given a chance to relax. The lasers converge in my direction and I run as fast as I can to the edge of the building and duck down behind a two-foot-high concrete lip. The north tower is a hundred yards away, its roof crowded with three copters and a dozen armed men and women.

They don't immediately open fire and that helps confirm my guess. The soldiers are worried about hitting the parked helicopter behind me. It's the one that counts because it's the one the three members of the Source are hurrying towards.

However, even if the three high-ranking Telar are presently in my building, they can always switch to the north tower. To discourage such a move, I rush towards the corner of the building and prepare to open fire on the north-tower roof. But since I'm no longer in the line of sight with their precious helicopter, they immediately start shooting at me, effectively pinning me down.

They switch from lasers to conventional weapons. It might be that the lasers don't work against concrete or else the Telar are skittish about melting the side of a well-known building. In either case a barrage of machine-gun fire erupts less than a foot above my head.

The bullets are of the armour-piercing variety. They begin to chew away my protective concrete, powdering the air with white dust, and I see I have only a few seconds before I will be exposed. Rolling vigorously to my right, I stand, take aim, and kill half a dozen people on top of the other tower. They drop suddenly, and the sound of silence, as their machine guns die, is just as abrupt. I use the time and the shock to blow out anything that looks like a radio. Then I run to the single waiting helicopter.

I disable it carefully by unplugging a chip attached to its ignition system. Who knows, I might need the helicopter later. I can always replace the chip. I work out of sight of the remaining Telar on the north tower. They're still trying to recover from my devastating attack. Fortunately, I don't see any of them on the radio or even a phone. I can only hope I've taken out their communication equipment.

I have lost the plug to my cell. It must have fallen out at some point.

Finally, I enter the building, taking a short stairway that leads down from the heliport. It doesn't take long for me to find a set of elevators. Neither appears to be in use, but I can tell at a glance they're too small to support the bulk of the building's traffic.

Sitting down in a windowless hallway and closing my eyes, I let my hearing expand downwards, floor by floor. I'm not just listening for people, I'm trying to detect a specific heart signature. The Telar have a powerful pulse; it separates them from normal people.

Ten floors below me, I hear a dozen people cleaning – vacuuming, sweeping, washing the toilets – while another two type on their computers. Letting my hearing drop further, I pick up fifteen more. Five are painting and plastering, two are typing while listening to music, six are arguing about future sales, and two are having extremely loud sex.

I drop lower. There are so many floors, it's a strain for even my ears to hear what's happening below the twentieth level. But I'm lucky because I become aware of three people in the stairway, climbing upwards, and I only hear them because sounds echo in that vast hollow chamber.

They climb at a steady jog, taking no breaks, but don't breathe as hard as they should for such strenuous exercise. Also, their pulses don't exceed a hundred and twenty beats a minute. These facts alone convince me they're Telar, but are they the three I'm looking for? That is the question.

I don't want to spend the whole night killing foot

soldiers. I have to get back to the IIC's headquarters to greet Umara and the others. Then I have to kill the top members of the Source, although according to Umara these three are crucial to its operation. I've already witnessed their amazing ability to link. It worries me how four of them were able to bloody so many of the kids. If Umara can't boost our power substantially, we're not going to win this fight.

The three Telar continue up the stairway. The more I listen, the more confident I become that they're the ones I'm looking for. They are sticking close together, like people would who have known each other a long time and are used to turning to one another in times of crisis. Also, there are two men and one woman in their group, just like at the hotel.

Standing, I push the button on the elevator and call it to the top floor. This is a calculated risk. It will probably warn the Telar where I am. At the same time, I might need the elevator if I'm to trap them in this building.

I listen closely as the cubicle rises. The system is old, it takes its time. The three Telar also appear to stop and listen. I want the elevator on my floor but I don't want to use it just yet. Fortunately, there's a garbage can in a nearby restroom, and when the elevator does finally reach my floor, I'm able to jam it in the doorway and secure the elevator in place.

The Telar don't seem to understand what I've done. Their desire to reach the helicopter might be overshadowing their reasoning. They continue their upward march.

I go in search of the stairwell. There are two, I discover, but only one is occupied. I know the Telar are still twenty-five floors beneath me. Yet I open the door as quietly as possible. I do a pretty good job until the lower hinge screeches. At that instant I hear the three stop jogging and go still. I have no choice. Moving forward, softly closing the door, I tiptoe to the edge of the stairwell and peek over. It's a long way down.

I can't see them but I can hear them. Breathing. Listening.

I have an opportunity here. I have grenades. The guys in the copter told me they have a standard five-second delay after the pin is pulled. I estimate it will take seven seconds for a grenade to reach my enemies if I simply let it go. Of course it will drop faster if I put some muscle behind it. But too hard a throw might cause the grenade to fall too quickly.

I calculate as best I can how much extra speed I need to add to my grenade. It is really no more than an educated guess. Pulling the pin, I step to the handrail and throw the grenade straight down.

I listen as it falls and note that those below me also seem to be listening. No one rushes for the door, at least not at first. But then there's a sudden shuffling of feet and I realize they've figured out what I'm up to. Far below I hear a door open, followed almost instantly by a loud explosion.

The grenade I dropped was different from the kind Darla used to kill the guards. This one throws off a brutal sphere of hot shrapnel. I'm not surprised when I hear a guy scream as his body is raked by pieces of metal. An unmistakable thud follows and I know he has fallen. But he's alone, I hear the other two running for their lives.

They appear to be heading for the main elevators. I race back to the elevator I have waiting for me and push the button that will take me to the lobby.

The slow ride down is maddening. If I can reach the bottom ahead of them, they'll have to go through me to escape.

At the same time, they could try for the roof. They might figure, even if I've sabotaged the helicopter, they have people on a tower just a hundred yards away. If they can signal them, they might get picked up before I can arrive and kill them.

Right now, anything is possible.

My elevator finally lands. I rush out into the main lobby and find two Telar guards waiting by the front door. I shoot them in the head before they know I'm there. I might have just chased them away but they had already shot the human watchman.

Studying the lights on the main elevator board and listening, I estimate my two remaining adversaries have stopped ten floors above me. I have already called for another elevator and have one waiting for me. I suspect the Telar heard me kill the guards and are thinking the roof is now a better bet.

Are the two remaining Source members in touch with their people in the other building? If they are, they will stand a better chance of escaping if their helicopter pilots on the north tower are waiting to lift them off our roof.

The Telar on the tenth floor finally reenter their elevator and head upwards. I watch them climb, for a second, before leaping into my own elevator and hitting the top button. Now I'm in the elevator shaft next to theirs. I can hear them talking to each other, a man and a woman, as they rise above me. That's how I know they haven't tricked me.

But as I pass the tenth floor, I hear something. Breathing, powerful heartbeats – I'm not sure. It makes me wonder why the couple above me is talking at all. They must know about my hearing. They should be silent.

Then I get it. These Telar are not just old, they're smart.

The voices I hear in the elevator above me, it's one cell phone talking to another. But they're not ordinary cell phones. Those wouldn't have fooled me for an instant with their poor sound. No, these are Telar cells, like the kind Matt gave me, their sound quality is perfect.

The two Telar never did leave the tenth floor.

I have been tricked.

I struggle to stop my elevator but it goes up another two floors and I get off on the fourteenth. I run like hell to the stairway and am not surprised to hear them galloping down the stairs ahead of me. But before I can uncork another grenade, they exit the stairway at what I estimate to be the third floor. Hell, they could jump through an office window at that height and survive.

Then the truth finally hits home.

That's what they're going to do!

They have me above them and they know exactly where I am.

This is their best chance to get out of this building alive.

I listen as they run to the far side of the tower, away from the stairwells and elevators. I hear them kick in a door. Damn, I totally underestimated them, they're going to get away.

Unless . . . what?

Unless I get to the ground floor the same time they do.

I rush to the window at the end of the hall. Before I jump, I wait a few seconds for the sound of another window exploding. There it is! On the other side of the building! I hear their weight as they land. They're outside! I have at most five seconds before they reach the north tower.

Backing up a few steps, I prepare to rush the glass and fall fourteen miserable floors. I can survive such a fall, I've done it before. Not that it's comfortable. I mean, I'm a vampire not a goddamn bat. I can't fly.

Something makes me hesitate. It's the idea that they would expose themselves by running between the two buildings, which jumping out a window would force them to do. By dumb luck, due to the layout of the hallways on my floor, I'm unable to glimpse the ground on their side of the building. However, they don't know that, which makes me wonder why they would expose themselves where I could just pick them off with my rifle.

Yet I heard their window burst open.

I heard the weight of their bodies hitting the ground.

But what if it was the weight of something else I heard landing?

A desk for example. They could have shoved two desks out their window. Now that I think about it, I didn't hear any running footsteps after they hit the ground.

Then the truth hits me again. A new truth.

They are *still* on the tenth floor.

They *still* haven't left the building.

Their goal is to get *me* to leave the building.

Smart. Very smart. They almost had me.

Yet two can play their game.

Picking up a desk, I throw it through a nearby window.

To them, they just heard me jump outside and fall fourteen floors.

I just stand there, waiting for them to make a move.

I hear two people enter the tenth-floor elevator.

They push a button and head up.

I run up two floors, before I return to the secondary elevators and call the elevator that took me to the lobby a few minutes ago. When it arrives, I ride it to the top floor. Climbing the stairs that lead to the helipad, I see a Telar helicopter swooping in to make a quick pickup.

Taking aim, I shoot off the tail rotor and the tail fin.

Nasty, trying to steer a copter without either of them.

The copter spins out of control and vanishes over the side.

I approach the two big shots carefully. The bald man with the big head, Mr Kram, and his daughter, Alia. I know of their relationship from the attack we made on them at the hotel. They're armed with handguns but they don't reach for them. The woman's left arm is bleeding, probably from the grenade I dropped in their path. I gesture to the wound.

'How did you hear it coming?' I ask.

'I felt it coming. It was a good shot,' the man says.

'Thank you,' I say.

Alia stares at me with dread. 'We don't support Haru. We told him not to take you prisoner.'

She's speaking the truth. I return the favour.

'You're members of the Source. It was the Source that ordered the creation of X6X6.'

'We never thought it would be used,' Kram says. 'Even now, it hasn't been released.'

'Can you guarantee it won't be released?'

'No,' he says.

I gesture with my gun. 'Then what can I do?'

'Spare my daughter, Alia. She opposed the virus from the start. Haru hates her. She's only a member of the Source because of me.'

'And because she's a powerful psychic.'

'She's a healer at heart,' Kram says.

I study Alia. 'Is that true?'

She shrugs. 'I do what I can.'

I shake my head. 'I have to destroy the Source.'

'Alia will never go back to the Source,' Kram begs. 'Not after tonight.'

'What's so special about tonight?'

'I finally saw the spirits Haru has attached to us,' Alia says.

'You must have known about them,' I say.

'I did. Alia did not,' Kram says. 'Please. We've heard you can be . . . merciful.'

'I can't let both of you go,' I say. The truth is, I need one of them alive. 'You may live, Alia.'

The man is grateful. 'Thank you.' He turns to his daughter. 'Go, Alia. Please.'

Alia weeps as she falls in his arms. 'No, Papa. I can't.'

He gently cups his daughter's face. She has inherited many of his features but not his huge head. With dark lustrous eyes, a mane of black hair, she is truly beautiful. He wipes away her tears.

'It's for the best,' he says. 'The things I've done, I deserve this.'

'No.' She looks to me. 'Please, for the love of God.'

'Don't push me, Alia,' I say. 'As it is, I want something in return for your life. When we attacked your Link, I glimpsed your minds and saw you have extensive relationships with generals and admirals in NATO. Both of you know the people who command the most powerful missile systems on earth.'

'That's true,' Kram says.

'I also saw that Haru has retreated to a temple in Egypt with his inner circle. When the time is right, I'm going to mentally contact you, Alia, and ten minutes later I want a barrage of cruise missiles to strike that temple.'

'Impossible,' Kram says. 'The remaining members of the Source expect your attack. They'll be in the Link, and in such a state no physical weapon on earth can harm them. The demons they're aligned with would instantly know about the danger and would avert it.'

'I'm aware of that. When I mentally contact Alia – and my contact will be some time in the next six hours and it will be crystal clear – it will mean the Source's Link has been broken and they're open to attack.'

'I can't imagine how you'll break them,' Kram says.

'Let me worry about that. Now, are there any codes or numbers or names you need to pass on to Alia so she can keep her end of the bargain?'

'Yes,' Kram says. 'Let me tell her what to do.'

They have a brief whispered conversation in ancient Egyptian. I hear and remember every word. Kram gives his daughter three separate ways to blow up the temple. When he is done, she starts to beg again for his life. I shake my weapon in her face.

'Walk away, Alia,' I say.

Kram kisses her cheek. 'Go, darling. Go with love.'

Alia finally appears to accept that her father's life is over. She hugs him and walks past me towards the door that leads to the stairs and the top floor. I point the rifle at Kram.

'Any last words?' I ask.

'There's a rumour you met Krishna. Is it true?'

'Yes.'

'Was he who they say he was?'

'I don't know. I like to think so.'

'Was he wonderful?'

'More wonderful than you could dream.'

The man smiles and closes his eyes. 'It's a good dream to have right now. Thank you for my daughter's life.'

I raise the rifle to shoot. Just then I hear a click behind me.

The cocking of a hammer on a pistol. I whirl and fire.

The bullet catches Alia in the heart.

She falls to her knees. 'Papa,' she whispers.

He rushes to her side but she's already dead.

There's nothing I can do to ease his grief except shoot him.

I would if I didn't need his help.

'Now it's you I'll be contacting,' I tell him as I walk towards the helicopter. A moment later, I reattach the ignition chip and fly away.

21 ~⌐

When I return to IIC's headquarters, the gang is waiting in my room. Except for Paula and John, they have all come: Matt, Umara, Seymour and Shanti.

Brutran is with them but I ask her to leave. She stands but holds her ground. 'I need to know what happened to the three Source members at the Century Plaza Towers,' she demands.

'I chased them into the south tower and killed them.'

'Our people haven't recovered their bodies. The Telar still have a presence in the north tower.'

'It doesn't matter. The Telar we were after are dead.'

'A Telar helicopter landed on the roof of the south tower minutes after you left. What do you know about that?'

'It was probably looking for survivors.'

'Our people say you were talking to a man before you left.'

'I spoke to him before I killed him.'

'You should have returned with the bodies.'

'For confirmation? What physical confirmation do we have that the Marherrs in Geneva are dead?'

'The Cradle gave a unified report on the Marherrs. The Century City operation was carried out by you alone.'

'Because you wisely took my advice and fled the scene, Cindy.'

The woman doesn't like being called a coward. She gestures to my friends. 'Why are these people here?' she asks.

Brutran does her best to pretend she doesn't know who they are but it is clear to me that she has identified Seymour, Shanti and Matt.

What is also clear is that Brutran doesn't recognize Umara for who she really is, but sees her as Mary, Freddy's girlfriend. The disguise won't last. When Umara joins me in the next attack on the Telar, Brutran's going to want to know why. Also, Lark and Jolie and the other kids are going to sense Umara's power, unless the ancient Telar knows how to cloak herself. Umara does have the advantage of having spent thousands of years involved with mental links.

'To assist me,' I reply.

'In what capacity?' Brutran asks.

'Don't push me, Cindy, not now. Mentally attacking the Telar, and then chasing after them, has worn me out. It's enough that these people are my friends and can help. But I can tell you that Matt and Seymour will be assisting Charlie with the inoculations.'

Brutran doesn't give up. 'And these two?' she asks, pointing to Shanti and Umara.

'They're none of your business.'

'This is still my firm. You're not in charge, Alisa.'

'I'm in charge wherever I am. When I decide to leave, you'll have your firm back. If you still want it.' I stop and stare at her and I cannot tame the heat in my eyes. I pity her but not nearly as much as I hate her. I know she struggles with the best way to kill me should I succeed with destroying the Source.

Brutran ignores my last remark and tries her best to deflect the heat I pour her way. She points to Shanti. 'She damaged the effectiveness of our Array. She's not to get anywhere near the Cradle.'

'That's for me to decide,' I say.

'I've done my best to accommodate you, Alisa, but this isn't open to discussion. The kids will reject her disruptive influence.'

'Everything is open to discussion!' I snap. 'We hit four high members of the Source and they hit back and killed how many trillions of brain cells in the Cradle? Half the kids have nosebleeds, and that's just the beginning. We have to go after Haru and his closest allies next. And if Shanti can help us with that, then so much the better.'

'She can't,' Brutran says.

My patience is as exhausted as I am.

'Get out of here,' I say.

She goes to protest but thinks better of it and leaves. But not before giving Umara another glance. It's clear the woman doesn't fit into Brutran's equations.

I cross the room and lie on the bed and stare at the ceiling. I'm glad my friends have arrived and wish I had more energy to greet them properly. Fortunately, we have Seymour to put everything into perspective.

'It's great you two have formed such a tight bond,' he says.

I chuckle. 'Ding dong, the Wicked Witch is almost dead.'

Shanti sits beside me and squeezes my hand. 'You can't keep this up. Even you have your limits. You have to rest.'

'She can rest later,' Umara says, sitting in a corner chair. 'The next attack is the key. We have to risk everything. Haru will do the same. He'll try to gather as many of the Source as are left.' She pauses. 'Did you kill the four?'

'I let Kram go.'

'Why?'

'Because I'd just shot his daughter in the heart. And because I need physical weapons to rain down on Haru and his pals after we have removed their psychic weapons.'

Umara frowns. 'Kram's a dangerous man. He's close to Haru.'

'I honestly think he's sick of Haru.'

'Let's hope you're right,' Umara says.

Seymour sits on my other side and studies me. He tries

to keep his smile warm but I can tell he's worried. 'Your left eye doesn't look so good. It's bloodshot,' he says.

'I got that fighting the bad guys,' I say.

Unfortunately, Umara knows better. 'You've got blood on your hands,' she says.

'I need a shower,' I say.

'That kind of blood doesn't wash off,' Umara says.

Her remark takes me back to the Middle Ages, to the time of Landulf of Capua, the evil necromancer, and Dante the leper castrato, the two who were really one. In those days I killed an innocent woman, ripped out her heart, so I could get to Landulf. But it was all a trick and my hands ended up with red stains I was unable to wash off. Until I was able to see through Dante's lies.

'Lisa,' I whisper.

'What's the matter with Lisa?' Shanti asks nervously.

'She was killed. It was an accident,' Umara says quickly, trying to save me the burden of explaining.

Shanti's eyes burn with tears. 'But she stayed in Truman. I thought she would be safe.'

'No place is safe these days,' Matt says, rubbing Shanti's shoulders. I take her hand.

'I'm sorry,' I say.

'It wasn't your fault.' Shanti's devotion to me never wavers.

'People who get close to me have a bad habit of dying young. Lisa was just another example. But at least I can protect you. I agree with Brutran. I don't think you should get near the Cradle.'

'But you need me to shield you from it.'

'That's the problem. I'm a part of it now. You would just get in my way.'

'I don't understand,' Shanti says.

'I don't either,' Umara says. 'Your decision isn't logical. You've explained how Shanti sheltered you from the negative effects of the Cradle. We might not understand how she does it, but if it works, we should have her present.'

'It's too dangerous,' I say.

'I'm not a child, I can make my own decisions,' Shanti says. 'If I can help, I need to help. I know you would do the same for me.'

I smile at the innocence of her love. 'But we're using demons to kill demons. How can we be sure an angel will be welcome in the room?'

'Put her in a nearby room,' Umara says. 'But keep her close.'

Love and logic are a hard combination to argue against.

'We'll see. I still want to think about it,' I say.

'While you're at it, give me something to do,' Seymour says.

'I have the perfect job for you. You're going to give the kids their vaccine shots.'

Seymour grimaces. 'I hate needles.'

I sit up. 'So do kids. Even these ones. You're the perfect one to take care of them. Find Brutran and ask her to help organize the children into a line outside the clinic. Matt will give you enough preloaded syringes to inject them. Work fast, we're going to start our next

339

session as soon as they're ready.' I pause. 'Now, Shanti, Seymour, I need to talk to Matt and his mother alone. Could you please excuse us?'

Shanti and Seymour leave reluctantly. Seymour in particular doesn't like being kept in the dark. From my position on the bed, I gesture to a box in the corner.

'Matt. That's the box I want you to give Seymour. Make sure he uses those needles and doesn't bum any off of Charlie. This is important.'

Matt goes over and picks up the box. He doesn't ask.

Umara taps on the super-hard plastic that acts as my window.

'It would take a tank shell to penetrate this,' she mutters.

I glance at her son. 'Did you happen to bring any Telar grenades with you?' I ask.

Matt nods. 'We have a few boxes in the trunk.'

'You plan ahead,' I say.

'What do you want to talk about that's so private?' he asks.

'We have a problem. Umara, I suspected it might be an issue when you gave me the vials of blood. But after the Cradle's last attack on the Source, I'm even more concerned.'

'What is it?' Matt asks. His mother has already filled him in on how we're going after the Source. I'm not surprised when she speaks up.

'It's Haru's blood,' Umara says.

Matt's puzzled. 'It's not authentic?'

'It's perfectly authentic,' Umara says.

'Therein lies the problem,' I say. 'In this last session, the Cradle had trouble penetrating the Source's Link. Then I noticed some of the blood we held was resonating with a guard outside their door. It was because she was the grandchild of one of the four. Of course her blood was not identical but it was close enough. We were able to invade her mind and force her to kill the other guards and blow open the door. She was only able to kill one of the four before they killed her but that's neither here nor there. The point remains that the grandfather's blood allowed us to home in on both of them.'

Matt nods. 'The blood bond between close relatives.'

'Haru is Umara's son,' I say. 'Matt, he's your brother. When the Cradle focuses everything we've got on him, you two are going to feel it. It could kill both of you.'

The room is silent a long time. Matt looks stunned.

'He's my brother?' he whispers, turning to his mother. 'Why did you hide it from me?'

Umara meets his pained gaze. 'You hated him so much.'

Matt shakes his head. 'You hate him as well.'

'I do. But I love him too.'

'Enough to protect him?' Matt asks.

'No. Never,' Umara replies.

Matt nods slowly, turns back to me. 'What's the risk here?'

'I don't think you're a major risk,' I say to Matt. 'Your father was Yaksha, the most powerful vampire who ever lived. Vampire DNA is much more complex than human DNA. When you rescued me in Arosa, I told you that you were your father's son and you thought I was flattering you. But I was telling you the truth. You're more vampire than Telar.'

He looks to Umara. 'Is that true, Mother?'

She turns to us. 'Yes.'

I can see she wants me to stop talking but I feel an obligation to continue. 'But like Haru, Umara, you're a hundred per cent Telar. The attack on him is going to resonate with every blood cell in your body.'

'It's like Matt says. It's a risk we have to take.'

'Not necessarily,' I say. 'We'll have the blood of the other Source members. If we can pierce their Link, we can get them to turn on Haru. We might not have to use his blood at all.'

'Too risky,' Umara says. 'You might kill everyone in the Source except Haru. He still commands the Telar. If he sees he's cornered, he'll definitely release the virus. I know him.'

'I'm sure you know him better than anyone. But you can't predict how the battle will go. Chances are, if we do manage to break their Link, we'll quickly focus on the weakest member of the group and try to force them to attack the others. We can have this person concentrate on killing Haru. Again, we can do this without bringing Haru's blood into the mix.'

'That sounds reasonable,' Matt says.

'I want to try it this way,' I say.

'You say that as if you're going to get a second chance,' Umara says. 'You're not. You have to attack what's left of the Source, using the blood of all its surviving members, otherwise it won't work.'

'Why not?' I ask.

'Words don't exist to describe how a psychic Link forms. But from experience I know if you don't attack from all sides, you'll fail.' She stops and stares at me, her eyes sad. 'You need to trust me, Sita.'

Her desire for my trust is sincere. Yet she is lying about the need to attack the Link from all sides. I hear the lie plainly, although it seems Matt believes his mother. At the same time he appears grateful to me.

'Thank you for explaining the dangers ahead of time,' he says.

'It was the least I could do.' I don't add, *after what I did to Teri.*

Matt continues to think. 'I might be able to help break the Source.'

'You have no experience with Links,' Umara says. 'Leave this to Sita and me. It will work out, I'm confident.'

Another odd remark from Umara. My confidence level is low. We couldn't pierce a four-person Link without outside help. How are we going to take down the last of Haru's people?

Umara knows something she's not saying.

'I need you to take charge of security,' I say to Matt. 'We have no idea what Brutran and her buddies will do if we fail.'

'Or succeed,' Umara adds.

'Do we want anyone leaving this building?' Matt says.

'A lot of good people work here,' I say.

'You didn't answer my question.'

He's right. I don't want to answer it.

22

I decide to introduce Umara honestly to the Cradle, even though I know Brutran and her people will eventually hear about it. I can only imagine the Wicked Witch's shock when she hears that the insignificant chick Freddy's been hanging out with is actually the oldest person on the planet.

In reality, I have no choice but to be honest with the Cradle. The moment we link, they will know there's something unusual about Umara. Also, the way I introduce her is designed to give the kids confidence.

'Umara has fought the Telar for thousands of years. She's the one who supplied us with the blood we're using to lock on to their oldest members. She's had centuries of experience with Links. We're going to need that experience this time around. More important she's the strongest natural psychic on earth. In a single stroke, she'll double our power.'

For the most part, the kids, on both floors, mutter their approval. But Lark has to stand and take the floor. He has changed his clothes and wiped away his blood but he's still looking shaky.

'Everything Alisa says sounds impressive. But she fails to mention several important points. Umara isn't a member of the Cradle. She hasn't been initiated. She hasn't made a sacrifice to the powers who stand behind us. Even you, Alisa, didn't try to avoid these requirements. Surely Umara can't be treated any differently.'

Before I can answer, Umara stands and speaks in a strong voice. 'I'm ready to abide by your initiation requirements. Let's begin and I'll offer you a sacrifice none of you will forget.'

The lights are dimmed, the candle is lit, the prayers are intoned. The power in the room is immense and we have hardly begun. With Umara on my left instead of Lark, and Shanti sitting out of sight in the room directly above, I feel almost no head pressure. Nevertheless, the room begins to spin as the etheric tornado enters and I feel the usual separation from my body. I am still a little dizzy when Lark stops and demands that Umara provide a blood sample of the person she intends to offer to the Familiars.

I have to struggle to open my eyes.

'How innocent does my victim have to be?' Umara asks.

345

Lark snickers. 'Not as innocent as Alisa's victim.'

Umara plays dumb. 'Excuse me, what does that mean?'

'No one is truly innocent,' Lark says impatiently. 'Give the person's blood to Jolie and let's continue.'

'As you wish.' Suddenly twisting her left hand counterclockwise, Umara snaps Lark's wrist so violently that his bone pierces his skin. With her other hand, she makes a fist and strikes him on top of the head, stunning him, probably with the intention of keeping him in place. Reaching past me to Jolie, she gives the girl a healthy sample of Lark's blood. The little girl licks it off Umara's hand and holds it in her mouth. Umara looks to me as if to say, *You better take over.*

I'm still reeling from the brilliance of Umara's choice.

Although Lark believed that he led the Cradle, it was obvious he was a cocky bastard with no friends. Furthermore, his refusal to obey my simple instruction during our last attack led to the most painful blow the Cradle had ever suffered. As the children settle down and prepare for the final battle, I don't sense a single thread of regret or sympathy in either room.

'Now let's close our eyes and join hands,' I say.

I repeat the original invocation and then concentrate on the three key phrases. 'Enter us now and forever so that we may do thy will. We invoke the power that destroys. For we are one with thy power.'

Soon I'm repeating them in my mind.

Yet I manage to say aloud one last line.

'We invoke the power that destroys against Lark.'

The pressure at the back of my skull suddenly arrives. I feel myself sucked straight up through a tiny hole at the top of my head. I have popped out of my body. I see us sitting below. My eyes are tightly shut but I see the Familiars standing behind the kids. I don't perceive one behind Umara, however, and when I try to catch a glimpse of my own, my vision grows cloudy.

Lark stirs to life as the might of the Cradle focuses on him. It's as if he's suddenly covered with bees or wasps because he begins to fight them off. But there's nothing there and I'm confused because I have not given the Cradle a suggestion as to how to attack him.

Then I realize no direction is necessary. Lark has murdered so many, his own mind is fully capable of inventing a nightmare worse than any of us could supply. His subconscious provides the form his death will take, the Cradle merely supplies the electricity.

Red welts appear on his face and he screams.

The rest of the kids don't seem to mind.

They act like they welcome the sacrifice.

Poor Lark. He definitely wasn't popular.

It takes a while for him to die. It's not a pretty sight.

Still, I don't see a Familiar appear behind Umara.

With that business out of the way, I instruct the Cradle to pick up the vials that contain the diluted blood of the remaining members of the Source. There are eight different samples in our individual vials and I'm not surprised when its touch transports us across land and sea to a lifeless desert burning beneath a blazing sun.

Egypt. This is where it all began.

But where is the Nile? Where are the pyramids?

From Umara, I know the Telar started beside the great river.

Then I understand. The Nile has shifted drastically over the last twelve thousand years. We're above the spot where Umara's culture truly began. The pyramids of her youth are buried beneath the sand and it is to the last of those ancient monuments that Haru has gathered the remains of the Source.

The temple stands atop a rugged hill, a collection of broken pillars and slabs of marble and baked clay. At first glance it's not very impressive, but then I realize what we are seeing is like the tip of an iceberg. Beneath the scattered ruins is a complex maze of tunnels and halls.

As a group, we plunge deeper into the ruins. I send out a mental message to the kids that Umara will know where to go even if we do not, and my faith in her is not unfounded. Soon we reach our goal, a vast black chamber whose dimensions cannot accurately be fathomed because the light cast by the Telar's burning candles is too feeble. Immediately I sense this is where the Familiars were originally invoked by human beings.

We see Haru and seven other members of the Source. They sit on a dirt floor around a stone circle, their eyes closed. They appear to be aware of our arrival. Yet I don't pick up any fear, which worries me.

Are they that confident in their Link?

There's a stone seat at the head of the table. At first

glance it appears unoccupied but then I see a glowing red figure. As it takes on shape and definition, I glimpse other similar figures standing behind Haru and his people. These Familiars are unlike any I've ever seen before.

They look more like human beings.

People who have been to hell and back.

Their skin is dark and crusty with roasted flesh. Their eyes shine red with hatred. Their every movement seems pained, yet a fire burns in them that cannot be easily extinguished. Except for the one who sits alone, they keep their palms on the shoulders of Haru and his people.

Bolts of flame continually flare above them.

That is their shield, the ultimate product of their Link.

I know without testing it that it's impenetrable.

My despair in that instant is a terrible thing. To have come so far and to be stopped. My feeling of hopelessness leaves me wide open. At least to the one person in the Cradle I care about.

'Sita,' Umara says in my mind.

'I assume you see what I see.'

'Yes. I notice you haven't given the order to strike.'

'I fear what will follow. Hundreds of gushing nosebleeds.'

'You're wise to wait. The Source has forgotten much. How it began. How it gained immortality. How it was once mortal. But they have never lost the power to link. That's how Haru and the others have managed to stay in control.'

'I can't leave here without putting up a fight.'

'I know. We're committed. If we flee they'll attack.'

'Who sits at the head of the table? He doesn't look human.'

'Maybe not now. But he was long ago. That's Hatram.'

'The one who raped you?'

'Yes. The father of Haru.'

'That means we hold his blood as well.'

'In a sense.'

'He appears to wield the fire. Or is that my imagination?'

'He's very powerful. He controls the fires of hell.'

'Is he really from hell?'

'Of course. Upon death, he was taken to where he belongs. Now he is a demon from the deep.'

'Has he risen because you're here?'

'Perhaps. He died hating me, and wanting me. You might have had more luck today without my company.'

'We need more than luck. We're not going to destroy the Source unless we get through his flames. There must be a way.'

Umara is a long time answering.

'There's only one way.'

'How?'

'You must find his master.'

'Are you talking about . . .' I don't want to finish.

'Yes.'

Now it is my turn to hesitate. 'How do I find him?'

'The same way anyone does. You die.'

'Die? Is that a joke?'

'It would be for anyone else. But not for you.'

'Because I have already died.'

'Yes.'

'But I didn't go to hell. I was sure I went to Krishna.'

'Do you remember seeing Krishna?'

'No! That's my problem. I can't remember what happened.'

'You blocked it out.'

I freeze. 'Are you saying I blocked it out because I couldn't bear what I saw?'

'It's time to go back, Sita. Time to remember.'

'But I don't know how!'

'Die.'

'No.' I feel dizzy and I have no body. 'Stop saying that.'

'You've died twice already. You can die a third time.'

'I don't want to. I'm . . .'

I'm afraid. That's why I can't remember.

Suddenly there's something wrong with my vision. I can't see the Source anymore, not Haru, or the demons standing around them, not even Hatram. All I can see are the flames, growing brighter and hotter. I don't know if I've dropped towards them or they've risen to catch me.

I don't suppose it matters.

I feel myself burning. I feel myself dying.

23

I stand in the beautiful mountains beside a sparkling blue lake laced with drifting patches of ice. The morning sun dazzles the eastern sky. The air is fresh, the stillness a wonder.

I hear someone saying my name and turn to see who it is. To my surprise I see Seymour and Matt. Seymour has his head bowed and is weeping. He keeps calling out to me. Matt is on his knees, silent, holding a body in his arms.

One that looks awfully familiar.

'Shit. Am I dead?' I say aloud.

The question is ridiculous. I can't be dead and talking to myself. If I was really dead I'd be talking to Krishna. I remember shouting his name a moment ago. I remember I called to him because . . .

Matt was firing his laser rifle.

He was going to shoot Seymour.

That's why I leapt in front of Seymour . . .

There's a dark red hole in the chest of the body Matt's holding. It looks serious; the hole pierces her heart; it's no wonder she's dead. And I should stop trying to think of her as someone separate from myself because it's obvious she's me and I really am dead.

OK, I got that settled. Sort of.

'Damn. I can't believe it,' I say.

I might have it settled on one level, but on another level I'm not buying it. This is like no death I ever imagined. Where is the bright white light? Where are the angels? How come Krishna hasn't come to take me to his abode in the starry sky?

'What am I doing with Seymour and Matt?'

The question feels kind of cold, even if it is coming from a dead woman. I mean, it's obvious the two of them are broken up over what's happened to me. I should be more sympathetic. On the other hand, Matt was the one who shot me. It's his fault I'm dead.

No, that's not fair. It was really that damn Array. It got hold of his mind and somehow transformed him into a nut who was jealous about his girlfriend being turned into a vampire when all I was really trying to do was keep her alive.

Which reminds me, how is Teri doing?

She's probably still up in the cave.

I want to check on her. But I feel guilty leaving Seymour and Matt. For that matter, I find it hard to leave my body. I keep thinking it's going to heal. I've been beaten up before and survived. I've been stabbed, shot, almost had different limbs blown off. I even got staked once, through the heart, when my old house exploded, and that didn't kill me. Maybe I can get over this latest injury and slip back inside my body. I should probably wait around and see what happens.

Then I notice something strange. The cave up on the hill. The one where Teri is changing into a vampire. The entrance is glowing. It's not giving off a bright white light like some kind of tunnel to heaven. But the glow is definitely there. It shines with a faint silver radiance. The color seems familiar. It's not something I can simply ignore.

Seymour and Matt continue to grieve over my body.

Christ, I feel so guilty leaving them to take care of it.

'Listen guys, I know you can't hear me, but maybe you can pick me up in your minds. If you can then I should probably stop rambling and get to the point. I'm pretty sure I'm dead, for real this time, and I want to tell you that I'm sorry. Not for the dying part, but for leaving you to take care of the Telar and the IIC. I assumed Krishna would keep me alive long enough to help kill the bastards but I guess he has other plans. Anyway, you both know how much I love you and how much I'm going to miss you. Seymour, meeting you made my life complete. I'm sorry I've got to go now. The light in the cave – I feel it calling me. If I don't go now, I don't think I'll have the strength to leave later.'

I give them both hugs, which they don't feel, and tell

them again how much I love them. Then I hike up the hill to the cave. The light continues to glow, although it doesn't get any brighter when I enter the cave. For a divine sign it isn't very impressive.

Yet a small miracle occurs when I reach the rear of the cave. Teri's where I left her, beside the burned-out fire, wrapped in Seymour's jacket. I can tell by her colouring and her rate of breathing that her transformation into a vampire is going smoothly.

Teri has nothing to do with the miracle. It's the cave itself. It no longer stops where it did before. It continues on, as does the faint silver glow. Finally, I'm beginning to get impressed.

I kneel and give Teri a hug and a kiss.

'I'm going to miss you. I hope you enjoy being a vampire. I only changed you because I figured it was better than being dead. Of course now that I'm dead I have to wonder if that was such a great idea. We won't be able to hang out together like we used to. But the way I figure it, you're too young to die. Matt needs you, and so do Seymour and Shanti. Take care of them for me. I love you.'

I kiss her once more and walk deeper into the cave.

The floor begins to slant downwards. Overall the terrain becomes more rocky. To my immense disappointment the silver light begins to fade. Here it's the only thing that vaguely resembles what people who have near-death experiences talk about and it's going away. It fades to the point where I can barely see where I'm going.

Just when the dark becomes almost impenetrable, I

spot a burning torch jammed in a crack in the wall six feet above the floor. Unsure if I'll find another light along the way, I grab it and continue on. The incline gets steeper and I have to be careful not to slip and fall.

The walls and floor of the cave are coated with a red dust that I would assume was iron oxide, if I was in the real world. I noticed the dust building up as the silver light failed, and wondered if it was responsible.

On the whole, the cave is bland. The only thing that interests me is my torch. I have no idea how it keeps burning. It's just a stick with a baseball-sized bump on the top that happens to spout orange flames. I wonder why God didn't give me a kerosene lamp or even a flashlight.

After about an hour of hiking, I run into a much larger cave that's also heading down, but at a more gentle angle. This subterranean passage is fifty feet across, with a ceiling that's at least twice that in height. The light of my torch struggles to illumine many details, not that I think there's much to see. The new cave is larger than the old one but just as boring.

I notice an occasional small cave converges with the larger one, and to my surprise a person suddenly walks out of one of these caves. He looks like a middle-aged Japanese businessman. Wearing a dark suit and red tie, he has a torch like mine and walks with it held aloft.

Unfortunately, when I try striking up a conversation with him I get nowhere. At first I figure it's because I'm speaking English, but when I switch to Japanese it makes no difference.

Then I notice how glazed over his eyes are. He appears drugged or else severely traumatized. 'Are you OK?' I shout at him.

He grunts and keeps walking.

I spot more caves, and every now and then another person walks out of one of them. Going by their nationalities and dress, they appear to be from all over the world. Most are older, sixty-five or more, but I do bump into quite a number of African children. They're generally more animated than the lobotomized adults, but they scurry away from me when I try to speak to them.

I hike for another hour, with my herd of zombie companions, before the tunnel finally opens into a massive cavern. The walls, the ceiling – I can't even glimpse them, although I assume I'm still underground. Yet the sight of the cavern causes me to increase my pace because a mile away from the end of the tunnel is a black river with several thousand people gathered on its shore.

Even though the majority of these men and women wander aimlessly about, the river still feels like a viable goal to me. For it's lined with giant torches, held high by arms carved out of stone, and I see small boats moving back and forth over the water, ferrying people to God knows where.

I assumed my travelling companions were semi-brain-dead, but that might not have been entirely true. Most of the people who exit the tunnel with me suddenly pick up their pace, as if they now have a purpose. They head straight for the boats that wait at the edge of the black river.

Yet the other class, those who wander the shore, look like they have been there a long time. As I approach, I see they're not just dressed in foreign clothes, a lot of them are clad in historical garments. There are plenty of people from the forties and fifties, and the early part of the twentieth century. Others have on buckskins, kilts, and even togas.

I realize I'm seeing people who have been dead for decades, if not centuries. For some reason, I feel the sudden urge to try to shake them out of their lethargic state. Climbing on to a nearby boulder, I shout at the top of my lungs.

'Does anyone know what's going on here?' I yell.

My shout draws the attention of a few, but only one guy seems alert enough to understand what I asked. Wearing a World War II uniform and chewing on a dead cigar, he walks over and offers his hand.

'Lieutenant Gregory Holden, Fifth Army,' he says. Taller than me by six inches, the man has a face so dirtied and bloodied from battle, his features are hard to distinguish. Yet his voice sounds clear and the blue in his eyes is visible even in the dim light. I shake his hand.

'Alisa Perne. Pleased to meet you, Gregory.'

He acts delighted. 'Lord, ain't you a looker. Where you from?'

'Los Angeles. And you're from Virginia, I can tell by your accent.'

'You have sharp ears. What were you doing out in LA?'

'Trying to break into Hollywood.'

His eyes widen. 'I knew I seen you before! You were in that film with Fred MacMurray and Barbara Stanwyck. That one she convinced him to kill her husband. You played her daughter.'

'That's right. Turned out in the end I was the only decent person in the whole film.' The movie came out the year before the war ended. It was probably the last film he saw.

He slaps his leg. 'Imagine that! Me meeting a famous movie star.'

'Tell me about this place, Gregory,' I say, pointing to the black river, the wandering mass of humanity, and the torch-lit ferryboats. 'What goes on here?'

'You must be a new arrival,' he says.

'I just walked out of the cave.'

'Lucky you. You get a fresh start.'

'What do you mean?'

Gregory points to one of the ferryboats, which all seem to be manned by old guys in black robes. 'You want to walk over there and see if you can get a ride across the river,' he says.

'What's on the other side of the river?'

'No idea. But you don't want to stay here. This is no place for a pretty girl like you.' He adds, 'Trust me, I've been here a long time.'

'Why don't you take a boat across?'

'Lord knows, I've been trying. Before they let you in

one of those boats, you've got to answer a riddle.'

'What kind of riddle?'

'It's different for everyone. But the answer's supposed to be something you learned when you were alive.'

'Wait a second, Gregory. So you know you're dead.'

'Sure. I'm afraid you are, too. You wouldn't be here otherwise. Best you accept that fact and move on. But I know how you feel. I felt the same way when I first got here.' He adds, 'I never even saw that bullet coming.'

'What was the riddle you didn't know the answer to? Or have they asked you lots of riddles?'

Gregory frowns. 'It could be the same riddle. Only, right after they ask it, if you don't know the answer, you forget it right away.'

'Why do you forget?'

'Beats me, I can't remember.'

'But they might ask more than one riddle?'

'Sure. Who knows? You just got to answer it right once and they take you over to the other side.'

'That doesn't sound so bad.'

'Trust me, it's hard. I keep trying and I keep getting it wrong.'

'Gregory, do you know how long ago World War Two ended?'

'No, and I don't want to know.' He turns away, frustrated, but has the decency to call over his shoulder. 'Good luck, Alisa.'

'Take care, Gregory,' I say.

I'm not 100 per cent sold on his advice. The more I

stare at the dark river and the old bony dudes in their black hooded robes guiding their ferryboats, the more I feel like I've fallen into a Greek myth. I still can't get over how every book I ever read on near-death experiences talked about travelling down a blissful tunnel filled with bright light and loving relatives. And this is what I get. Of course, the people who wrote those books, none of them had really been dead.

'To hell with it,' I swear, and walk over to a ferryman that isn't busy. I might have made a bad choice. The guy's hood is hung so low I can't see his face, beyond a pit of wrinkles and a row of yellow teeth. As I draw near, the ferryman doesn't look at me, he just goes very still.

'Hey. Can I hitch a ride to the other side?' I ask.

The guy nods and I swear I hear his neck creaking, even though he is hardly moving. He speaks in the kind of dry rasp a mummy might make if you gave him CPR and he suddenly came back to life.

'What's the most useless human emotion?' he asks.

'That's an interesting question. It's sort of broad. Can you give me a hint?'

To my surprise, the ferryman helps me out. 'Several words describe the emotion. They are all correct. Pick one.'

'Does this useless emotion apply to women as well as men?'

'Yes.'

'Who suffers from it more?'

'It depends on who raised you. Now answer the question.'

I recall Krishna speaking of the three qualities in the heart: love, hate, fear. He said hate could overcome fear. A warrior could do anything if he really believed in his cause. He could sneak into an enemy camp with just a sword and start killing people and not worry about what happened to himself. A more modern example would be a suicide bomber getting on a bus and blowing himself up, along with a bunch of innocent women and children. The point being that if someone was pissed off enough, fear wasn't going to stop them.

But love could also conquer fear. Every day soldiers laid down their lives to protect their loved ones. And love was also capable of overcoming hate. Love allowed for forgiveness, which negated anger. Therefore, of the three, love was the strongest emotion and fear was the weakest because love could defeat the other two, while fear could be removed by the others.

I feel pretty confident with my chances with the ferryman.

'Fear is the most useless emotion,' I say.

'Wrong,' the ferryman says and raises a hand. His robe briefly slips up his arm and I see his fingers are made of bone. 'Forget,' he whispers as his palm passes over my eyes.

I stagger back, dizzy. Up until then, I hadn't noticed that the grim underworld had a particular temperature, yet suddenly I'm aware of just how stuffy the cavern is. Sweat drenches my brow. The heat and humidity remind me of a dragon's lair. I struggle to hold on to the riddle in my mind but I feel distracted and it slips from my grasp. Bowing my head, I walk away from the ferryman and try to collect my wits.

I can't remember when or where I set down my torch, but wish I had it with me. The water in the river is so dark, it gives me the creeps. I try keeping a distance from it. At the same time, the wandering horde is poor company and I avoid them as well. A few talk to themselves, muttering a series of questions, and possible answers. At least they have some life to them. But the others – it's like most of them have given up.

I don't know how long I walk around. But eventually I run into a young woman dressed in contemporary clothes. On the thin side, she has blonde hair and blue eyes and a winning smile. I could swear she looks familiar but I can't place her. Whatever the ferryman did to me is still messing with my mind.

'How did you do?' she asks.

'I don't know. I think I got the wrong answer.'

'That's OK. I answered wrong the first time. You just got to try again. Let me give you a hint. Think before you respond, don't rush yourself. They give you plenty of time.'

'You act like you already got it right.'

The woman nods. 'I did. The last time I spoke to the ferryman.'

'What did he ask you?'

'That doesn't matter. My question might confuse you. Just focus on what he asks you the next time.'

'But if you gave the right answer, how come the ferryman didn't take you to the other side?'

'I'm with the same ferryman as you. So is a friend of mine. We're not going to cross until you're ready to come with us.'

'Why are you waiting for me?'

She smiles. 'The ferryman usually takes three at a time.'

'I didn't know that. Where's your friend?'

'She's around. You'll meet her soon.'

'Has she already given the right answer?'

'Yeah, she got it the first time. But she's wise, you can't compare yourself to her, none of us can.'

'I'd like to meet her.'

'You will.'

'I'd like to talk to her before I go back to the ferryman. If she's so wise, maybe she could give me some hints.'

'The most important thing to know is that you already know the answer to the question he asks you. Otherwise, he wouldn't ask it.'

'Does he ever ask trick questions?'

'Well, they're riddles so they're all kind of tricky.'

'You look like you just got here,' I say.

'I did. I got here not long after you did.'

'How long after?'

'A week or so.'

'Hey, hold on. I haven't been here a week.'

'Time is hard to keep track of in this place. That's why you see people from hundreds of years ago. A lot of them feel like they just got here. But some of them have been asked hundreds of questions.'

'The ferryman gives you that many chances?'

'I was told you can't go on until you get one of them right.'

'God. I hope I don't end up like one of those losers.'

'Relax, you'll do fine. You're pretty wise yourself.'

'How do you know?'

'Because I know you.' She leans over and hugs me but before I can ask another question she slips away and vanishes in the crowd. Her kind words have given me renewed confidence. I head back to the ferryman I spoke to before. I think it's the same guy, although they all look alike.

He stands in his boat with his hood covering his head, a long black pole in one hand, a torch in the other. Like before, he seems to freeze as I draw near. I don't understand how I can remember that little detail when I can't remember what he asked me the last time.

'I want to go to the other side,' I say.

'What's the greatest quality a human being can have? That can also turn out to be the most dangerous quality?'

'That's a hard one.'

'Yes.'

'Can you give me a hint?'

'Perhaps.'

He doesn't offer one so I assume I have to take the initiative.

'There are many human qualities that can be both good and bad.'

'Yes.'

'Being a hard worker can be good. But if you work all the time, you never get to spend time with your family. You can get fat and out of shape and die of a heart attack in your fifties and you end up here.'

'Is that your answer?'

'What?'

'Being a hard worker.'

'No. I just used that as an example. You said you'd give me a hint.'

'Perhaps.'

'Well, can you tell me what's wrong with my answer?'

'Being a hard worker is not the greatest quality a human can have. Nor is it the most dangerous.'

'I see what you're saying. You're speaking in absolutes here so I need to raise the bar and go for the one thing that can either totally make your life or totally screw it up. Is that correct?'

'Yes.'

'Can you tell me where you get these questions?'

'Yes.'

'Where do you get these questions?'

'From you.'

'I don't understand.'

'You bring them with you.'

'Do I bring the answer as well?'

'Yes.'

'Why did I bring such hard questions?'

'Because you're going to need the answers.'

'Need them for what?'

He gestures with his pole, although he does not take

it out of the water. 'You will need the answers when you reach the other side.'

'What's over there?'

'You'll see. Now answer the question.'

'Wait. You have to give me time to think.'

'Think. Then answer.'

The greatest human quality versus the worst human quality. To me, the ferryman is clearly implying they're one and the same thing. I struggle to remember anything Krishna might have said on the subject. I didn't get to hear him talk much, but I read the Gita and I read Yaksha's book and Yaksha wrote down several lectures Krishna gave.

I suddenly remember one Krishna gave on love.

He said how love was the sweet expression of life. The one thing that made life worth living. Love made difficult tasks easy. Raising a family could be a great burden, but if there was love, the sacrifice was a pleasure. And when love matured into devotion then everything you did for your lover was a joy. You would give up your life to save those you loved.

On the other hand, if love did not mature it could lead to bondage, to jealousy. If you loved someone, but felt possessive of them, you could end up treating them like an object that belonged to you. Just as bad, with your children, if you showered them with too much love, and never disciplined them, they would grow up weak and spoiled. At times, love had to be tough, or it could end up wrecking those dearest to you.

Krishna's lecture was very insightful. That's why I

remember it so well, and that's why I feel confident when I turn back to the ferryman.

'The answer is love,' I say.

'Wrong,' the ferryman says and raises his hand. Before I can stop him, his bony arm reaches up and his skeleton fingers pass over my eyes. 'Forget,' he whispers.

Like before, I stagger back and feel stung by a wave of dizziness. The ferryman's question and my answer just slip away. The weight of the underworld suddenly descends on me and I feel trapped. The place is too hot, too claustrophobic. Bowing my head, I stumble away from the river.

I wander far from the spooky water, trying to escape the confused throng. At the same time, I'm afraid to go too far in the dark because I don't want to get lost. I have yet to replace my torch. The only sources of light I can depend on are the huge torches that burn above the ferryboats.

I finally find a rock and sit down.

Eventually, a beautiful woman approaches, wearing a silk robe and exquisite jewels. Her skin is like copper, her eyes like coal, and when she smiles at me I know she is a friend, even if I can't remember her name.

'Hello,' she says.

'Hi.'

'May I sit beside you?'

The boulder is hard but at least it's clean. That's the reason I chose it. 'Sure. I don't mind,' I say.

The woman sits and stares off into the distance,

occasionally playing with her necklace, a gold chain filled with diamonds and rubies. There is something about the sparkling rubies that reminds me of another cavern I once visited but I can't remember it clearly enough to make the connection. Nor do I know who the woman is. But I suddenly recall the blonde girl who spoke to me.

'Hey, are you friends with that blonde I spoke to earlier?'

She stares at me. 'We are friends through you.'

'Did I introduce the two of you?' I ask.

'In a manner of speaking.'

'When?'

'You don't remember?'

'No.'

'It doesn't matter.'

'She told me we're all supposed to ride across the river together, with the ferryman.'

'That's true.'

'Have you been to the ferryman?' I ask.

'I went after you did.'

'What did he ask you?'

'That's not important. All that matters is I gave the right answer.'

'That's what the other woman said. That's why I went back and gave it another try. But I must have given the wrong answer because the ferryman brushed my forehead and I forgot everything.'

'That's his job. He's doing you a favour, you just can't see that yet.'

369

'Will his questions come back to me later on?'

'The questions and answers should return when you need them. So it doesn't matter how many times you fail. It just means you're going to leave here with what you need to know.'

'Have you ever left here?'

'What are you asking?'

'Do you know what's on the other side?' I ask.

The woman takes a long time to answer. 'I saw it once in a vision.'

'What did you see?'

'It's different for everyone. But you'll see it soon, when you're ready to leave.'

'I feel ready now. I'm sick of this place. But I don't want to fail another test.'

'Don't see the questions as tests. See them as lessons you learned on earth that you want to take with you to the other world.'

'Can't you give me a hint what this other world is like?'

She smiles at my persistence. 'For some it's wonderful. For others it's not so nice. It all depends on the sum total of the lives you've lived.'

'Lives? I think I've lived only one life.'

'You're like me in that respect. I just lived one long life.' She smiles again and reaches out and squeezes my hand. 'You're going to be all right. You'll see, everything will be fine.'

With that the woman gets up and walks away.

Yet her words stay with me, and once more I feel the courage to approach the ferryman. This time I find him reclining in his boat, as if he was taking a nap. His robe is bunched up around his legs and I notice he doesn't have much skin down there. But he quickly stands as I come near, waving his torch close to my face as if he is trying to get a better view of me. He stands and goes very still.

'I'm ready for another riddle,' I say.

'What is the greatest secret in the universe?'

I feel my heart pound, and I'm surprised because I know I'm dead and I'm pretty sure my heart shouldn't be beating at all. But it doesn't matter. Finally, I know the answer to the question. I heard Krishna give it a long time ago.

Yet I caution myself to move carefully. The question isn't worded the way I would like it to be.

'By secret do you mean mystery?' I ask.

'Yes.'

'So you could be asking what is the greatest mystery in the universe?'

'Yes.'

'Great. I've got it. The greatest mystery is that even though every man and woman know they're mortal, they wake up every morning and know they're not going to die that day.'

'Wrong.' The ferryman raises his bony arm and his skeleton fingers are about to brush against my forehead. I know what will happen next. He will tell me to forget and then, a few seconds later, I won't even remember what he asked, never mind what the answer is supposed to be.

But this time I've had enough.

I reach up and block his arm.

'Stop!' I snap. 'You're making a mistake. Krishna himself said this was the answer to that question, and he was supposed to be an avatar, or a divine incarnation. How can you say my answer's wrong?'

The ferryman struggles with my arm for a few seconds. It's like he's surprised at my strength. But when I refuse to let him touch my forehead he finally lowers his arm and answers me.

'The question was, "What is the greatest secret in the universe?" You came close with your answer. It would have been the correct answer if I had asked, "What is the greatest mystery in the world?"'

'But I had you clarify your question. You said "secret" and "mystery" were synonymous in this case.' I pause. 'You do know what synonymous means, don't you?'

'Yes.'

'Then explain how my answer can be wrong.'

'Your problem was that the question was about the "universe", not the "world".' The ferryman goes to rub his bony hand across my forehead. 'Now for—'

'Wait!' I yell. 'I was close, you admitted that.'

'Yes.'

'I deserve another chance at the same question.'

'We don't give second chances.'

'You have to give me one. I deserve it.'

'Why?'

'Because you tricked me. You asked a question I

372

knew the answer to. But you changed one little word at the end to throw me off. That's not fair.'

'Who says death is fair?'

'I don't know. I've never been dead before. But you hear what I'm saying and I think you're afraid to give me another chance because you're afraid I know the answer.'

'Very few people know the answer to that question.'

'You've asked it before?'

'A long time ago. Almost no one got it right.'

'Ask me again, right now.'

'You already gave your answer. It was wrong.'

'I'm telling you, you cheated! I deserve a second chance.'

'No one ever gets a second chance.'

'Well, I want one. I'm sick of this black river and all these zombies wandering around talking to themselves. And I'm tired of you. I mean it. I don't think you're playing by the rules.'

'That's a serious accusation.'

'Well, I'm a serious kind of chick. Now do what I say. Ask the question again, and if I answer it correctly, then you have to take me and my two friends across the river. Deal?'

The ferryman bows his head and considers for a while. Finally he nods. 'Deal,' he says.

I rub my hands together. 'Ask away.'

'What is the greatest secret in the universe?'

'That the Lord and his secret names, his mantras, are identical. In other words, when I say, "Krishna", then Krishna is present. Correct?'

'Correct.' The ferryman gestures with his pole. 'Get in the boat.'

'Thanks,' I say.

While I'm getting settled, my two friends appear. The young one, the blonde, sits near me at the front, while the wise one sits in the centre, which is smart. Her position helps distribute the weight in the boat. Standing at the other end, the ferryman pushes off the shore with his pole.

'We're finally on our way,' I say, excited.

My blonde friend smiles. She looks glad for me.

The wise one simply nods. She appears more cautious.

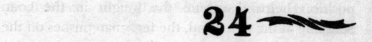

24

The boat itself is a curiosity. Except for a heavy pole fastened to the rear, and the oars, the craft appears to have been carved from a single thick tree. The wood's a deep grey, the texture surprisingly soft. Except for the sombre colour, it reminds me of balsa wood.

The ferryman uses his pole to get us going then switches over to his oars. The river's current is sedate. Facing away from the shore, it slowly pulls us to the right. The black water is like a stream of ink. Even with all the boats coming and going, it hardly ripples. For some reason, I can tell it's deep, and that it would be impossible to swim across.

My mind begins to clear the moment we leave the shore.

I ask the others if they feel the same and they say yes.

'But don't count on it to last,' the wise one says. 'This is a place of transition. What I think, even what I see, is not necessarily going to be the same as you.'

'Why's that?' I ask.

'It's just the way it is.'

'How do you know so much about this place?'

'I told you, I've seen it before in visions.'

'You're lucky. I feel like I'm lost in a weird Bardo realm.'

'That's one way of looking at it,' she says.

The blonde speaks up. 'But we passed the riddles. We're on our way.'

'I wish I knew where we were going,' I say, as I stare out over the bow of the boat. The black is like a thick cloud, sprinkled with burning lanterns. It makes me wonder if the river even has another shore. Still, a part of me is relieved. It's good to be away from that haunted beach.

I can only hope Lieutenant Gregory Holden of the Fifth Army finally figures out his riddle. I have an affinity for men who fought in World War II. I was in Europe at the time and helped kick the Nazis' butts. Plus Gregory seemed like a nice guy, and he died fighting for his country. You'd figure the ferryman would give him a break and ask him something easy. Like who General George Patton was.

Eventually, after an hour or so, we catch sight of a massive mound dotted with thousands of red lights. As we come closer, I see that each light is a torch, burning darkly and hanging at the end of an endless number of tunnels that burrow deep into the hill, or whatever the hell it is. Most of the tunnels are located at water level, but a few are up high, definitely out of reach, at least from the river.

I can't see any stairs or paths on the side of the mound. More than anything, it looks like a gigantic stone that somehow thrust its way up from the bowels of the earth. Assuming, of course, that the earth is still a factor in this crazy twilight zone.

The ferryman steers us to a tunnel that's only two feet above the water and beckons the wise woman to climb out. I try to follow – I want to stick with her – but the ferryman stops me. It's only then I realize he's going to drop each of us at our own tunnel and break up our happy family.

Naturally, I protest, but at that instant the ferryman lifts his head and his hood falls back and I see that his eyes are . . . well, the guy doesn't have any eyes, just black holes in his head. I decide to sit back down.

The ferryman spends a long time locating the next tunnel, where he deposits the blonde. I'm not surprised that he leaves me until last. I'm having that kind of day. By now I'm anxious to get away from the guy. Besides creaking when he moves and having no eyes, he starts to make a weird clicking sound with his teeth. It's probably his version of singing along with the car radio. I'm relieved when he finally finds my tunnel. It's five feet above the water line but I don't care, I jump into it, and don't bother to wave goodbye to the ferryman.

The tunnel, although narrow, is an improvement

from the original cave I found myself in, the one where I said goodbye to Teri. It appears to have been constructed. The curved walls and flat floor are made of tightly fitted stones, each engraved with runes and symbols that I don't recognize.

Like at the start of the first cave, I see a burning torch and grab it, not sure what kind of light I'm going to find along the path. The flames give off a bloody hue; they're more red than orange.

I talk to myself as I hike through the tunnel, just a bunch of nonsense, but the sound of my voice hardly carries beyond the reach of my arms. The stone appears to have a dampening effect and it freaks me out enough that I soon shut up. The place is so silent all I can hear is my heartbeat.

Except I no longer seem to have a heart.

I stop to check my wrist but can't find a pulse.

'Great,' I whisper.

There's nothing to do, I have to keep going. Once again, like on the shore of the river, I feel a palpable heaviness that might be signaling an approaching storm if only there were sky. I walk for what feels like hours before I come to the end of the tunnel.

But it's an end that brings no relief because the tunnel terminates in a precipice, a cliff, nothing. Yet a hundred yards away, across the abyss, I see that my tunnel does in fact continue. Unfortunately, there's no bridge, not even a piece of rope, to help me to the other side. It makes me wonder if I pissed off the ferryman by demanding a second chance. Or maybe the bony dude was able to read my mind and he heard exactly what I thought of his clicking teeth routine. Whatever, the ferryman has chosen a rotten tunnel to dump me at.

Above and below is black.

I have absolutely no idea what to do next.

I mean, if I was alive, and feeling my usual vampire self, I'd take a running start and leap across the chasm and probably make it to the other side. But since I don't have a beating heart, I figure I'm nowhere near strong enough for such heroics.

'That goddamn ferryman,' I mutter.

Propping my torch up against the opposite wall, I sit on the floor and stretch out my legs and pray for help. Even though all the books I read on near-death experiences were turning out to be wrong, I was hoping they were right when it came to the power of prayer. For they said that no matter how lousy a place you ended up in when you died, you could always pray your way out of it.

I recite every prayer I know and nothing happens.

'At least send someone to ask me a riddle!' I yell.

Maybe the prayers work, after all.

A few minutes later something happens.

A figure appears at the end of the tunnel, across the way. She isn't carrying a torch but I can see her clearly, maybe because she glows with a greenish light. Her eyes are also green, her hair long and black, and her skin is so white it looks as if she only bathes outside when the moon is full. Her beauty is undeniable. She has sharp features and not a single wrinkle. To top it off, her long white gown has been cut from a fairy tale. She smiles and waves to me and I wave back.

Privately, I hope she's not into riddles.

'Hello!' she calls. 'Do you want to come across?'

I stand. 'Do you have a rope?'

She laughs at my question, like I'm being silly, and then steps over the edge. Inside, I cringe, expecting a catastrophic fall, but she doesn't go anywhere. Rather, her bare feet appear to step on to an invisible bridge that responds ever so faintly to the pressure of her pale skin. Wherever she puts her toes, for an instant, a bunch of green sparks flash. It takes her only a few seconds to cross the chasm.

'Do you want to come across?' she repeats shyly, and I expect a blush but her skin remains as white as snow. I feel the coolness of her breath, and her eyes are no ordinary green. They could have been cut from the coral of a tropical lagoon. Staring into them, I feel my thoughts begin to swim . . .

'Yes,' I reply, shaking my head to clear it. I gesture to the invisible bridge, if that's what it is. 'I just have to walk across like you?'

She comes near, lightly brushing my right arm with her green nails. 'For you, that won't work, you'll fall. I'll have to lead you across.'

'OK.'

She comes closer, until I feel the soft pressure of her breasts on my chest. Tilting her head to the side, she closes her eyes and says in a husky whisper, 'Give me a kiss.'

I pull back. 'I'm sorry?'

Her eyes spring open. 'Don't you find me attractive?'

'I don't know you. I don't know who you are.'

She grins mischievously. 'You're a woman and I'm a woman. What does it matter? There are no rules here.'

'Why don't we talk about it on the other side?'

She giggles and shakes her head. 'First a kiss, then we'll talk.'

'Just one kiss? Then you'll help me across?'

'Yes.' She puts her palm over my heart and bats her dark lashes. 'Then you'll be safe with me.'

The way she says 'safe' makes me cringe.

Her touch feels . . . mouldy.

The woman senses my reluctance. With a sweeping motion, she gestures to the gorge. 'I'm the only one who can rescue you. Otherwise, you'll be trapped here forever.'

'But why the kiss?'

She laughs like I'm being foolish. 'There is no why. Not here, not now.'

I hesitate. She's an attractive woman, and although I'm primarily heterosexual, I have no inhibitions about swinging the other way. Humans make too big a deal about sex, how it should be performed, whereas to me sex is the one area of life that should be free of rules.

But there's something about her that disturbs me. For example, her mocking demeanor makes me feel nothing she says or does is genuine. I'm just a pawn for her to play with for a while and then discard. Also, she's got that Emerald City green-glow thing going. It reminds me too much of Dorothy and the Wicked Witch of the West.

If I didn't know better, I'd swear she was a witch.

'I don't believe you,' I say.

My remark doesn't offend her. Licking her lips, she stares at me as if I were the best thing to come along since Hansel and Gretel. Her grin swells.

'Belief doesn't matter, either,' she says, trying to lick my face. I take a step back and feel the wall of the tunnel on my shoulder blades. The edge of the precipice is three feet to my left, she's two feet in front, her white dress scraping the floor of the tunnel, her green eyes as cold as ice carved from a Neptunian glacier.

It might be my imagination but in the blink of an eye her face changes. I had thought her features flawless but now I see scarring on her right cheek, stretching from her mouth to her eye, and I realize at some point in her past she was severely burned. Ordinarily the sight would evoke pity in me, yet the way she keeps staring at me, the smacking sound her lips keep making, leads me to believe her lust for me is actually closer to hunger.

'I'm not going to kiss you,' I say.

She keeps her grin but it looks stiff and artificial.

'Why not?'

'Like you said, there is no why. Not here, not now.'

She doesn't get angry, at least she doesn't show it. From the folds of her white gown, though, she draws a silver needle and holds it up for me to see. The metal glitters in the light of the torch I left propped up against the wall and I see the tip is stained with blood. She brings it near my right eye.

'Do you know what this is?' she asks.

'No.'

'Your destiny.'

'I don't understand.'

'It's your last and future sin.'

'How can it be my last sin if I haven't committed it yet?'

'Because your course is set and you're caught in a circle. With this needle you'll damn your soul for eternity.'

Finally, she seems to be telling the truth. But I refuse to admit that, even to myself. 'You're lying.'

'No,' she gloats, lowering the needle and letting its tip play across my neck, scratching the skin above my jugular. 'You know what you put in this needle, and who you chose to give it to.'

I don't have a clue what she's talking about.

'If it hasn't happened yet, I can change it,' I say.

The witch, and I'm now certain that's what she is, presses her face so close to mine I feel her breath. With every inhalation and exhalation, I see the wounds on her face deepening. Her breath is like acid, her own saliva burns her from the inside out. Her tongue stretches out and she licks the tip of my nose and I feel its sting.

'Your only hope is to kiss me and let me lead you across the bridge,' she says, and the words appear in my mind before she speaks them. 'Then when you reach the Scale, you'll be under my protection.'

'What Scale are you talking about?' I ask.

'The Scale of right and wrong. Of good and bad.'

'Are you talking about my karma?'

She throws her head back and laughs. 'Your karma! You've lived so long you have mountains of karma. No, I'm talking about now, and what follows it.'

'You mean, tomorrow?'

The witch ignores my question. 'There's poison in these needles.' Her needle comes to rest above my jugular and I fear she's going to push it in. Even without a heart, I'm afraid.

'I didn't put it there,' I say.

'Not yet. But you will.'

'I'm not going to do anything any more! I'm dead!'

'Try telling that to the Scale.'

'That's what will judge me?' The way she says the word, I just know it's a really big deal, like God or something.

'The Scale is both judge and jury. It pronounces your . . . doom.' Her choice of words amuses her and she laughs loudly,

'Shut up!' I snap.

Except for a soft sick chuckle, she falls silent.

'If I kiss you and go with you, I can avoid this doom?'

'That's right,' she says.

She lies now. She is the worst of liars because she mixes in so much truth. 'How do I know I can trust you?' I ask.

Her green eyes sparkle with an eerie light. 'Oh, Sita,

that was the second question. Don't you remember? You failed that one.'

'The second question?' I don't need her to respond. Suddenly I know she's referring to the ferryman's second riddle. It comes back to me.

'What's the greatest quality a human can possess? The one quality that can be the most dangerous?'

Since this witch knows my name, I suspect she knows the answer to the riddle. The wise woman had warned me that the ferryman would only ask what I needed to know . . . later.

'What does it mean?' I whisper.

'A kiss,' she says as she licks the left side of my face. 'And we'll cross the bridge together and I'll whisper the answer in your ear.'

I hear the falsehood in her words. Worse, I smell it in her saliva.

'No!' I shout, and suddenly push her back. 'You're a liar!'

Fury grips her face and tears her wounds wide open so that I can see her sharp teeth waiting inside. The change in her is breathtaking.

'You dare to defy me? You who are already damned.'

'Maybe I am.' I pause as the answer to the riddle comes to me. 'But I'd be a fool to put my faith in you.'

Faith was the answer to the riddle. Faith was the greatest human quality. It could move mountains. It allowed me to trust Krishna. It gave me the courage to trust my friends, and to seek out John and listen to his words.

But faith could also be dangerous. Faith in the wrong person. And blind faith in a sect or creed could often lead to dogma and bondage.

Faith is indeed a coin with two sides.

To know what side is right, I have to trust my heart.

She stares at me, her needle held ready. She can read my mind, she knows she has lost me. But she still wants a piece of me. I have to laugh.

'What's the matter, witch? Black cat bite your tongue?'

She stabs at me, she's fast. I barely escape her thrust. Yet that's the crux of my dilemma – I have nowhere to go. But maybe life has taught me a thing or two. As she strikes again, I dodge to the left, close to the edge. A dumb move, on the surface, but I've finally decided that it's time for a leap of faith.

'You're mine!' she screams, approaching for what she's sure will be the decisive blow.

'You're so full of shit,' I say.

My heart, and my head, tell me a dead person can't die.

I jump over the side of the cliff.

I don't scream as I fall.

I don't want to give the witch the satisfaction.

I fall a long way, in utter darkness.

Before I strike something hard and black out.

When I come to, I'm lying on my back on large grey marble tiles, staring up at the night sky between the edges of two very close-together cliffs. The stars are faint and far off and they confuse me because I wasn't able to see any stars when I stood at the end of the tunnel. I don't see how, in this underworld, I am able to catch even a glimpse of the heavens.

As I lie there, I hear the clink of metal hitting stone. Looking over, I'm pleased to see it's the witch's silver needle. For some reason the blood is gone from the tip. I wonder if it wiped off on my clothes when she tried to stab me that last time and missed. Rolling over, I sit up and grab the needle and slip it in my pocket. I might need it later.

I'm surrounded by torches. They burn in twin lines away from where I sit, held in place by gigantic metal sculptures that writhe in the flickering shadows like snakes in passion. Standing, I can make out a distant structure that bears a vague resemblance to the Greek Parthenon. It could be miles away but it's not as if I have any other place to go. Feeling good about my escape from the witch, I set off at a brisk pace.

It takes me an hour to reach the white building.

On the steps of the structure, there's a bustle of activity. I'm glad to discover this crowd is not brain-dead like the one back at the river. At the same time it's not a major social scene. As I get in line, I notice how orderly the group is. The line leads straight up the steps towards the dimly lit interior but no one pushes to get to the front.

Maybe they have their reasons. I can't see what's going on inside but every now and then I hear two loud sounds reverberate from the heart of the Parthenon's cousin. A beautiful melody of chimes blowing in a breeze and a despairing wailing noise.

The second sound worries me.

The wait is long. There's no table with magazines to read and the people around me, although polite, all seem to be caught up in their own thoughts. I get the impression most have heard about the Scale. To be frank, it's hard to imagine a more heavy place. It's not an evil spot, but it is a crossroads of immense significance. For we're about to be judged, our souls are, and the Scale will determine where we spend the rest of eternity.

I pick up that much from listening to the others.

Everyone seems to know it's the Scale that makes the sounds.

The sweet chimes mean you're going to heaven.

The screeching wail means you're going to hell.

I look for the women I crossed over the river with but don't see them. I wish at least one was nearby. I'm anxious; I long for companionship. Just meeting them, I could tell they were kindhearted. For sure, they didn't have the blood of thousands on their hands.

I wish Yaksha had never turned me into a vampire.

I would have been in and out of this place centuries ago.

No sweat. I had been a good mother and wife.

I feel as if I stand there for hours. It's difficult to gauge the passage of time. Overhead, the stars remain fixed in place. Either the earth has stopped rotating or else we're no longer on it. I try without success to find a familiar constellation. I keep thinking about my friends and how much I love them.

I pray Matt learns to accept Teri as a vampire.

I hope he's able to find his mother.

Umara. I would have loved to have met her.

Finally, the slow-moving line leads me inside. Two groups of characters – one in white-hooded robes, the other red – direct the traffic. Someone refers to them as *Caretakers*. The Caretakers in white are the good guys. The ones in red . . . I hear you don't want to get too close to them. Both move about silently, their faces largely covered, without making a fuss.

For the first time I realize there are many rooms inside the structure. A white-hooded Caretaker places me in a small area behind a dozen people. Inside the room is a black marble table, on which sits a gold Scale as large as a desk. Numerous candles light the room but the Scale has no need of them; it possesses its own lustre. Its design is simple and elegant. Two circular plates hang by three sets of chains each, which are attached to a sleek pole that sits atop a square bar. It's the bar, welded tight in a heavy cube, that supports the whole thing.

Behind the Scale, on the right, is a doorway filled with a golden light. I can't see any particular object in the light but it's enough to be near it, to stare at it and feel its soothing warmth. On the left is another doorway, only the light coming from it is a terrifying red. It makes my eyes ache to look at it.

Inside the room, the line isn't exactly straight, it's spread out. When it comes to the final step, it appears people are given a choice of when to take it, within reason. There's no pushing or jockeying to get ahead. But I watch, fascinated, as a young African girl approaches the Scale. She's pretty but far too thin. It's possible she starved to death. She announces herself when she reaches the Scale.

'My name is Batu Sangal. I am fourteen years old.'

Batu must have arrived before me and studied the proper protocol; she knows what to do. I watch as, closing her eyes, she stretches out her hands so one hangs above each of the Scale's plates. I marvel how steady she keeps her arms, but it's possible they're under the control of an invisible force. Her hands seem to hover for ages. Finally, as if by magic, jewels begin to form beneath her fingers.

On the right side of the Scale, a small pile of diamonds begins to appear. On the left plate, a smaller collection of black pearls materializes. For a moment the Scale teeters, as if deciding which side is heavier. But since the amount of diamonds is so much greater, I'm not surprised when the gold plate settles down on the right side.

At that instant the sound of chimes fills the room.

The enchanting melody causes everyone to sigh with relief.

Clearly the diamonds represent our virtues.

While the black pearls are symbolic of our sins.

A white-hooded Caretaker takes Batu's hand and leads her towards the door on the right, where she disappears into the golden light. I feel happy for her and wish I was following in her footsteps. It doesn't take a genius to figure out what the two doors represent.

Next up is a well-dressed woman from Los Angeles. I recognize the accent.

'My name is Sharon McCloud. I am seventy years old.'

Sharon stretches out her arms, palms up, and closes her eyes and waits. Me, I think I would keep my eyes open in case the pile of black pearls on the left starts piling up. I'm not sure how the Caretakers deal with runners and I hope I never find out. Still, I would want to see what is materializing beneath my hands. I suppose Sharon is certain she is going to paradise.

Sharon ends up with six bright diamonds on the right plate. But so many black pearls form on the left side that it quickly causes the Scale to tilt in that direction. It strikes the table beneath the plate with an audible bang, which causes her eyes to fly open.

'No,' she whispers. 'There must be some mistake.'

The screeching wail seems to come out of the walls.

Everyone groans; the sound makes our heads ache.

'No!' Sharon screams. 'I'm a Christian! I renounce Satan and all his works! You're making a mistake! I didn't do anything wrong! You can't put me in there!'

The red-robed Caretakers are experienced. Three of them descend with amazing speed and grab Sharon by her arms and legs and lift her off the floor. They carry her towards the left door and the wicked bloody light.

'Please!' Sharon begs. 'Don't put me in the fire! I don't want to go in the fire!'

The Caretakers go as far as the threshold of the left door, but don't cross inside. Dark arms with burned flesh reach out and grab Sharon. The sight of the arms causes me to do a double take.

I swear I've seen them before.

The Caretakers let go and Sharon's screams slowly fade away.

'Jesus,' I whisper. She's gone but the sound of her cries haunts me. The diamonds and pearls disappear before another person steps forward.

The guy in front of me goes next. He looks like an Eskimo. He still has on a heavy seal coat and, incredibly, has a raw fish in his pocket. He must have drowned while ice fishing.

His case is maddening. He holds out his hands and closes his eyes and an equal number of bright diamonds and black pearls materialize. At least to the eye. But the gold plates, after fluctuating up and down on both sides for what seems like forever, finally settle on the right side.

The chimes fill the room.

The collective sigh of relief is loud.

The Eskimo is led off to the golden light.

Suddenly the young blonde woman comes up beside me.

'How are you doing?' she asks.

'I've been better.'

She nods toward the Scale. 'You're going to be all right.'

'I don't know. My history, it's complicated.'

'But your heart is good. I can tell.'

'Do you know how far they go back?'

'What do you mean?'

'Does this Scale weigh everything you've done in life? Or are more recent events more important? You see what I'm asking.'

'Sure. Maybe a person got off to a bad start but then they found their path in life and became a better human being.'

'Exactly. It seems to me that where you end up should carry more weight.' I say this because my behaviour improved as I went along in life, even for a vampire. Indeed, towards the end, I saved a lot of lives.

Of course, in the beginning, I took a lot of lives.

The blonde shakes her head. 'I can't say for sure how it works.'

'You look awfully optimistic. Have you gone yet?'

'I was waiting for you and that other woman.'

'That's nice of you. Have you seen her?'

'No. But I'm not surprised. She told me when we were crossing the river with the ferryman that her case is different.'

'What do you mean?' I ask.

'She said her path depended on what you decided.'

'She didn't tell me that.'

'I might have misunderstood her.'

'Besides, there's nothing left to decide. What's done is done.'

The blonde is distracted, excited to move on. 'Hey, are you ready to give it a go?' she asks.

I hesitate. 'Are you?'

'I can go first if you want.'

'Great. I'll root for you.'

There's a man already in front of us. He looks like a European businessman. I can tell he's nervous. His face is intelligent but maybe that's his problem. He might have made too many shrewd decisions in his life, ones that cost others but not himself. He introduces himself before the Scale.

'My name is Roberto Vion. I am forty-nine years old.'

I lean over and whisper to the blonde. 'Why do you have to state your age?'

'I heard if you're older, the Scale expects more of you.'

'Oh shit.'

Roberto stretches out his arms and closes his eyes. Immediately the diamonds begin to pile up at a fast rate. Then, halfway through the process, probably halfway through his life, the pearls start to pour out at high speed. It's like he hit a bad stretch.

Near the end, the diamonds start to increase.

When it's over, the Scale wobbles back and forth.

But it settles on the left side. Under the weight of the pearls.

The room is dead silent. Except for the Caretakers. The red-hooded and white-hooded ones whisper back and forth to each other.

The tension is unbearable. My partner and I exchange looks.

The wail finally starts. It's so loud.

Roberto takes it like a man. He's quiet as he's led away.

'Damn it. There's no mercy here,' I swear.

'There is,' a voice says at our backs. We turn to find the wise woman has found us. Her company is reassuring but my nerves are still taut.

'Glad you could make it,' I say with feeling.

She smiles as she pats me on the back. 'Whose turn is it?'

'I'm going next,' the blonde says.

Neither of us tries to stop her. The small crowd parts as she makes her way up front. She nods to both coloured Caretakers, and to the Scale itself.

'My name is Teresa Raine. I am nineteen years old.'

Closing her eyes, she stretches out her hands.

'It's Teri!' I gasp. 'Why didn't I recognize her?'

'You knew her,' the other woman says.

'But what's she doing here? She's not dead.'

'How do you know when she died?'

'I just made her into a vampire!'

'There is no before or after here. There is only now.'

I shake my head. 'This place is not natural.'

Teri holds her palms above the gold plates. Things start slow for her, I'm not sure why. A few small diamonds appear, followed by a couple of black pearls. But then the pile of diamonds begins to grow. The size and brightness of the stones increase. No more pearls appear.

Her plate comes to rest on the right side.

The chimes sing louder than ever.

The woman and I cheer. Teri calls to us as a white-hooded Caretaker takes her away. She doesn't struggle with the guy, but tries her best to tell him that she wants to wait for us. He shakes his head. As she's being led to the right door, she shouts to me, 'I love you!'

Teri disappears into the golden light.

I discover I'm weeping.

I'm so happy for her, and so scared for myself.

The woman squeezes my hand. 'It's time,' she says.

'What happens if I fail?'

'Your path has always been difficult. Don't falter here at the end.'

Her advice sounds like something Krishna would say.

I step up to the front and nod to the Scale and the Caretakers.

'I am Sita. I am five thousand one hundred and fifty-two years old.'

A stir fans the room. Voices murmur all around.

A tall red-hooded Caretaker orders everyone to hush. Something about his voice sounds familiar.

I hate him. He's not indifferent like the others. He's evil.

Keeping my eyes open, I stretch out my arms. As I place my hands above the plates, palms upward, I feel as if something reaches out and locks them in place. The invisible grip is strong enough to hold a normal human in place. Of course, I'm not human, yet I suspect that even I could not break free. Plus I see no point in fighting the process. I mean, where am I going to run?

Diamonds begin to collect on the right side, small ones. This goes on for a while and I feel encouraged but then black pearls start to pour on to the left plate. I realize this must be a result of when Yaksha changed me into a vampire. Back in the days when we killed whoever crossed our path.

Then something miraculous happens.

A single giant diamond appears above the right plate. It drops on to it from a height of several inches and heavily weighs it down. In an instant I know the precious jewel is from the day I met Krishna and took my vow not to make any more vampires. The diamond is so large it must weigh several pounds. I suddenly feel good about my chances.

Then fate or destiny intervenes.

Pearls and diamonds begin to pour out of the thin air at an incredible speed. Since the Scale has so many years to cover, I can understand the need for haste. But this is ridiculous.

There are so many pearls and diamonds on each side, they begin to fall off the plates on to the table, and I have to ask myself how I managed to commit so many good and bad deeds. Frankly, most of my life I just kept my head down and tried to keep people from noticing that I never aged. Yet the Scale acts like I never stopped killing or saving people.

Near the end, the flow begins to slow.

Especially on the diamond side. The pearls take over. The left side looks like it's going to win.

Then a handful of extra large diamonds appear.

The Scale wobbles back and forth, up and down. More than half the pearls and diamonds, half my life, lie spread over the black table. There's no room on the plates to measure all that I have done or failed to do. It's not fair but I realize this isn't a place where you get to argue your case.

At some point, I'm not exactly sure when, the invisible grip releases my hands and my arms fall to my sides and I finally close my eyes. But I feel my fingers touch the Scale plates as they drown in the piles of black pearls and diamonds. My heartbeat has finally returned, I feel that too, I feel it breaking. Especially as the red and white Caretakers begin to whisper to each other. Yet eventually even they stop.

The room falls dead silent.

Please, Krishna.

A screeching wail suddenly fills the room.

I open my eyes and see the left plate is lower.

The black pearls have won.

The tall red-hooded Caretaker grabs my left arm.

I try to shake him off and fail. He is very strong.

'I know what bloody door I have to take,' I snap.

He speaks in a voice I know. A voice I heard in a crummy motel in London just before I skinned an innocent woman and ate her alive. The voice is soft-spoken but firm; it carries the weight of authority and I have no reason to doubt what he says.

Yet he doesn't raise his hood, and I cannot see his face.

'You have been judged and there is no escape from

that judgment. You are damned. A word from me and you will be taken through the red door, where there is only fire and pain. There you will burn. But not like you burned on earth. In the world of the living you were a vampire. There you would heal quickly. But in the world of fire, there is no relief. There is only agony.'

I cower. I want to tell him to forget his silly speech and get on with it but I feel as long as he's talking, I'm not suffering. In that moment, even an instant without pain feels like a blessing. So I listen, I listen closely, for he appears to be implying that he has the power to change my fate, or at least postpone it for a time.

I bow my head respectfully. 'I am listening,' I say.

He comes near so that only I can hear, and his words seem to cast shadows over my thoughts. This speech of his is not new. I suddenly realize it is very old, and I know before he says it that he is going to offer me a deal.

'I have the power to give you a respite from your judgment,' he says.

'How long a respite?'

'Does it matter? Say no to me now and you will burn.'

I swallow thickly. 'What do you want?'

'Kill the Light Bearer.'

'Who is the Light Bearer?'

'You will know her when you meet her.' He pauses. 'She is wise.'

'How am I to kill her? I'm dead.'

'You will be sent back. I will send you.'

'Why don't you kill her yourself?'

'Enough!' he shouts. 'I have already spent more time with you than you're worth. Do as I command or your torment will begin. Decide now.'

I can't just murder this Light Bearer. That's not who I am. Also, she sounds like someone the world needs. Like another John.

But I can't allow this monster to put me in the fire.

After suffering such agony, I'd never be myself again.

From the shadow of his hood, his eyes bear down on me. Once more, my spirit cowers. My fear is too great. I choose without really choosing.

He has hold of my left arm so I offer him my right hand.

'Deal,' I say.

25

Suddenly, I'm back in the room in Malibu. Umara has opened her eyes and is studying me. The others sit with their eyes closed, deep in a trance state. I sense they are still in Egypt, in the temple.

'What happened?' she asks.

'How long have I been gone?' I'm not afraid that Brutran and her cronies are spying on us. Matt has taken charge of security. For his sake, though, I hope he's not recording this conversation.

'A few seconds. But something's changed. Sita?'

'I remembered what happened when I died.'

'Good,' Umara says.

I feel like a child, no different from the children around me. Lowering my head, I barely hold back the tears. 'It isn't good. My life, my whole life, has been

401

nothing but a sham.'

'Why do you say that?'

'You wouldn't understand.'

'Try me.'

'I went before the Scale and was judged.'

'And?'

'You know what it is?'

'Yes. What happened?' Umara asks.

'I failed.'

Umara puts a hand to her lip. 'Oh my.'

'Don't act surprised. You knew something terrible would happen when you forced me to recall my death.'

Umara considers. 'I knew the answer to our problem with the Telar was stored in the memory of your death experience. And since you had blocked out the experience, I feared it would be traumatic.'

'It was traumatic all right. It's not every day you discover you're going to hell.'

'You saw a portion of the truth. That's all.'

'How do you know about the Scale? You've never died.'

'What comes before or after has no meaning in that place.'

I'm shocked. 'That woman I kept running into. That was you.'

Umara hesitates. 'It's possible it will be me.'

'I don't understand.'

'Whether our brains are Telar, human, or vampire, they all struggle when it comes to dealing with time paradoxes. The visions you were shown are mysterious.

That's why I warn you against jumping to any conclusions.'

'Umara, I appreciate the pep talk but when I stood before the Scale, the results were clear cut. My virtues and vices were weighed and I was found wanting. I'm damned.'

'Did you actually enter the inferno region?'

'I got scared and made a quick deal.' I stop and sigh. 'I know I'm only postponing the inevitable.'

'Who offered you this deal?'

'I suspect it was the Familiar who haunts me now. But I suppose we should be grateful to him. What you sensed was true. I was given the key to destroying the Telar.'

'What is it?'

'You mean *who* is it?' I pause. 'You.'

Umara is silent a long time. 'I suspected,' she whispers.

'I should have guessed the truth when you explained how the Telar became immortal. When you tapped into that high spiritual plane and that white light descended, it transformed all the Telar. You said it yourself, that is what made your people immortal. That light was brought to earth during that first Link, and as far as I can tell you're the only surviving member of that group. True?'

'Yes.'

'You anchor that light to this world. When I was in the underworld, it became clear to me that if the Light Bearer was killed, the Telar would become vulnerable.'

Umara frowns. 'How can I be the Light Bearer?'

I look at my dear friend. How much I wish she could embrace me and allow her magical white light to flow into my heart and make me immortal like the angels in heaven. Yet to keep the demon at bay for the time being – for however long he'll let me walk the earth – I have to hold her in my arms and break her neck.

'The demon is a liar. He tried to confuse me by casting you in his place. Yet he knows you carry the light that protects the Telar.' I pause. 'So in a sense he told me a great truth.'

Umara nods. 'If it has to be done, then do it. Make it quick.'

'You misunderstand me. I'm not going to kill you. Get out of here while you can. I'll return to the kids. They're waiting for their leader. The final battle with Haru and the Source still has to be fought.'

Umara smiles at me and shakes her head and I know that she has no intention of leaving.

'Thousands of years ago,' she says, 'when I was part of the original Link, and we were able to explore higher dimensions, it was said that even the Lord's most powerful archangels feared to double-cross Tarana.'

'Are you saying that's the Familiar I met?'

'I fear it is. You can't make a deal with him and then ignore it. You can't imagine the horror of the revenge he will take. Besides, the Telar must be destroyed. Be strong, Sita, kill me.'

'I'm not strong!' I say bitterly. 'If I wasn't damned before I died, I am now. You're my friend. I haven't known you long but I feel in time we could have become close friends. Yet when the Scale pronounced my doom and I came face to face with the demon, and he threatened me with the fire, I immediately turned on you. I'm a coward. I gave you up.'

'I'm sure you did what you had to do.'

I snort at the irony in her words. 'Where I'm going, that's probably their favorite excuse.'

Umara takes my hand. 'What exactly did Tarana ask for?'

'Your head on a platter.'

'Like John the Baptist?'

'Yes.'

Umara strokes my palm. 'I was there in those days, in Jerusalem. I saw what happened. I admired John. When Herod took him captive, all the king demanded was that John renounce Christ. And Herod said he would let him go. Herod meant it, too; he didn't want to make John into a martyr. He knew it would just stir up his kingdom. But John refused his offer.'

'He was a braver soul than me.'

'No, Sita. Did Tarana ask you to renounce Krishna?'

'No.'

'He didn't ask because he knew you would refuse.'

'I called to Krishna when I stepped in front of Matt's laser rifle. As the blast tore through my chest, I focused on Krishna and nothing else. But when I died, I was forced to wander lost in the dark underworld. And when I was finally judged, I failed. The Lord's name proved useless in the end.'

'The knowledge of his name helped you cross the river.'

I snicker. 'What good did that do me? Haven't you heard a word I've said since we opened our eyes?'

'You're alive now. Where there's life, there's hope.'

I take back my hand and gesture to the silent kids, the ones on our floor and the larger group below. 'These children are my final testament. Those who survive our attack on the Telar will exit the session and discover they have blisters. They'll scratch them but the itch won't go away. Soon the blisters will cover their bodies and ooze a black fluid. Then the real fun will begin. They'll start vomiting and have convulsions. They'll die in agony.' I pause. 'You can see why I don't think my karma's going to improve in the short time I have left.'

'You can still give them the vaccine.'

'If I do that, I'd be like Hercules walking away from the Hydra and saying maybe I should kill the monster some other day.'

'Don't be Hercules. Be Iolaus.'

'You are Iolaus!' I snap. 'At least when it comes to Haru and the other Telar waiting in Egypt. But only if you're dead. Only if you let me snap your neck. Otherwise, we'll never kill Haru and his partners. It's not Hatram that protects them. It's you.'

She nods. 'I know. It's why I've come here.'

I shouldn't be stunned and yet I am. 'To sacrifice your life?'

'To follow in John the Baptist's footsteps. When they brought Herod his head, on a silver platter, I knew that one day that would be my destiny.'

I shake my head. 'I told you, I have no intention of fulfilling the deal I made with Tarana.'

'Then he'll come back for you.'

'He's going to do that anyway.'

'Sita, you're not listening to me.'

'I'm not killing you. Forget it. If you want to die, jump off a bridge.'

'There's isn't a bridge or building tall enough to kill me.'

'Then buy an axe and pay a guy on skid row a thousand bucks to chop off your head. Just don't ask me to do it.'

'My death will delay Tarana's revenge on you.'

'I don't care about pleasing Tarana! I want to please Krishna! I want him to save me!' I stop and press my hand to my aching head. 'Why didn't he save me when it mattered?'

'I don't know. But kill me and you'll destroy the Source, and perhaps the Cradle, and you'll have time to find out.'

I stare at my stained palms and then at Umara's kind face.

'What about Matt? First I kill his girlfriend and then his mother. Excuse me but I think I've exhausted my forgiveness quota with him.'

'I told Matt on the way here that this was my last day.'

'He would never have accepted that.'

'He did. I told him he had to accept it.'

'How?'

She rubs my shoulder. 'Would it help if I told you I'm

407

ready to die? That my life's gone on too long.' She pauses. 'That I'm lonely without Yaksha.'

I briefly close my eyes. 'I miss him, too.'

'Send me to him. That's the greatest gift you can give me. And when you've learned all you need to know, find a way to follow me home.'

I reach over and caress her neck. 'You're a brave woman. I can see why Yaksha loved you.'

She presses my hand to her neck. 'Your face was the last face he saw. Your face is the last I'll see. So our destinies are entwined. Don't lose faith, Sita. Krishna hasn't forgotten you.'

I want to thank her for her kind words but don't know how.

I break her neck, instead. She dies instantly.

In the blink of an eye I'm back in the underground chamber in Egypt, hovering above Haru and the remaining members of the Source. The power of the Cradle continues to wait to attack. The kids don't even know that I've been gone. For them nothing has changed, although with Umara gone our power has diminished.

I feel her loss, even if I'm not allowed to mourn it.

I struggle to focus on the task at hand.

'Stand back while I speak to their head Familiar,' I instruct the Cradle. The children acknowledge the order with a mental nod.

Carefully, I detach from the group and float down towards the Telar's Link. Not far above the bolts of flame and Hatram's massive head, I halt. I notice him watching me and bow in his direction.

'It's a pleasure to meet you, Hatram,' I say by way of telepathy. 'I have heard of you and your many extraordinary exploits.'

He studies me. 'Why have you come?'

I have no choice, I have to play it by ear and act like I know more than I do. Since I'm conversing with a demon, it feels only natural that I should lie.

'To set you free of the tedious task of guarding these boring mortals. I have just met with Tarana and he and I have reached an agreement. He asked me to dispatch the Telar who preserved the lives of this miserable group and I have done so. In return he said you would help my people.'

Hatram is not impressed. 'Your group is made up of children.'

'These children are under the direct protection of Tarana.'

'He has never said this to me.'

'He keeps his own counsel. Surely you must know of Umara.'

He raises his head. 'Of course.'

'She's the sacrifice I offered Tarana for your help.'

Hatram is stunned. 'Umara is dead?'

'Yes. Note how the light that surrounds this group has faded.'

Hatram studies the mortals who sit around the stone table.

'It is true,' he says.

'You have a keen eye.'

'Umara was old and powerful. How were you able to destroy her?'

'First I gained her trust. Then I betrayed her.'

Hatram nods. 'She did the same to me, long ago.'

'She got the punishment she deserved. Now I would appreciate a small favour in return. Remove your mighty flames and let my children feast on their prey.'

'What is your name?'

'Sita. Some call me the Last Vampire.'

'I have heard of you.'

'You flatter me,' I say.

'I have heard you're not to be trusted.'

'If you are reluctant to help me, I understand. Perhaps you feel the need to consult with Tarana. But I was told to deliver this message to you and I have done so. If you wish to disturb him further, that is up to you.'

Hatram considers. He obviously fears Tarana. I find that interesting. I'm still trying to ascertain how high Tarana's position is in the hierarchy of demons. It's not like the creatures wear badges or stripes.

'I wish I could have been present at Umara's execution,' he says.

'I assure you it was both bloody and painful.'

'You handled it yourself?'

'Yes,' I say.

'If I drop my protective flames, what will you do to the Source?'

'I would be flattered if you would stay and watch. I think you would find our attack . . . creative.'

Hatram flashes a hungry grin. 'You are sly, Sita. I'm

glad to see that aspect of your reputation has not been exaggerated.'

'Thank you.'

'What help can I offer?'

'The Cradle and I are invisible to Haru and his partners. They can feel us but they're confident we can't pierce their Link. They have grown cocky after being in control for so many years. With your help, I'd like to burst their pride. I want to appear before them as if I'm physically present in this chamber. Can you make this happen?'

Hatram looks aroused. 'I know a secret magical working that can make that possible.'

'Hatram, you are a wonder.'

'But tell me, what will you do for me in return?'

'What do you wish?'

'Umara's head.'

'I'll give you her heart. After all, it was her heart that betrayed you.'

'Well said. When do you wish to appear?'

'Now.'

Moments later, I sit at the head of Haru's table in the stone chair he reserves for his most powerful Familiar. Because their eyes are closed, the group isn't aware I'm in the room until I speak.

'Hello, people,' I say cheerfully.

Their eyes snap open. Including Haru, there are four men and four women present. Most are dressed in casual attire but Haru has on the same black suit and a red shirt as before. He's squat and strong. He has a long torso that reminds me of a gargoyle. His beady eyes belong to a demon. For a guy who has ruled the world for ages, he's one ugly bastard.

'How did you get in here?' he demands.

'Does it matter? I'm here and I'm not leaving until I get what I want.'

'What do you want?' a beautiful woman on Haru's left asks. She is pure Egyptian. Her black hair is thick and shiny, her copper skin is without blemish. I realize I'm looking at Haru's wife.

'Revenge,' I say.

'Isn't such an emotion beneath you?' Haru asks, and I can see he is scared. They all are. The last thing they expected has occurred. Despite all their planning, all their layers of physical and psychic shields, their great enemy has suddenly materialized before their eyes.

My voice hardens. 'The last time we met, Haru, you tortured me so viciously that I passed out from the pain.'

Haru shrugs but his fear remains. 'You refused to talk.'

A part of me pities him. With Hatram's protection out of the way, I can feel the power of the Cradle's focus on this chamber. It reminds me again how dangerous these kids can be. They wait with bated breath to torture the Telar. Like Hatram, they crave the pain, it feeds them.

'It's over,' I say. 'Your thousands of years of subjugation. Look at the way you sit here, so smug and confident in your hidden temple. Did you meet here when you decided to create a virus that would wipe out the bulk of humanity?'

'We haven't released the virus,' Haru's wife says. 'Not so far. But if you force our hand, we can't be responsible for what happens.'

'How quickly you resort to childish threats. You're not going to be giving any more orders. In fact, none of you are going to leave this room alive.'

Haru struggles to keep his composure. 'Surely we can reach an agreement. The virus is like the American and Soviet nuclear arsenals during the Cold War. They were never meant to be used. They only existed as instruments of deterrence.'

'Then why did you lecture me endlessly about how overpopulation was destroying the earth? Let's be honest. You created the virus to kill billions. Not for a moment did you stop to consider how much suffering you would cause. For that reason you deserve no more sympathy than the Nazis who ran the death camps. Of course, Haru, you'll recall that you boasted to me that you and your group were behind the Nazis.'

The others glare at Haru, including his wife.

'We apologize for how Haru treated you,' a kindly-looking woman on my right says. 'Most of us were opposed to the Arosa operation. We saw no point in taking you captive. Certainly, we were appalled at your torture.'

'Are you saying it was all Haru's fault?' I ask.

'That would not be far from the truth,' a man says from across the table. He's the only other one who wears a suit. He looks like a banker.

'Then why didn't one of you try to rescue me?' I ask. 'Or better yet, warn me before I was taken captive.'

Haru's wife speaks. 'We discussed the issue at length but Haru insisted that you were dangerous and needed to be broken. We weren't allowed to vote on the matter.'

I nod to Haru. 'It looks like your people are hanging you out to dry.'

'Umara put you up to this, didn't she?' he snaps.

'No.'

'Now you lie, Sita. You recall how sensitive I am.'

'I recall how arrogant you are! You know nothing about Umara. You never will.' I stand and stroll around the table. 'As of this instant, you will discover that the Familiars that were protecting you have turned against you. The IIC is ready to psychically attack with their Array. Indeed, that's why you'll notice that your bodies are paralyzed from the waist down.'

As a group, they struggle to stand. They fail.

'Please, show mercy,' Haru's wife begs.

I respond angrily. 'I begged for mercy from Haru and all he did was keep turning up the dial on the Pulse. Maybe the rest of you wouldn't have been so cruel, I don't know. But I do know you represent the cream of the Telar and yet none of you has a conscience. Just now, not one of you has even tried to take responsibility for your crimes. You just keep trying to pass the blame to Haru.'

Several of them try to speak at once but I silence them.

414

'There's no point to this discussion. I'm not sure why I bother to speak to you. Already I have given Kram the order to fire a barrage of cruise missiles at this temple. The weapons are in the air, they will be here in ten minutes. And if you think I'm no better than Haru, then try to imagine what the IIC could do to you now that they have shattered your Link. Honestly, you should thank me for my mercy.'

'Are the missiles loaded with nuclear warheads?' Haru's wife asks.

I shake my head. 'I saw no reason to contaminate this area with radiation.'

Haru summons his most persuasive tone. 'Then there's still time. If you release us now, we can take shelter deep beneath this temple.'

'I'm not going to release you.'

'Think, Sita. We can help each other,' Haru pleads. 'I'd be willing to work with you to remake this world into a paradise. The last time we spoke, you had some wonderful ideas. They've stayed with me, I swear it.'

'Petty revenge is unworthy of you,' his wife says.

'You're probably right,' I say. 'But, you know, after all I've been through, it feels pretty good.'

I stay long enough to see the missiles arrive.

The temple is engulfed in flames.

Again, I pity them, even Haru, but not for the fire that kills them in this world. No one knows better than I how small a matter that is compared to the suffering that awaits them in the next world.

26 ━━━━

When I return to the room in Malibu, I find the majority of the kids still deep in a trance, although a few are starting to scratch. I can only assume the Cradle is psychically attacking the Telar who were protecting Haru and his inner circle, or at least the men and women who were related by blood to them. From working with the kids, I know they have a deep distrust of any Telar and would just as soon kill them all.

Leaving Umara's body beside Lark's, I flee the room and hurry upstairs. I want to get out of the main building before the children start dying. I don't want to see them suffer. But I run into Matt, who is armed to the teeth, and he tells me that Seymour's looking for me.

'He discovered you switched the vaccine for the virus,' Matt says.

'I stained the virus blue so it looked the same as the vaccine. How did he find out?'

'Remember, this vaccine works as an antidote, too. You get a shot, you should begin to feel better right away. Seymour believed he was giving out the permanent cure. He'd give the kids a shot and a few minutes later he'd ask how they were feeling. The kids kept saying they felt the same. That made him suspicious, but he wasn't given a chance to drill them. You swept in and gathered the kids together for your last session. So Seymour went looking for Charlie. He found him in the bottom basement and showed Charlie a sample of what he'd been injecting the kids with. You know Charlie, he invented this stuff. He just had to smell it to know you had tricked Seymour into shooting the kids up with a pure strain of the virus. Seymour freaked out, he tried to burst in on your session. If I hadn't stopped him, he would have disrupted your attack on the Source.'

'Did you see everything that happened in the room?'

'Not in your room. I was too busy keeping order. I had Seymour and Charlie screaming at me, along with Cynthia and Thomas Brutran. I was lucky to keep them at bay without hurting them.'

'Thanks for backing me up,' I say.

Matt shakes his head. 'I can't say I agree with how you handled the situation. Why use Seymour? He has a soft heart. I would have hated it but you should have had me give the kids the shots.'

'The kids in the Cradle are sensitive. The ones in the

Lens can almost read minds. I know you can block your thoughts, but there was a chance they would have picked up that you were hiding something. To be safe, I chose Seymour. He loves kids. I'm sure he felt good about giving them the shots, protecting them from the virus. I wanted the kids to sense his goodwill and nothing else.'

Matt nods his approval. 'Clever. But now you've got a problem. Seymour's demanding that you immediately give the kids the vaccine.'

'Does Charlie support him?'

'Sort of. He wants to talk to you first.'

'Then we've got to get them both out of here, and fast.'

Matt is torn. 'Isn't it enough to leave the kids in the Lens infected? According to what Freddy told us, the Cradle needs them to focus its power. Otherwise, the Cradle should be harmless.'

'The psychic gap between the most powerful kids in the Cradle and those in the Lens is not as great as you think. Even if we kill all the kids in the Lens, there's no guarantee that Brutran or the remaining children won't create another Lens in a few months. We can't take that risk. We have to follow Hercules' example and destroy all the heads of the monster.'

'But even he ran into a head he couldn't destroy.'

'I can't worry about that part of the story right now.'

Matt is a mass of emotion. Like Seymour, I know he's always had a soft spot for kids. 'Has Charlie told you how they're going to die?'

'I know it ain't going to be pretty.'

'It's going to be bloody awful. It might be more merciful if I stayed behind and took care of them.'

'No. Some of these kids are related to adults who work in this building. They are 'planned children.' The IIC paid the parents extra to have the kids on special days and in special places. It goes back to what Freddy told us. But their parents love them just the same and they're not going to stand by and let you put a bullet in their little darlings.'

'But they'll convulse and haemorrhage. They'll die in agony.'

'More reason to get out of here now.'

'Wait. You want us all to leave?'

'Except for the infected kids, I want the building evacuated.'

Matt finally gets it. 'Are you saying the war's over? That the Source has been destroyed?'

'They're all dead and buried under a mass of sand.'

Matt smiles. 'My mother will be pleased. She's been fighting those bastards for thousands of years.'

I put a hand on his shoulder. A Telar grenade hangs loose from a clip and bumps against my hand. 'Matt. I don't know how to tell you this.'

He lowers his head. 'No,' he says.

'She told me she talked to you about it on the ride down.'

He turns away and my hand falls uselessly at my side. He pounds the wall. 'This can't be happening! Not again!'

I stand there feeling utterly useless, extremely vulnerable, and totally damned. 'She died to disrupt the Telar Link. She sacrificed herself so they could be killed.'

'I don't know what you're saying.'

'I'm not sure I understand it myself. It seems that long ago the Telar developed a remarkable Link and tapped into a spiritual realm of light and joy. And they were able to channel that light into the lives of their people. It was only later they discovered that they were immortal.'

'My mother told me this story last night.'

'Did she tell you that she was the last member of that original Link? The reason the Telar were immortal was not because they possessed some secret knowledge. It was because they were blessed from this high realm. To this day, it's like your mother functioned as a vehicle for this blessing.'

'Are you saying that she protected them?'

'Yes. Just by being alive, she made them virtually impossible to kill. That's why she had to give up her life to stop them.'

His pain turns ugly. 'How?'

'Excuse me?'

'How did she die?'

'She asked me . . . I killed her. I broke her neck.'

The look of horror on his face takes me to the time outside the cave. When I told him I was trying to transform Teri into a vampire to save her. He killed me then and it looks like he could kill me again. He is so strong. Yet he gestures helplessly.

'You couldn't have done that, Sita. Not you, not again.'

'I can't tell you how sorry I am. I know apologies are useless. All I can say is that I did what I had to do.'

'Did you leave her down there? With the sick kids?'

'Yes. But as far as I know, most of the kids are still in a trance.'

Matt reaches out a trembling hand and touches my neck. I can't bear to see the pain in his eyes and so I close my own. I feel his fingers touch my skin. It's possible I have a second left to live, and afterwards an eternity of fiery damnation to look forward to. Yet, whatever he does to me, I feel I will deserve it.

His touch turns to a gentle caress. 'I'm proud of you,' he says.

I open my eyes. 'Matt?'

'Everything you've done so far ... I would never have had the courage. That includes what you did to my mother.'

I swallow. 'If there had been any other way.'

'There wasn't.' He takes back his hand and stands at attention. 'Tell me what you want me to do.'

'Have all the adults been inoculated?'

'Charlie says we have a hundred per cent containment of the virus when it comes to the adults.'

'We have to isolate the kids in the bottom level of the basement.'

'Those in the Lens or all of them?'

The question and answer to that will haunt the rest of my life.

'All of them,' I say. 'First isolate the kids and then enlist the help of IIC security and start moving the adults out fast. Lie if you have to. Say the vaccine isn't working the way we expected on the children and we have to quarantine them more carefully.'

'Keeping IIC security in line will be difficult.'

'It's why you're here. It's a job only you can do. I'll get Seymour and Charlie and we'll meet outside. Oh, where's Shanti?'

'I assume she's where you left her.'

'I put her in an empty room above the Cradle. She's probably still there. I'll get her.'

'What about Cynthia Brutran and her husband?'

'Order them out of the building.'

'Their daughter is one of those who's going to get sick. I don't care how evil Cindy is, she's not going to leave Jolie. Not without a fight.'

'I'll take care of Brutran. The key is to move fast.'

Matt fiddles with the Telar grenade pinned to his chest. 'I understand what has to be done.' He leans over and gives me a quick kiss on the lips. 'You didn't have a choice.'

'How can you be so understanding?'

'I don't have a choice.'

Matt tells me about a van he's placed outside the main entrance and gives me several sets of keys. He explains about the vehicle's cell phones and hidden weapons. But I know he has something up his sleeve he's not telling me about.

I run towards the isolated room where I left Shanti but bump into her in the elevator. She was on her way to see me. Her eyes are big and red and I can see she's been crying. She hugs me when we meet.

'Did it work?' she asks.

'It worked.'

'Is Umara OK?'

'She didn't make it.'

'What happened?'

'I don't have time to explain. I need you to get to a black van that's parked out front.' I hand her a set of keys. 'Wait there until I arrive. I won't be long.' I turn to leave.

'Wait! Sita, there's something wrong with the vaccine. The kids are coming out of the session. I saw their hands and legs. They've got worse blisters than Seymour and I had. They're real sick.'

'Trust me, I'll handle it. Right now I need you to get to the van.'

'Is Seymour coming?'

'I'll get him. Now go!'

Unfortunately, it's the Brutrans I run into next, not Seymour and Charlie. We meet in a stairway between the basement floors. Tom and Cindy are both armed and have half a dozen guards with them. They plant themselves firmly in my way. But they're below me, I have the high ground, and that makes a bigger difference than they realize.

Cindy and Tom have semi-automatic handguns.

They don't point them at me but they don't exactly avoid me either. They look tired and desperate.

'Where are you going?' Cindy demands.

'To the basement to get Charlie and Seymour.'

'They're there but I've placed them under guard.'

'Why?'

'This is still our building,' Cindy says. 'I've been monitoring you the last ten minutes. You're gathering your friends and preparing to leave. In all this time, you haven't stopped to call me. I haven't been debriefed.'

'You want a debriefing, I'll give you one. The Source has been wiped out. Our business is finished. My people and I are getting out of here. Do you have a problem with that?'

'You're damn right we do,' Tom says. 'You're leaving behind hundreds of sick kids, and as far as we can tell, no cure. One of those kids is our daughter.'

I pause. 'Has Jolie begun to show symptoms?'

Cindy nods. 'Many are sick. I moved Jolie to our clinic and sedated her to decrease her pain. But Matt has managed to collect all the vaccine. We're not sure how. We only know we can't find any. Even Charlie is out.'

Matt is strong and capable of making his own decisions. While I was travelling through the underworld, he must have guessed my general plan and taken control of the vaccine.

'Release Seymour and Charlie and I'll see what I can do about getting more vaccine.'

'No,' Tom says. 'They're the only insurance we have.'

424

'In other words, we don't trust you,' Cindy says.

'I just destroyed the Telar. That's why we decided to work together, isn't it? I have also inoculated the bulk of your people against a potentially fatal virus. From my perspective, I've upheld my end of the bargain. Now, in return, you put a gun in my face and tell me my friends are hostages.'

Tom sweats over the trigger on his gun. 'Give us the vaccine for the children and you and your friends will be free to go.'

'Those kids are assassins. They can strike the mind of anyone in the world. I can't just leave them here in your hands. They're too powerful.'

Tom frowns. 'Are you saying you're going to kill them?'

I turn to Cindy. 'How should I answer that?'

Cindy studies me and suddenly the light dawns inside. 'You want me to decide,' she gasps.

I shrug. 'I'm not Jolie's mother.'

'But you care for her,' Cindy says.

'You can give the children the vaccine on one condition. You've got to separate them. You've got to spread them across the globe and make sure they have no contact with each other. You have the resources to do this. But if you deviate from this rule, I'll hunt them down and kill them. After I kill you.' I pause. 'That's my deal. Take it or leave it.'

Tom's trigger finger shakes with anger. 'You're in no position to dictate what direction our firm must take. Especially when it comes to our children.'

'They're not your children. They're no longer under your control.'

Tom is ready to explode. 'What are you talking about?'

'Ask your wife.' I turn to her. 'Cindy?'

She points her gun between my eyes. Her arm is steady but her gaze is distant. It is not an easy decision to make, and I sympathize. That's why I'm dumping it in her lap. Jolie is a monster and she's a little girl. She is both and she is what they made her to be.

Cindy doesn't answer. But she pulls back the hammer on her gun.

Her husband stares at her in wide-eyed amazement. 'Cindy?'

'I'm thinking,' she whispers.

'About what?'

'Love.'

Tom snorts. 'Don't fall to pieces on me right now. I need you. Jolie needs you. We have to secure a supply of that vaccine. Until we do, we'll always be at the mercy of this witch.'

'The effects of the last vaccine we gave you are permanent,' I say.

He glares at me. 'Like we trust you.'

I don't respond. His remark is irrelevant. His wife is in charge. I have given her more authority than I ever imagined I would. She continues to stare at me, her gun held ready. Even if she pulls the trigger, she'll miss. All of them combined are no match for me.

'Tom,' Cindy says quietly.

'What?'

'Shut up.'

His handsome face swells with blood and his gun trembles. 'Jolie's life is in jeopardy! If you think you can choose this time to talk to me like that, then you—'

Cynthia Brutran shoots her husband in the forehead. Her handgun is a .45; it has heavy stopping power. A spray of bloody brains explodes out the back of his skull and paints the stairway wall. His body drops and rolls down a flight of stairs. It comes to a halt in a pool of blood, his eyes wide open, staring at nothing.

The IIC guards come to full alert. The stakes of our confrontation have risen. Cindy turns the gun back on me. 'I've come to a decision.'

'I can see that,' I say.

'I leave here with you and Jolie. You find the real vaccine and give her a shot. Her symptoms better fade in a few minutes.'

'Why follow us? What's your purpose?'

'You know our business is far from over.'

She refers to the game, CII, Cosmic Intuitive Illusion, and whatever else the kids have programmed onto the Internet.

'Release Seymour and Charlie,' I say.

'Agreed.'

'What do you want me to do with the rest of the children?'

'You made them sick. You decide.'

She tries to throw the responsibility back at me.

'Call your guards and tell them to let Seymour and

Charlie go,' I say. 'Get your daughter. I'll meet you outside the main entrance in a few minutes.'

She taps my forehead with the tip of her gun. 'Sita?'

'Cindy?'

'No tricks.'

'Sure.' But I suspect it won't be up to me.

27 ～

We're outside in the black Mercedes van that Matt has procured for us. This is Malibu, home of the world's most famous celebrities. Armoured vehicles can be rented at the last minute with a call and a credit card. The vehicle has three rows of seats. Matt climbs behind the wheel. I'm beside him in the passenger seat. Behind me are Cindy, Jolie and Charlie. The Telar scientist has just given Jolie a shot of the C-1 vaccine and the child rests in her mother's lap. She's still groggy from the pain medication she received at the IIC clinic.

Shanti's way in back, lying down, resting her head on Seymour's lap. She doesn't want to complain but it seems the last session sucked the life out of her. She has a pounding headache. Seymour tries to comfort her but at the same time he fumes.

Matt has started the van and is about to drive away.

Seymour wants to talk. Hell, he doesn't want to leave.

'We're abandoning a lot of sick children,' he says. 'I don't care who they are or what they've done in the past. They're kids and they're in pain.'

'Most of the adults have left the building,' Matt says. 'There are only two doctors taking care of the sick. They know the kids can't be exposed to the outside environment.'

'What's that supposed to mean?' Seymour demands.

When Matt doesn't respond I know exactly what it means.

Matt has rigged the place to blow with Telar weapons.

'What do you have to say, Cindy?' I ask.

The woman strokes her daughter's head. 'We've lost control of the Cradle, in more ways than one. We should start over fresh.'

'Let's get out of here,' I say to Matt.

'Wait!' Seymour shouts. 'This isn't like you, Sita. We can save everyone. We can make this right.'

Matt glances at his watch as the van eases down the long driveway. 'We have less than a minute to fix anything,' he mutters.

'Let me out, I'll stay with them,' Seymour says, not understanding Matt. 'If all I can do is help stop their pain, then so be it.'

Matt accelerates. We approach Pacific Coast Highway.

'Their pain will soon be over,' I promise him.

Seymour pounds the back window in frustration. 'I'm serious, let me out,' he yells.

'Go right. Head north,' I tell Matt.

We turn on to the highway and roar north at eighty miles an hour.

'How come no one's listening to me?' Seymour complains.

The explosion, when it comes, is much larger than I expect. Matt must have planted his Telar grenades throughout the structure. Fortunately, the building is surrounded by plenty of land. There's no danger to any other homes or businesses.

Glancing back, it looks as if the top of the hill has been struck by an asteroid. The debris cloud is half earth, half glass. It glitters with red and green sparks from the exotic explosives. At its heart glows a fireball as hot as the surface of the sun. It's hard to imagine a virus, no matter how deadly, surviving such a blast.

'Damn you all,' Seymour swears.

There's nothing I can say. He's right, I have damned us all.

The sound of sirens begins and yet quickly fades as we drive further north. Disgusted with us, Seymour stops talking, while Shanti falls asleep in his arms. Cindy eases Jolie into her own seat and fastens her seat belt. The woman reaches for her laptop. Charlie stares out the window at the ocean. Matt drives. I close my eyes and try to forget I'm going to hell when I die.

We're thirty minutes north of Malibu and about to turn inland when Cindy hits a key on her laptop and lets out a groan. 'Oh no,' she says.

'What's wrong?' I ask.

'This is going to be hard to believe.'

'Nothing can surprise me at this point,' I say.

'Our pictures are on the FBI's Ten Most Wanted list.'

I whirl. 'What are you talking about?'

Cindy turns her laptop screen towards me. I see my photograph, followed by Matt's and Cindy's. Seymour's face is in a small row on the bottom of the page. According to the US government, we're the most dangerous criminals in the nation.

'But the building just blew up,' Matt says.

'No one paid any attention to us leaving,' I agree.

'This makes no sense. The FBI can't work that fast,' Seymour says.

Cindy shakes her head. 'We're not on this list because the FBI saw us blow up IIC's headquarters. Nor has anyone at IIC spoken to the FBI. This list was generated higher up the food chain. It was already in place and was just released now to make it difficult for us to travel.'

'How do you know?' I ask.

'Because it takes time to get the warrants from a judge that would put us on this list.'

'It must be the Telar,' Seymour says. 'Sita and Umara took out the Source, but there are still thousands of them alive all over the globe. Some have got to be in positions of power. They're probably angry.'

'I've checked with my Telar contacts,' Matt says. 'The group is in complete disarray. But one thing is definite – they're delighted that Haru and his inner circle are dead.'

'Then who's after us?' Seymour says.

Cindy and I stare at each other. She nods. I shake my head.

'Are you thinking what I'm thinking?' I ask.

'It's the only logical explanation,' Cindy replies.

'It's not logical at all. It's impossible,' I say.

'What are you two talking about?' Matt demands.

Cindy taps her laptop. 'The Cradle's Internet program. Someone just activated it.'

'How?' Matt asks.

'You mean why,' Cindy says. 'Because we killed the Cradle.'

Shanti sits up and rubs her aching head. 'Who activated what?' she mumbles.

'But if they're all dead,' I say, 'then who's left alive to turn it on? Cindy, are you absolutely sure you had every member of the Cradle in that facility?'

'Yes. I even forced kids who were not feeling well to attend your sessions. When the bombs exploded, it was like the Array's head was chopped off.'

'Then it can't be the program,' I say.

'What if they designed it to take over if they ever stopped feeding it fresh data or new lines of code?' Cindy says.

'They didn't know anything about computers,' Matt protests. 'They were just a bunch of kids.'

'What about the intelligence they were channelling?' Cindy asks. 'We have no idea what it was capable of. I find it fascinating that it's chosen to go after us only minutes after we killed its main mouthpiece.'

'You speak of the program as if it's alive,' Matt says.

'Maybe it is,' Cindy says.

'That's science fiction,' Seymour says. 'We're decades if not centuries away from developing intelligent machines.'

'I'm not talking about human programmers,' Cindy says. 'I'm talking about an intelligence that might have existed before our sun was even born. We have no idea how old the powers are that the kids were in contact with.'

'Tarana,' I say.

Cindy nods. 'He taught us stuff no one in the world knew. He was the real president of IIC. He helped us make trillions and it was always obvious to me that he was just the beginning.'

'Hold on a second,' I say. 'Let's not get carried away. I have no trouble with the idea that the kids were trying to install a gigantic program on the Internet. But I'm with Seymour and Matt. The program can't be conscious.'

Cindy frowns. 'I have a slightly different problem I'm struggling with. I'd expect that no matter how sophisticated the program is, it must still need a biological link to connect to the spiritual realms.'

'Huh?' Shanti says.

'She's saying the program still needs a person to help it channel the evil spirits,' Seymour says.

'Then we're back to the possibility that the Cradle must have members we don't know about,' I say.

'If they existed, the IIC had no record of them,'

Cindy says.

'That counts for nothing,' Matt says. 'Those kids could have been meeting behind your backs for years. There could be another three hundred of them out there for all we know.'

'I don't think I'd go that far,' I say. 'The Cradle was anxious to destroy the Telar's Link. It was an obsession. That was the only way I got them to accept me and Umara. They wanted all the help they could get. If they had another group, they would have brought it to aid with the attack.'

'Did you ever sense another group when you were connected to the Cradle?' Shanti asks.

'No,' I say.

'But you were definitely aware of evil spirits?' Seymour asks.

'Absolutely,' I say.

'Who is Tarana?' Matt asks.

'A powerful Familiar,' Cindy replies.

'Could he be something more?' I ask.

Cindy shrugs. 'You have more experience with these realms than I do. But I wouldn't be surprised if the Familiars are tightly organized in a hierarchal fashion. If that's the case, then it stands to reason the ones on top may have evolved into something greater than our small human brains can even imagine.'

We hear a siren at our backs. I look in the rearview mirror. A police car is trying to flag us down. I glance at Matt, who shakes his head.

'I wasn't speeding,' he says.

'What name did you rent this van under?'

'Robert Reeve. The ID is squeaky clean.'

'This van was parked outside the entrance to the IIC's headquarters,' Cindy says. 'Its plates could have been picked up by our remote cameras.'

'And fed to the Cradle's Internet program?' Seymour asks. 'I doubt it.'

'See what the cop wants,' Cindy says. 'But I suggest we all be ready to move fast, if necessary. We can't be taken in for questioning. We'd never be released.'

Matt pulls the van over to the side. The police car parks and we note we're dealing with two officers. One comes up on Matt's side, the other on mine. I'm surprised to see they have already drawn their weapons.

'Can I help you, officer?' Matt asks the policeman after rolling down his window.

'License and registration please.' Matt's cop is older, sun-beaten, carries a gut from too many doughnut stops over the years. He has the face of a bulldog, he looks angry at the world. He takes Matt's paperwork in his left hand while he continues to hold his gun in his right.

The cop outside my window is young and gawky. He has nervous blue eyes that remind me of a fish out of water. His gun looks like it might break his frail arm if he ever summoned the nerve to fire it. I push a button and my window rolls down and I smile.

'Beautiful morning, isn't it?' I ask, and it's true. Locked in IIC's headquarters, I had lost all awareness of what time of day it was. The cop wants to return my smile because I'm cute but he's got something else on his mind.

'Where you folks from?' he asks me.

'Lots of places. We're old friends. We're just passing through.'

He nods nervously but doesn't respond. He keeps looking to the other cop for directions. Bulldog finally takes a step back and orders Matt out of the vehicle.

'Why, officer?' Matt asks calmly. 'What have I done wrong?'

'Listen, punk, I just gave you an order.'

Cindy leans forward. 'Don't listen to him. By law, he has to tell you why he's stopped us and why he wants you to exit the vehicle.'

Matt stares at Bulldog. 'Did you hear that? This woman is a lawyer. I demand to know why you pulled us over.'

Bulldog raises his gun and puts it to Matt's head. 'Get out now. Last warning.'

'We can't let this escalate,' Cindy says. 'Alisa, use your powers.'

Cindy isn't aware of the extent of Matt's power so it's natural she should turn to me to get us out of this jam. I'm happy to oblige. I turn to the nervous guy on my right and catch his eyes.

'Go back to your vehicle and forget all about us. Treat yourself to a milkshake this afternoon. You need to gain some weight.'

As the young cop turns back towards the squad car, his partner gets more nervous. He rams the gun up against Matt's skull and pulls back the hammer. 'You want to die, huh? You want me to blow your brains out?'

'Stop,' I say calmly. 'Relax and lower your gun.' The angry cop does as I say and I continue. 'There's no reason to get excited. You don't want to hurt anyone. You're a good man and a fine officer.'

'I'm a great police officer,' the man mumbles.

'That's right,' I agree. 'Now tell us why you stopped our van?'

The tension flows from the man's face. He stands swaying like an unsupported mannequin. A breeze could blow him over. He speaks like a robot.

'An all-points bulletin has been issued for a vehicle of this make and license-plate number. We were warned that you are armed and dangerous. We were told to approach you with extreme caution.'

'Do you know what crime we are supposed to be guilty of?' I ask.

'No, Miss.'

I hold the cop's eye and heat up his synapses. 'None of these orders have anything to do with us. Return to your car and forget you ever saw us. Also, erase meeting us on the digital tapes you keep in your vehicle. Do you understand?'

'Yes.'

'We're going to leave now and you two are going to take the rest of the day off. Go to the Chumash Casino outside Solvang and have some fun at the blackjack tables.'

'Go to the casino. Play blackjack. Thank you. Goodbye.'

The cop walks away and I order Matt to get back on the road.

'We have to get another car,' Cindy says.

'Do you think?' I say sarcastically.

'Why so testy, Alisa? It's unlike you.'

Because I'm damned. Because it's all hopeless.

I dislike using my psychic abilities. I feel as if Tarana is attached to every subtle act I take. My soul is still connected to his. We are like allies, only he believes he's in charge. The feeling of being watched persists.

'I was looking forward to relaxing after we destroyed the Source and the Cradle,' I say. 'Now we have the Internet sending complete strangers after us. It kind of wrecks your day, you know.'

'We have to get out of the city,' Matt says. 'The more isolated we are, the more off the grid, the safer we'll be. I have a feeling it's going to take time to figure this one out.'

'To live off the grid we need cash,' Seymour says.

'I've got plenty,' I say.

'So do I,' Cindy says.

'What does it mean to live off the grid?' Shanti asks.

'It means we don't pay for anything with credit cards,' Seymour says. 'We don't go anywhere with security cameras. We don't even use a phone or log on to a computer. And we'll have to change our appearance.'

Shanti is dismayed. 'Can a person live like that nowadays?'

'Not easily,' Seymour says with disgust.

28 ～～

We end up in a hole-in-the-wall motel in the Nevada desert, in a small town called Baker. The town is famous for being a place to drive through while on the way to Las Vegas, it being only a half an hour outside of Sin City. In the summer the average temperature is a hundred and ten. In the fall – the present – it drops to a comfortable ninety-nine. I can only assume the people who live in Baker are preparing for an eternity in hell.

We rent three rooms for twenty-five dollars each. Since we stole the truck we arrived in, we park it a mile away to disassociate ourselves from it.

Each room has either twin beds or a queen-sized bed. Shanti and I end up with the latter. We'll be sharing the same mattress, although I doubt I'll sleep much.

Our room comes with a creaky air conditioner that blows freezing air for fifteen minutes before stopping for the rest of the hour. It is like it knows how little we paid for the room and it doesn't want to overwork itself.

I offer to go out and get Shanti a bag of ice.

'You can sleep with it near your head. It will keep your blood from boiling.'

'I'm from India, I don't mind the heat,' she reminds me. She has just come out of the shower and is combing her long black hair. I've showered as well and am sitting in an oversized Lakers T-shirt I bought at a nearby gas station. It's all I wear, I'm not shy, but Shanti has on a cotton robe she'd be better off without.

'I'm sorry about the mess we're in,' I say. 'I keep fighting to get rid of our enemies, but no matter how many battles we win, the situation keeps getting worse.'

Shanti shakes her head as she presses her dripping hair with a towel.

'I think the situation's improving,' she says. 'A month ago we had the Telar and the IIC both trying to kill us. Now they're largely out of the picture and we just have a computer virus to worry about.'

'It's not a virus, it's a program. And it's probably smarter than us. I can't begin to imagine how we can destroy it.'

'If the story about the Hydra's true, then maybe it's the immortal head that never dies, and the best we can do is bury it somewhere.'

'Hopefully in a mainframe in Antarctica.'

'If that's what it takes,' Shanti says.

'I can see a computer program being written so that it could infiltrate the FBI and all the other law enforcement databases and convince them that we're dangerous people that need to be tracked down and arrested. But what I don't understand is how fast it went into operation. We blew up the kids and half an hour later we're on the FBI's Ten Most Wanted list. It's like someone tipped the program off.'

'A lot of IIC people escaped the blast.'

'I arranged for most of them to escape. But how many of them knew about the Cradle's Internet program?'

'It sounds like the thing's haunting you,' Shanti says.

'It is. Cindy's remark about a program, no matter how sophisticated it is, still needing a human liaison stuck with me. The woman might be a monster but she's insightful.'

'So you're saying there is another Cradle out there?'

'No. Like I said in the van, I think the Cradle would have called in all its resources to fight the Source. Plus, when I joined with the kids, I never sensed them thinking about another Cradle.'

'Could you read their thoughts?' Shanti asks.

'I had a sense of the sum of their minds. Trust me, that last time we went after the Source, they were scared. They thought the Link was going to fry them.'

'Maybe they sensed the virus working in their blood.'

I lower my head. 'Maybe.'

Shanti drops her towel and looks distressed. 'I'm

sorry, I said that without thinking. I know how hard it was for you to give the order to inject them with the virus. That's the kind of decision I could never make.'

'What would you have done in my shoes?'

'I'm the wrong person to ask.'

'Why?'

'Because I'm weak, I can't hurt a fly.'

'Making life-and-death decisions doesn't make a person strong. But when I weighed the risks of letting the kids go, it just felt too dangerous.'

'I understand.'

'How did you feel during the final session? You came out of it looking like hell.'

'Just sitting near it gave me an awful headache.'

'So you did link with us?'

'Yes.'

'What did you experience during the session?'

'I didn't see things as clearly as you. But I did see images of Egypt and how the Telar were hiding in a temple beneath the sand. I guess because I've spent time with her, I felt Umara close at hand. I sensed when she spoke to you.'

Her clarity surprises me. 'I didn't know your intuition was so sharp.'

'I thought you did. Wasn't my intuition the reason the IIC paid Marko a ton of money to whack me?'

'You have a point. Tell me more about what you saw during the session.'

Shanti returns to drying her hair. 'Like I said, I could hear you and Umara exchanging thoughts. You said something about having to die to know the truth and she said you had already died.'

'Then what happened?'

'It was strange, I felt like I was back on that mountain where Teri broke her leg. You were there, and Seymour and Matt. Only it was right after you got shot. You were lying on the ground, dead.'

'Did you see anything else? Did you see my spirit?'

'I think I felt it nearby. But I'm not sure.'

'That was the start of my journey into the underworld.'

'Really? What was that like? Did you see Krishna?'

'My whole experience, it was like a Greek myth. I took a tunnel down into the underworld. There I met people who had recently died, and others who had died ages ago, all wandering beside a black river. It was like the River Styx. There were ferrymen that would take you across the river, but only if you answered the riddle they asked.'

'What did they ask you?'

'That part's hard to recall. When they would ask a question, if you didn't get it right, you'd forget it right away.'

'How many riddles did they ask?'

'Three. I remember that much. I got the last one right. That's why the guy took me across the river. He asked, 'What's the greatest secret in the universe?' I told him that Krishna's name was identical with Krishna. That's why repeating it was so magical.'

Shanti is impressed, which is understandable, given

the fact that she is a Hindu. 'That's straight out of the Vedas.'

'I know,' I say quietly.

'What's wrong?'

'Nothing.'

'You suddenly look sad.'

'I'm not sad.' *I'm doomed*, I want to scream. The answer got me across the river but that's as far as it got me. It was all a bunch of lies, what the Vedic scriptures said, a monster like me could never be saved.

'Try to remember another riddle,' Shanti says.

'I told you, I got them wrong so I forgot them right away.' I pause. 'But I do remember this witch. I wasn't sure why I ran into her. She was in charge of an invisible bridge that crossed a chasm. She kept pushing me to kiss her. If I did, she promised to take me to the other side of the cliff. But there was something wrong about her. I didn't trust her. Her face was all scarred . . .' I stop. 'Oh, Shanti, I'm sorry. I didn't mean that her scars made her a bad person.'

Shanti's lower lip trembles but she hides it by quickly shaking her head. 'That's all right. People are always judging others by how they look. It gets programmed into everyone that beautiful is good and ugly is evil.'

'I really am sorry.'

'Continue with your story. It's fascinating.'

'There was something else about the witch. She was beautiful to start with. It was only when I got close to her, and said no to her offer, that she changed.'

'Did she ask you a riddle?'

'The ferryman was the only one who did that. But I was told each riddle was supposed to be important. They were supposed to be clues to help a person on their way.'

'How did you get past the witch?'

'It's funny you should ask. The second riddle came back to me when I was wrestling with her. The ferryman asked, "What's the greatest quality a human can possess? The one quality that can be the most dangerous?"' I pause. 'Do you know the answer?'

Shanti makes a face. 'That's tough. There are so many good qualities that, when you take them too far, end up being bad.'

'Say you didn't take the quality too far. Say you just interpreted it backwards.'

'I don't understand.'

'I didn't either. That's why I got it wrong.'

'Then how do you remember it?' Shanti asks.

'Like I said, the answer came to me later, when I was with the witch. It helped me get away from her.'

'What's the answer?'

'Come on, Shanti! You have to at least guess.'

She laughs as she combs her hair. 'I'm going to say discipline. If you're disciplined, you can accomplish almost anything in life. But if you're too disciplined, you never take time off to enjoy yourself.' She giggles. 'Am I right?'

'You're close.'

'How close?'

'Well, not that close. The correct answer is faith.'

Shanti frowns. 'How can faith be bad?'

'Krishna gave a talk on faith. It's in Yaksha's book. It's brilliant. First he describes how faith can allow you to accomplish anything in life. How a deep confidence in oneself allows you to overcome all obstacles. He explains how absolute faith can even lead to God.'

Shanti nods. 'That's what I was taught growing up.'

'There's another side to faith. Krishna was probably the first person to use the phrase "blind faith". He said that faith without experience was useless. To believe something just because you're told to believe it leads to dogma and deeper bondage.'

'But isn't that the point of faith? No one can be sure if there's a God or not. You just have to believe in him.'

'I believe Krishna's approach to spirituality was more scientific. He said that whatever path you follow in life, you should uncover small proofs along the way so you know you're going the right way. Otherwise, you could end up chasing illusions.'

'I can't imagine a talk like that being in the Vedas,' Shanti replies. She continues to look unhappy and I can only assume I've trodden on sacred ground.

'I don't want to get into a religious argument with you. I just want you to understand how the riddle saved me from the witch. When I stopped to consider that I was dead, I realized I could no longer be hurt. That gave me the faith or the courage to jump into the chasm.'

'Where did you fall to?'

'I don't want to talk about that.'

'Why not? Your story keeps getting better.'

'Trust me, you wouldn't like the next part.'

The fan inside our air conditioner suddenly screeches to a halt and the cold air stops. This time it's only been on for five minutes. The room isn't cool yet, and even Shanti looks unhappy.

'It would be hard to live here. It's like this place is surrounded by fire,' she says.

The remark rings a bell. I've heard it before.

Something like it. About a world filled with fire.

There's not much to do in the tiny room. Shanti prepares for bed. She brushes her teeth and finally takes off her robe and crawls under the sheets. I sit in the corner with Yaksha's book. I don't need the light on to read. I review Krishna's version of the Hydra myth.

'As Hercules fought the monster, he was almost killed by its deadly breath, but eventually he removed all but one of the Hydra's heads. The last one could not be destroyed by any man-made tool, so, picking up his club, Hercules crushed it and tore it off with his bare hands. With Iolaus's help, he wisely buried it deep in the ground and placed a huge boulder over it lest it be disturbed by the future races of man.'

Today, I reflect, I destroyed two Hydras, the Source and the Cradle, and in a sense I cut off many heads. But only with the Source did I follow Krishna's directions to the letter. When I killed Umara and removed the Telar's protection.

But what of the Cradle?

They seemed to have no immortal head.

At least none that I knew about.

Unless it was their damn computer program.

'Does my reading bother you?' I ask.

'No,' Shanti mumbles from the bed. 'What are you reading?'

'Yaksha's book.'

'I'm glad you found it.'

'I have you to thank for it. You're the one who flew it away from Arosa to safety.'

Shanti yawns and turns over in bed and readjusts her pillow. 'That's nice. Good night, Sita.'

'Good night.' I continue to stare at Yaksha's book, not really reading it, just happy to have the original in my hands. Because I was sure the Telar had taken the original back. That I had only given Shanti a copy to take to the States.

'Shanti?'

'Hmm.'

'When you flew home with the book, and you showed it to Seymour, what form was it in?'

'Huh?'

'Was it the original or was it a copy?'

'I thought you gave me the original.'

'I gave you a copy.'

'I thought you wanted me to protect the original. In case it had secret messages hidden inside it. A copy wouldn't have those.'

'I didn't say anything about secret messages,' I say.

449

'Seymour told me about them. I hope that's OK. We've become close. He shares stuff with me. He likes me to feel like I can help you and the others when I know I really can't do much.'

'Gimme a break. You're the one person who could protect me from the Cradle.'

'But I didn't do anything to protect you.'

'You just had to be nearby. In that way you were like Umara. She just had to walk the earth and all the Telar could live forever.'

'Now that she's dead, do you think they'll start to die?'

'I believe so, yes.'

'That's sad,' Shanti says.

'Not really. Many have lived for thousands of years.'

'I guess.' Shanti yawns. 'Good night, Sita. I love you.'

I go to tell her I love her but something holds me back.

It bothers me, her story about Yaksha's book.

Because it's not true. I gave her a copy.

I had promised the man at the Swiss hotel, Herr Reinhart, that I would return the original to him intact. At the time I didn't know he was Telar, and there's no way I would have pawned off a bunch of photocopied pages on him and tried to convince him that it was Yaksha's original manuscript. The idea was patently absurd.

Right now, though, I have the original in my hands.

But the Telar never gave it to me. Why should they?

It's a mystery. One I can't solve.

It strikes me then how close mysteries are to riddles.

In a sense, they are identical.

A strange déjà vu sweeps over me, and I feel as though the answer to the mystery surrounding Yaksha's book can be found in the first riddle the ferryman asked me. On the surface, there is no logical link between the two questions, other than the fact that I don't know the answer to either. In fact, I don't even know what the first riddle was . . .

Then, just like that, sitting in this hot room, I remember.

Somehow the heat helps.

'What is the most useless human emotion?'

That was it! I told him fear. But that was wrong.

What was the right answer? Everyone in that place agreed that the ferryman wouldn't ask a riddle that your life hadn't taught you the answer to. That meant I must know the answer. Why won't it come to me?

'Shanti?'

'Hmmm.'

'I want to apologize again for comparing you to a witch.'

'You didn't compare me to her.'

'I meant her scars. I didn't mean to say they reminded me of your scars.'

'Mine are all gone thanks to you.'

'I know. Your face looks great.'

Shanti hesitates. 'Yeah.'

'What's wrong?'

'Nothing.'

'Is something about your face still bothering you?'

'Well, I don't want you to take this the wrong way.'

'I won't.'

'But sometimes I feel like all the work the doctors have done is just an illusion.'

'I don't understand.'

'I still feel ugly inside.'

'You're not ugly. Don't be ridiculous.'

'Not outside, inside. Don't you ever feel that way?'

'I did today.'

'When you injected the virus in the kids?'

My turn to hesitate. 'Yes.'

'How do you feel about that?'

'I have tons of guilt. Regret. Remorse.'

'Don't those words all mean the same thing?'

'Yes, they're synonyms.' I pause. 'It's odd, I had a talk with the ferryman about synonyms.'

'That must have been amusing.'

'There was not necessarily one answer for each riddle. You just had to get the meaning right.'

'That makes sense.' She pauses. 'Sita?'

'Yes.'

'I'm exhausted. Can I sleep now?'

'Sure. Sorry to bother you. Sweet dreams.'

'Same to you. Good night.'

I sit in the dark. The air conditioner remains silent. It continues to get warmer. All I have on is a thin T-shirt and the sweat drips off of me.

'*A word from me and you will be taken through the red door, where there is only fire and pain. There you will burn. But not like you burned on earth. In the world of the living you were a vampire. There you would heal quickly. But in the world of fire, there is no relief. There is only agony.'*

It was Tarana who said that.

'Shanti?' I say.

She sits up in bed and stares at me.

'What's bothering you?' she asks.

'Why did you lie to me about Yaksha's book?'

'Lie to you? Why would I lie to you?'

'I don't know. That's what I'm trying to find out.'

'Sita, honestly, I brought the original home. It's sitting right there on your lap.'

'The first time we talked about this issue, I was in Teri's body. I was confused. But now that I'm whole again, I'm a hundred per cent sure I gave you a copy.'

'Then how did you end up with the original?'

'The question should be, how did you end up with it?'

'I don't understand. Are you accusing me of stealing it?'

'That would be an amazing trick, to steal it from the Telar.'

Shanti stands, puts her robe back on, and comes over and sits on the seat beside me. Her plastic surgery doesn't look so good when she's tired and not wearing makeup. Her scars are much more visible. She reaches for my hand but I don't take hers.

'What's wrong?' she asks, worried.

I shrug. 'Just asking a few questions is all.'

'No, you're not. It's like you suddenly don't trust me.'

I stare at her. I don't speak. Silence can cut the deepest.

Shanti grows restless. 'Ask your questions and get it over with.'

'How did you block the Cradle?'

'I told you, I don't know.'

'I thought perhaps it was your goodness.'

'But you've changed your mind?'

'You know, the first time I was attacked by the Cradle, in Brutran's house, it used you as an object of focus.'

'I don't know what you're talking about.'

'The Cradle struck and suddenly you were on her TV. You picked up a gun and forced it deep into your mouth. You pulled the trigger and blew away half your face. You ended up looking like, well, the day we met.'

Shanti nods sadly. 'I remember that day. You were very kind to me.'

'You're right, I fell for you immediately. That was unusual for me. Normally I warm up to people slowly. But right from the start, I wanted to take care of you.'

'I suppose I cast a spell on you.'

'Like a witch.'

Shanti glares. 'If you're going to sit there and insult me . . .'

'How long were you outside that London motel before you rushed in and saved me?' I interrupt.

'Seymour and I had just got there.'

'I always wondered about that morning. That was the worst time the Cradle ever struck me. I felt like I was in hell, literally. It was worse than when I was sitting in

Brutran's house. That always puzzled me. After all, Jolie was in Brutran's house, and she was one of the leaders of the Cradle.' I pause. 'You see what I'm getting at?'

'No.'

'I wonder if you were outside that motel room for an hour.'

'With Seymour?'

'Yeah.'

'Doing what?' she asks.

'I don't know.'

'What was Seymour doing during this hour?'

'Maybe nothing. Maybe he didn't know what he was doing. Just like I didn't know what I was doing.'

Shanti is annoyed. 'Are you done?'

'How did you get hold of Matt's blood?'

'I don't know what you're talking about.'

'The Cradle needed a sample of his blood to attack him. But when I was in the Cradle and we attacked Lisa, I saw she hadn't stolen it. I saw she was completely innocent.'

'Are you the one who killed her?'

'Yes. She was my sacrifice.'

Shanti stands and there appear to be real tears in her eyes. 'You say that so casually. Like her death meant nothing to you.'

'You're wrong. I feel terrible about her death. Now wipe away those fake tears and sit back down and answer my question. Did you steal Matt's blood that day he slipped on the pool deck and cut his scalp?'

Shanti sits back down and wipes at her eyes.

'It was Lisa who bandaged his head,' she says.

'I know. That's why I thought she was guilty. She threw away a lot of blood-soaked gauze when she was done with it. Tell me, did you take it?'

'No.'

I smile. 'You know what's weird?'

'What?'

'I can always tell if a person's lying or not.'

'So you're absolutely sure I'm lying about the blood.'

'Not at all. I can't tell with you. I get no clear signal at all. It's like you're not really in this room. But it was odd Matt was so careless with his blood. I think you had something to do with that. I'm sure it was you who stole it. It wasn't me. It wasn't Seymour or Teri or Lisa. You're the only one left.'

Shanti acts bored. 'Anything else?'

'You told Brutran I was dead. From the start, you were the mole. But for some reason she doesn't know you're the mole. It's like you implanted the info in her head. Her whole attitude towards you is bizarre. It's like she's afraid of you but doesn't know why.'

'Do you know why?'

'I'm beginning to get an idea. I think you're the head of the Cradle. Its immortal head. Oh, I suppose your body can be killed and that would be a pain in the ass for you because it's a useful tool when it comes to spying on us. But I think deep inside, what you are, can't be destroyed so easily.' I pause. 'Isn't that true, Tarana?'

Finally, I have spoken the demon's name, and just as

the Lord's name chanted aloud has immense power to bring light and love, the demon's name can alter the room so that it feels like it's filled with poisonous snakes and other vile creatures. The temperature appears to rise twenty degrees in a heartbeat and a smothering heaviness chokes the air.

Shanti smiles, or perhaps it is a sneer.

'Very good, Sita. If you had just named me from the start, you could have avoided all this useless talk.'

'Because when you expose a demon, it loses its power?'

'Who told you that?'

'Umara.'

'Only the host body can be harmed by exposure.'

'So I haven't actually hurt you?'

Shanti grins and raises her hand and snaps her fingers.

'Nope,' she says.

I blink. An instant passes.

Suddenly I'm standing in the living room of an expensive hotel suite overlooking a large city. It's nighttime, the skyscrapers are all lit, and even though I know every major skyline in the world, I don't recognize this one.

The suite itself is five-star. It has the finest accommodations. There's a wet bar stocked with liquors that cost a mint, a sunken sauna that gives off perfumed waves of steam, two adjoining bedrooms, and huge flat-screen TVs.

Standing by the door is Tarana.

He does not look like I expect.

Does it matter? He can assume any form he chooses.

He is a young man of thirty. He wears a beige suit and has a strong handsome jaw. His hair is black, neither long nor short; he combs it straight back. His eyes are large and dark. They are his most striking feature and perhaps his worst. When I look directly into them, I don't feel so good.

Yet he smiles when he sees me and crosses the room to shake my hand. His grip is firm but he does not try to crush my fingers. He's much too subtle for that. You see, I know him, he has been watching me for days, and I have been feeling him. This is the one who has been standing behind me, the man in the mirror so to speak, a very powerful Familiar. How much more he might be, I'm not exactly sure, but I hope to find out.

'Sita. I've looked forward to this meeting for ages.'

'I didn't expect we'd ever meet,' I reply, playing along. Of course we have already met. In front of the Scale, where we consummated our deal to kill Umara. Yet this Tarana acts more cheerful than the Caretaker in the red robe. The key word is 'acts'. I know his behaviour, like his appearance, can change in an instant.

'Life is like that. Impossible to predict. Can I get you a drink?'

'No, thanks.'

'Have a seat,' he says, gesturing to a chair, while sitting on the couch across from me. Out of nowhere a

Scotch and soda with ice appears in his right hand. 'So how did you know it was me?'

'Shanti?'

He acts disappointed. 'Shanti was just a tool, a convenient puppet I decided to use for a while. Frankly, I'm surprised it took you so long to see through her disguise. That saccharine personality I used around you should have given you a clue. Didn't I make her just a tad too perfect? I even had her worshipping the same god as you.'

'I admit, I should have spotted her sooner. But how did you two get hooked up? Young Indian girl. She doesn't seem like your type.'

Tarana gestures upwards, as if he's pointing to the surface of the earth. 'One thing you have to know is that they're all my type. Shanti is a perfect example. That history she fed you was all lies. She didn't get trapped in one of those arranged Indian marriages where she had to agree to spend the rest of her life with the biggest asshole who happened to come up with the biggest dowry. In reality, Shanti's fiancé refused to marry her because she scared him. She didn't spend her days reading the Gita. She was into what you would call the left-handed path. She loved nothing more than to go out late at night and hang around graveyards and perform ceremonies designed to reanimate corpses. Oh, that must sound familiar to you. Isn't that how Yaksha came to earth?'

'Yaksha started as a demon but redeemed himself in the end.'

'Good for him. I doubt Shanti has much chance of doing that. To make a long story short, it was while she was in the midst of conversing with one of her excited corpses that I took over and we struck up a deal. Nothing too fancy, but you see, I already had my eye on you and I figured she might come in handy later on. She ended up being more useful than even I planned. She was my principal alter ego when it came to the Cradle. She could cast a spell on any of them: Haru, Cynthia Brutran – it made no difference.'

'Is that how she got Yaksha's book from Haru?'

'Naturally.'

'Is that why Cindy feared her?'

'Brutran never understood why she felt so uneasy when Shanti was around. It was Brutran that ordered the hit on Shanti, not me. But that didn't worry me. I knew you would protect her.'

'But Shanti's uncle backed up her story. Or was he just another of your pawns?'

'What do you think?'

'How did Shanti get the acid burns on her face?'

'She did those to herself. It was a requirement on my side to make sure she was serious about our relationship.' Tarana chuckles. 'To think how frightened Shanti's fiancé was of her to start with. Once she fried off half her face, he tried to escape her by moving to England. Too bad she got to him before he could get away.'

'I assume he came to a bad end.'

'Worse than Numbria, if you can imagine. I'll spare

you the gory details. If you'll answer my original question. How did you know I was the immortal head?'

He is not asking about being Shanti. He is asking how I knew he was Tarana. Indeed, he wants me to think of him as Tarana.

Why?

So I will not guess who he *really* is?

'Who else would know to come running when human beings started experimenting with arrays, cradles and links? To be blunt, Tarana, I think you're the cosmic expert at establishing contact with mortals and feeding them the information they need to know to totally screw up their lives.'

'That's high praise coming from a monster like you.'

'I was a monster once. I retired from that position long ago.'

'Did you? What about the three hundred syringes you prepared for Seymour to inject? I understand you switched the vaccine for the virus.'

'I did what had to be done.'

Tarana smiles. 'A lot of people down here say that.'

'I imagine they do. But if I hadn't done it, would we be having this conversation right now?'

'I'm sure the question weighs on your heart. A part of you wonders if the Scale would have treated you better if you hadn't chosen to murder those kids.'

I stop, he's got me. 'I confronted the Scale before I killed them.'

'Surely you realize time has no meaning in that place.'

He's trying to confuse me, to make me doubt myself. The trouble is, he's doing a damn fine job of it.

'I'm not here to talk about the kids,' I say. 'We had a deal and I kept up my end. I killed Umara. I want to be compensated.'

'You already have been. I've kept you from burning.'

'I want more.'

He smiles and takes a sip from his glass. 'I admire a greedy woman. What do you want?'

'The Cradle's Internet program destroyed.'

'Sorry, no can do.'

'It's just a bunch of code.'

'Code that I happened to write. Let's be blunt, Sita, you only killed Umara so you could destroy the Telar. I didn't interfere because it worked to both our advantages. The Telar had run the world for so long they had begun to bore me, and there's nothing I hate worse than someone who bores me. But the Cradle were my kids. I honestly didn't think you had the nerve to inject a bunch of children with a deadly virus.'

'Since you hate boring people, I'm glad I was able to surprise you.'

Suddenly angry, he slams down his drink on the glass coffee table, chipping the edge. The outburst reminds me how unpredictable he can be.

'You did more than that! In a single stroke you wiped out years of preparation. Next to the code I loaded on the Internet, the Cradle was my strongest link to the world.'

'You can always create another.'

'Not easily. Matt, Brutran and the rest of your clowns will be on the lookout for another one. They'll probably stop it before it can get started.' He pauses. 'Unless of course you stop them.'

'What are you offering?'

'The obvious. To continue our relationship.'

'Why should I want to do that?' I ask innocently.

'In case you've forgotten, you've already been judged. You're damned, Sita, which means you either play by my rules or you burn.' He glares as he gestures out the window, his anger not far away. 'This whole city is surrounded by fire.'

'It sounds like Baker.'

'I assure you it's a lot hotter than that hick town.'

'Fine, I'll make another deal with you.'

My quick response seems to take him by surprise.

'Excellent. Your greed grows. Tell me what you want and I'll get it for you. Then I'll tell you what I want and you obey me without question.'

'That sounds too much like our last deal. Where I was forced to agree to a contract I never got a chance to read.'

'No one ever gets to read my contracts.' He pauses. 'What is it you want?'

'The answer to the first riddle the ferryman gave me.'

Tarana snorts and takes a large gulp from his drink. 'You can't even remember the question. Why should you care about the answer?'

'Humour me.'

'No.'

'I'll help create another Cradle for you.'

He whirls the ice in his glass. 'You're not asking much in return for such a huge task.'

'Then give it to me.'

He shakes his head. 'I'm disappointed in you. I would expect your desires to match your abilities. That Greek myth – the ferryman and his riddles. What a waste of time, even for the dead. One would have thought they could have come up with something better after all these years.'

'I think the riddles endure because they work. They help remind a person what he or she learned in a particular life.' I pause. 'As does the Scale.'

He sneers at the mention of the Scale. 'We both know how it treated you. Loved your expression when it began to wail. You have to admit it, Sita, it took a pretty dim view of your time on earth.'

Mocking me appears to improve his mood. Still, I feel he is trying to steer the conversation away from certain directions. He is used to being in total command and this moment he is not.

'The answer to my first riddle, tell me,' I demand.

'No.'

'Why not?'

'I told you. You don't even remember—'

' "What is the most useless human emotion?"' I say.

He blinks, surprised, but then settles down and finishes his drink. Yet when I gesture for him to respond, he shakes his head. 'The answer can't help you,' he says. 'Only I can help you.'

'Since it was the first question the ferryman asked, I suspect it could help me a great deal. But if you're not ready to answer, let's leave *my* riddle aside for a moment. Let's talk about yours.'

He acts amused. 'I've never stooped so low as to ask a ferryman for a ride across that disgusting river.'

'Maybe you should have. You know what those fire-and-brimstone ministers always say. "Pride goeth before the fall." In other words, you might benefit from a dose of humility.'

He suddenly stands, his glass still in his hand.

'Need I remind you who you're speaking to?' he asks.

I carefully shake my head.

He continues. 'Then I suggest, if you want to make a deal, make it. Otherwise, you're beginning to bore me, and you know what becomes of those who displease me.'

I stand and speak in a firm but reasonable voice. If I provoke him too soon, he won't allow me to finish, and this being his world, he probably will crush me like an insect. On the plus side, I have two cards to play. Both are aces but both have to work.

'Pride goeth before the fall,' I repeat. 'That's the answer to your riddle. That's the answer you accidentally showed me in that motel room in London. You wanted to take me to the depths of hell to break me. Only you took me so deep I saw who you really are. I discovered your little secret. Only it's not so little, after

465

all. Actually, it's so important mankind's greatest minds have struggled with it since the beginning of time.'

'Stop!' he screams, and throws his drink at my face. His reflexes are extraordinary, greater than my own. The glass hits my chin, where it shatters and tears a three-inch gash in my flesh. My blood gushes out but I ignore it. Already, I fear, I have pushed him too far.

'You're the one who took me to that place where I saw the truth.'

'Be silent! I command you!' he shouts.

I take a step towards him. 'You must have wanted me to see. You weren't really talking about Umara when you ordered me to destroy the Light Bearer. You were talking about yourself. It's time to quit hiding behind that silly name, Tarana. I mean, it's just an invented word, it doesn't explain who the Light Bearer is and why he fell. If humility is out of your reach, and you must be proud of something, then admit who you really are. We both know who the real Light Bearer is.' I stop. 'Don't we, Lucifer?'

The whites of his eyes vanish. There is only black. I cannot bear to look at him and yet he forces me to do so. I feel I will be sick. The nausea arises from a sudden pressure at the back of my skull.

He speaks softly, in a deadly tone. 'Last warning, Sita.'

I smile and raise my arms as if to applaud him. 'You are the greatest of the great. The one who was given the divine light. But it wasn't enough for you. You wanted more. Unfortunately, when you went to war to get it, you had to call upon your great light. You had to dive deep into it. So deep you discovered, quite by accident, that the Lord you were fighting was the same as yourself. Most would have rejoiced in such a discovery, that they were one with God. But you . . . it just made you want to run and hide.'

He turns away so I can't see his face.

I come close so I can whisper in his ear.

It is the bravest thing I have ever done in my life.

'That is why you ended up in this godforsaken realm. You were too proud to admit you were no different from the Lord. Yet you never told the truth to the others who fought by your side. You damned them for no reason. You fell for nothing, which makes you nothing in my eyes.'

He slowly turns and grips my neck.

'You think you can mock me? How will your Hydra look without its immortal head?' he asks as he flexes his fingers as a prelude to decapitating me. He chokes off my air, and I don't know how I manage to get out my last words.

'You no longer have any power over me,' I gasp. 'You never did. You see, I remember the answer to the riddle, and what it means for me.'

My remark shocks him. He blinks.

His spell wavers as another instant passes.

Suddenly Shanti and I are back in the motel room.

She has her hands around my neck.

I knock them loose and grip her throat.

Finally, my hands are clean.

'Guilt,' I say. 'That is the most useless of all emotions. No matter how many people I've saved in my life, I still felt guilty about those I killed. It was my guilt that made me feel I didn't deserve to see Krishna. But it was all a lie, and you, the father of lies, exploited my weakness when you caused me to remember only a portion of what happened when I died.'

Shanti stares at me with genuine fear in her eyes.

Her master has left her all alone.

'What you say is true,' she says, fighting to sound sincere. 'Show me mercy now and you will definitely see Krishna when you die.'

I laugh. 'You fool! What I do with your miserable life won't change what happens at the Scale. Don't you understand? I'm already dead.'

I'm sick and tired of this bitch and her lies.

I rip off her head and throw it out the window.

Epilogue ～～

Suddenly I stand before the Scale.

Judgment has been passed. There are no beautiful chimes to welcome me into paradise. A forsaken wail echoes through the ancient structure. The left door and the burning light await me. The tall Caretaker in the red robe with the searing grip takes hold of my left arm, ready to drag me through the door from which no one ever returns, unless I agree to do his bidding. All this I recognize. All this is as it was before.

The devil gives his speech about me being damned and how horrible it will be to burn. But just when he's talked me into a state of total despair, he offers me a deal. Kill the Light Bearer and you will have a respite from the agony that awaits you. In my fear I offer my right hand and accept his deal.

Then I realize I'm holding down the left plate. That I unconsciously pushed it down after the invisible force released my hands, while the Scale was still bobbing up and down. Guilt caused me to do it. It's like I felt the pain of every single person I hurt during the thousands of years I walked the earth.

Yet suddenly I am able to let go of the guilt, and when I do, I remove my thumb from the edge of the left plate, and its right counterpart, loaded with diamonds, sinks down.

Delicious chimes fill the air. The crowd sighs with relief.

My own relief could fill the sky. I weep with joy.

The red-hooded Caretaker releases my left arm.

'Almost, Sita,' he whispers. 'Almost.'

I smile. 'Go to hell,' I say.

A white-hooded Caretaker takes me by the arm and leads me towards the door on the right from where the golden light emanates. Before I leave the room and the others waiting to be judged, the mysterious woman reaches from the crowd and our fingers touch.

'Will I see you soon?' I ask.

She smiles and in that moment I almost know her name.

'Of course,' she says.

My Caretaker leads me to the door on the right and I enter the golden light. The change I feel in that instant fills me with wonder. Suddenly I'm no longer bathing in the light, I feel as if it enters me and I become one with it.

Once again, I pass through a long tunnel. I assume I'm still walking but at the same time I glide along without effort. The tunnel is neither big nor small, it's just the right size, and as I sweep through it I see different coloured caves. Some give off a white light that fills me with amazement. Others shine with a green glow that reminds me of everyone I ever loved in life. Still other tunnels radiate a combination of colours and I know it is to these realms the majority of people are drawn. Yet I see no one along the way, and I know that's because I have yet to reach the place where I belong.

Finally I come to a tunnel filled with an intoxicating blue light.

As I turn into it, I feel my feet and legs return and I recognize the body that carried me through my journey on earth. Suddenly I'm wearing a blue gown with a yellow sash tied at my waist. Around my neck is a gold chain, which holds a single indigo-coloured jewel.

It reminds me of the famed Kaustubha gem Krishna often wore on earth but it is a darker hue. The jewel hangs above my heart and seems to emit an energy that fills every cell in my body with joy.

The tunnel ends in an ordinary door with a domed top.

A man not much taller than myself, with long black hair, stands to the side of the door. He wears loose-fitting gold trousers and an open saffron shirt. His chest muscles are smooth and strong, his smile inscrutable, his blue eyes as bewitching as a night sky filled with a galaxy of newborn stars. The sight of him sends a thrill through my heart but I hesitate to let myself accept who he is. He stares at me with such love, and yet a part of me, a small childish part, feels afraid, or unworthy.

I hesitate. 'My Lord?'

He nods. 'Sita.'

My name, he has said my name, and my doubt lessens. Yet I begin to weep and don't know why. I couldn't be happier, however, I feel sad, too, consumed with sorrow. Both emotions feel very old. He reaches out and strokes my hair.

'Welcome home, Sita.'

'Lord,' I say, struggling to find the words to explain my confusion. 'Do I really belong here?' I ask.

He gives a faint smile, he has the most seductive lips. 'The choice is yours. You feel there's much you still have to do to atone for those you hurt. But there comes a time when even the last vampire is permitted to leave the world to its own destiny.'

'But I did leave so much undone,' I say, wiping at my tears. 'I just changed Teri into a vampire. She'll need my guidance. And Matt and Paula and Seymour are left to face the Telar and the IIC. It doesn't feel right that I should get to enter paradise while they struggle against such evil.'

'That evil is finished. You already defeated it.'

His words make no sense. Or maybe they do and it's my memory that's at fault. For as I move closer and stare at his face, I catch glimpses of myself linking minds with a bunch of disturbed children as I psychically try to hunt down Haru and his followers. I also see images of a pretty woman more than twice my age, who possesses more wisdom than anyone I have ever met, except for Krishna.

I realize it is the woman I met on the banks of the river.

The one who bid me farewell after I passed the Scale.

'Umara,' I say aloud.

'She waits for you inside.'

'But I don't know her. I never met her.'

'Are you sure?' he asks.

Three simple words but they feel as if they unlock a whirlwind inside of me. Especially as I focus more tightly on Krishna's eyes. As I gaze into them, I feel as if I lift into the air and exchange positions with him. Now I see through his eyes, and see myself, and all the things I still want to do.

If I decide to return to earth.

I realize it is Krishna who is making me the offer to extend my life. Not that demon in the red robe. However, even though I see with his eyes, not all of my confusion vanishes. For they are so mesmerizing, their blue so deep and dark, they seem to gaze in all directions at once. The past and the future have no meaning to him. They are linear, he is infinite.

But they still have meaning to me. The simple remembrance causes me to shift positions again, and once more I find myself back in my body, wondering if I really want to ask if I should go back or not. To leave him feels like an impossibility.

Before I can speak the question aloud, Krishna smiles.

'It matters not, Sita. Stay or go, you will always be with me.'

His words heal my last shred of doubt.

I have faith. It doesn't matter what I decide.